"Very well, Valerian, I *will* tell you of Korhal, what I know of it and what I have pieced together over the years, but I'll tell you more than that if you've the wit to hear it," said Arcturus, standing and draining the last of his port.

"What do you mean?" asked Valerian.

"The story of Korhal is the story of your grandfather and what it means to be a Mengsk. Korhal was the forge in which our dynasty was hammered into shape, raw and bloody upon the anvil of history."

Valerian felt his heart quicken. "Yes, that's what I want."

Arcturus nodded towards the woman in the holographic plate upon the mantelpiece. "And I'll tell you of your mother."

"My mother?" said Valerian, instantly defensive.

"Yes," said Arcturus, making his way towards the door. "But first we have to bury her."

STARCRAFT™

I, MENGSK

GRAHAM McNEILL

POCKET STAR BOOKS
New York London Toronto Sydney

Pocket Star Books
A Division of Simon & Schuster, Inc.
1230 Avenue of the Americas
New York, NY 10020

First Pocket Star Books paperback edition January 2009

POCKET STAR BOOKS and colophon are registered trademarks of Simon & Schuster, Inc.

For information about special discounts for bulk purchases, please contact Simon & Schuster Special Sales at 1-800-456-6798 or business@simonandschuster.com.

Cover art by Mark Gibbons
Cover design by Richard Yoo

Manufactured in the United States of America

10 9 8 7 6 5 4 3 2 1

ISBN-13: 978-1-4165-5083-9
ISBN-10:   1-4165-5083-6

There are a number of people who deserve thanks here, as without them, it's doubtful I'd have written *I, Mengsk*. First off, the biggest thanks to my friends at Blizzard Entertainment, Mark Gibbons, Andy Chambers, and Jay Wilson, for singing my praises to Chris Metzen, who was good enough to take a chance on a guy like me getting his hands on the Starcraft lore. The actual writing of *I, Mengsk* was a genuine pleasure, largely thanks to the help and humour of Evelyn Fredericksen, who made sure I kept to the path and provided invaluable feedback along the way. A novel's journey to the bookstore shelves has just begun when you type "The End," so for his patience and advice during the book's editing and production, I'd like to thank Marco Palmeri for making me look like I know what I'm doing. Cheers, guys, I hope I've done your worlds proud.

Graham

STARCRAFT™

I, MENGSK

BEGINNINGS

VALERIAN HEARD THE KNOCK AT THE DOOR, BUT ignored it, concentrating instead on the tawny port that swirled in the expensive cut-crystal glass held in one manicured hand. The knock came again, more insistent this time, and the tone and impatience of the sound told Valerian Mengsk who was on the other side of the door without his having to answer it.

He smiled as he sipped his drink, the gesture out of place on his handsome features this day, or any other day recently, for that matter. Valerian settled into the deep leather upholstery of the chair, enjoying the heat of the room's coal fire and the warmth of the drink in his belly.

Precious little else had given him enjoyment these last months, for they had been thankless and pain-filled. The pain had not been his, at least not physically, but it had been hard watching his mother suffer as the wasting sickness melted the flesh from her bones and unraveled her mind.

Valerian stared into his glass of port, a fine blend with a rich, fulsome flavor that lingered long on the palate and was the perfect accompaniment to the wildfowl being served to the guests awaiting him in the main chamber of his home.

His home.

The words still felt unusual, the fit not yet settled upon him.

Valerian looked up from his drink and cast his eyes around the room, taking in every exquisite detail: the fine mahogany paneling that concealed sophisticated communications arrays and elaborate countermeasures against electronic eavesdropping, the silken wall hangings, the gold-framed portraits, and the tasteful uplighters that bathed the high-ceilinged room in a warm, restful illumination.

But pride of place on the walls was reserved for the many weapons of Valerian's collection that hung between the more archaic decorations. A long-bladed falx rested on silver hooks, curved swords hung by their quillons, and a multitude of punch daggers and bizarre circular weapons with blades protruding from leather handgrips were set on concealed hooks. Glass cases against the walls contained antique pistols of wood with gold inlay and long-barreled muskets with battery packs fitted to their skeleton stocks.

A marble surround contained the crackling fire and a grainy holo plate sat upon the mantel. It shimmered with the ghostly image of a woman with wistful eyes from which Valerian studiously kept his gaze averted.

He stared into the fire and sipped his port as the door opened behind him.

Only one person would dare enter the chambers of Valerian Mengsk without invitation.

"Hello, Father," said Valerian.

A shadow fell across him and Valerian looked up and saw his father's stern, patrician features staring down at him. Though he had seen the face of Arcturus Mengsk a thousand times in holographic form, his father's sheer physical presence had a powerful charisma that no mere technology could capture.

Arcturus was a big man, broad of shoulder and thick of waist, with hair that had once been dark and lustrous but was now streaked with silver. His beard contained more white than black and where age might weary other men, it had only enhanced the natural gravitas and dignity with which Arcturus had already been generously endowed.

His father's black frock coat, similar to the one worn by his son, did nothing to disguise his bulk and only emphasized his power. Gold frogging edged the coat and wide, bronze epaulettes framed his shoulders. A basket-hilted sword and magnificently tooled pistol hung from his belt, but Valerian knew it had been many years since his father had had cause to draw either of these weapons in anger.

"I knocked," said Arcturus. "Didn't you hear me?"

"I heard you," said Valerian, nodding.

"Then why didn't you answer the door?"

"I didn't think you'd need an invitation, Father,"

replied Valerian. "You *are* the emperor, aren't you? Since when does an emperor wait on the pleasure of others?"

"I may be the emperor, Valerian, but you are my son."

"I am that," agreed Valerian. "Now that it suits you."

"You are angry," said Arcturus. "That's understandable, I suppose. It's only natural for people to behave irrationally over these kinds of things."

"'These kinds of things'?" snapped Valerian, rising from his chair and hurling his glass of port into the fire. "Show a bit of damned respect!"

The glass shattered and the fire roared as the alcohol burned ruby red in the flames.

"Have you no feelings for others?" cried Valerian. No sooner had the words left his mouth than he realized what he'd said and to whom he'd said it.

Valerian laughed. "What am I saying? Of course you don't."

Arcturus remained unmoved by Valerian's outburst and simply laced his hands behind his back. "That was a waste of good port," he said. "And a nice glass, if I'm any judge. I thought I had taught you better than to show anger. Especially when it serves no purpose."

Valerian took a deep breath and turned away from his father, making his way to a drinks cabinet set into the wall. His precious malts and ports were protected from the attentions of poisoners by reflective glass sheathed in an impenetrable energy field, the installation of which had been at the behest of his father, since anyone who knew anything of the Mengsk dynasty would know of their love for quality liquors.

Valerian paused for a moment and studied his reflection as he reached for the recessed brass button that would disengage the security field. Valerian's blond hair spilled around a face that was handsome to the point of beautiful. His features were unmistakably his father's, but where Arcturus wore his hard edges plainly, Valerian's were softened by the influence of his mother's genes.

Full lips and wide, storm-cloud eyes that could charm the birds from the trees sat within a face of porcelain-smooth skin and noble features. At twenty-one he was a beautiful young man, and he knew it, though he was careful to keep that knowledge hidden beneath a veneer of modesty. Which, of course, only served to heighten his appeal to the opposite sex.

He pressed his thumb against the button, the gene-reader on its surface comparing his DNA with the hourly updated records held within the building's mainframe. Though the technologies of the modern world were commonplace to him, Valerian detested the idea of function overwhelming form.

A slight ripple in the air was the only sign of the protective field's disengaging. Valerian opened the glass door to pour two fresh drinks, selecting another tawny port for himself and an expensive ruby vintage for his father.

Valerian returned to the fire, where his father had taken one of the two chairs. His basket-hilted sword sat propped up against the armrest. Arcturus nodded appreciatively as Valerian handed him the glass.

"Calmer now?" asked his father.

"Yes," said Valerian.

"Good. It does not become a Mengsk to openly display his thoughts."

"No?"

"No," said Arcturus. "When men think they know you, they cease to fear you."

"What if I do not want to be feared?" asked Valerian, sweeping his coattails beneath his rump and sitting opposite his father.

"You would rather be loved?" countered Arcturus, sipping his port.

"Can't one be both?"

"No," said Arcturus. "And before you ask, it is always better to be feared than loved."

"Well you'd know," replied Valerian.

Arcturus laughed, but there was no warmth to the sound. "I am your father, Valerian, and cheap gibes will not change that. I know you do not love me as a father ought to be loved, but I care little for that. However, if you are to succeed me you will need to be tougher."

"And if I do not want to succeed you?"

"Irrelevant," snapped Arcturus. "You are a Mengsk. Who else is there?"

Anger touched Valerian. "Even a Mengsk you called a bookish, effeminate weakling?"

Arcturus waved a dismissive hand. "Words spoken

in haste many years ago," he said. "You have proved me wrong, so move on. Scoring points over me does you no credit."

Valerian covered his irritation at his father's stoicism by drinking some port, letting the aromatic liquid sit in his gullet a while before swallowing. He watched as Arcturus used the pause to look around the room at the weapons hanging from the walls, the one point of common ground upon which they could converse without the threat of argument or resentment rearing its ugly head.

"You have made a fine home here, son," said Arcturus, apropos of nothing.

"'Home'?" said Valerian. "I don't know what that word means."

Seeing the puzzlement in his father's eyes, Valerian continued. "Until a few months ago, home was simply where we settled until we had to move on. From one crumbling Umojan moon to another. Or one of the few orbitals the UED or the zerg hadn't destroyed. You must know the feeling, surely?"

"I do," conceded Arcturus. "Though I'd forgotten it. For a long time, home was the *Hyperion*, but then with all that happened with Jim. . ."

"What about Korhal IV?" said Valerian, not wishing to endure another tirade regarding the treachery of Jim Raynor. Over the last few years, Valerian had thrilled to the adventures of Jim Raynor and had secretly admired the man as the thorn in his father's side the former marshal had proved to be.

Arcturus shook his head, quickly masking his irritation at the interruption. "Vast areas of the planet are habitable again and we have rebuilt much of what was destroyed, but even I don't have the power to undo in so short a time the damage done by the Confederacy. Korhal will be great again, I have no doubt, but it will never be what it once was."

"I suppose not," agreed Valerian. "I should have liked to see Korhal before the attack."

"Ah, yes, you would have liked it, I think," said Arcturus. "The Palatine Forum, the Golden Library, the Martial Field, the summer villa . . . yes, you would have liked it."

Valerian leaned forward. "I would like to learn of Korhal," he said. "From someone who was there, I mean. Not dry facts from a digi-tome or holo-cine, but the real thing. From someone who walked its surface and breathed its air."

Arcturus smiled and nodded, as though he had expected such a request. "Very well, Valerian, I *will* tell you of Korhal, what I know of it and what I have pieced together over the years, but I'll tell you more than that if you've the wit to hear it," said Arcturus, standing and draining the last of his port.

"What do you mean?" asked Valerian.

"The story of Korhal is the story of your grandfather and what it means to be a Mengsk. Korhal was the forge in which our dynasty was hammered into shape, raw and bloody, upon the anvil of history."

Valerian felt his heart quicken. "Yes, that's what I want."

Arcturus nodded toward the woman in the holographic plate upon the mantelpiece. "And I'll tell you of your mother."

"My mother?" said Valerian, instantly defensive.

"Yes," said Arcturus, making his way toward the door. "But first we have to bury her."

Book 1.

Angus

25 years earlier

CHAPTER 1

THE VILLA WAS DARK, ITS OCCUPANTS ASLEEP. From the outside it looked peaceful and quiet. Vulnerable. He knew, of course, that it was not; laser trips surrounded the villa in an interconnected web, motion sensors swept the high marble wall that surrounded it, and tremor alarms were set into the floors and walls around every opening. It wasn't the most expensive security system money could buy, but it wasn't far off.

To penetrate the Mengsk summer villa, a white-walled compound perched on a headland of white cliffs overlooking the dark waters of the ocean, would be no easy feat, and the silent figure took his time as he approached the farthest edge of the system's detection envelope.

The scanner attached to his belt, used by prospectors of the Confederate Exploration Corps, was a modified geo-survey unit, a harmonic detector set to read the electromagnetic returns of vespene gas. It had been a simple matter to adjust the sensors to pick up the security lasers and link its display to the goggles he wore over his young, handsome face.

For such a device to work, you had to know the frequency of the lasers and the exact mineral composition of the crystals that produced them. All of which had been simplicity itself to obtain from one of the techs who had installed the system only the previous summer.

The goggles bleached everything of color. The midnight blue of the sky was rendered a flat, rust color, the mountains to the north a deep bronze, and the sea a shimmering crimson.

Like an ocean of blood.

The walls of the villa were dark to him, the lasers and sensor returns gleaming like cords of silver strung like a hunter's trip wires.

"Too easy," he whispered, then inwardly chided himself for the unnecessary words.

The figure dropped to his belly and slithered around the northern side of the villa, avoiding the road that ran all the way to Styrling and keeping to the tall grass that waved in the brisk winds blown in off the sea.

The net of lasers moved regularly, but preprogrammed algorithms in the survey unit meant that by the time they shifted, he was already in a patch of dead ground.

Of course, no algorithm was completely perfect and there was always a chance that he would be detected, but he was confident in his abilities and wasn't worried about failure.

In truth, the prospect of failing was something that hadn't occurred to him. Failure was something that happened to other people, not to him. He was good at what he did and knew it. It gave him a confidence that reached out to others and made it all the easier to ensure he always got what he wanted.

Well, almost always.

He eased ever closer to the villa, keeping his movements slow and unhurried. He knew that to rush things would be to invite disaster, and it took him nearly two hours to come within six meters of the wall.

Passive infrared motion sensors were built into the eaves of the wall, but these were old systems, installed nearly a decade ago, and were about as sophisticated as those you'd find protecting some fringe world magistrate. It was most assuredly not what you'd expect to find protecting the summer villa of one of Korhal's most renowned senators and his family.

The figure was rendered invisible to these sensors by the coolant systems of the black, form-fitting bodysuit he wore. He had fashioned it in secret from the inner lining of a hostile-environment suit used by miners when prospecting high-temperature sites, and he smiled as he rose to his feet and the beams swept over him without detecting him.

Once again the laser net shifted, and he froze as the new pattern was established. He let out a breath as he saw a glimmering, hair-thin beam of light at his calf, and carefully eased away from it. It would be another seventeen point three seconds before they changed again, and he shimmied up to the wall, careful not to touch it for fear of setting off the tremors.

He was within the laser net, and so long as he kept close to the wall—but didn't touch it—he would be invisible to the villa's security. Taking a moment to compose himself, the figure eased around the compound, heading for the delivery entrances.

He froze as a patch of light was thrown out onto the ground.

A door opening.

A man came out, followed by another, and he felt a flutter of fear.

Then they sparked up cigarettes and began to smoke and gossip.

He let out a breath, his heart hammering against his ribs.

Kitchen porters, nothing more.

They moved away from the door, taking refuge from the cold wind behind a lean-to, and he took this golden opportunity to sneak forward and slip through the door, flipping up the lenses of his goggles as he entered the kitchen.

Warmth assailed him from the large, stone-built ovens, and the air was redolent of the lingering aroma of the Mengsk family's last meal. This time of night, the kitchen was empty, the cooks and skivvies retired for the night before rising early to prepare breakfast, and he briefly wondered what the two smokers were doing up this late.

He dismissed the matter as irrelevant and continued onward, moving from the kitchen to the door that led toward the main entrance hall, easing it open, and looking out into the shadowed chamber.

Portraits of Angus Mengsk's illustrious ancestors lined the walls and a number of tasteful statuettes, vases, and weapons, chosen by his wife, Katherine, were displayed on fluted columns. In contrast to the dignity of these objets d'art, a number of toys belonging to Angus's youngest child, Dorothy, were scattered at the bottom of a flight of carpeted stairs that led up to the family bedrooms.

The tiled floor was a black-and-white, checkerboard pattern, and he waited as a guard entered from across the hall and checked in with his compatriots in the security room on a throat mike.

Angus Mengsk kept only a handful of armed guards within the summer villa, claiming that he came here to get away from the trouble Korhal was having with the Confederacy, not to be reminded of it.

The guard turned from the front door and started toward the dining room, shutting the door behind him. With the guard gone, the figure swiftly entered the hall and made his way up the stairs, pausing at the top to glance along the wide corridor.

The bedroom shared by Angus and Katherine was to his left, but the figure set off in the opposite direction, toward the bedrooms of the Mengsk family children.

The floor was wooden, covered with thick rugs, and he walked carefully on it, avoiding the places in the floor where he knew the wood creaked. He stopped before a thick door with a bronze "A" fixed to the wood and smiled to himself.

He gripped the handle, softly opened the door, and ghosted inside the room.

The room was dark, with long benches strewn with dismantled equipment and rock samples lining the walls. Framed images of geological strata and rock compositions hung from the walls and a lumpen, sheet-covered form rested in the large, iron-framed bed.

He took a step into the room and a voice said, "I suppose you think that was clever."

Turning around, he saw Achton Feld, head of security for the Mengsk family, seated on a plush leather chair in the far corner of the room. Dressed in a dark uniform jacket and loose-fitting trousers, Feld's hand rested on the butt of a heavy pistol. He was tall and powerful—built exactly as one would imagine a head of security would be proportioned.

The figure in black relaxed and removed the goggles, revealing patrician features, a strong jawline, and the wide, eager gray eyes of a seventeen-year-old boy.

"I thought it was very clever of me, as a matter of fact," said Arcturus Mengsk.

Achton Feld examined the geo-survey unit with a critical, and not unimpressed, gaze. The boy had managed to put together quite an infiltration package, and Feld was going to have to thoroughly review the security procedures in place at the summer villa.

He put the geo-survey unit down. If Arcturus could get this far, there was no telling how far someone with more malicious intent might reach.

Feld didn't want to the think about the consequences of that. Korhal was in a volatile enough state as it was without something happening to Angus Mengsk. To have so outspoken an opponent of the Confederacy murdered in his bed would be a blow from which the fledgling independence movement on Korhal might never recover.

"Shouldn't you be at the academy in Styrling?"

"I got bored," said Arcturus, sitting on the edge of the bed and pulling the covers back to reveal a series of pillows arranged to give the semblance of a human being. "They weren't teaching me anything I didn't already know."

That was probably true, reflected Feld. Arcturus Mengsk was many things, including a truculent teenager and a selfish rogue who possessed a confidence some called arrogance. But he was also fiercely clever and excelled at everything to which he turned his hand.

"Your father won't be happy about this."

"When is he ever happy with what I do?" countered Arcturus.

"Once a rebel, always a rebel, eh?" said Feld.

"What's that supposed to mean?"

"Nothing. Forget it," replied Feld. "So why break into your own house?"

Arcturus shrugged. "To see if it could be done, I suppose."

"And that's all?"

"Well, maybe to annoy my father." Arcturus smiled. "That never gets old."

"Oh, I have no doubt it'll annoy him," said Feld. "Especially now. And after he's gotten through chewing me out, I'm sure he'll have some choice words for you, too."

"So how did you do it?" asked Arcturus. "Find me, I mean? The bodysuit kept me off the infrared and I know the laser net didn't get me. So how did you know?"

"And why should I tell you? If anything I should be hauling *you* over the coals to find how you got this far. You had help, didn't you?"

"No," said the boy, but Feld knew he was lying. Having a senator for a father had schooled the boy in many of the political arts, and he was almost as skilled a dissembler of the truth as a seasoned veteran of the Palatine Forum.

Almost, but not quite.

"There's no way you could have known how to avoid the laser net without help."

"All right," admitted Angus. "I had help. I persuaded Lon Helian to give me the specs for the lasers so I could modify that geo-survey unit to make them visible. I told him it was for a school project."

"Then Lon Helian will be looking for a new job in the morning."

"Yes, I suppose he will."

Anger touched Feld at Arcturus's lack of concern for the man whose life he had just ruined for the sake of a prank and at the boy's need to challenge the limits of his abilities.

"Come on," said Arcturus. "Tell me. How did you find me? Some new system I didn't know about? A biometric reader? A DNA scanner?"

Feld looked at the young, eager face and felt his anger melt away. Angus Mengsk's son had a quality that caused those around him to forget their ire and want to please him. Only his father and mother seemed immune to his charms.

"It wasn't a new system, it was an old system you forgot about."

"An old system? What?"

"EB Mark 1," said Feld, picking up the geo-survey unit.

"EB Mark 1?" repeated Arcturus. "I've never heard of that one? Is it LarsCorp? No, wait, it has to be Gemini, yes?"

"Neither," said Feld, pointing to his eye. "Eyeball. Mark 1. I saw you on the spy-cams as you came in through the kitchen."

"Spy-cams? What spy-cams?"

"The new Terra model spy-cams your father had installed last week in time for that Umojan ambassador's visit."

"Who?"

"Do you listen to anything that goes on in this house that doesn't involve you?"

"Not if it's anything to do with my father. It's all politics and business, far too boring to pay attention to," said Arcturus. "So who's here?"

"A man named Ailin Pasteur and his daughter," said Feld. "Apparently he's some sort of bigwig on Umoja, and he wants to talk trade with your father."

That wasn't entirely true, but Arcturus had displayed little enough interest in the senator's dealings before now for Feld to bother with explaining further. World-changing events were in motion and all Arcturus wanted to do was piss his father off and spend his time with his coterie of sycophants at the academy or his collection of rocks and gems.

With the geo-survey unit confiscated, Achton Feld turned and made his way to the door.

"Oh, and you'd best tell your friends the game's up."

"My friends?" said Arcturus. "What do you mean?"

"Don't," warned Feld. "Just tell them to go home. It's late and I'm too tired to deal with any more nonsense."

"Honestly, Feld, I have no idea what you are talking about."

Achton Feld stared hard at the boy, looking past his glib exterior and power to make the unbelievable believable. Arcturus Mengsk could, with a few words, get techs with ten years' experience to give up the specs for a laser net, but Feld knew that what he was hearing now was the unvarnished truth.

Which meant . . .

"Crap," said Feld, activating the comm unit on his wrist. "All units, condition black; I repeat, condition black."

Feld turned back to Arcturus. "Stay here," he said. "And hide."

"What is it?" cried Arcturus as Feld ran for the door.

Feld drew his pistol and said, "Intruders."

Arcturus watched Feld disappear through the door, and it took a moment for the implication of the head of security's words to penetrate.

Intruders? Here?

Arcturus now wished he had not thought to try and test himself against the defenses of his father's home; it seemed suddenly foolish and childishly impulsive. Close on the heels of that thought was the idea that his family might actually be in danger, and he felt a knot of warm fear settle in his belly.

The emotion was quickly suppressed, and contrary to Feld's instructions, Arcturus bolted from his room into the corridor. Lights were coming on throughout the house and shouted voices were rousing guards from their posts. As doors slammed, Arcturus was suddenly rooted to the spot with indecision.

The hard bang of a pistol shot echoed in the hallway and a man's scream galvanized him into motion. He set off farther down the corridor and skidded to a halt beside a door hung with paper flowers and a child's drawing of a pony tacked to it.

Colorful paper letters declared that this was "Dorothy's Room," and Arcturus pushed it open. The lights were on, and he pulled up short as he saw his four-year-old sister sitting in bed, her long dark curls spilling messily around her shoulders as she sleepily rubbed her eyes.

Sitting next to her in the bed was a young girl, roughly Arcturus's age, whose blonde hair shone like honey and whose face was as beautiful as it was unexpected.

"Who are you?" demanded the girl, putting protective arms around Dorothy.

"I could ask you the same damn thing," said Arcturus. "What are you doing in my sister's room?"

"I'm Juliana Pasteur," said the girl. "Dorothy asked me to stay and read her a story. I guess we must have both fallen asleep. You must be Arcturus, but what's going on? Was that a gunshot?"

"Yes, and I'm not sure exactly what's going on," said Arcturus, rushing over to the bed. "I think we might be under attack."

"Attack? From whom?"

Arcturus ignored the question and knelt beside the bed. "Little Dot," he said, keeping his voice even and using his sister's pet name. "You have to get up."

At the sound of Arcturus's voice, Dorothy looked at him and his anger rose as he saw the tears in her eyes. Arcturus did not care much for his father or his dealings, but he doted on his sister. Her smile was able to melt the hardest of hearts and not even Angus could resist giving in to her every whim.

"Where are we going?" said Dorothy, her voice drowsy.

Before Arcturus could answer, more gunshots boomed. Dorothy squealed in terror. Arcturus looked up at Juliana Pasteur and said, "Look after her. I'll see what's happening."

Juliana nodded and clutched the little girl tightly as the door to the room opened and two people burst in. Arcturus leapt to his feet, but let out a relieved breath as he saw that one of the figures was his mother.

Katherine Mengsk was tall, beautiful, and slender, but she was no shrinking violet who spent all her time at needlepoint or recitals. A core of neosteel ran through her, and with her children threatened, that quality was in the ascendancy. She blinked in surprise to see Arcturus, but overcame that surprise in a heartbeat and quickly gathered her children as the man next to her ran over to Juliana.

"Are you all right?" asked Katherine. "Arcturus? Dorothy?"

"We're fine, Mother," said Arcturus, prizing himself free of her embrace. "Where's Father?"

Katherine lifted Dorothy to her breast. "He's with Achton. Some men are trying to get inside and they've gone to stop them."

More shots sounded from beyond the door, and Dorothy burst into tears.

His mother turned to the man who had entered the room with her and nodded to Juliana. "Is she okay?"

"She's fine," said the man, his voice strong and lyrical.

Arcturus thought the man looked around the same age as his father, which put him in his mid-forties. His concern over Juliana identified him as Ailin Pasteur, and Arcturus thought him an unimpressive man for an ambassador from so important a world as Umoja.

Receding gray hair and a weak chin conspired to make Ailin Pasteur look timid, but from an early age, Arcturus's father had warned him that where politicians and men of words were concerned, it was almost always the ones you underestimated who would bring you down.

"What's going on, Mother?" asked Arcturus. "Are we really under attack?"

"Yes," said Katherine, nodding. His mother was never one to sugar the pill—it was one of the things Arcturus loved about her. Ailin Pasteur took his daughter by the hand as Katherine Mengsk said, "Now we need to get to the refuge. Everyone follow me, and no dawdling."

The bark of automatic weapon fire roared from somewhere nearby. The noise was so loud it was impossible to pinpoint the source of it, but Arcturus thought it was coming from this floor.

He heard booted footsteps and more shouts.

Arcturus hauled on his mother's hand as more shooting exploded nearby.

The wooden frame around the bedroom door splintered as gunfire tore through it. Everyone screamed and dropped to the floor. Arcturus covered his ears as a clatter of metal and wood rained down from the shattered door.

A twisted spike of silver rolled across the carpet, a thin cone of metal as thick as the tip of his pinkie.

Arcturus recognized it immediately: ammunition fired from a military-grade assault rifle. A C-14 gauss rifle, to be precise. An Impaler.

He heard thumps from outside and two men spun around the doorway. One was Achton Feld, his slugthrower smoking and blood pouring from wounds in his arm and chest. The other was armed with the Impaler rifle, and Arcturus recognized him as one of his father's security guards, a man named Jaq Delor.

As Feld's gaze swept the room, he spoke hurriedly into his shoulder mike. "Angus, it's Feld. I've got them. We're in Dot's room."

Arcturus missed the reply as another roar of gunfire sounded. Delor quickly leaned around the door and fired off a couple of shots. The noise of the gun was deafening, especially mixed together with Dorothy's sobbing cries.

"Achton," said Katherine. "Where is my husband?"

"Downstairs organizing the defense, but he's on his way," said Feld, slamming a fresh magazine into the butt of his pistol and awkwardly racking the slide. "And we have to get out of here. We're too exposed. The refuge is just along the hall."

"We can't go out there!" said Ailin Pasteur. "We'll be killed."

"We'll be killed if we stay here, Ailin," replied Katherine.

"No time to argue," said Feld, his face pale with blood loss. "They have men coming in from both sides. Jaq, how's it looking?"

Jaq Delor raised his rifle and leaned around the door, checking left and right. He fired a burst of Impaler rounds along the length of the corridor, and Arcturus heard a scream of pain.

"Clear now," said Delor as the sound of gunfire intensified.

Arcturus could make no sense of this. All he could hear was a meaningless cacophony of cries for cover, medical attention, or mothers.

Who was winning this fight? Did anyone know?

"Now!" shouted Feld. "Let's go!"

Feld was first out of the room, his pistol extended, as Delor hustled Katherine—still with Dorothy clutched to her chest—Ailin Pasteur, and Juliana through the door. Lastly came Arcturus, and Delor remained with him as they sped along the corridor toward the refuge.

Smoke from the gunfire filled the hallway and Arcturus could see little beyond the floor in the dim glow of sputtering lights that had been shot out. He passed a bulky shape lying on the ground, a body with a bullet wound in the neck.

Blood squirted onto the floor from the ragged crater in the man's throat and Arcturus gagged at the horrid, burned-metallic smell of the man's death. Another man's body lay farther along the corridor, this one with his chest torn apart by Impaler spikes. It looked like he'd been sawn in two.

Delor kept watch on their rear as Feld haltingly led the way to the refuge, a fortified bolt hole constructed in the heart of the house with comm systems capable of reaching Korhal's orbitals and enough supplies to last four days.

Arcturus's mother had objected to the idea of installing such an ugly thing in her summerhouse, but had reluctantly consented to its construction after a crazed psychopath had murdered Senator Nikkos and his family in their beds a few years ago.

A crazed psychopath who was probably now a neurally resocialized Confederate marine.

Arcturus stumbled, but Delor held him upright.

The refuge was up ahead, its neosteel door open and a cold fluorescent light spilling from inside. The wounded Achton Feld lay slumped in the doorway, his face ashen as he tried to hold his slugthrower level.

Shouts sounded behind Arcturus, urgent and demanding.

Jaq Delor released him and spun around, dropping to one knee and bringing his rifle up. The barrel exploded with noise and light, and Arcturus cried out at the unimaginable volume of the weapon. Gauss spikes roared from the barrel and more screams of pain followed.

"Go!" shouted Delor.

No sooner had he given this last instruction than Jaq Delor was struck by a burst of Impaler fire.

It was as if a giant fist had hammered into his side and hurled him against the wall. Blood spattered Arcturus, and he watched in horror as Delor's head lolled down over his chest, almost severed by the impact of the Impaler spikes.

"Arcturus!" screamed his mother from the refuge, but her voice seemed tinny and indistinct. All he could hear was the last rasp of Delor's breath and the sound of his blood as it sprayed from his ruined neck.

Without conscious thought, Arcturus knelt down and lifted Delor's fallen rifle. He'd never fired such a weapon before, but figured all you needed to do was point it at what you wanted to kill and pull the trigger.

How hard could it be?

A shape resolved itself from the smoke of the corridor, a gunman dressed in dark fatigues, body armor, and a strange helmet. It had a number of projecting attachments jutting from the side and a matte black visor, upon which Arcturus could see his own face reflected.

The rifle was a dead weight in his hands, but he raised it without conscious thought.

The gunman already had his rifle aimed, and Arcturus knew he would not be able to pull the trigger before he was torn apart.

The thought made him more angry than fearful.

Before the gunman could fire, Arcturus's reflection

in the helmet's visor exploded in a mist of Plexiglas fragments, bone, and brain matter.

Another shot struck the gunman's helmet, then another and another. The man dropped to his knees as high-velocity slugs tore into his chest and legs.

Arcturus turned and saw his mother marching toward him, Achton Feld's slugthrower held out before her in both hands. With her long black hair unbound and her nightdress flaring behind her like a cloak, she looked like some warrior woman from the old myth stories.

The gun boomed in her grip and she never once broke step as she fired.

Arcturus watched the gunman die and dropped the gauss rifle as his mother's hand clamped on his shoulder. He looked up and saw that her face was thunderous with anger—not at Arcturus, but at the man who had dared threaten one of her children.

Katherine pulled Arcturus to his feet and all but dragged him into the refuge. With help from Ailin Pasteur, she hauled the heavy door of the refuge shut, then punched in the locking code to a keypad set into the wall. Arcturus took heaving gulps of clean, recycled air, feeling his hands shaking at how close he'd come to death. He clenched his fists, angry at such a display of weakness and fought down his fear through sheer force of will.

In control of himself once more, he took stock of his surroundings.

Achton Feld lay slumped against one wall, his chest and shoulder a mass of sticky red fluid, but Arcturus couldn't tell whether he was alive or dead. Juliana Pasteur sat against the opposite wall of the refuge, holding Dorothy tight, and Arcturus went to them. He stroked his sister's hair and smiled reassuringly at Juliana.

"Little Dot," said Arcturus. "It's me. We're safe now."

Dorothy looked up and Arcturus smiled, putting every ounce of sincerity into his words. "You were very brave, little one. No one is going to hurt us now."

"We're safe?" said Dorothy, between snotty exhalations. "You promise?"

"I promise," said Arcturus, nodding. "I won't let anything happen to you. Ever."

"Never ever?"

"Never ever," promised Arcturus.

With the door to the refuge sealed, there was nothing to do but wait, and waiting was something Arcturus Mengsk wasn't particularly good at. He sat on a fold-down cot bed with his legs crossed and Dorothy's head resting on his thigh, her thumb jammed in her mouth and a stuffed pony named Pontius clutched tightly beneath one arm.

Despite all that had happened, she had fallen into a deep sleep, and Arcturus smiled as he ran a hand through her dark hair.

As it turned out, Achton Feld was still alive, and Arcturus's mother was doing her best to treat the Impaler wounds in his shoulder. With the practical mind-set that had made her such a formidable matriarch of the Mengsk family, Katherine set about assigning them all tasks, as much to keep their minds busy as to actually achieve anything useful.

Arcturus was told to look after Juliana and Dorothy, while Ailin Pasteur was ordered to keep watch on the vidcams to get a better idea of what was happening beyond the refuge. The Umojan ambassador nodded, taking a seat by the wall of monitors that displayed a multitude of images of both the exterior and interior of the Mengsk summer villa.

Arcturus wasn't surprised that his mother had taken charge, or that Pasteur had so readily acquiesced to her, for Katherine Mengsk had an aura that conveyed absolute authority, confidence, and credibility. Even at seventeen, Arcturus was old enough to appreciate his mother's strength of character and knew that his father had learned, over the years, not to underestimate her.

Without looking up from Achton Feld's wound, Katherine said, "Ailin, what's going on out there? Can you see Angus?"

Arcturus watched as Pasteur scanned the images before him—empty corridors, dead bodies, and black-clad figures dashing furtively from cover to cover. But the ambassador couldn't tell whether the figures were the attackers or Angus's security forces.

Some of the cameras had been disabled, the screens displaying a hash of static, so that it was impossible to tell exactly what was happening.

"There's still men with guns on the ground floor, but I can't see Angus, no."

"Well, keep looking," said Katherine.

Pasteur nodded and returned his attention to the screens as Katherine stood and wiped her bloody hands on the front of her nightdress. His mother's face was strained, yet beautiful, and Arcturus smiled as he remembered the sight of her standing over him with Feld's pistol blazing, as she killed the man who was about to shoot him.

"Your mother seems very calm," said Juliana Pasteur beside him. "Does she know something we don't?"

Arcturus turned his head to face Juliana. With time to think, he made a fuller inspection of her. He'd thought she was beautiful when he'd first seen her, but now, looking more closely, he saw that he had done her a disservice.

Juliana Pasteur was more than beautiful; she was absolutely stunning, and made all the more so because she plainly had no idea of how attractive she was. The girls at the academy were either driven politicos who bored him or academic types who were no challenge to seduce.

He sensed Juliana would fit into neither of these camps.

The nightdress clung to the curves of her body and his seventeen-year-old mind pictured what she looked like underneath it.

He shook off that image, knowing that this was

neither the time nor the place for such thoughts. "My mother is a strong woman," he said at last.

"My mother got sick and died when I was very young," said Juliana. "I barely remember her."

Arcturus heard the weary sorrow in her voice, but did not know what to say. He did not deal well with grief, for he could never empathize with those who had suffered loss and found them unpleasant to be around.

"I'm sorry," he said at last.

Juliana nodded, seemingly oblivious to his discomfort. "Are we safe in here?" she asked.

Arcturus nodded, pleased the conversation had shifted to a subject he could speak on with some authority.

"Yes, we're perfectly safe," he said. "The walls of this refuge are three feet of plascrete with neosteel reinforcement bars. It would take the Mining Guild's biggest drills—at least a BDE-1400—to get through. Maybe even the 1600."

"You know a lot about drills?"

"A little," he said, with just the right hint of modesty for her to infer that he knew a *lot* about drills. "I plan on becoming a prospector someday."

"Aren't you going to go into one of your father's businesses?"

Arcturus's face darkened at the mention of his father. "No, not if I can help it. I wouldn't be surprised if it's his speaking out against the Confederacy and meddling in things that don't concern him that's gotten us into this mess."

"What the Confederacy is doing should concern everybody," said Juliana.

"Maybe," said Arcturus with a shrug, looking over to Ailin Pasteur to find some clue as to the state of affairs beyond the refuge. "I don't really know and I don't really care. I just want to be left alone to make my own way in the galaxy."

"But if the Confederacy goes on the way it is, no one will be able to do that."

Arcturus glanced over at Ailin Pasteur. "Did your father tell you that?"

"As a matter of fact it was your father," said Juliana archly.

"Then I have even less interest in it."

"You aren't very polite, are you?"

"I don't know you," pointed out Arcturus. "Why do I need to be polite to you?"

"Because even fringe worlders know it is good manners to be polite to a guest."

He saw the color in her cheeks and realized she was right—he *was* being rude, and being rude to such a pretty girl seemed like the behavior of a savage, not that of a senator's son.

Arcturus took a deep breath and flashed his most dazzling smile, the one that melted the hearts of the girls at the academy who briefly piqued his interest. "You're right: I am being rude, and I'm sorry. This has been an . . . unusual evening. I'm not normally like this. Normally I am actually quite pleasant to be around."

She stared at him, trying to crack the mask of his handsome sincerity, but even the most desirable of Styrling socialites had tried and failed to do that.

Juliana Pasteur would have no chance beneath the glare of his charm.

"Apology accepted," she said with a smile, but Arcturus knew she wasn't yet hooked.

"You're a sharp one, aren't you? I like that," he said, more interested in Ailin Pasteur's daughter now that she had displayed a measure of resistance to his wiles.

"Korhal may be one of the jewels in the Confederate crown, but Umoja isn't without culture and breeding."

"I've never traveled there," said Arcturus. "Maybe I will soon, if all its maidens are like you."

"They're not, but I think you would like it there."

"I'm sure I would. Would you be my guide?"

"Perhaps," said Juliana. "I could show you Sarengo Canyon."

"Where the supercarrier crashed," said Arcturus. "It's said to be breathtaking."

"You have no idea," promised Juliana.

"Well, if we live through the night, I'll be sure to take you up on that," said Arcturus, his light tone robbing the comment of any danger.

Juliana smiled, but before Arcturus could say any more, Ailin Pasteur said, "Katherine! The door!"

Arcturus looked over to the bank of monitors, but the vidcamera showing the corridor had been shot out in the fighting. A series of clicking beeps came from the keypad next to the door, and Katherine bent to examine the sequence before typing in her own code.

This was in turn answered by another series of key punches from the other side, which was again answered by Katherine. His mother nodded to Ailin Pasteur and then typed in a last key sequence that disengaged the locks.

Arcturus felt a mixture of relief and disappointment that their time here was to be cut short, but smiled as he felt Juliana's hand take his and squeeze it in nervous anticipation.

The thick neosteel door of the refuge swung open and Angus Mengsk, senator of Korhal, father to Arcturus and Dorothy, and husband to Katherine, entered with an Impaler rifle cradled in his arms.

Angus was a broad, powerfully built man, his dark hair pulled into a long ponytail that, like his beard, was lined with silver streaks. His features were strong, gnarled with age, and a pair of cold gray eyes stared out from beneath a bushy set of eyebrows.

He swung the rifle over his shoulder and took his wife into a crushing bear hug.

"Thank God you're safe," he said. "I knew you'd look after them."

"We're all fine," said Katherine. "Achton's been hit, but he'll live. Is it over?"

Angus released his wife from his embrace and nodded. "They're all dead, yes."

Arcturus swallowed nervously as he saw his father finally notice him sitting on the bed.

Angus prized his gaze from Arcturus and shook hands with Ailin Pasteur, his scowl replaced with the practiced smile of a politician. "Good to see you're still alive, my friend."

"And you, Angus," said Pasteur. "A bad business this and no mistake. Confederates?"

"Maybe," said Angus. "We'll talk later, eh?"

Pasteur nodded, and Angus moved past him to stand before Arcturus, the politician's smile falling from his face like a discarded mask.

"What in the name of the fathers are you doing here, boy?" demanded Angus. "Have you been thrown out of the academy again?"

"Nice to see you too, Father," said Arcturus.

CHAPTER 2

ANGUS MENGSK POURED HIMSELF A GENEROUS measure of brandy from an expensive crystal decanter and downed the amber liquid in one swallow. He closed his eyes and allowed the molten taste to line his throat and settle in his stomach before pouring another glass. He lifted up the bottle inquiringly toward Ailin Pasteur, but the Umojan ambassador shook his head.

"No thank you, Angus."

"I know you don't drink, Ailin," said Angus. "But under the circumstances . . ."

"Angus, I can't."

"Come on, man," cajoled Angus. "Surely one won't hurt?"

"He said he didn't want one," said Katherine, replacing the stopper in the decanter and glaring sternly at her husband.

"There's no such thing as just one for me. Not anymore," said Pasteur.

"Fine," said Angus, shrugging and taking his own drink back to the table.

In the aftermath of the attack, Angus had gathered the occupants of the summer villa in the main dining room, a long, oak-paneled room dominated by an exquisite rosewood table carved with pastoral scenes of a rustic Korhal that had probably never existed.

An exquisite chess set with pieces carved from jet and ivory sat next to the drinks cabinet, the pieces apparently arranged in mid-game, though the white king was in checkmate.

Angus's wife took a seat at the end of the table, next to Dorothy and Ailin Pasteur's daughter, and he allowed himself a moment of quiet relief that his girls had been spared the worst of this night's bloodshed. His mood darkened as he shot a glance over to Arcturus, the boy sitting with his arms folded across his chest and his eyes steadfastly refusing to meet those of his father.

Achton Feld had managed to haul himself from his sickbed to join them. The man looked terrible, his skin gray and greasy with sweat. Everyone knew he should have been resting, but, to his credit, he had found the strength to be part of their debate as to what was to be done about this terrible night and how best to repay those responsible.

Angus paced the length of the table, his expression murderous, his eyes smoldering with anger.

"Angus," said Katherine. "Sit down before you wear a hole in the carpet. And calm down."

"Calm down?" exploded Angus. "They tried to kill us in our own house! Armed men came into our house and tried to kill us all. I swear I'll lead the army to the Palatine Forum and strangle Lennox Craven with my bare hands if he had something to do with this. For God's sake, Kat, how can I be calm at a time like this?"

"Because you need to be," said Katherine firmly. "You are a senator of Korhal and you don't have the luxury of anger. It achieves nothing and only clouds your judgment. Besides, you don't know yet *who* was behind this. It might not be Craven and his Confederate goons."

Lennox Craven was the senior consul of the Korhal Senate, the man tasked with ensuring that the will of the Confederacy was carried out, upholding its laws and providing a controlling influence on the unruly senators below him.

Angus loathed the man, believing him to be little more than a stooge for the corrupt Old Families that governed the Confederacy from the shadows. But for all that, Craven was a formidable senator and canny businessman, and Angus had exchanged many an incendiary barb with him across the marble floor of the Palatine Forum. The Mengsk family was one of the Old Families too, one of the oldest in fact, and Craven never tired of reminding Angus that he was spitting in the eye of the establishment that had given him such power and wealth.

Angus took a deep breath and nodded, smiling at Katherine as he took a drink.

"You're right, my dear," he said, "I need to think this through clearly. Achton? Do you have any thoughts on what happened here tonight? Who were these men?"

"Professionals," said Achton Feld. "They were good, but we got the drop on them, thanks to Arcturus's stunt. A few minutes more and, well, I don't like to think what might have happened."

"And you and I are going to talk about the security here later," promised Angus, staring at his son. "But who were they?"

Achton Feld chewed his bottom lip for a moment, then said, "Everything about them leads me to think they're a corporate death squad, a black-ops unit used to kill off business rivals and engage in corporate espionage, kidnapping, and that kind of thing."

"Why would anyone want to target Angus?" asked Katherine. "And why now?"

"Perhaps someone got wind of the things Angus is going to address in his Close of Session speech to the Senate?" suggested Pasteur.

"It's sure to ruffle some feathers, to say the least," agreed Angus.

"But that's not for months," protested Katherine. "And your business interests only benefit Korhal."

"A lot of people on Korhal have become very wealthy thanks to their dealings with the Confederacy," said Pasteur. "Plenty of organizations have ties to both Korhal and the Confederacy, and Angus is stirring up trouble for them. If the Confederacy were to be kicked off Korhal, they would stand to lose millions."

"I know it's a long shot, Achton, but is there anything on the bodies that might tell us who sent them?" asked Angus.

Feld shook his head. "The kit they used is all ex-military stuff, the kind you can pick up easily enough if you know where to look. It looks like something local, but I don't buy it. My gut's telling me something different."

"And what is your gut telling you?" asked Katherine.

"That this is bigger than some corporation trying to hold on to its savings."

"Why do you think that?" said Angus.

"Because all those dead men are marines. Or at least they were."

"Marines? How do you know?"

Feld reached up and tapped the back of his neck. "They've all been brain-panned. All six of them have got neural resocialization scars."

Ailin Pasteur cleared his throat. "Well, naturally that leads us to the Confederacy."

"You're probably right, Ailin," said Angus, "but it seems heavy-handed, even for them."

"Really? You heard about the rebellion on Antiga Prime?"

"No. What rebellion? I didn't see anything about that on the UNN."

"Well, you wouldn't, would you?" pointed out Katherine. "Aren't you always saying that the Old Families control the corporations that run the news channels? They broadcast what they want you to see, their version of the truth in twenty-second sound bites."

"That's true enough," replied Angus. "But what of Antiga Prime?"

"Yes, well, apparently the people of Andasar City kicked out the Confederate militia and held the local magistrate hostage. They demanded an end to Confederate corruption, and whole districts rallied to their call to arms. The city was as good as in open revolt, but two days later, a troop of marines under a Lieutenant Nadaner went in and took the place back. And they didn't leave any survivors."

"Good God," said Angus. "How many dead?"

"No one knows for sure, but my sources say the figure is in the thousands."

"And that's exactly why we need to be careful here," pointed out Katherine. "If the Confederacy isn't shy about perpetrating a massacre like that, then clearly they don't have any compunction against killing a senator and his family, do they?"

"But why send resocialized marines?" asked Arcturus, lifting his head up from staring at the table. "Surely any dead bodies would be easy to trace back to the Confederacy?"

"Because they didn't expect to fail," said Angus, returning to the crystal decanter on the drinks cabinet and pouring himself another glass of brandy. "Their paymasters expected them to kill us all and not leave any of their own dead behind. The damned arrogance of it!"

"Then why bother making them look like corporate killers?" said Arcturus.

"Plausible deniability," said Achton Feld. "In case the assassins were caught on any kind of surveillance. Corporate-sponsored murders are terrible, if not exactly uncommon, but if it was discovered that the Confederacy was complicit in the murder of a prominent senator . . ."

"The planet would erupt in revolt," finished Katherine.

Angus laughed without humor. "Almost makes me wish they'd got me after all."

"Don't say that!" snapped Katherine. "Not ever."

"Sorry, dear," said Angus, standing behind his wife and kissing her cheek. "I didn't mean that, but I feel it's going to take something truly dreadful to bring the Confederacy to its knees. We won't beat them overnight, but we *will* beat them, and I'll tell you how."

Once again Angus paced the length of the table as he spoke, allowing his voice to become the rich baritone he used when speaking in the Forum. "It's their arrogance that will be their undoing. They can't see how they can possibly do anything wrong, and when you can't see that, you make mistakes. My father once said that when all you have is a hammer, everything starts to look like a nail."

Angus paused and turned to address his audience. "We'll show them what happens when the nail hits back."

• • •

The dining room was empty save for Angus and Arcturus, the two sharing an uncomfortable silence as the elder Mengsk poured out two snifters of brandy. Angus took one for himself and walked over to where his son sat to offer him the other.

Arcturus looked askance at the glass, clearly wishing to reach for it, but unsure as to whether or not he should.

"Go on, take it," said Angus. "I know you're too young, but on a night like this it hardly matters, does it? There's a lesson for you right there: sort out what matters from what doesn't. Act on the things that mean something and discard the rest."

Arcturus took the glass and tentatively sniffed the expensive drink. His nose wrinkled at its potency, and he took an experimental sip. His eyes widened, but he kept it down without coughing, and Angus felt his anger loosen its hold on him as he sat across from his son.

Achton Feld had explained what Arcturus had done and, as much as he wanted to rage biliously at his son, Angus couldn't help but be proud of the lad's inventiveness and sheer brio in pulling off a stunt like that.

But despite his grudging admiration, Angus couldn't allow Arcturus off the hook too easily.

"Do your tutors at the academy know you are gone?" he asked.

Arcturus looked at the timepiece on his wrist and smiled. "They will in a few hours," he said. "I sent a message with an attached comm-virus to Principal Steegman's console. He'll open it with his morning java, and it'll really spoil his day."

Angus shook his head. "They'll expel you for this."

"Probably," agreed Arcturus, and Angus fought the urge to slap him.

"Have you any idea of how much your place at Styrling Academy cost?"

Arcturus shrugged. "No."

"A great deal, and there are plenty of prospective students just waiting to take your place."

"So let them have it," said Arcturus. "I'm not learning anything there anyway."

Angus bristled at his son's belligerence, forcing himself to remember what he had been like on the verge of manhood: his entire life ahead of him, and the sense that he knew all there was to know about the world. Arcturus was no different, and he began to appreciate the patience his own father had displayed.

He took a deep breath before speaking again. "Listen to me, son. You live a privileged life here, but it's time you learned that it is a harsh world out there beyond these walls, and that you are not prepared for it."

"I'll survive."

"No," said Angus bluntly. "You won't. I can't pretend I'm not impressed by what you did tonight, but stunts like that will see you dead sooner or later."

Arcturus laughed and said, "Now you're being melodramatic."

"No," said Angus. "I'm not. It's the truth, and now I have to discipline you."

"Why?" said Arcturus. "If it weren't for me, those men would have killed us all."

"I think you'll find it was Feld catching you that alerted us."

"It was just a joke," said Arcturus. "And anyway, isn't that something that doesn't matter after what happened tonight? Or don't your own lessons apply to you?"

Angus put down his glass and leaned over the table, lacing his hands before him. "You've the seeds of a debater in you, son, but you have to be punished. To allow youth to run unchecked is to invite a recklessness of spirit and disregard for the proper order of things that is anathema to any ordered society."

"You're one to talk," said Arcturus. "You disregard 'the proper order of things' all the time. All I ever hear the other students at the academy say is how you're stirring up trouble for Korhal with all your speeches about the corruption of the Confederacy and how we'd be better off without it. Why do you have to be such an embarrassment?"

Angus sat back in his chair, surprised at Arcturus's outburst and angry at how little his son understood of the world beyond his own little bubble of reality.

"You have no clue what you're talking about, son," said Angus. "What the Confederacy is doing on Korhal is criminal. Corruption, backhanders, and bribery are everywhere, and if you have money the law is a joke. Virtually every penny earned by the citizens of Korhal swells the coffers of some Confederate puppet corporation while our own, independent industries wither on the vine. Tell me how *that* is the proper order of things?"

"I don't know," said Arcturus. "All I want to do is become a prospector."

"A prospector? Grubbing in dirt and rocks like some Kel-Morian pirate? Hardly. You are the son of a senator, Arcturus, and you are destined for greater things than prospecting."

"I don't *want* greater things. I just want to do what *I* want, not what you think I should do."

"You're too young to really know what you want," said Angus.

"I know that I don't want to follow in your footsteps," snapped Arcturus. "Hell, I might even join the military."

"You don't mean that; you're just angry," said Angus. "You don't know the reality of life, what the Confederacy has done and what they're going to do if someone doesn't stand up to them. In the centuries since the supercarriers crashed, the Old Families have been taking over everything by force, guile, and corruption. Soon there won't be anything left they don't control."

"So what? Who says that's a bad thing?"

Angus fought down his anger, but he could feel his temper fraying in the face of his son's obstinacy. Didn't the boy understand the scale of the Confederacy's corruption? Couldn't he see the terrible fate that awaited all right-thinking people if they didn't take a stand against the all-controlling, all-pervading influence of a remote, unthinking, unfeeling government?

Looking into Arcturus's face, Angus could see he did not, and his heart sank.

Speaking in the Palatine Forum, Angus Mengsk had swayed recalcitrant senators to his side, won hopeless causes through the power of his oratory, but he couldn't convince his own son that the Confederacy was a great and terrible evil that threatened everything the free people of Korhal prized.

Angus Mengsk, firebrand senator and son of Korhal, might yet save his planet—but might lose his son in the process.

The irony of it all was not lost on him.

The following morning, with the sun rising over the mountains, Arcturus yawned as he heard the door to his room open. He rolled over and smiled as he saw Dorothy standing in the doorway, the bright blue form of Pontius the pony clutched in her arms.

"What is it, Little Dot?" he said, propping himself up in bed.

"Why do you fight with Daddy?" asked Dorothy.

Arcturus laughed. "That's a big question for such a little girl."

"But why?"

Arcturus swung his legs out of bed and opened his arms, whereupon Dorothy ran to him and jumped up onto his lap.

"Ow, you're getting bigger every day," said Arcturus. "You're getting fat."

"No I'm not!" squealed Dorothy, jabbing her fingertips into his ribs.

"All right, all right! You're not fat!"

"Told you," said Dorothy, satisfied she had won the argument. She looked up at him, and he knew she hadn't forgotten that he hadn't answered her question.

"I wish you didn't always fight with Daddy," said Dorothy.

"I wish we didn't either."

"So why do you?"

"It's hard to explain, Dot," he said. "Father and I . . . well, we don't agree about a lot of things and he's too stubborn to admit that he's not always right."

"Are you always right?"

"No, not always, but—"

"So how do you know Daddy's not right then?"

Arcturus opened his mouth to answer her child's logic, but floundered when he couldn't think of an answer that would satisfy them both. "I suppose I don't. But he wants me to do things I don't want to do."

"Like what?"

"Like not be who I want to be," said Arcturus.

"Who do you want to be? Don't you want to be like Daddy?"

Arcturus shook his head. "No."

"Why not?"

Arcturus was spared from answering by a gentle knock, and he looked up to see his mother standing in the doorway. Katherine Mengsk was dressed in a long cream dress with a midnight blue bodice and looked as fresh as if she had had a full night's rest and not been hunted by armed soldiers.

"Dorothy, it's time for breakfast," said Katherine.

"But I'm not hungry," said Dorothy.

"Don't argue with me, young lady," warned her mother. "Go down to the kitchen and have Seona fix you a bowl of porridge. And don't turn your nose up at me. Go."

Dorothy leaned up and planted a small kiss on Arcturus's cheek before dropping from his lap and running off, Pontius dragging on the floor behind her.

With Dorothy gone, Arcturus stood and pulled on his shirt and a pair of dark britches, hiking the braces up over his shoulders.

"You didn't answer her question," said his mother.

"What question?"

"Why you don't want to be like your father."

Arcturus ran his hands through his dark hair and poured himself a glass of water from a silver ewer beside the bed. He took a drink and swilled the water around his mouth before answering.

"Because I want do something with my life that's mine, not his."

His mother swept into the room, graceful and

strong, and placed a hand on Arcturus's shoulder. The touch was maternal and comforting, and Arcturus wished he could be as close to his father as he was to his mother.

"Your father just wants what's best for you, Arcturus," she said.

"Does he? Sometimes I think he just wants a carbon copy of himself."

Katherine smiled. "I see a lot of him in you, it's true, but then there's too much of me in you to ever be *that* much like your father."

"That's a relief," said Arcturus, but the smile fell from his face as he saw the hurt in his mother's face.

"I'm sorry," he said. "I know he's a good man, but he doesn't understand me."

"You think you're the first seventeen-year-old who's said that about his father?"

"No, I suppose not."

"You are a brilliant boy, Arcturus; you could achieve great things if you allow yourself to. Everything you turn your hand to you master within days, and your father just wants to make sure you make the most of your talents."

"I remember you telling me I was going to be a great leader when I was Dot's age," said Arcturus. "But I grew out of that a long time ago."

His mother took his hands in hers and looked straight at him. "No. It was true then and it's still true."

Uncomfortable with his mother's grandiose dreams for his future, Arcturus changed the subject. "Do I really have to go back to the academy?"

"Yes, you do. I know you don't like it there, but it means the world to me that you finish your education. You *did* recall that message with the comm-virus you sent to Principal Steegman's console, didn't you?"

"I did"—Arcturus grinned—"though it would have been worth getting expelled just to have seen the look on his face as the virus sent his private files to the parents of every student at the academy."

His mother shook her head in exasperation, but he could see that she too was amused at the thought of Steegman's humiliation. "I don't even want to think what might be contained in that odious little man's 'private files'."

"Are Ailin Pasteur and his daughter going to be staying with us for a while yet?" asked Arcturus, hearing movement from another part of the house.

Katherine's eyes narrowed as she sensed his interest. "Yes, they will be our guests for a spell. Your father thinks it wise for them to remain with us until he can recall some more guards to escort us all back to Styrling."

"That sounds sensible." Arcturus nodded, trying not to sound too interested, though of course his mother saw through his nonchalance in a heartbeat and smiled.

"She's very pretty," said his mother. "Juliana."

"Yes, she is," agreed Arcturus. "And I think she likes me."

His mother leaned down and kissed his cheek. "Who could not love you, my handsome boy? Now go and get some breakfast with your sister; I've no doubt she'll be trying to talk Seona into giving her something so laden with sugar it'll keep her awake for days."

Arcturus made his way downstairs, along the corridor that had only the previous night been filled with gunsmoke and the sound of battle. The bodies that had lain here, pumping their lifeblood over the carpet, had been removed and the domestics were cleaning the stains they had left behind.

It still seemed unreal to him that people had tried to kill them last night. The idea that people would kill helpless civilians for the sake of something as prosaic as money seemed ludicrous, but if his reading of history had taught him anything, it was that entire cultures had been wiped out for far less. Killing for honor, glory, land, or freedom seemed more noble ideals to kill or die for, but Arcturus Mengsk planned on doing none anytime soon.

He set foot on the stairs, the wood creaking and the banister splintered by Impaler spikes. Entire sections had been blasted away and the marble and plaster walls were stitched with impact craters.

When he reached the bottom, Arcturus heard voices coming from the dining room. The door was ajar, and he paused as he recognized his father's stentorian tones and the more mellifluous sound of Ailin Pasteur's voice.

Curious as to what they were talking about, Arcturus edged closer to the door.

". . . exactly why we need your help more than ever, Ailin," said his father. "Korhal can't do this alone. We're gathering strength, but without the support of Umoja, the Confederacy will crush us."

"I understand that," replied Pasteur, "but you have to understand the precariousness of our position. Umoja can't be seen to be openly supporting you, Angus. We have a hard enough time fending off the Confederate influence as it is, and to be publicly linked with a rabble-rouser like your good self would give them an excuse to increase their pressure. The Ruling Council is willing to supply your men with what they need, but our involvement can't be made public."

"That's a given, Ailin, but matters are coming to a head. The attack last night only goes to show how desperate they're becoming. I have supporters within the Senate and all over Korhal to make this work, and you know well enough that brushfire rebellions are erupting throughout the sector. All it needs is one shining example that the Confederacy can be beaten and the old order will be swept away. Korhal can be that example, but only if you support us."

"And we will, but what you are talking about . . . you'll be called a terrorist."

"I prefer the term 'freedom fighter,'" said Angus.

"That depends on whether or not you win."

"Then I'll need to make sure I win."

Arcturus knew he was hearing words of great import, but the sense of them washed over him. What was his father planning that might have him labeled a terrorist? The word itself was a powerful one, conjuring up images of secretive men who met in shadows to plot the death of innocents to achieve their diabolical ends.

The idea that his father might be such a man repelled Arcturus, and his previously solid notion of Angus Mengsk as a powerful and controlling, yet mostly benign, presence in his life now seemed as fragile as glass.

As these thoughts surged through Arcturus's head, he heard footsteps, realizing too late that they were approaching the door at which he listened. He turned away, but was too slow, and a heavy fist took hold of his shirt and dragged him into the dining room where they had met last night.

"Spying on me, are you?" roared Angus. "What did you hear?"

Arcturus struggled in his father's grip. "That you're a terrorist!" he shouted.

Angus spun him around and pushed him down into one of the chairs.

"You heard nothing, son," said Angus. "Those words were not meant for the likes of you."

Arcturus looked over to Ailin Pasteur, the man

clearly surprised and worried that Arcturus had overheard their discussions.

"What are you going to do?" asked Arcturus. "Are you going to kill people?"

His father stared hard at Arcturus, and the father's cold gray eyes saw deep into the heart of his son.

Arcturus saw his father come to a decision within himself.

Pasteur saw it too and said, "Angus . . . are you sure?"

"Aye, he'll be eighteen soon. It's time he started acting like a man, so I'm going to treat him like one."

Arcturus felt a nervous thrill at his father's words, wondering if all those years of wanting to be treated as an adult were about to blow up in his face.

"Well, boy, are you ready to become a man?"

Arcturus hesitated for the briefest second before answering. "I am."

"Good," said Angus. "I'll respect that. But you have to understand that what I'm going to tell you can't leave this room."

Angus held out his hand to Arcturus. "Swear that to me and I'll tell you everything."

"I swear it," said Arcturus, shaking his father's hand.

"Very well," said Angus, taking a seat next to Arcturus and sitting with his legs crossed. "You know, of course, that I detest the corruption of the Confederacy with every fiber of my being, but it runs deeper than that. The Old Families control everything from their capital world of Tarsonis, and the entire apparatus of the Confederacy is geared to keep them in power, exploiting the planets under their control and stealing their wealth. Well, no more."

"You're going to fight the Confederacy?" asked Arcturus. "Why?"

"Because someone has to," said Angus. "They've overstretched their empire and, like a house of cards, all it needs is one push in the right place to make it fall. People are tired of the yoke of the Confederacy around their necks and rebellion's in the air—you can feel it."

"You're going to declare war on the Confederacy?" said Arcturus incredulously.

"Well, not war exactly," replied Angus. "Not yet, at least."

"Terrorism," said Arcturus. "Is that it?"

"I have no doubt some will call it that, yes, but if you think about it, what the Confederacy is doing can easily be construed as terrorism."

"Surely that's not the same thing?"

"Isn't it?" asked Angus. "Isn't the purpose of terrorism to kill and maim people so that whoever it's directed against will bend to your will? And doesn't the Confederacy engage in military operations designed to coerce people into bending to their will through fear?"

"But that's different," said Arcturus. "That's war."

Angus shook his head. "No, it's not. After all, the purpose of war isn't, or at least shouldn't be, about killing every last man in the enemy army. It's about killing enough of them that their leaders are more afraid of continuing the war rather than of surrendering."

"Then, by your definition, every act of war could be called an act of terrorism, since it's coercion through fear by the use of violence."

"Exactly," said Angus, pleased he had made his point.

"But you're still going to kill people," pointed out Arcturus.

"In war, people die. It's unfortunate, but inevitable," replied Angus. "I wish it were different, but the Confederacy has brought this on itself. Unlike them, however, we won't hurt innocent civilians; we'll only be targeting military installations."

"It's still wrong," said Arcturus. "People will still die and you'll have killed them."

Angus leaned back in his seat, his face lined with disappointment. "I thought you would be man enough to understand what needs to be done, Arcturus, but I can see I was wrong. You're still a child and you still think like a child, unable to see the truth of the world beyond your own selfish little bubble."

His father's words stung like red-hot whips, and Arcturus felt his resentment flare. He stood up and turned on his heel, marching toward the dining room door.

"Angus . . . ," hissed Ailin Pasteur.

"Son," barked Angus. "You are never to speak of this. You understand me? Never."

"I understand," snapped Arcturus.

CHAPTER 3

SUNLIGHT RIPPLED THROUGH THE CANOPY OF treetops and made the landscape glow as the convoy of silver groundcars sped along the road to Styrling. Altogether there were six cars, one conveying the Mengsk family, another Ailin Pasteur and his daughter, and the other four bearing armed men.

The cars were '58 Terra Cougars, an older model of groundcar, yet a mode of transport favored by many of Korhal's senators, thanks to the heavy steel undercarriage and thick side panels that had foiled more than one assassination attempt.

Two of the cars were equipped with turret-mounted Impalers, and the convoy moved at speed along the wide strip of road. Half a kilometer ahead, three vulture hovercycles ran point, herding what little traffic there was on the road out of the convoy's path.

This time of the morning, traffic was light, but Achton Feld was taking no chances and had ordered his men to shoot first and ask questions second—

assuming anything survived a grenade barrage from the vultures. The Confederacy had already tried to kill Angus Mengsk once, and Feld wasn't taking any chances that they might try again.

Arcturus watched the countryside flashing past, lush greens and sumptuous golds as the autumn tones blended together in a swirl of color like a painting left out in the rain. The Mengsk summer villa was built sixty kilometers to the south of Styrling and the countryside separating the two was amongst the most verdant and lush of Korhal, yet it was shrinking every year as the industrial complex of the city spread farther and farther.

His father had chosen the site precisely because it was far enough from Styrling to feel like he could escape the day-to-day running of his many businesses and the politics of the Senate, but close enough that he was never too far out of the loop.

Arcturus felt his mood sour with every kilometer that passed beneath the groundcar and brought him closer to the academy. His father sat opposite him, his face unreadable, though he smiled whenever Arcturus's mother looked at him. Dorothy was on her knees on the backseat next to him, Pontius clutched tightly as she peered out the polarized, armored glass of the window.

He smiled at the simple joy on her face, wishing he could go back to a time when life had been simpler. All Dorothy cared about was Pontius, sugary sweets, and being close to her father. She didn't yet have to worry about disappointing anyone or being forced into a role she didn't want.

Little Dot would be the apple of Angus's eye no matter what she did, and Arcturus felt a twinge of irritation, but quickly shook it off, recognizing that it was foolish to be jealous of a four-year-old.

Despite his mother's pleasant ramblings on the colors of the leaves and the beauty of the scenery and Dorothy's enthusiasm for the journey, the interior of the groundcar was tense. Arcturus and his father had not spoken since their harsh words in the dining room the previous morning, and no amount of calming words from his mother could bridge the gulf, which grew wider with every minute of silence.

Arcturus kept his gaze fixed on the landscape unfolding around them as the groundcar wove its way though the low hills to the south of the city. Despite the inevitable growth of business, Korhal remained a defiantly green world, the planetary authorities long ago having had the foresight to invest in renewable energy sources and enforce stringent clean air laws.

As a result, Korhal was one of the few planets in the Confederacy to be a thriving hub of trade and industry that was also actually a pleasant place to live and visit. Arcturus had not yet ventured off world, but he had ambitions beyond Korhal's skies. He longed to travel between the stars and explore new worlds and *earn* his fortune with his skills, instead of simply inheriting it as his father had done.

That his father had also worked tirelessly since he had achieved adulthood never occurred to Arcturus. Not that Arcturus disapproved of inheriting wealth, title, and position—the dynastic traditions of Korhal were well established—but he wanted to be known as a man who had gotten to the top by virtue of his own abilities. He wanted people to look at him and know that he had achieved what he had through blood, sweat, and sacrifice.

His thoughts of the future were interrupted when he caught sight of a shimmering lattice of silver through the branches of the trees, the first signs of civilization. Despite his foul mood, he smiled as he caught tantalizing glimpses of Styrling through the wide canyons of the hills.

It was a huge city, a mecca of commercial interests and a glittering symbol of all that had been achieved in the two centuries since the planet's settlement. Arcturus loved the opportunities the city offered: the wealth, the entertainment, the bustle, and the sheer, vibrant *humanity* of it all. Everything a person desired, and more besides, could be found in Styrling if you knew where to look.

The groundcar swept over a ridge that curved along the road, and then the city was laid out before him.

No matter how many times he saw it, it never failed to impress.

Styrling was like the frozen aftermath of a droplet that had fallen into a petri dish of mercury, a silver crown of soaring structures that stood tall and majestic in the center and which gradually diminished in size toward the edges.

A dizzying web of flyovers surrounded and penetrated the bright metropolis, like a hundred threads of dark wool woven through it, and the city shone with dazzling reflections from the mass of neosteel and glass that made up the bulk of the buildings.

The architecture of Styrling was not subtle. Most of the towers and spires belonged to one of the megacorporations or to representatives of one of the Old Families, and each of the owners sought to outdo the others with the height and magnificence of a given structure. Graceful curving walls had once bounded the extreme edge of the city, but the pressure of commerce had driven a great deal of the city's infrastructure beyond them.

The wealthiest families of Korhal kept their headquarters within the walls of Styrling, and the Mengsks were no exception.

The Mengsk Skyspire was a mighty, fortresslike edifice that towered over its nearest rivals: the Continental Building, the LarsCorp Tower, and the Korhal headquarters of the Universal News Network. Arcturus hated the Skyspire, its angular lines and neo-Gothic stylings appearing at odds with the sleek, graceful designs of its neighbors.

As far as Arcturus was concerned, it was the architectural embodiment of his father: cold, stern, and uncompromising.

The city drew closer and the traffic grew heavier, the vultures drawing back to surround the groundcars like mother hens protecting their chicks. Arcturus watched the traffic flow like a living thing around them, moving to its own internal rhythms, and as he looked at the faces within each car, he wondered at the lives he saw passing him.

Each one represented a self-contained world, around which the universe revolved, and Arcturus idly tried to fit histories to each face—trying to imagine what lives these people lived. What were their dreams and ambitions? What made them rise from their beds each day to toil in the factories and offices of Styrling?

Love? Ambition? Desire? Greed?

Watching the people as they made their way to work, Arcturus saw all human life before him—laughter, quarrels, stolid silences, and a thousand other things. He saw conversations between men and women, fathers and children, lovers and colleagues, each small world with its own hopes and dreams for the future.

A young girl with a yellow ribbon in her hair sat in the passenger seat of a car two lanes over. She noticed Arcturus looking at her and waved to him. He smiled and waved back, feeling an unaccountable closeness to these people of Korhal, feeling that in some small way they were *his* people. He sensed a kinship with the faces he saw around him, a bond with the people with whom he shared his homeworld that he had never felt before.

The girl's car drifted away, vanishing down an off-ramp, and Arcturus returned his attention to the city around him as they were swallowed up by its glass and steel canyons.

The tense silence in the groundcar was broken only when their journey took them around the chaotic site of the new Korhal Assembly Forum.

Or what was *supposed* to be the new Korhal Assembly Forum.

Towering cranes and enormous earthmoving machines stood idle around a monstrous, half-finished building of concrete and exposed steel that looked as though it had been stripped by an army of looters. A number of prefabricated cabins were arranged around the perimeter of the site, but there appeared to be no men or robots working there.

Arcturus was no judge of aesthetic, but even to his untrained eye, the building looked as though it had been spawned in the worst nightmares of a demented architect.

"Look at that," said Angus Mengsk, jabbing a finger at the unfinished building. "If there's a more visible symbol of the moral decay and corruption at the heart of the Confederacy, I don't know what it is."

"Oh, please, not this again, dear," said Katherine.

But Angus was not to be denied venting his outrage.

"I ask you, why do we need a new building for

the Senate anyway? What's wrong with the Palatine Forum? Granted, it's old, but it's got character and tradition behind it. This new fiasco of a building sums up everything that's wrong with the Confederacy: money siphoned off into the pockets of corrupt officials, perverse priorities, and an arrogant indifference to public opinion. Did you know that the costs have soared to over five hundred million and counting? Oh yes, and that's from an initial estimate of sixty-three million! And where's that money gone? On insane expenses like a Chau Saran sunwood reception desk or bribes to Confederate city officials. They've been 'working' on it for the last six years, and it never seems to get finished. Oh, they say it'll be finished later this year, but look at it. . . . Does it look like that's realistic?"

"No, dear, it doesn't," said Katherine dutifully.

"The truth is that the one thing people know about the Confederacy is that everything costs quadruple what it ought to, thanks to the bribes you need to pay to get anything done and the dozens of new 'taxes' that suddenly seem to apply to any project that isn't intended to line the pockets of the Old Families."

"Then you should be thanking the Confederacy for the ammunition," said Arcturus.

"Oh, I am, son," said Angus, forgetting the tension between them in the fiery heat of his ire. "This whole project has been a public relations disaster that, thank God, even the UNN isn't afraid to report on, and one upon which I fully intend to capitalize."

His father continued to list the many faults of the building and the process by which it was being built, or rather *not* being built.

Arcturus tuned the words out as the unfinished building passed from sight.

This deep in the city, the colossal scale of the towers was much more apparent. Shadows enveloped the convoy, and Arcturus felt a chill travel down his spine as the driver expertly wound the groundcar through the streams of traffic.

People thronged the streets, well dressed and healthy, but only a few turned to watch as the convoy sped by. To see such things on the streets of Styrling was not unusual, for many captains of industry or senators traveled in this manner.

His father reached over and activated the comm unit on the armrest beside him.

"Ailin," said Angus. "We're coming up to the academy to drop Arcturus off, so we won't be far behind you. Let's just hope he stays here this time."

This last comment was directed squarely at Arcturus, who ignored his father's barb, though his mother placed her hand on her husband's forearm and frowned sternly at him.

"Very well, Angus," replied Ailin Pasteur. "I shall await you at the Skyspire."

The comm unit was shut off and Arcturus sighed as they passed alongside the lush parkland and playing fields of Styrling Academy. Here, the buildings thinned out and became less vulgar in scale, for this was a district of culture and breeding, where the young minds of the future were molded into compliant citizens of the Confederacy.

Arcturus knew the area well, despite the fact that students were forbidden to venture from the walled, security-patrolled campus of the academy by Principal Steegman. That such petty regulations needn't apply to him was a decision Arcturus had long since come to, and he—and a select band of adventurers—had often visited the exotic, neon-lit depths of the city's night.

Of course, his mother and father knew nothing of this, but the less they knew of what he got up to the better. In Arcturus's opinion, it was best that parents know as little as possible about their offspring's doings, since they'd only try and put a stop to them if they had any idea.

The great clock spire of the academy loomed large over an immaculately manicured line of trees in the distance, and Arcturus sighed as he contemplated another six months of sitting in sterile classrooms being "taught" by morons who knew less than he about politics and history, while blathering about the great destiny that awaited the school's alumni.

He shook himself from that bitter reverie as the groundcar slowed and turned down a graveled drive-way that led to the academy's security checkpoint.

That checkpoint consisted of an old, brick-built gatehouse and a couple of wooden sawhorses that blocked the road to the campus proper, with a handful of plastic orange cones scattered in front of them. The car slowed as it reached the gatehouse, and Old Rummy emerged from within, leaning down to examine the occupants of the vehicle.

Old Rummy was the name the students gave to the venerable gatekeeper, and Arcturus had never bothered to find out his real name. He reeked of liquor from the middle of the morning onward and his swollen nose and puffy cheeks were rife with the ruptured capillaries of a professional alcoholic.

Arcturus could smell the drink on his breath, and wrinkled his nose.

He'd started early, Arcturus reasoned.

"Morning, Mr. Mengsk, sir," said Old Rummy, doffing his peaked cap as he saw Angus. There were few people on Korhal who didn't know Arcturus's father, thanks to reports on the UNN of his political grandstanding and near-constant berating of the Confederacy.

Angus was popular in most quarters of Korhal, but where his money was spent freely—and the academy was such a place—he was feted and fawned over like royalty.

Old Rummy shuffled over to the sawhorses, clearing them from the road with grunting heaves before picking up the cones and waving the groundcar through. The driver gunned the engine and the car passed onward.

"Ten million for 'enhanced security measures' to protect the sons and daughters of Korhal from rebel attacks," said Angus, shaking his head as they swept past the grinning, idiot face of Old Rummy and onto the grounds of the academy. "You remember the fund-raising ball the academy held to raise money to implement these security measures, dear?"

"I do indeed," said Arcturus's mother with a shiver of distaste. "That frightful Principal Steegman preened like some oily salesman, begging his betters for money. A most distasteful evening."

Angus nodded. "I pledged over half a million to that fund, and look at the security it's bought: a few planks of wood and some cones shifted by a fat man in an ill-fitting uniform. I'd wager the same again that the best part of that fund-raiser went into Steegman's pockets."

Arcturus stored that nugget away and watched as the great mass of Styrling Academy hove into view around the perfectly maintained woodland and expanse of lush green grass. The finest examples of the topiarist's art decorated the lawn, and a number of youngsters were already practicing with foils and rapiers under the watchful supervision of Master Miyamoto.

"If it weren't for the quality of the tutors, I'd school the boy myself," continued Angus, and Arcturus stifled a horrified laugh at *that* idea.

The building, nearly a hundred years old, had been built from polished gray granite and positively reeked of money. A grand, columned portico sheltered the entrance, and the triangular pediment was decorated with heroic individuals and symbols of academic and martial excellence.

Carved statues sat in niches along the building's length and elaborate carved panels filled the spaces between each of the tall, narrow windows. Though the building was old, amongst the oldest on Korhal, its eaves and roof were fitted with recessed surveillance equipment and sophisticated eavesdropping equipment, though why the faculty should feel the need to spy on the students was a mystery to Arcturus.

The groundcar crunched to a halt on the gravel at the bottom of the wide stone steps that led up to the main doors of the academy. A liveried porter descended and opened the back door of the groundcar.

"On you go, dear," said his mother.

Arcturus nodded and turned to Dorothy. "See you soon, little one," he said. "I'll write you lots of letters and Mummy can read them to you."

"I can read, silly," pouted Dorothy. "I'll read them myself."

"Well aren't *you* the smart one?" he said, laughing.

Dorothy threw her arms around him and hugged him tightly. "I'll miss you, Arcturus."

He blinked in surprise. Normally Dorothy had difficulty in pronouncing his name, mangling the syllables and calling him 'Actress' or 'Arctroos,' but this time she said it without fault.

Arcturus untangled Dorothy's arms from around his neck and handed her off to his mother, who smiled warmly at him.

"It's only one more term, dear," said Katherine

Mengsk. "And then the world will open up for you, I promise. If not for yourself, do it for me. Please?"

Arcturus took a deep breath and nodded. He could disappoint his father without fear of guilt, but every time he felt he'd let his mother down, it cut him to the quick.

"Very well," said Arcturus. "I'll finish the term."

"You'd damn well better," snapped Angus. "Because I don't want to see you again until I'm watching you graduate. Understand me?"

Arcturus didn't deign to furnish him with an answer as he stepped from the groundcar, taking a small measure of satisfaction from the withering glare his mother shot his father.

As satisfying as that was, it was small recompense for the bitter seed planted in his heart.

Still, once he had graduated, he could go anywhere.

Somewhere that was as far away from Angus Mengsk as he could get.

Three months later, his promise to see out the term was being tested to the limit.

Principal Steegman had made it clear that Arcturus remained a student of Styrling Academy thanks only to his father's generous patronage of many of the school's facilities, and repeatedly informed him that he was skating on thin ice, walking a tightrope, balancing on a knife's edge, and performing numerous other well-worn clichés.

Lessons had continued much as they had before, and with all the extra attention being lavished upon him (no doubt at his father's insistence) Arcturus could not even find a way to relieve the crushing boredom of the academy by escaping into the city for an evening.

Arcturus Mengsk was, it seemed, a marked man at Styrling Academy, and even his former cohorts appeared to have been warned of the dangers of associating with him.

As a result, Arcturus spent the majority of his time during his last term at Styrling Academy in the school's library, reading and rereading every digi-tome he could find on geology, politics, psychology, and warfare. Many of these books he had already memorized, but each rereading brought fresh insight and understanding.

Arcturus wrote to Dorothy as promised and her return letters were among the few sources of comfort and amusement left to him. In these letters his mother informed him of the workings of the world beyond the walls of the academy, and he was surprised at the frankness of them, talking as they did of revolts in the outer colonies and fringe worlds (of which there was a growing number) as well as relating the latest society gossip. Her letters skirted carefully around the subject of his father, but Arcturus needed no letters from home to know all about Angus's dealings.

The UNN broadcasts were replete with stories of his fiery speeches denouncing the corruption of the

Old Families and the Council. Though Angus publicly condemned the rising tide of violence engulfing Korhal, which had seen hundreds of Confederate marines dead in rebel bombings and ambushes, Arcturus knew his father *had* to be part of it.

The objective part of Arcturus actually admired the skill with which Angus was able to distance himself from the violence while subtly implying that it was the inevitable result of the Confederacy's oppression and engendering sympathy for the rebel cause.

As much as he was now regarded as something of a pariah at the academy, this did not stop his fellow students from making their feelings about his father plain to him. Many of them came from wealthy families with close ties to the Confederacy, and were suffering daily embarrassment thanks to the withering scorn of Angus Mengsk's rhetoric.

Though Arcturus wanted nothing to do with his father's politics, he was savvy enough to recognize that what he said made a great deal of sense. Still, the retaliatory humiliations heaped upon him by his fellow students only served to further his resentment toward the Mengsk paterfamilias.

But Arcturus's resentment was made bearable by the stimulating diversions offered in the letters he was now exchanging with Juliana Pasteur.

Within a day of his arrival back at the academy, Arcturus had received a letter from Juliana, politely inquiring after his health and the possibility of setting up a meeting during one of the periods he was allowed off the campus. With the precision of a razor, Arcturus had dissected the true meaning within her letter and seen the naked interest beneath the platitudes.

Clearly the rapport established in the short time they had spent in the refuge of his father's summer villa had blossomed despite his absence. Or perhaps because of it.

In return, Arcturus replied with a missive brimming with the foibles of his fellow students, the foolishness of the masters, and his trials within the prisonlike walls of the academy.

His words were well chosen, witty, erudite, and filled with enough self-deprecation to puncture any sense of self-importance his letters might convey that might make him seem arrogant. That such self-deprecation was entirely contrived did not strike Arcturus as false in any way, and the effusive letters he received in return were proof positive of the success of his writings.

As they corresponded over the course of the term, it became increasingly clear that Juliana Pasteur was smitten with him. In marked contrast to their initially frosty meeting in the refuge, it appeared that Juliana now appreciated his brilliance and was assessing his suitability as a consort.

Though he remembered her intoxicating beauty, it had become a detached memory to Arcturus, and he indulged her letters as an outlet for his polemics and occasionally grandiose predictions of his future power. Truth be told, his desire to maintain the friendship had begun to wane, yet Arcturus continued to write to Juliana in the interest of eventually bedding her.

It would be the final act in the completion of a challenge that had once seemed difficult, but which he now knew had been simplicity itself.

The weeks and months passed in a gray blur, lectures boring him and insultingly easy assignments completed with barely a hint of effort. The end was in sight, and with only two weeks to graduation, Principal Steegman summoned the entire senior year to the grand assembly hall in the main block of the academy.

The assembly hall was a grand, vaulted chamber of cedar-paneled walls, gold-framed portraits of illustrious former students, high ceilings, and soaring oak beams. Every morning, Steegman would mount the stage to stand behind his lectern and address the entire upper school, announcing the results of the academy's sporting endeavors and notices of supposed importance.

Occasionally the assembly hall was also used for scrupulously chaperoned balls or played host to visiting dignitaries who would speak to the student body on the virtues of civic service or some other similarly dull subject.

The identically uniformed students filed drearily into the hall, and Arcturus briefly wondered what manner of speaker they were to be subjected to today. As he drew closer to the assembly hall's doorway, the excited hubbub of voices from within told him that whatever awaited them was something beyond the run of the mill.

He passed beneath the arched entrance to the assembly hall and the academy's motto of *Aien Apisteyein*, which meant "ever to be the best" in one of the dead languages of Old Earth.

The vast floor space in front of the stage was filled with uncomfortable chairs, each one occupied by an excited student. Principal Steegman was at his lectern, looking very pleased with himself, but it was the three hulking figures standing at attention behind him that captured Arcturus's attention.

They stood several feet taller than Steegman, their backs ramrod straight and their bulk enormous, thanks to the heavy plates of neosteel armor they wore.

Arcturus recognized the armor from the technical manuals he'd read in the library.

They were CMC-300 Powered Combat Suits, a brand-new design that was replacing the dated CMC-200 series.

Powered Combat Suits . . .

As worn by soldiers of the Confederate Marine Corps.

CHAPTER 4

PRINCIPAL STEEGMAN WASTED NO TIME IN GETTING the proceedings started. Once every boy in the upper year was seated, he clasped the lectern with both hands and leaned forward, in what Arcturus knew he hoped was an authoritative stance. In reality, it just emphasized how short he was, but either no one else had noticed or no one had thought to tell him.

"We are fortunate indeed," began Steegman, his nasal tones grating on Arcturus's nerves, "to have representatives from the brave Confederate Marine Corps here to talk to you today. It is a great honor for us to have them here, and I know you will give them a rousing, Styrling Academy welcome."

This last comment was clearly an order, and the assembled boys gave an enthusiastic round of applause as Steegman retreated from the lectern and one of the marines stepped forward, his heavy steps booming on the wooden floor of the stage.

He reached the lectern and removed his helmet, revealing that he was, in fact, a she.

And a strikingly pretty *she*.

The marine placed her helmet on the lectern and smiled at the assembled boys, who now appeared even more interested in this morning's talk. Behind her, the curtain parted to reveal a large projection screen, upon which the red and blue Confederate flag was displayed, billowing dramatically in the wind against a golden sunset. Stirring music played in the background, piped over the assembly room's PA system.

"Good morning, my name is Angelina Emillian," began the marine. "I'm a captain with the 33rd Ground Assault Division of the Confederate Marine Corps, and I'm here today at your principal's request to talk to you about a career in the Marine Corps."

Captain Emillian marched to the front of the stage and planted her hands on her hips. "I know what you're thinking."

A nervous titter ghosted around the assembly hall, suggesting that Emillian might not want to know what many of the boys were thinking right at that moment. "And it's *'Why in the name of all holy hell would I want to join the Marine Corps?'* Right? After all, as graduates of this school, you'll no doubt be expecting to go into some cushy, well-paid job. And it's dangerous, isn't it? You might get killed. The Corps is for losers who don't have any other options open to them, isn't it?"

Arcturus saw Principal Steegman's eyes widen in surprise. Captain Emillian's presentation obviously wasn't starting in the way he had imagined and for that reason alone, Arcturus found himself warming to this pretty marine captain.

"Well, if you're thinking that, I've got some news for you, boys. You're dead wrong."

Captain Emillian swept her gaze around the room, her confidence and steely demeanor capturing everyone's attention.

"The Confederate Marine Corps embodies three principals," said Emillian, slapping her fist into her palm to emphasize each one. "Strength. Pride. Discipline. Those ideals have enabled the Confederate Marine Corps and the Colonial Fleet to defend Confederate interests along the galactic rim for more than a century and a half. And right now, you're thinking that marines are just resocialized panbrains, but I'm here to tell you that's just not true. Marines come from all walks of life, from every level of society, but they are united by one thing—their devotion to the preservation of the Confederate way of life."

As Emillian spoke, the projection screen behind her displayed images of laughing marines as they abseiled down cliffs, played padball, or skied down snowy mountainsides. To Arcturus's eye, they appeared to be having so fantastic a time it was a wonder they managed to do any soldiering at all.

"The Corps offers countless opportunities for young men and women to see the sector and gain valuable *real-world* experience. We will train you. We will teach you. We will shape you into an efficient warrior, garnering respect and admiration from your peers. During your service, you can choose where and what you learn. And when you come out after your short service period, you'll have a strength of character that you'll find nowhere else."

The projection screen now showed marines working through an assault course, men and women with rippling muscles and movie-star good looks. Once again, they appeared to be having the time of their lives, despite the rigors of the physical exertion, and Arcturus wondered who had shot this promotional film—clearly someone not averse to incredible visual hyperbole.

"The Corps has an honorable tradition of service and there are a great many benefits to joining up. Pay and conditions in the Marine Corps have steadily improved over the years and barely fifty percent of recruits ever see active combat. But armed with the latest weaponry and armor technology, a marine has little to fear from the kinds of folk that need fighting. And don't forget that your service becomes part of your permanent record. Combine that with the reputation of this fine institution and you have the key to open any door you want once you muster out. A life in the Marine Corps is one lived without limits, a life lived for the greater good of the Confederacy and everyone in it. You can be part of that, boys. You can make a difference. You can be all you can be."

Despite himself, Arcturus found himself swept up in the general enthusiasm that filled the assembly hall. The endlessly repeating images of handsome, fulfilled soldiers and Emillian's charismatic delivery combined to make him feel that a life in the military might not be such a bad option.

Captain Emillian stood back and saluted the assembled boys, and the two marines standing behind her repeated the gesture. Thunderous applause erupted and Arcturus found himself standing with the other boys as they rose to their feet to give Captain Emillian a standing ovation.

She smiled and gave a short bow, turning to shake Principal Steegman's hand. Arcturus wanted to laugh at how ridiculously insignificant the man looked next to the armored marine.

Steegman returned to his lectern and raised his hands for silence, which was forthcoming only after a few minutes of clapping and wolf whistles. When the boys sat down, Steegman said, "Thank you, Captain Emillian, for those stirring words. I'm sure you have given our senior year a lot to think about."

Again, scattered sniggers broke out amongst the assembled boys.

"And now," continued Steegman, oblivious to the effect his ill-chosen words were having, "I want you to take some time to collect some of the literature kindly provided by the Confederate Marine Corps. Classes will resume in one hour, so you'll have plenty of time to gather anything you wish and talk with the marine recruiting sergeants."

Arcturus followed Steegman's gaze and saw a number of tables stacked high with pamphlets and books set out along the side of the assembly hall. He'd not noticed them before, his attention captured by Captain Emillian and her dog-and-pony show. Tall, attractive marines of both sexes in immaculately pressed dress uniforms of navy blue and gleaming brass stood behind each table, hands clasped tightly behind their backs.

"Dismissed," said Principal Steegman, and there was a rush of bodies as the boys of the academy stood and made their way eagerly over to the tables.

Arcturus followed the herd, curious to see what might be on offer.

"Hold still, will you," said Katherine Mengsk, fastening the red toga around her husband's shoulder with a bronze clasp. "This is hard enough as it is without you fidgeting all the time."

"Pain in the damn neck is what it is," said Angus. "Remind me why I need to wear this?"

"Tradition," replied his wife.

"Tradition," spat Angus, as though it were the filthiest swear word he knew.

"You can't very well give the Close of Session speech to the Senate in that old suit of yours, now can you, dear?"

"Fine," said Angus. "But why are you making me wear it now? The speech isn't for another two months."

Achton Feld concealed a smile at Angus's pouting and complaining as his wife turned him this way and that to alter the cut and hang of the ceremonial robes of a senator of Korhal. The robes were heavy and uncomfortable-looking, but the governmental apparatus of Korhal had a long tradition of pomp and ceremony where its procedures were concerned.

"Because, dear," said Katherine patiently, "it needs a few adjustments. It's been a few years since you wore it and you are not as sylphlike as once you were."

"So you're saying I'm fat," said Angus.

"Not at all," replied Katherine lightly. "Merely more statesmanlike."

Angus looked unconvinced, and Feld rose from his chair and made his way to the Skyspire's balcony window as he felt his employer's gaze linger on him, daring him to laugh at his discomfort.

Feld shifted the holster beneath his jacket, wincing as his shoulder pulled stiffly from where the doctors had removed six Impaler spikes from him. He'd been told he was lucky to be alive; four inches to the side and his lungs would have been perforated.

Months of agonizing skin grafts and bone reconstruction surgery had given him plenty of opportunities to curse that luck when the pain meds wore off and left him with a bone-deep ache that not even scotch could obliterate.

Katherine continued to fuss over Angus and Feld left them to it, activating the force field that protected the balcony and heading outside. The energy shield had cost a small fortune and not only protected the balcony from ballistic projectiles, energy weapons, and electronic surveillance, but also kept out the winds that howled around so high a structure.

Feld made his way over to the handcrafted ironwork barrier at the edge of the balcony and gently rested his elbows on it as he leaned out and admired the view.

As far as views went, it was up there with the best of them.

The upper balcony of the Mengsks' tower was on the one hundred and sixtieth floor of the building, some eight hundred meters above street level. The mountains to the north reared up like the ramparts of a giant's castle and to the south the landscape became progressively greener until it reached the azure line of the ocean.

On a clear day such as this, the distant coastline was visible and you could see the summer villa as an oblong of white through the optical viewer that sat on its tripod on the edge of the balcony.

The city of Styrling was laid out before Feld in a grid of silver, with soaring towers rising to either side of the Skyspire like stalagmites of steel and glass. From here, the sheer scale and life of the city was apparent, and that such a vast conurbation had been built in so short a time was testament to the ingenuity and dedication of the people of Korhal.

That it had been achieved in the face of rampant Confederate corruption made it all the more impressive. Feld loved Styrling; from here he could see the green of the Martial Field, the site of Korhal's establishment as a member planet of the Confederacy. That day had been filled with so much promise so many years ago, but now, as a parade ground for Confederate marines, the Martial Field served only as a bitter reminder of how bad things had become.

Across from the Martial Field was the Palatine Forum, home of the Korhal Senate. Its bronze roof shone like a beacon, shimmering like molten gold in the sunlight.

"Inspiring, isn't it?" said Angus, appearing at Feld's side on the balcony. "Reminds you what we're trying to achieve."

For a big man, Angus Mengsk could move silently when he wanted to. Feld hadn't heard him approach.

"Yeah, it's some view," agreed Feld.

"The jewel in the crown of the Confederacy, they call it."

"I've heard. And now you want to pluck that jewel."

"Right from under them," said Angus with a smile. "It's not their jewel to keep. Not anymore."

"And what will we do if we win?" asked Feld.

"*If* we win?" said Angus. "Don't you think we can defeat the Confederacy?"

"I don't care anymore," said Feld, standing up straight and stretching his shoulder. "I just want to hurt them."

"Oh, we'll do that, my friend. Have no fear of that," promised Angus.

"You really think we can bring them down?"

"I do," Angus said, nodding. "I wouldn't be doing this if I didn't believe that. It may not happen in our lifetimes, but what we start here will be the beginning of something truly exceptional. Even a landslide has to start with a single pebble, eh?"

"That's true," conceded Feld.

"The influence of the Confederacy is spreading," continued Angus, warming to his theme as he always did when talking of his hatred of corruption, "but the people with the power to take action are the very ones who won't recognize that there's a terrible malignancy at the heart of that power."

"Why do you think that is? It must be obvious, surely?"

"Of course it is, but recognizing the problem creates a moral obligation to then *do* something about it," said Angus. "And too many people have too vested an interest to take action."

"But not you?"

"The Old Families and the Council can make things difficult for me, yes, but all the Mengsk businesses are largely self-sufficient. We own every part of the process involved in my factories, from the hovercar plants to the AAI production lines. There's nowhere for them to squeeze us."

"Not legally."

"I've no doubt that the Confeds will throw money at any number of pirate bands or mercenary troops to cause us trouble off world, but we've come too far to give up now. Pretty soon we'll be able to do more than plant bombs or ambush lone squads of marines. Soon we'll be able to declare war."

Feld heard the unmistakable relish in Angus's tone and wondered if the senator truly appreciated what was at stake in taking on the awesome power of the Confederacy. Lives had already been lost, and Confederate troops were cracking down hard all across Korhal.

Early morning raids on those they suspected of terrorist activities were commonplace, and only Feld's rigorous insistence on watertight security and isolation among the various active cells had kept the integrity of the fledgling resistance movement intact.

Though Korhal wasn't yet under anything that resembled martial law, it wouldn't take much to force the Confederates' hand.

"Let's walk before we run," cautioned Feld. "If we rush things, we risk losing everything."

"You're right, of course," said Angus. "But the moment is coming where the scales will start to tip, and if we don't act when it comes we'll miss it. And it's coming soon, Achton. The guns and tech being brought in from Umoja makes us stronger every day. Our men are now almost as well equipped as the marines."

That was true, reflected Feld. Every day, shipments of "industrial parts" for the Mengsk factories came from Umoja via a number of dummy corporations and along circuitous freighter routes. Innocuously labeled and accompanied by all the correct documentation, these freighters' cargo containers were laden with the guns, ammunition, explosives, armor, and technology that allowed the Korhal freedom fighters to wreak havoc on the Confeds at the behest of Angus Mengsk.

"I never thought Ailin Pasteur would come through like he has."

"He's a good man, Ailin, and not to be underestimated," said Angus. "I've no doubt he's helping us more for the Umojan cause than our own, but I'll take whatever I can get."

"He's still coming back for your Close of Session speech?"

Angus nodded. "Indeed. He and Juliana are returning to Korhal at the end of the week."

"His daughter's coming?" said Feld, making no effort to hide his irritation. "That wasn't in the security briefs. It'll complicate things. Why wasn't I told?"

"I just heard this morning," said Angus, his tone neutral. "Apparently my son has asked Ailin's daughter to accompany him to his graduation ball. And, irritatingly, she has accepted."

Feld looked away, cursing Arcturus for adding this unnecessary burden to his already overworked security staff. In addition to the extra security measures he had

instituted since the attack on the summer villa, Feld
had assigned men to keep watch on each member of
the Mengsk family.

Katherine was relatively easy to protect, as she
kept close to Angus, and Dorothy was escorted to and
from her preschool playgroup, but Arcturus seemed
to delight in making Feld's life difficult, and this was
surely another of his schemes to test Feld's patience.

"Great," said Feld. "Another problem I could do
without. As if you weren't making things difficult
enough."

"I know what you're going to say, Achton, and the
answer's still no."

Feld knew he was fighting a losing battle with
Angus, but that didn't stop him from trying.

"Look," said Feld. "You need more guards when you
make your walk to the Forum. You're too exposed,
and if you don't let me put more men on the ground
beside you, I can't guarantee your safety."

"I told you," said Angus, his tone suggesting he was
growing weary of having this argument. "I won't walk
to the Senate surrounded by armed soldiers. I can't
look as though I'm traveling as a war leader. For now
I need to be seen as the voice of peace."

"But—"

"But nothing," said Angus. "That's the end of it. I've
already consented to the ruinous cost of a personal
force field, which I'm not happy about, but I *will not*
be surrounded by soldiers. The Forum is a place of
democracy and debate, and Lennox Craven will call

me a tyrant or a usurper if I walk in with armed men at my back."

"It's your funeral," said Feld. "I'm just telling you what I think. Hey, I could have taken a cushy job on Brontes getting paid a fortune to babysit rich kids, you know."

"So why didn't you?"

Feld sighed. "Hell, I'd have died of boredom, you know that."

"You're a man of action," agreed Angus. "And you are my friend, so it means a lot to me to know how worked up you're getting over my safety."

"Just remember, that force field's going to give you only a few minutes' protection, just enough to get you to the Forum."

"Yes, so you've told me a dozen times already."

Feld shook his head with a rueful smile. "I still get paid if you die, right?"

"Honestly, Feld, I swear you're worse than my mother ever was."

"She was a sensible woman, your mother," said Feld.

"Pah, there's nothing to worry about, Feld," said Angus. "You're jumping at ghosts, nothing more."

The press of bodies around the tables had eased now and Arcturus lifted one of the pamphlets. An animated graphic of the Confederate flag billowed beneath the words, "The Confederate Marine Corps—A Place for Heroes."

The two marines who had stood immobile behind Captain Emillian circulated throughout the assembly hall, demonstrating aspects of their armor and allowing students to handle their AGR-14 gauss rifles.

Arcturus replaced the pamphlet as the marine recruiting sergeant loomed over the table. He could smell the polish of the brass on the man's uniform and the sweet, slightly sickly aroma of gun oil. The marine's face was open and earnest, but devoid of any real personality.

"Thinking of joining up, son?" asked the man.

"Maybe," said Arcturus. "I haven't decided."

"It's an honorable profession, son," said the marine, and Arcturus noticed the telltale bump of resocialization scars just above the neckline of his uniform's collar as he bent down.

"When did you enlist?" asked Arcturus.

"Six years ago, and never looked back," said the marine automatically, and Arcturus caught the whiff of words said by rote. "Best decision I ever made, son, let me tell you. I've traveled all over the Koprulu sector, seen all kinds of worlds, and met me plenty of interesting folks."

"And killed them?" finished Arcturus mischievously.

"Well, let's put that to one side just now," suggested the marine. "What's your name, son?"

"Arcturus Mengsk."

"Pleasure to make your acquaintance, Arcturus. Now, what you need to think of are all the opportunities the Corps can offer you. Travel, self-respect, honor, discipline—"

"Well, have you?" interrupted Arcturus. "Killed anyone, I mean?"

"See here, Arcturus," said the marine sergeant. "Being a marine means you got to kill people sometimes, but only those as deserve it. When bad folks are trying to kill me or my buddies, it ain't no choice. When someone's got a gun pointed at you, well, there's only thing you can do, right?"

"I suppose it depends on why they're pointing the gun at you," said Arcturus.

"Making trouble, are you, Mengsk?" said a voice behind him, and Arcturus recognized the supercilious tones of Principal Steegman.

"Not at all, sir," said Arcturus, turning on his heel. "Just finding out what I'd be getting into."

"A stint in the military would do you a power of good, Mengsk," said Steegman. "Knock some of the smart-ass out of you. Bit of military discipline would soon sort you out."

"I wasn't aware I needed sorting out, sir."

Steegman leaned in close, and Arcturus had to resist the urge to cough at the overpowering reek of the man's aftershave.

"I know your type, Mengsk," hissed Steegman. "If I had my way, I'd have you all drafted. A dose of military training is just what a boy needs to turn him into a man."

Before Steegman could press his point, a shadow fell over him and Arcturus looked up into the face of Angelina Emillian. Up close, she was even more impressive, the bulk of her combat armor giving her an extra foot of height over Arcturus, who wasn't exactly small.

She absolutely towered over Principal Steegman.

"And what unit did you serve with, Principal Steegman?"

"Excuse me?"

Captain Emillian smiled sweetly, displaying perfect teeth in a perfect smile. "I merely asked what unit you served with. In *your* time with the military."

"I, uh . . . haven't," said Steegman. "I mean, that is to say, I couldn't."

Arcturus bit his lip to hide his amusement at Steegman's discomfort and kept his eyes downcast. When he looked up, he saw Steegman staring at him, his face florid with embarrassment.

"I wonder if I might have a word with Mr. Mengsk," asked Emillian.

Steegman nodded curtly and all but fled from the marine captain.

"I think I love you," said Arcturus with a broad grin.

"You wouldn't be the first," returned Captain Emillian.

Arcturus watched Principal Steegman's departing back and said, "He's always made out he served in the military, but I'd always suspected he was lying."

"To be fair, he did apply to join the Colonial Fleet, but he failed the entrance exams and couldn't pass the physical. And between you and me, the physicals for the fleet are a cakewalk."

"Well, thank you for sparing me from him, Captain," said Arcturus.

"Mr. Mengsk?" said Emillian as he turned away.

"Yes?"

"I didn't save you from your principal's attentions out of the goodness of my heart. I do actually want to speak with you."

"Oh? Well, of course," said Arcturus, pleased the captain had singled him out. He could see his fellow students looking over with envious eyes and relished the attention being lavished upon him.

"Thank you, Sergeant Devlin," said Emillian, addressing the marine still standing to attention behind Arcturus. "That will be all."

The marine sergeant snapped a smart salute. "Yes, ma'am."

With that, Captain Emillian strode off, her hands clasped behind her back, and Arcturus was forced to step lively to catch up with her.

"Do you always bring resocialized marines to recruitment drives?" asked Arcturus.

"Most of the time," said Emillian. "They don't make great speakers, but they do a good job in giving the right answers to students' questions."

"So what did he do?" asked Arcturus. "Sergeant Devlin, what did he do?"

"I don't know," replied Emillian. "Those files are sealed. Once you're a marine, resocialized or otherwise, your past life is irrelevant. You're a marine, plain and simple."

"How very egalitarian, but I don't think that's entirely true, is it?"

"No, it's not, but would you rather hear how he murdered his entire family with a butcher knife? Or maybe that he enjoyed molesting small boys in the park?"

"I see your point," said Arcturus, looking over his shoulder at the bland face of Sergeant Devlin and imagining it contorted with rage, a bloody knife in his hand.

"The few, the proud, the psychotic . . ." said Arcturus.

"You're trying to make fun of us, but it won't work, Arcturus," said Emillian with a smile.

"No? Why not?"

"Because I already know you're thinking of joining up."

"I am?" said Arcturus. "And how would you know such a thing?"

"I know more about you than you think. I've seen your test scores and read your psych profile. I know you have fine leadership skills and a confidence that makes people want to follow you. I know that you have a problem with authority figures you consider your inferiors and that your IQ is at the upper end of genius level."

"Those files are classified," said Arcturus, more

irritated at her spot-on assessment of his personality than at the violation of his privacy. He didn't like to be so easily read by others.

"Yes they are, but Principal Steegman allowed us to read up on his final-year students before we came here today. Makes selecting likely candidates for recruitment much easier."

"Isn't that against the law?"

"Almost certainly."

Arcturus was surprised at Emillian's easy admission and smiled as he realized why she'd allowed it. "You're trying to put me at ease by sharing a secret," he said. "If you've read my psych profile, then you think I'll trust you more if I think you're being honest with me and appeal to my sense of rebelliousness."

Captain Emillian nodded. "Very good. Is it working?"

"A little," admitted Arcturus, enjoying the back-and-forth he was sharing with this attractive warrior woman.

"So tell me, Arcturus," said Emillian, stopping at one of the sergeants' booths and lifting a handful of different flyers. "What do you want to do with yourself once you leave the academy?"

"I was thinking of becoming a prospector, traveling to the fringe worlds and exploring the edge of space. There's planets there that even the Confederacy hasn't set foot on. I want to leave my mark on history—name a planet, discover something no one's ever seen before. You know, the usual . . ."

"A prospector," said Emillian. "That's an honorable

profession. Did you know the Corps can help you with that?"

"Really? How?"

"Most of our tours take place out on the fringe worlds. We deal with miners all the time. You'd be able to pick up some real firsthand experience dealing with mines, miners, and the like. Not to mention the training you'd get on your downtime. The further education facilities on our fleet ships are second to none, equipped with the very best in neural interface mnemo-tutors. You could learn entire new skill sets while you slept."

"Sounds interesting," said Arcturus, surprised to find he *was* actually intrigued.

"You could do a lot worse than the Corps," said Emillian, handing him the flyers she'd picked up. "With your test scores, you easily qualify for officer training. And once you've completed your basic service, you're free to leave if you want and use the skills you've learned in the military and apply them in civilian life."

"Ah . . . my 'basic service' . . ." said Arcturus. "How long would that be?"

"The Corps offers a range of flexible terms," said Emillian smoothly. "It all depends on your circumstances and the current threat level as defined by High Command."

"And what's the current threat level?"

Emillian smiled. "Low," she said.

CHAPTER 5

GRADUATION DAY. ARCTURUS FELT A NERVOUS thrill of excitement coursing though him at the thought of finally escaping the confines of Styrling Academy. After the Marine Corps recruitment morning, Arcturus had found his thoughts returning more and more to the idea of joining up. He had even filled in the electronic application form, though he had not yet submitted it.

The idea of learning the skills of a prospector while being paid by the Confederacy appealed to him, as did the idea that it would drive his father up the wall. And given the current low level of threat in the Koprulu sector, it seemed likely that he would need to serve only a minimum of three years before he was eligible to resign his commission and begin his life as a prospector.

Yes, the idea had its merits, but in the back of his mind, he couldn't shut out the idea that his life would be at risk, and Arcturus hated the idea of placing himself in physical danger.

Wasn't that what the marines were for, to keep danger *away*?

He put the military from his mind and concentrated on the day at hand. He had enough to concentrate on without creating distractions.

Styrling Academy was bathed in sunlight, the gray granite shining like marble and imparting a sense of modernity to the building. A wide stage had been set up on the lawn before the main portico, with row upon row of seats facing it.

The hundred and fifty-six students of the senior year who were graduating (and that was all of them, for an institution of the stature of Styrling Academy did not allow its students to do anything so prosaic as fail) sat in these seats, dressed in long black capes edged with pale blue silk and wearing mortarboard hats.

Bleachers had been set up on either side of the seats in the center of the lawn, and proud parents sat watching their offspring finally graduate from school. Behind the lectern at which Principal Steegman handed out gold-edged scrolls containing diplomas sat the tutors and masters of the academy. Accompanying them were distinguished alumni of the academy, CEOs of major corporations, noted academics, patrons of the arts, senior marine commanders, and even the chief of the Styrling Police Force.

The principal of Styrling Academy was dressed in his full ceremonial robes of black and gold, complete with scarlet chasuble and tall, conical hat—which made him look like a cockaded martinet—and Arcturus was sure he was concealing height augmenters beneath his robes.

The school band played rousing tunes as the students walked toward the stage one by one and accepted their diploma from Steegman to the hearty applause of their parents and the curt applause of those whose sons or daughters had already accepted their diplomas or had yet to receive them.

By virtue of his surname, Arcturus was in the middle of the list of names being called out by a lower school prefect, and he eagerly awaited his turn to take the walk to the stage. He glanced over at the bleachers, smiling as he saw his family watching with pride.

Dorothy saw him looking and waved enthusiastically. His mother gave a more restrained wave, and even his father gave him a proud nod of acknowledgment.

Sitting next to his father was Ailin Pasteur and beside him was Juliana. It was the first time Arcturus had seen Juliana since the attack on the summer villa, and he was struck again by her stunning beauty. Aside from her being someone to write to, Arcturus hadn't thought of her much, but seeing her here in the flesh reminded him of the desire she had stirred in him upon their first meeting.

The student next to him, a panbrained moron by the name of Toby Mercurio, followed his gaze and said, "Who's the curve, Mengsk? Sweet looker."

Mercurio was from one of Styrling's nouveau riche families and had little in the way of breeding, still using slang imported from the Gutter of Tarsonis. Despite that, Arcturus couldn't fault his conclusion.

"Yes," agreed Arcturus, looking forward to the graduation ball that evening. "Sweet is exactly what she is."

"You taking her to the ball tonight?"

"I am indeed, Toby."

Arcturus tuned out Mercurio's nonsensical banter and concentrated on the names being called out. He smiled as he heard names beginning with K being called out.

Not long now . . .

The K's didn't last too long, and Arcturus felt his heart rate flutter as his own name was called. He rose from his seat, glancing over his shoulder to where his family watched, and strode out into the aisle between the two rows of seats. The clapping of the students was somewhat muted, but Arcturus knew they would soon be changing their tune.

He walked with his head held high, reaching the front of the stage and making his way to the steps at the side. The school photographer took a vidsnap and Arcturus lifted his gaze toward where he knew his mother and father would be recording the event on holocam.

Arcturus smiled for the photographer, then ascended the steps and walked casually across the stage to where Principal Steegman waited with a gold-rimmed diploma. Arcturus fixed his most ingratiating smile across his face and extended his hand to receive the scroll.

It was traditional for the principal to congratulate a graduating student and wish him well in his future endeavors, but Arcturus had no illusions that Steegman would make any such gesture. He was not to be disappointed.

"You'll come to a rotten end, Mengsk," said Steegman, handing him the diploma. "I can always tell the bad ones. And you're the worst of the lot."

Arcturus took the proffered scroll in his left hand and offered his right to Steegman, which, his being unwilling to appear ungracious before the parents and alumni, the principal shook.

"Thank you," said Arcturus. "I hope you enjoy your new residence."

Steegman's face registered confusion, but he quickly recovered and waved Arcturus off the stage. Arcturus swiftly made his way around the back of the seated students, holding his diploma up with a smile for his mother and father to see.

Juliana was on her feet, clapping and staring at him with rapt adoration, and Arcturus smiled. He walked back to his seat and quickly fished his remote terminal console from within his coat pocket.

Little more than a simple communications device with an optical reader, the console nevertheless had the capability to tap into computer networks remotely. So long as you had the connection key and authorization codes, you could get into pretty much any network without too much trouble.

Arcturus quickly tapped in the codes for Steegman's

console, long since having memorized the details from the many times he had been summoned to the principal's office and seen them entered in the mirror behind the idiot's desk.

Numbers and letters flashed across the screen for several seconds until a small square appeared on the screen with a line of text beneath it.

DNA verification required.

Arcturus pressed a fingertip onto the optical reader and a green light flashed on the screen.

Identity Confirmed: Isaac Steegman.

He laid the console down on his knee and peeled off the thin, transparent coating he'd coated his right hand with before walking out onto the graduation field. The one-way bio-mimetic gel had been simplicity itself to create in the academy's chem-labs and would disintegrate in the sunlight within a few moments now that he'd removed it.

Arcturus picked up the console once more and opened Steegman's private directories. Using a linguistic algorithm based on a few well-chosen keywords, he quickly discovered the files he'd known he'd find.

"My God, he didn't even *try* and hide them." Arcturus laughed.

"What's that?" asked Toby Mercurio, sitting back down next to him with his diploma.

"You'll see," Arcturus said with a smile. "Just wait."

Quickly and methodically, he highlighted every file his algorithm had turned up, then set his console to scan the surrounding area for fones and other personal consoles. Hundreds of personal designations scrolled past on the screen, his father's and the SPF chief's amongst them, and Arcturus set the console to send the selected files to every one of them.

Arcturus's finger hovered over the Send icon and he hesitated for the briefest second, savoring the moment.

"To the victor go the spoils," he whispered, and pressed Send.

Angus rested his arms on the balcony of the Skyspire as he stared out over the nighttime cityscape of Styrling. During the day, the view was impressive, but at night it was something truly spectacular. An ocean of light spread across the hinterlands that sprawled from the mountains, a web of interconnected light that reflected on the underside of the clouds with a warm, golden glow.

Despite the turmoil engulfing Korhal, the bombings, the unrest, and the Confederate crackdowns, being up here at night always brought Angus peace. Looking over the city from the balcony gave him a sense of perspective he often lacked when dealing with the minutiae of the life he had chosen.

Sometimes it was good to step back from what you were doing and look at the larger picture. Yes, things were hard just now, but with every blow struck against the tyranny of the Confederacy, their hold on Korhal slipped a little further.

Angus scratched a long-ago-healed scar on his forearm, earned on a hunting trip with his father in the forests of Keresh Province to the east, which had taught him that there was no more dangerous a beast than a cornered one. Achton Feld had called Korhal the jewel in the Confederates' crown, which was an apt description, and the Council and the Old Families weren't going to give it up without a fight.

Well, they were going to find out just how much the people of Korhal wanted them gone.

Angus could feel his anger growing as he turned the many injustices inflicted upon the people of the Koprulu sector over in his mind.

On Tyrador X, Confederate meddling and illegal financial dealings had caused the planetary economy to collapse, resulting in mass unemployment on a global scale. Only extensive loans (complete with ruinous rates of interest) and economic restructuring that placed the entire system in the hands of the Old Families had prevented entire continents of people from starving to death.

Another favorite tactic was to set up loss-leading businesses on the fringe worlds—where the Old Families' monopolies were not ironclad—to run local competitors out of business. Once any competition was eliminated, those same businesses would begin charging extortionate prices for basic necessities.

While the use of corrupt business stratagems was the Confederacy's preferred modus operandi, the Old

Families were not above using force to take what they wanted.

A prospecting team from the Kel-Morian Combine exploiting the Paladino Belt, an asteroid field containing huge mineral reserves within the larger rocks, had been eliminated when CMC forces launched an assault to capture its leader, a man apparently wanted for murder on Tarsonis. The deaths were described as a tragedy, but within days, a Confederate mining team was working the field, complete with marine garrison and battlecruiser support.

Hundreds of similar stories were the common currency of the Confederacy, tales of greed, bribery, corruption, and nepotism told over a drink with a resigned shrug and a shake of the head. The injustice of it all screamed out for someone to fix the problem, but the scale of the Confederacy was such that no one could do anything. It was the way of things, said people.

Angus Mengsk was going to prove that belief wrong.

He did not relish the thought that he had brought violence to the streets and cities of Korhal, but he knew that it was the only way to wake people up to what was going on around them.

Already things were beginning to change here. Angus was bringing the flagrant abuses of power perpetuated by the Confederacy to light, and the people were finally opening their eyes.

And they did not like what they were seeing.

When you watched a tale of misuse of power on the UNN, it was far away and thus easily forgotten, but when trouble hit close to home it was harder to ignore.

And when those misuses of power began to threaten your livelihood and the future of your family, even the most torpid of viewers would be forced to take a stand.

Angus did not want power for himself and he had no desire to replace the faceless, conscienceless Council with a tyrant of his own making. No, when the Confederacy fell, he would become part of the process of creating a democratic government that sought to benefit all mankind, not one that served the will of one man.

He sensed a presence behind him and smiled as he caught the fragrance of Epiphany, his wife's perfume. Angus turned to see Katherine standing in the green dress of shimmering taffeta with navy bodice she had worn to Arcturus's graduation ceremony earlier that day.

"You look beautiful, Kat," said Angus, accepting one of the thin-stemmed wineglasses his wife carried.

"You've told me that already today, but don't let that stop you." Katherine smiled.

"Never," said Angus. "How did I ever convince you to marry me?"

"You didn't. I asked you, remember?"

Angus sipped his wine. "I maneuvered you into a position where you had no choice."

"You keep on thinking that."

It was a familiar pantomime, one he and his wife often played out in the few moments they had together in private, away from prying eyes and the needs of business and revolution. Theirs had been a tempestuous courtship, for both were passionate, independent individuals who did not like to be overshadowed by another.

But through it all, they had felt a shared need for companionship, recognizing that being one half of a couple could be as liberating as freedom.

Their wedding had been the most glorious day of his life, and throughout their entire married life they had been pillars of strength for one another, supporting each other through times of bliss and despair, and never wavering in their love.

Katherine leaned her head on his shoulder, and Angus kissed the top of her head.

"Dorothy asleep?" he asked.

"Out like a light," said Katherine. "Today really took it out of her, bless her."

"I'm not surprised."

"Yes, it was quite a day, wasn't it?" said Katherine, and Angus laughed so hard tears rolled down his cheeks.

When he had composed himself, he said, "You always did have a knack for understatement, dear."

It had indeed been quite a day, a day that had seen his son finally graduate and the principal of Styrling Academy hauled off to jail by a former student.

When Angus's fone had trilled in his pocket, he

had been irritated at the interruption of his son's graduation day, for he had left strict instructions with all his subordinates that he was not to be disturbed.

Then he had heard a multitude of clicks, bleeps, and whistles of hundreds of fones and personal consoles receiving incoming data streams. A ripple of consternation spread throughout the crowd and Angus felt his stomach lurch as he saw that the originating signal belonged to Arcturus's console.

"Oh God, what's he done now?" Angus whispered as his fone's screen lit up and a number of files opened. His practiced eye quickly scanned the contents and his anger built as he flipped though the various statements and account records.

"The thieving little bastard . . . ," hissed Angus, looking up and seeing that same anger on scores of other faces now staring in fury at the principal of Styrling Academy. "I *told* you he was nothing more than a damn crook!"

"Who?" asked Katherine, puzzled at the suddenly tense atmosphere.

"Steegman," barked Angus, making Dorothy flinch. "These are his private accounts. The little toad's siphoned millions from the school treasury and fund-raisers over the years."

People were getting to their feet now, an angry hubbub of voices cutting through the sound of the band and the shouted names of graduating students.

Onstage, Steegman looked puzzled and angry at the disruption, calling for quiet and order. But as an irate school governor marched over and thrust a portable console in front of him, his face blanched in horror as he realized what the entire audience had just read.

Looking back over the day, Angus chuckled as he remembered Steegman's halfhearted attempts to calm the situation. Violence had been averted only by the chief of the SPF's hauling the principal away and bundling him into his groundcar, to the uproarious cheers and applause of the entire student body.

The news had traveled fast, for Arcturus had been thorough in his dissemination of Steegman's files, and within the hour the scandal was being reported on the UNN. Steegman was not connected to anyone of influence, and a great deal of the money he had stolen had come from some very wealthy, very powerful families.

They would throw Steegman to the wolves, and the courts were sure to show him no mercy.

In the aftermath of Steegman's arrest, the vice principal had tried to calm the situation, but gave up in the face of a horde of angry parents and jubilant students, who cheered and hurled their mortarboards into the air.

A near riot had only been avoided by the contagious glee of the students, who danced and laughed and sang as Steegman was driven away in disgrace. Recriminations and a thorough investigation of the depths of the principal's corruption were sure to follow.

With Steegman's departure, the staff and parents

milled around in confusion until the vice principal led them off into the main administration block like a marching mob, leaving the jubilant students to continue the party on the main lawn.

Some of the academy's masters had wanted to cancel the graduation ball planned for the evening, but after the day's amusements, it was clear the students weren't going to allow this day of festivities to end so quickly.

Now, with the day behind them, Angus and Katherine stood and drank wine as the architect of the day's mischief enjoyed his graduation ball.

"I should be angry at him," said Angus.

"Who?" asked Katherine.

"Arcturus, who else?"

Katherine chuckled. "I know, but it's hard to be angry with him for today. After all, he's graduated now, and you can't say Steegman didn't deserve what happened."

"Oh, he deserved it all right," agreed Angus with a smile. "And to get his just desserts so publicly . . . I almost don't mind losing the money to have been there to see it."

Katherine leaned up and kissed him on the cheek.

"What was that for?"

"Do I need a reason to kiss my husband?"

"No. Never."

"Good. I'm proud of you," said Katherine. "You know that, don't you?"

Angus nodded. "I know that."

"I'm proud of you both, you *and* Arcturus. You're very alike, you know?"

Angus furrowed his brow and turned to face his wife. "The boy is willful."

"He's his father's son." Katherine pointed out, laughing.

Angus grunted, unwilling to concede the point. "He has a fine mind and the capacity to achieve anything. And he wants to waste that talent on prospecting, flying around the fringe worlds, and associating with backwater hicks and Kel-Morian pirates? It's no life for a Mengsk. We're made for bigger and better things than that."

"If I didn't know you better, I'd say that was arrogance speaking," said Katherine.

"You know it's not, though," countered Angus. "I know you see it too—you've told the boy often enough that he can be great if he wants to be."

"That's just it, isn't it? It has to be if *he* wants it. You should know by now you can't make Arcturus do anything he doesn't want to. The more you try and force him down a path, the more he'll resist you."

"Willful," said Angus again, though his tone was mellow this time.

"Just as you were," pointed out Katherine. "Until you met me."

Angus took a drink of wine and leaned down to kiss her. "Then let's just hope that the women in his life are as wise and calming as you."

Katherine smiled at him, and Angus Mengsk knew he was the luckiest man alive.

The assembly hall had been transformed.

On every other day, it was an austere, cold place of announcements, the news of sports results, and dull speeches, but now it was a place of festivities. Hundreds of students filled the hall, drinking, dancing, and reveling in the sheer *fun* of the day. Of course, the only topic of conversation was Steegman's arrest and Arcturus's part in his downfall.

Music pounded from the stage, colorful lights flashed from the ceiling, streamers trailed from every wall, and even the portraits had been hung with fake beards and noses.

The ball's theme was aliens from another world, and a floating banner of light shone with the words: "Class of '78! They Came From the Stars!"

Papier-mâché creatures of all descriptions hung from the roof beams on wires, reared from punch bowls, or emerged from lovingly detailed lairs set against the walls.

The students' imaginations had run riot and the past week had seen a frenzy of creation in the art classes. A carnival of grotesque creatures filled the assembly hall: giant lizards, bulbous floating jellyfish with multiple eyes, snakelike creatures with whipping tails and tentacles for mouths. At the edge of the stage, sharklike creatures mingled with hairy, multilegged spiders with long necks and terrifying mandibles.

Arcturus knew the subject of alien life had been an obsession with mankind ever since it had first looked up into the night sky in fear and wonder. Thus the abject failure of the Confederacy's science and exploration vessels to find any sign of surviving intelligent alien life was a source of constant frustration to those who believed that the human race was not alone in the galaxy.

Of course, a few explorers were said to have unearthed ancient ruins they claimed were the remnants of alien civilizations, but most people believed these to be elaborate hoaxes. Then there were the big insect creatures on Umoja, which had been domesticated by the people of that world, but they hardly counted as intelligent life.

Even the band was dressed in alien costumes, made up with latex prosthetics to look like fearsome creatures with gnarled foreheads, long hair, and jagged, spiky armor. The effect was more comic than frightening—something Arcturus suspected was half the point.

He normally detested such events, but had to admit he was enjoying himself immensely.

Perhaps he was still on a high from this afternoon's unmasking of Steegman's crimes. After all, it had been deeply satisfying to see the odious little man led away, and he had made sure the principal knew exactly who'd uncovered his crimes and destroyed his life.

It might also have been due to the attractive girl on his arm, for Juliana Pasteur was, without fear of contradiction, the most beautiful creature in the room.

But, if he was honest, Arcturus knew it was none of these things—it was the acclaim accorded him by his fellow students and the near worship in which he was now held. His former status of pariah had been forgotten now that Steegman was gone, and Arcturus suddenly occupied a position more akin to a war hero.

It was quite intoxicating.

"Arcturus?" said Juliana as the volume of the music dropped.

"Hmmm?" he said.

"You looked miles away," she said, offering him a glass of punch.

"Sorry," he said with a winning smile, accepting the glass as he returned his attention to the beautiful girl standing next to him.

Juliana Pasteur wore an ankle-length gown of ivory silk with a velveteen bodice that hugged her budding figure and which accentuated her delicate features. Blonde hair spilled around her bare shoulders in golden ringlets and a fine silver necklace set with an Umojan sapphire hung down her neck.

He took a sip of the punch and raised an eyebrow. "There's alcohol in this."

Juliana nodded. "I saw some students emptying some bottles in earlier, but I don't think anyone's going to mind. Not after today."

"No," Arcturus grinned. "I suppose not."

Juliana took his hand and smiled at him. Over the months they had corresponded, he had reveled in the power he seemed to have over her, but with her here next to him, he now fully appreciated the reality of what he had done.

Everything in Juliana's body language told Arcturus that she had fallen for him, which was ridiculous given the few times they had actually met. Truth be told, he didn't know quite what to do with that, for, while he liked her and found her engaging company, he certainly didn't reciprocate the strength of her feelings.

"Dance with me," said Juliana as the band struck up the opening bars of a song with a more relaxed tempo that saw couples all over the room make their way to the dance floor. With no chaperones present, the students of Styrling Academy weren't about to waste this opportunity for some dancing that involved full body contact.

"Dance?" said Arcturus. "I don't think that—"

Juliana took his drink from him before he could protest, then put her own down as well.

"That wasn't a request," she said, leading him onto the dance floor.

Arcturus followed her, nervous at the prospect of making a fool of himself, but pleased at the attention he and Juliana were garnering. Arcturus had to admit they made an attractive couple, Juliana in her ivory gown and he in his exquisitely cut tuxedo and golden cummerbund.

The idea of kissing her leapt to the forefront of his mind and suddenly the idea of dancing close to Juliana didn't seem nearly so bad.

She turned to face him, holding up her arms. "You *do* dance, don't you?"

"Not for a long time," he admitted, taking her left hand and placing his right hand on her hip. "My mother made me take lessons when I was young, in preparation for my entrance into society. I always hated them."

"Don't worry," promised Juliana, moving his hand to her backside. "You'll be fine."

"I fear I may not be the dancer you hope for."

"Trust me, Arcturus, it'll all come back."

"Well, don't say I didn't warn you if I trample those expensive shoes."

Juliana smiled, and they began to move in time with the music. Arcturus thought he'd forgotten the steps of those long-ago lessons, but, sure enough, after his first faltering steps, he began to move with the music instead of against it. He and Juliana flowed naturally into the rhythm of their shared movement, and he felt like he'd just stepped out of dance class.

A series of dancers spun past them, the girls offering compliments to Juliana on her outfit and the boys hearty congratulations to Arcturus for having Steegman sent down.

"They really like you here," said Juliana, looking up at him. "You must be sad to leave."

Arcturus laughed and shook his head. "Not even a little bit," he said.

"Really? I think I'm going to be sad when I leave the Umoja Institute next year."

"That's because you are well liked and don't have a troublesome, embarrassing father."

"Well, since you're so glad to get out of school, what are you going to do with yourself?"

Arcturus didn't answer at first, wondering how much he should tell her of his plans for the future, for she clearly wanted to be part of them.

"I still want to be a prospector," he said. "But I don't think that's what I'll do first."

"No? Then what?" said Juliana, pressing herself closer to him.

"I think I might join the Marine Corps."

Juliana looked up sharply at him. "The Marine Corps?"

"Yes, I think it would be good to have some military service on my record," said Arcturus.

Arcturus could see she was uncomfortable about his joining the Marines, but whether it was from any concern for his safety or through moral objections, he couldn't yet tell.

"What do you think?" he asked.

"I . . . I'm not sure," said Juliana. "It sounds dangerous, but if it's what you want to do . . ."

"It's a stepping-stone, nothing more," said Arcturus. "It's not like I plan to stay in the military. Once I'm done I'll muster out and be a prospector, just like I always planned."

"Your father won't like it."

"I don't give a damn if he likes it or not," snapped Arcturus. "It's my life and I'll do what I want, not what he thinks I ought to do. I'll be eighteen next week and there's nothing he can do to stop me."

Juliana looked into his eyes, seeing the steely determination there, and nodded. "Then I think it's wonderful. I just know you'll be the best soldier they've ever had."

Arcturus wanted to laugh at how easily Juliana had come around to his way of thinking, despite the anti-Confederate propaganda her father was no doubt feeding her.

"You'll be a general within six months," she said. "My hero."

Sensing a moment of opportunity, Arcturus let go of Juliana's hand and tilted her chin upward with a light touch of his fingertips. She guessed what he was doing and closed her eyes, her lips parting slightly as he leaned in.

Their lips met, and they kissed.

Juliana's skin was warm to the touch and her lips were soft. She held him tightly, as though afraid to let him go, and the students closest to them cheered at the sight.

Arcturus felt a surge of vindication at the sound, understanding exactly what it meant.

It meant he could have anything he wanted.

CHAPTER 6

THOUSANDS OF PEOPLE LINED SENATORS' PARADE, the marble-paved street that led from the Martial Field to the Palatine Forum. Their cheers were deafening, and Achton Feld had to concentrate to hear the updates from his men over the mike nestled in his ear.

He had been awake since dawn, overseeing the last-minute preparations for Angus Mengsk's walk through the heart of the city. After the attack on the summer villa, Feld had increased security around the senator, but this had been the moment he had been dreading for weeks.

Angus's natural disregard for any threats to his person had given Feld dozens of sleepless nights as he worried about Confederate assassins, lone nutcases, or simply a zealous supporter of Lennox Craven. To watch for such a threat, Feld had men spread throughout the crowd, equipped with detectors attuned to the spectral frequency of the alloys used in the ammo of slugthrowers and spike pistols.

That would detect the most common firearms, but he knew that if anyone in the crowd carried a more sophisticated weapon, it would need to be visually recognized.

The atmosphere was electric and the mood of the crowd was jubilant (which was something to be thankful for) as they awaited Angus's arrival. Today was the final day of the Korhal Senate's sitting for the year, and it was traditional for a senator chosen by popular acclaim to deliver the Close of Session speech.

Ever since he had taken a stand against the tyranny of Confederate rule, it had been clear that it would be Angus Mengsk the people of Korhal would choose to deliver the speech.

Feld looked along the length of Senators' Parade, steel barriers keeping the crowd from the road. Banners with Angus's name on them were held high alongside flags with the wolf-head emblem of the Mengsk family crest. The route itself was clear and the gleaming white structure of the Forum shone like a beacon of light at its end. The roof blazed in the summer sunlight as though afire, and even Feld had to admit that it was an impressive sight.

All being well, Angus would walk through the great oaken doors of the Forum and stand before the assembled senators and visiting planetary dignitaries to deliver his speech. And after that . . . well, after that, the dynamic between Korhal and the Confederacy would be changed forever.

Feld heard a double click in his earpiece and felt a jolt of adrenaline hit his system.

Angus was on his way.

Sure enough, Feld saw the silver '58 Terra Cougar as it pulled slowly around the curve of the road that led to where he awaited his employer and friend. The groundcar moved slowly and Feld silently willed it to hurry up as the noise of the crowd grew louder with word of Angus's arrival.

At last the groundcar pulled up, and Feld moved quickly to open the door. The door slid upward and Angus Mengsk emerged from within, resplendent in his bright red toga. Angus stood tall, waving to the crowd with his head held high, his smile warm and genuine.

Katherine Mengsk followed him from the car, and Feld did a slow double take at the sight of her. She was dressed in a simple yet elegant dress of cornflower blue, her long dark hair bound up in a flattering style that brought out the classical lines of her cheekbones.

Angus turned back and took Katherine's hand, but before he could walk to the end of Senators' Parade, Feld stepped close and said, "What the hell are you doing, Angus?"

"I'm walking toward the Forum, Achton," said Angus through his smile. "What does it look like I'm doing?"

"It *looks* like you're blatantly disregarding the security plan we discussed. What is Katherine doing here? She was supposed to meet you at the Forum."

"I didn't like that plan," said Angus. "Now get out of my way. I'm going to walk to the Forum with my wife, and I don't want you next to me like a guard dog at my heel."

"Do you want to get killed?" asked Feld. "Is that it?"

"Don't be ridiculous—even the Confederacy wouldn't try anything today," scoffed Angus. "And we're both shielded by that force field of yours. Nothing's going to happen."

Feld stepped back and allowed Angus to walk past him, angry beyond words that the senator had so casually thrown out the security plan designed to keep him safe. Angus was probably right that nothing would happen today, but in Feld's experience it was usually just at that moment—when you lowered your guard—that your enemies struck.

Cursing Angus's need for dramatic gestures, Feld quickly broadcast an update on the security situation to his men in the crowd and closed the groundcar's door, thankful that Angus hadn't gone the whole hog and decided to bring Dorothy along. The vehicle would follow a discreet distance behind Angus in case a speedy exit was called for, and Feld just hoped it would not be needed.

Setting off alongside the groundcar, Feld scanned the crowd as Angus began his walk to the sounds of

ecstatic cheers and howls of support. Every face was
fixed on Angus and his glamorous wife.

Any one of them could be a potential threat, Feld
knew.

I should have taken that job on Brontes, he thought.

Angus felt the mood of the people surging through
him and knew he'd made the right decision to bring
Katherine along with him. He was just sorry he hadn't
decided to ask his wife to bring Dorothy and Arcturus,
but quickly discarded that thought.

Bringing a child as young as Little Dot to an event
like this would be foolish, and Arcturus . . . well, his son
would never have agreed anyway. They had spoken
little since the events of Graduation Day, his dealings
with Ailin Pasteur and preparations for today's events
taking up the bulk of his time.

In any case, Arcturus had been spending most of his
time since leaving the academy with Pasteur's daughter.
The only real time Angus and his son had spoken had
been yesterday at breakfast, where, despite his wife's
warning glance, Angus had broached the subject of
what Arcturus was planning on doing with his life.

"I haven't decided yet," said Arcturus, and Angus's
political instincts sensed evasion.

"I could set up an interview with Nestor Jurgens,"
said Angus nonchalantly. "He runs one of my machine
tooling factories in Fairstens. He's a good man—you
could learn a lot from him."

"What would I want to learn from a factory manager?" said Arcturus.

"Nestor's more than just a factory manager," replied Angus, irritated at his son's ingratitude. "All my managers effectively run their businesses autonomously. They're CEOs and financial managers all in one, though, of course, they answer to me. You're eighteen now, and you'd learn the ropes of what it takes to succeed in the industrial marketplace and acquire the skills you'll need if you're going to succeed me."

"Succeed you?" spat Arcturus. "I have plans of my own."

"I thought you said you hadn't decided on what you wanted to do."

"Well, I have."

When Arcturus didn't continue Angus sat back. "Are you going to keep us all in suspense?"

"You'll find out," said Arcturus, and Angus hadn't liked the sound of that one bit. After Arcturus's stunt at Graduation Day, Angus knew his son's mind could work in the most devious ways.

Arcturus had excused himself from breakfast at that point, and only Dorothy's spilling her cereal over the table had prevented Angus from going after him and demanding to know what was going on.

Angus pushed thoughts of Arcturus from his mind as Katherine gave his hand a squeeze.

He turned to her and kissed her cheek, and the crowd went wild.

They walked along Senators' Parade, the shimmering whiteness of the Forum drawing them ever onward. A tall figure in a red toga stood at the top of the steps and Angus smiled as he recognized Lennox Craven, the senior consul of the Senate and the man who would formally welcome him.

"This must be killing him," said Angus. "Having to welcome me in personally."

Katherine didn't need to ask who he meant, and smiled back. "I'm sure it is, but I can't say I have any sympathy for him."

Angus heard the steel in her voice, knowing that Katherine believed with utter certainty that Craven had dispatched the men who had come to kill them in the summer villa. She was probably right, but without concrete proof, there could be no public accusations.

"I'm going to enjoy watching that bastard squirm," said Angus.

"Careful, dear," cautioned Katherine, waving to the crowd. "There are a dozen holocams on you, and it would be bad form if someone lip-read that from you."

"Very true," said Angus. "As always, you are the soothing wind to my raging storm."

"Such is my role." She smiled. "But just make sure you *do* make the bastard squirm."

Lennox Craven was not a man given to public displays of emotion, but as he watched Angus Mengsk march toward him with barely disguised relish, it was all he could do to keep the anger from his face.

Dressed in a red toga identical to Mengsk's, Craven knew he was nowhere near as imposing or impressive a figure as his nemesis, but then, he had never set out to make himself a self-styled man of the people.

He knew for a fact that Mengsk's public face was as manufactured as that of any of the dozens of vacuous actors and actresses that UNN's celebrity channel broadcast day and night. Mengsk might pretend to be the champion of the common man, speaking out against the perceived injustices of the Confederacy, but hadn't he in fact benefited massively from all the Council of Tarsonis had done?

Wasn't Mengsk a wealthy man thanks to the very apparatus he so gleefully attacked with his speeches in the Forum and his incessant interviews on UNN? No, Lennox Craven knew the true face of Angus Mengsk, which made it all the more galling that he had to stand here as though they were the greatest of friends.

It made him want to throw up.

Even with bribes and calling in the many favors he was owed, he had not been able to prevent Angus from winning the hearts and minds of the people and the right to speak at the Close of Session. The Council had been most insistent: Angus Mengsk must be silenced. If one of the Confederate's most treasured and pampered worlds was seen to turn against them, then it would only be a matter of time before others attempted to follow its example.

And that could not be allowed to happen.

His paymasters were demanding results, and Lennox Craven had singularly failed to deliver them.

Thousands upon thousands of people lined the streets, and Craven could not remember a time when such numbers had come out to watch a senator march to the Forum. He remembered the year he had been chosen to make the Close of Session speech, and his bitterness at the apathy the people had displayed threatened to choke him in the face of Angus's popularity.

He drew himself up to his full height as Angus and his wife reached the bottom of the wide steps that climbed to the columned portico and the great black doors, beyond which lay the grand debating chamber.

Angus turned to give another wave to the cheering crowds, raising both arms above his head and accepting their adulation. He then turned and, taking his wife by the hand, began his ascent of the steps.

Craven could see the relish in Mengsk's eyes and prayed the man would stumble and fall flat on his face—anything to puncture the pompous arrogance that surrounded him. But Angus reached the top of the steps without mishap, and Craven fixed a practiced smile across his features and assumed the dignified mien of a seasoned senator who was about to welcome one of his dearest friends.

"Angus Mengsk, you've brought quite a crowd with you," he said by way of greeting. "And Katherine, you look radiant. A pleasure to see you, as always."

Mengsk's wife curtsied graciously and said, "Thank you, Lennox."

Angus Mengsk came forward with his arms open, and Craven's smile faltered.

Dear God, was the man expecting an embrace?

The crowds roared, and Craven knew he would have to play along with this charade of friendship. He opened his arms as Mengsk swept him up in a crushing bear hug, then awkwardly patted Mengsk's back in a suitably brotherly fashion, hoping that this would suffice.

"I know it was you who sent those men to kill me," whispered Mengsk. "I just wanted you to know that before I destroy you in there."

Craven stiffened, but before he could reply, Mengsk released him and made his way to the great doors of the Forum. Katherine Mengsk swept past Craven, locking her eyes with his as she went to join her husband. Though she said nothing, her cold gaze pinned him like a butterfly on a collector's wall.

Taking a deep breath to compose himself, Lennox Craven turned and followed Angus Mengsk into the Forum, already dreading what the damnable man was going to say in his speech.

The interior of the Palatine Forum was no less magnificent than the exterior, the floor of the vestibule fashioned from great slabs of black marble veined with gold and its columns fluted and rising to dizzying heights. The alabaster walls were painted with great murals depicting the pioneers of Korhal's heroic past: revered senators, intrepid space-farers, great architects, military commanders, and far-seeing philosophers.

Angus and Katherine crossed the vestibule and approached the bronze doors of the great chamber of the Forum, behind which could be heard the animated buzz of voices.

Lennox Craven caught up to them, but Angus did not deign to glance in his direction.

Katherine squeezed his hand. Once again, Angus was thankful for her steadying presence.

She turned to him and said, "I love you."

"I love you too," said Angus without hesitation.

Katherine smiled and made her way to a door at the side of the vestibule, which Angus knew led up to the viewing gallery. Tradition demanded that only senators enter the main chamber through this door, so Katherine would need to view proceedings from above, with the rest of the families and invited guests.

He waited for a few minutes—pointedly ignoring Lennox Craven—until he was sure Katherine would have reached her allocated seat. Then he approached the door.

It swung open smoothly, and Angus felt his heart race as he saw the assembled senators and dignitaries awaiting his arrival.

Yes, he thought, *this is my moment. . . .*

"There's your mother now," said Ailin Pasteur, and Arcturus turned to see Katherine Mengsk threading her way through the assorted family members gathered in the viewing gallery. She saw him sitting there, her eyes bright at this unexpected pleasure, and Arcturus felt a genuine moment of regret at what he was about to do to her.

Juliana sat behind her father, full of nervous excitement at the thought of seeing Angus Mengsk give the Close of Session speech in the Korhal Forum. In the time since graduation, she had spent a great deal of time with Arcturus, though thanks to the constant presence of a chaperone he had not had a chance to take her to his bed.

Instead, they had spent most of their time in closely supervised walks through Styrling, and though he never tired of filling her head with his grandiose dreams of the future, he *had* begun to tire of her company.

Not that that would be a problem soon, he thought, picturing the sheaf of papers nestling in his coat pocket. Only Juliana knew what he planned, but he knew she would say nothing.

His mother smiled as she negotiated her way toward their little group, obviously pleased to see him there. She smiled at people she passed, and Arcturus could see the genuine affection in which his mother was held. In addition to being the glamorous wife of a senator, Katherine Mengsk was a patron of numerous charities and spoke out on many issues that affected people from every strata of society.

She had been the first to address the subject of child trafficking between worlds, had opened people's eyes to the plight of the homeless in Styrling, and had set up numerous health organizations to aid the many victims of war. His mother offered kind words to everyone she passed, and watching her easy smile and natural grace made Arcturus realize why she was so beloved by the people of Korhal.

At last his mother reached them, and Arcturus shifted up on the wooden bench to allow her to sit next to him. She leaned over and kissed his cheek.

"I'm so glad you came, Arcturus," she said, her smile warm and genuine.

"So am I," said Arcturus.

She directed her attention to the Pasteurs and said, "Ailin, it's wonderful to see you here. And Juliana, Angus will be so pleased you came to see him deliver his speech."

Juliana smiled shyly at Katherine, and Arcturus could see she was a little in awe of his mother. "Thank you, Mrs. Mengsk."

"Call me Katherine, dear, please." She smiled, patting Arcturus's knee. "You're practically family now."

Ailin Pasteur returned Arcturus's mother's smile and said, "I wouldn't have missed this for the world, Katherine. People are going to remember this day for a long time to come."

"I have no doubt of that," said Katherine, beaming as the master of ceremonies rapped his bronze-tipped staff on the tiled floor of the Senate floor.

The senators below stood a little taller and everyone in the gallery leaned forward as the bronze doors opened and Angus Mengsk made his entrance.

Angus raised his arms in triumph as he stepped into the vast domed chamber of the Senate, recognizing that this was a symbolic as well as a literal crossing of a threshold. Like the most alluring woman, the Palatine Forum saved its most majestic treasures for last and, as always, Angus felt a deep sense of pride, awe, and reverence for what this chamber represented.

Democracy, free will, and freedom from oppression.

The central floor was paved with panels of opus sectile, in which porphyry and serpentine figured prominently. To either side were three broad, low, marble-faced steps, and on the level nearest the floor sat the more notable senators upon their curule chairs.

The two top steps were broader than the others, and upon them stood hundreds of richly dressed men and women, the entire body of the Korhal Senate and assorted dignitaries granted special leave to attend the Close of Session.

Gray marble wainscoting ran along each wall, finished with a molding above which marble panels were rhythmically placed with only the interruption of three statue-filled niches to break the pattern. As the wall rose toward the dome, it was faced with tall gray rectangular panels with golden lettering: the constitutional tenets set down by Korhal's earliest settlers and the principles by which its people were to be governed.

The dome itself was made up of heavily gilded lacunaria consisting of square coffers set with golden discs at their centers. Just below the dome was the viewing gallery, where those important enough to be allowed into the Palatine Forum yet not of sufficient stature to set foot in the main chamber could be seated.

Ailin Pasteur watched from here, as did Katherine, proudly awaiting Angus's arrival. He resisted the urge to wave to her. Looking farther along, he was surprised and pleased to see Arcturus next to her.

Katherine had probably emotionally blackmailed their son to get him here, he figured. Briefly he wondered why Katherine hadn't told him that Arcturus was going to be here, but put the thought from his mind. Where Arcturus was concerned, Angus would take what he could get.

He looked up into the dome as thunderous applause swelled from the assembled senators, and let the moment stretch as he reveled in the acclaim of his peers. When he judged the moment right, he slowly lowered his eyes to the Confederate flag hung opposite the entrance, below which sat the senior consul's plinth.

It was from this plinth that Angus would deliver his speech, and he marched across the floor of the Senate chamber toward it. With applause still ringing in his ears, he stepped up onto the plinth and stared up at the red and blue of the flag.

His scathing look made no secret of his loathing for all it represented.

Greed, corruption, and moral stagnation.

With one swift movement, he reached up and ripped it down.

The cheers of the assembled senators doubled in volume.

Arcturus watched the faces of the people below in the Senate hall and gathered around him in the gallery as they clapped and cheered. He was amazed they could be so enamored of his father. Could they not see him for what he was—an ordinary, stubborn man who didn't know how to listen? In that moment, a realization crystallized in Arcturus.

It didn't matter what the reality of a person was, it was what he showed the world that mattered. The people of Korhal didn't know the real Angus Mengsk; they knew the reality he *gave* them, the manufactured persona calculated to win them over to his cause. It didn't matter that his father was as human and as fallible as them; all that mattered was what he *meant* to them and what he promised them.

Arcturus had always known that ordinary people were easy to manipulate, but to see supposedly educated men and women so easily swayed was a revelation.

He sat back as his father strode across the Senate floor toward the senior consul's plinth, basking in the applause of his fellow senators. This was a salutary lesson in the power of perception versus reality, but Arcturus had no wish to sit through another of his father's impassioned rants about the iniquities of the Confederacy.

He'd heard enough of those over the course of his young life to last him a lifetime.

It was time.

Arcturus took a deep breath and reached inside his coat pocket, removed the sheaf of crisp papers he'd signed earlier this morning, and laid them on his lap. He looked over at his mother, again feeling slightly guilty about what he was about to do, but knowing that this was the right thing for him to do simply because it was what he *wanted* to do.

Sensing his scrutiny, his mother glanced over at him, and her clapping faltered as she saw the papers laid out before him and the insignia emblazoned at the top.

"Arcturus . . . ," she said hesitantly. "What's that?"

"Enlistment papers, Mother," he said. "For the Confederate Marine Corps. I went to the recruitment offices this morning."

Katherine looked down at the papers, her confusion turning to cold dread in the space of a heartbeat. "Oh Arcturus, no . . . please, no . . . What have you done?"

She went to lift the papers from him, but he was quicker, and snatched them up before she could take them as the cheers of the crowd suddenly swelled in volume.

"Arcturus, what did you do?" cried his mother. "Tell me!"

"I joined up," he said.

"No, no, you didn't!" said Katherine. "You didn't. Arcturus, if this is a joke, it's in very poor taste."

"I'm not joking, Mother," said Arcturus. "As of this morning, I'm part of the officer corps of the 33rd Ground Assault Division under Commander Brantigan Fole."

"No, no, you're not. This is some kind of prank, isn't it?" said his mother, and Arcturus saw real panic in her eyes. "Isn't it? Tell me it's one of your stupid pranks!"

People were turning from watching his father below on the Senate floor to the growing commotion in the gallery as Katherine's voice rose in pitch and volume. The applause was still loud and cheering echoed around the chamber, drowning out their words to all but the nearest spectators.

"It's not a prank, Mother," said Arcturus, cold fury entering his heart at the idea that something this important to him would be dismissed as a prank. This was his *life*, and she thought he was joking?

"I'm leaving this afternoon," he said.

His mother slapped him across the cheek.

Gasps of surprise spread like ripples in a pond at the sound of her palm connecting with his cheek.

"You stupid, stupid boy," stormed Katherine. "You stupid, selfish boy. Is this your way of hurting your father? Of hurting me? Do you have any idea what you've done?"

"I know exactly what I've done," said Arcturus, his resolve now hardened in the face of his mother's insulting slap. "And you've just made it easier for me."

Katherine reached for him, but he batted her hands away and rose to his feet. His mother looked up at him, tears spilling down her cheeks, but Arcturus didn't care anymore. He slid his enlistment papers back into his coat pocket and said, "Good-bye, Mother. Tell Dorothy I'm sorry I didn't have a chance to say good-bye to her. Tell her I'll write."

"No!" wept Katherine, her heartbroken cry swallowed up by the clapping that still filled the Senate chamber. "Oh God, please don't do this! Arcturus, please, please . . . wait!"

Arcturus ignored his mother's terrible, aching grief and strode through the astonished crowd sitting in the viewing gallery. He could feel their eyes upon him, but kept his head held high, determined to leave this place with dignity.

A strong hand gripped his arm, and he turned to berate the person for this impudence.

Ailin Pasteur stood behind him, his face a mask of anger. "Your father will never forgive you for this, Arcturus."

"I'm not asking him to," snapped Arcturus, shrugging off the Umojan ambassador's hand.

"Of all the days you could have done this, why today?" demanded Pasteur.

Arcturus returned Pasteur's stare with a steel gaze of his own. The man recoiled from the determination in Arcturus's eyes as though struck.

"Sometimes you have to do something dramatic to make your point," said Arcturus.

Pasteur shook his head sadly, turning to look at his weeping mother.

"Well, boy," he said sadly, "you've certainly done that. I just hope you don't live to regret what you've done today."

"I won't," promised Arcturus, turning and walking away.

Book 2.

Arcturus

CHAPTER 7

THE DROPSHIP SCREAMED THROUGH THE UPPER atmosphere of Sonyan, trailing fire from its wings like a swooping phoenix. The armored plates of its heat-shielding rippled with blazing orange fire and left a streaking contrail of vapor in the craft's wake as it dropped rapidly toward the planet's surface.

As flying machines went, it was proof that with a big enough pair of engines, you could get anything to stay in the air. Its front wings were stubby, swept forward and down, behind which enormous jet engines coughed to life as the craft hit the atmosphere.

Dropships were designed to carry Confederate military forces into battle in safety and at speed—though they achieved neither objective particularly well—and as Arcturus gripped the metal stanchion next to his head he knew that, regardless of any other considerations, comfort had certainly not been uppermost in the designers' minds.

Dropships could carry anything from troops to siege tanks in their transport compartments, and thus the cavernous bay housing Arcturus's armored marines—designated "Dominion section"—was an oily, dust-filled metallic cavern.

The dropship shuddered as it leveled out, wind roar and engine noise making conversation impossible unless carried out over the helmet comms. As well as the six armored soldiers, the dropship carried a huge siege tank, its colossal, groaning mass held fast with clanking chains and filling much of the dropship's internal space. It was breaking regs putting this many soldiers in with a siege tank, but the orders had come from on high to get them there like this, and Arcturus wasn't about to question orders this early in his career.

His five soldiers sat toward the rear of the red-lit compartment on uncomfortable metal benches that looked as though a blind welder had attached them to the fuselage's interior.

"So what's the situation, LT?" asked Yancy Gray for the hundredth time. "What are we flying into?"

Arcturus sighed. The irrepressible kid from Tarsonis never let up until he got an answer and he had a strange, naïve belief that the chain of command would keep him informed at every stage of what was going on. He hadn't been with the military long enough to know that the grunts on the front line were like mushrooms: kept in the dark and fed shit.

"Aw, man, how many times you gonna keep asking

that, Yancy?" said de Santo, her face belligerent. "LT's gonna tell us what's up when he knows. Right, LT?"

Diamond de Santo (or Dia, as her section-mates knew her) was a dark-skinned girl who had grown up on Tyrador IX, the daughter of indentured workers who toiled in one of the many spas and resort cities that made the planet such a refuge for the scions of the Old Families. Armies of men and women who owed money to one of the many Confederate financial institutions were forced to work there to repay their debts and ensure that guests didn't need to lift so much as a finger.

Needless to say, Diamond de Santo hadn't enjoyed that life much, and she'd signed up at the first recruiting office she could find on her eighteenth birthday. In the six months Arcturus had known her, he had seen the core of a good soldier, but one who had such a chip on her shoulder that it kept her mouth truculent and her manner rebellious.

Arcturus liked her immensely.

And by some strange, inverted magnetism, de Santo recognized a kindred soul and displayed a loyalty to Arcturus that reminded him of the bond between his father and Achton Feld.

"Hey, I'm just asking," said Yancy. "Nothing wrong with wanting to know what's going on, is there? I was supposed to be on leave until this new assignment came down the pipe."

"We were *all* supposed to be on leave," said de Santo pointedly, making no secret of her irritation at that particular stroke of genius from the brass.

She wasn't the only one annoyed that their leave had been postponed. Arcturus had planned to return to Korhal to see his mother and Little Dot. He hadn't been back to see them since he'd joined up, though he had written to them plenty of times over the Confednetwork.

His mother had eventually answered, though her words didn't have the same openness and warmth as did the letters she had sent him at the academy. Her correspondence was filled with news of his sister and of Korhal (and its troubles) but made little mention of his father beyond his continued good health.

Dorothy hadn't replied to him at all, and he knew she was probably still smarting with annoyance at his sudden departure. Hopefully, once this mission was over, he'd have a chance to patch things up with his family, as the last year and a half had made him realize how much he missed them.

Even his father, which surprised Arcturus immensely.

Of course, there had been a great deal of correspondence between Arcturus and Juliana, and it seemed she remained interested in him though light-years separated them.

They had arranged to meet on Tyrador IX before he headed onward to Korhal when his next period of leave eventually came through, and he was forced to admit he was looking forward to seeing her again.

Arcturus's reverie ended when Yancy nodded his helmeted head toward him and said, "I'll bet you anything LT already knows where we're headed. Yeah, a hundred credits says he already knows."

"Hell, I'd take that bet if I thought you had the damn cash," said Chuck Horner, his broad, fringe world grin robbing the comment of malice. Horner was what Arcturus's father would have disparagingly called "a good ol' boy," a thick-shouldered, broad-featured hayseed from one of the outlying worlds in the Confederacy where they counted themselves lucky if they had electricity throughout the day.

On the surface, that's exactly what Charles "Chuck" Horner was, and Arcturus had been surprised to find a sharp mind and quick wit behind his "aw shucks" exterior.

"But you ain't got two cents to rub together," continued Chuck. "Leastways not after me and Chun Leung won everything but your panties the other night at poker."

"You got lucky," said Yancy.

"Lucky?" drawled Chuck. "My daddy and his daddy before him was playing army poker before you was a glint in your mama's eye. Taught me everything I know, son."

"Oh yeah?" countered Yancy. "Wanna try your luck again tonight?"

"What you got to bet with?" put in the aforementioned Chun Leung. "I already got your money and your chocolate rations for the next week. You don't got anything else the Big Dog wants to take off you."

"I'll clean Mayumi for a month," offered Yancy.

"Boy wants to gamble," de Santo said with a laugh.

"No way," said Chun Leung, hefting his Impaler rifle across his lap to stroke the gleaming, oiled barrel. Mayumi was the name Chun Leung had given to his rifle, his pride and joy. He kept the rifle obsessively oiled and cleaned, and where everyone else's gun was battered and scratched, Leung's weapon looked as though it had come straight from the factory.

"*I'm* the only one who handles my weapon," said Leung.

"Yeah, that's what the girls on Pridewater said too," quipped de Santo.

Leung flipped her off. "You want a piece of me?" he said. "I'll show you why they call me the Big Dog, little girl."

Arcturus listened to the banter, sensing the undercurrent of fear behind their easy back-and-forth. Thus far, the commanders of the 33rd hadn't seen fit to post them anywhere too dangerous, but even though his soldiers had only mess tent scuttlebutt to go on, they could sense this assignment would be different.

Only one member of the section didn't join in on the banter, and Arcturus knew that if there was a God somewhere in the heavens, he had a strange sense of humor.

Toby Mercurio, another graduate of Styrling Academy, sat across from Arcturus, his face downcast and his shoulders slumped. Having spent the last six months trying to bring Mercurio up to the standard of the rest of the section, Arcturus knew that the life of a soldier was not for his fellow alumnus.

Though Mercurio's parents had been wealthy enough to send him to an expensive school, the boy wasn't really Styrling Academy material. He'd scraped by academically, but it had been his above-average performance on the padball courts that had allowed him to graduate.

But above average didn't cut it in the professional circuit and without the safety net of any real qualifications, Toby had floundered in the real world. A series of meaningless, paper-shuffling jobs at one of his father's plants had ensued—all of which he'd spectacularly failed at—followed by a drunken afternoon that had seen him wake with a crushing hangover and a sheaf of signed enlistment papers.

In the eighteen months since Arcturus had joined up, he'd found that a soldier's life consisted of long stretches of boredom, followed by frantic periods of deployment and shouting. Which, in Dominion section's case, had been followed by yet more periods of boredom.

This assignment looked as though it might involve some action and, as surprising as it was to him, Arcturus realized he was looking forward to the prospect of combat. He'd trained to fight in combat armor and could fire a gauss rifle with a reasonable degree of accuracy, but it was his understanding of battlefield tactics, combined with his talent for inspiring those around him and making the impossible sound plausible, that had seen him rise to the level of lieutenant. Senior officers had their eye on him to ascend the promotions ladder, but before he could really embark on that climb, he needed some real combat under his belt.

Hence Dominion section's deployment to Sonyan.

"So come on, LT," said Chuck Horner. "Is the kid right? You know why we're out here?"

Arcturus felt the eyes of his section turn on him, their faces blurred slightly through the low-grade plasteel of their helmet visors.

"Yes, Charles," said Arcturus, knowing the others got a kick out of his using Chuck's full name. "I *do* know why we're out here. I'm an officer—it's my job to know."

"So what's the skinny?" asked Yancy, leaning forward. "Pirates? Rogue merc bands terrorizing helpless colonists and their pretty daughters?"

"Something like that," agreed Arcturus.

Whoops and hollers echoed over the comms at the prospect of actually putting their training into practice. Arcturus held a hand up to quiet his section and said, "We're dropping on a planet called Sonyan, specifically Camp Juno, where we're to rendezvous with other elements of the 33rd and facilitate the evacuation of personnel involved in illegal deep-core mining operations."

"We gonna get to kill anyone?" asked Chun Leung, patting Mayumi's muzzle.

"I hope not," said Arcturus, "but it's likely many of

the people on Sonyan aren't going to want to leave their holdings."

"Well, damn, we got to show them the error of their ways," said Chuck Horner, high-fiving with Chun Leung. Yancy and Dia looked excited at the prospect, but, as usual, Toby Mercurio didn't join in.

"I bet I kill more than you, Dia," said Yancy.

"Sure you will," sneered de Santo. "Boy, you barely know which end of that gun to point at the enemy. We get into a firefight, you make sure you stay in front of me, you hear?"

Lines of scrolling text flickered onto the HUD of Arcturus's armor and the red light of the compartment began flashing.

"Quiet down," he said, his voice easily cutting through the good-natured sparring. "We're coming in to land, so look sharp."

Before Sonyan, Arcturus had seen precisely three other planets. Growing up on Korhal, a lush, temperate world of balmy summers and mild winters, he had assumed that most other habitable worlds in the Confederacy would be much the same. His training on the colossal orbital shipyards of Dylar IV and his first tour on Pridewater had quickly disabused him of that notion, emphasizing the point that humans could live pretty much anywhere with enough perseverance.

But Sonyan was a world you'd have to have a serious reason just to visit, let alone live on.

As the assault ramp clanged onto the sandy hardpan

of the planet, hot, biting winds howled inside the dropship, instantly blinding Arcturus and his soldiers.

As they disembarked, a group of engineers barged past them to get to the siege tank, and Arcturus fought the urge to shout at them. Instead he marched down the ramp and onto the gritty surface of another world.

The visor of Arcturus's helmet darkened in response to the sudden brightness as he took his first look at their new posting.

Camp Juno nestled in the rocky foothills of a broken series of valleys in the middle of a soaring range of reddish brown mountains. Dust devils blew down from the high peaks and the sky was the color of flaking rust. A jaundiced orb of a sun hung low above the tops of the mountains, casting long, thin shadows down the mountains and over the camp.

In the middle of the camp sat a modular command center, its pressed metal plates scoured and distressed by the constant assault of wind-borne grit. The rotating dish of a comsat swept the terrain and a number of depressingly identical buildings surrounded the command center, the standard pieces of kit you'd expect to find around any Confederate military establishment—barracks, mess halls, infirmary, and landing platform, as well as portal-framed hangars, supply depots, and training facilities.

Coils of wire looped between six missile turrets spaced at regular intervals around the camp's perimeter, their own dishes sweeping the skies for aerial threats. Squads of marines jogged through the camp and industrious SCVs effected repairs to damaged buildings.

Despite the number of people he saw, Arcturus sensed a relaxed, unhurried air to the camp. There was no urgency to the training, nor any sense of wariness in the posture of those marines that stood sentry over the camp. A few heads turned as he led his men from the belly of the dropship, but any interest in their arrival quickly passed.

"So what now, LT?" asked Yancy, slinging his rifle over his shoulder. "Where's our reception committee?"

Arcturus was wondering the same thing, but didn't reply. It didn't become an officer to admit that he didn't know what was going on. They were supposed to have been met by the camp's head of security, but they were completely alone on the landing platform.

"Watch out on the ramp!" shouted one of the engineers inside the dropship, sparing Arcturus from thinking of an answer for Yancy.

No sooner was the warning given than the throaty rumble of the siege tank's engine bellowed. Jetting filthy plumes of blue oilsmoke, the tank lurched from the darkness and jerkily drove out onto the sand.

Arcturus watched as the tank rumbled away from the dropship with the engineers in tow.

"Damn, that thing's probably older than you, Chuck," said Dia de Santo.

"Dia, honey," drawled Chuck. "You call it old; I call it experienced."

"Well that is one *experienced* tank," said Yancy.

"Screw you, son," said Chuck with a knowing wink to de Santo. "Gimme the choice between a filly and a mare, I'll take the mare every time. She knows what she's doing and she'll make sure you do it right."

"We still talkin' about tanks?" asked Yancy.

"Ten-hut!" shouted Chun Leung, and the marines of Dominion section snapped to attention. Arcturus turned to see a fully armored marine marching toward them from the command center. He saw the insignia of a captain on the marine's shoulder, and a security detail of two soldiers marched at the officer's back.

Arcturus pulled himself to attention, squinting through the glare and dust haze as he saw a familiarity to the marine's posture and walk. The captain halted in front of Arcturus and gave him a quick once-over.

"Lieutenant Arcturus Mengsk reporting for duty, sir," he said, saluting smartly. "Dominion section is ready for action, sir."

"At ease, Mengsk," said the captain, and Arcturus smiled as he realized why his superior had seemed so familiar.

The glare visor on the captain's helmet snapped up and Arcturus found himself staring into the face of Captain Angelina Emillian, the very woman who'd planted the seed of his enlistment, so long ago it seemed, at Styrling Academy.

Arcturus relaxed, but only a fraction. Emillian might have been a familiar face, but she was still a captain and he a lieutenant. Even he had to respect the chain of command.

"Good to see you again, Mengsk," said Emillian. "So they made you lieutenant?"

"Yes, sir," said Arcturus. "All the generals' jobs were taken."

Emillian smiled. "I see you've not lost that smart mouth of yours. Maybe your principal was right about you. They still letting him teach there?"

"No, sir," said Arcturus. "Last I heard he was doing sixty years in Bhar-el penal colony for embezzlement and fraud. I gather he wasn't a suitable candidate for resocialization."

Emillian caught the pride in his tone and said, "And I suppose you would've had nothing to do with that?"

"I couldn't possibly say," he replied, leaving Emillian in no doubt as to his complicity in Steegman's fall from grace.

"I thought so," said Emillian, jerking a thumb in the direction of his marines. "So what's their story?"

"Dominion section," said Arcturus. "Ready for action, sir. Just give us the word."

"Dominion section?" repeated Emillian. "Nice name. You choose it?"

"I did," said Arcturus with a nod. "I thought it sounded appropriately grand."

Emillian shook her head with a grin and walked along the line of marines, her stern gaze boring into each soldier and leaving no doubt that they were less than nothing to her.

"Okay, listen up, marines!" she shouted. "Welcome to Sonyan, the most miserable crap-hole this side of the core worlds. This ain't boot camp and it sure ain't paradise, so wherever you've been stationed before and thought was bad, forget it, this is worse. The chow sucks, the barracks have got more holes that an Impaler target, and you won't be leaving without at least one trip to the infirmary. Any questions?"

Most of the marines of Dominion section met her stare stoically, understanding that the best response to this kind of rhetorical question was silence.

Yancy Gray was, however, apparently oblivious to this piece of soldier's wisdom.

"Why will we be visiting the infirmary, sir?" he asked.

Captain Emillian rounded on him, the visor of her helmet barely an inch from her questioner. Arcturus winced, irritated that one of his marines had embarrassed him.

"Did you say something, soldier?" she said.

"Uh . . . you asked if anyone had questions," replied Yancy. "I do. Have a question, I mean."

"That's enough, Gray," said Arcturus. "The captain will brief me and then I'll tell you what you need to know. For your sake, you'd better hope your trip to the infirmary is because you've been killed so you won't go asking any more stupid questions."

Emillian continued to stare hard at Yancy, who kept

his gaze fixed on a point somewhere over her right shoulder. Eventually the captain turned away and stood before the section with her hands laced behind her back.

"In answer to Private Gray's question, you will most likely visit the infirmary because you will be getting shot at by disgruntled miners who have illegally begun deep-core operations on this rock, which just so happens to be a Confederate-owned piece of real estate."

Arcturus hadn't known that Sonyan was a Confederate world, that nugget of information not having been part of his briefing prior to their departure from Pridewater. Not that his briefing had said much more than "Go to Sonyan and await orders."

In any case, this far out on the rim, who claimed a world was largely a factor of who had the most men and the biggest guns. With the arrival of Dominion section and the siege tank, it appeared that honor now belonged to the Confederacy.

"Most of these miners have already been relocated," continued Emillian, beginning to pace as she spoke, "but there are a few stubborn holdouts, and it's going to be your job to flush them out. It's going to be bloody work, because these miners are dug in deeper than a Tyrador blood-shrike, but you'll have help. There are thirty marines and a handful of firebats here that'll be going in with you. And now we have a siege tank. But make no mistake, marines, you *will* be shot at and we will take casualties.

"That last part, I can guarantee," finished Emillian. "Since you lucky bastards are going to hit Turanga Canyon at 06:00 tomorrow."

The sun was already bright and hot when Arcturus rose from his bunk at 05:00 and made his way to the mess hall to grab some breakfast and gulp down some A-grade military caffeine. Breakfast consisted of high-calorie gunk that tasted foul, but provided the energy a marine would need for combat operations.

As he sat contemplating the brownish sludge spooned onto his tray, Captain Emillian took the seat opposite him.

"Morning, Lieutenant," she said, nodding toward the food. "Not what you're used to, I bet."

"Not exactly," he agreed. "Though the refectory at Styrling Academy could give this place a run for its money."

"I can see why the Marine Corps would be appealing to you then."

They ate their breakfast in silence, and Arcturus took the opportunity to study Angelina Emillian in more detail. She was still pretty, but he noticed a scar that hadn't been there before, which traced a pale line above her ear before disappearing beneath her hair.

"Got it on Chau Sara," she said without looking up. "There was a prison riot in one of the penal colonies where they keep the worst of the worst—the mass murderers, rapists, and serial killers. We were on rotation there to pick up a batch for resocialization when it happened. I was in solitary evaluating an inmate by the name of Wyan Schaen when he got one of the guard's weapons and shot me in the face."

"Nasty," said Arcturus, appreciating the ridiculous understatement of his remark as he said it. But Emillian appeared not to notice.

"Yeah, it was, but I was lucky. The bullet ricocheted from the interior of my helmet and grazed me before exploding out the back."

"So what did you do?"

"There was so much blood around me, the dumb-ass thought I was dead," said Emillian. "I guess I was out for a few seconds, but once I came to, I saw he was standing at the bars with his back to me. So I got up and broke his neck, and then got the hell out of there."

"I'm impressed," said Arcturus, genuinely meaning it.

"It's nothing," she said. "Anyway, we got our recruits and I got a new scar I could use to impress greenhorn lieutenants. So tell me about your section, Mengsk. Are they any good?"

Arcturus looked down the length of the table, where the marines of Dominion section sat chatting with the marines who were going to be flying up to Turanga Canyon with them.

"Yes," he said. "Until this mission came up, they were looking forward to going on leave. We all were, but they're good soldiers. Some are better than others, but they'll follow orders and they'll fight hard."

"Good enough," said Emillian.

Arcturus had seen the telltale scars of neural resocialization on the marines his men were talking to and said, "Tell me something, Captain. You have thirty marines here already, all resoced to follow orders without question."

"Yeah? So?"

"So why do you need us?"

Emillian answered between mouthfuls of scrambled egg. "You ever fought alongside a resoced marine?"

"No."

"You wouldn't ask that question if you had," said Emillian. "Don't get me wrong, they're perfectly good soldiers and they'll do anything you order them to, but they don't have initiative and don't react too well to changing battlefield situations. Give 'em an order that's easy to follow and there's no problem, but the minute things start to get a bit screwy, well, they get a bit lost. I keep asking for marines that aren't brain-panned, but they keep sending me more of 'em."

"And you think six of us can make a difference?"

"Six of you and a siege tank, let's not forget."

"Of course," said Arcturus. "These miners, they must be a tough bunch."

"What makes you say that?"

"You clearly don't think they'll surrender as soon as they see us. Am I wrong?"

"No, you're not wrong."

"I didn't think so," said Arcturus. "Why won't they surrender?"

"Because they didn't the last time we came for them. They fought back with goliath walkers, antiaircraft missiles, and a whole lot of guns. Then again, we didn't have a siege tank last time. Or Dominion section," she added with a smile.

The siege tank had left the previous evening and was to rendezvous with them at the mouth of Turanga Canyon, where it would provide artillery support as the marines moved up toward the miners' base.

"Do you remember when we spoke back at Styrling Academy?" asked Arcturus.

"Sure," said Emillian. "Why do you ask?"

"You said barely fifty percent of marines ever actually see combat. Seems like that might have been a slight . . . exaggeration."

"Not at all," replied Emillian. "About fifty percent of recruits to the marines either wash out of boot camp, are killed in training accidents, get their brains fried by the resoc, or otherwise end up invalided to desk jobs."

"So basically if you survive boot camp you're almost *guaranteed* to see combat?"

"Pretty much," agreed Emillian, with a wry twitch of her eyebrows.

"Doesn't sound quite as appealing when you put it like that."

"Hence the shift of emphasis," said Emillian, standing and carrying her breakfast tray to the racks. Arcturus followed her and slid his tray in below Emillian's.

"I can see that. Now."

Emillian turned, and from the steel in her eyes

Arcturus could see that the informality of breakfast was over.

"Right. Time to get busy, Lieutenant. Get your men together and be on the launchpad in ten minutes. We dust off at 05:30, so don't be late or I'll court-martial your ass. Now move it!"

Arcturus moved it.

Arcturus sat with his gauss rifle against his shoulder and his body braced against the craggy rock protecting him from the stream of bullets that sawed down from above. The sun blazed high above them, a sour lemon yellow orb that looked close enough to reach up and touch. His breath came in ragged spurts and he could taste blood in his mouth from where he'd bitten his tongue in the crash.

The members of Dominion section huddled in the rocks with him, each one looking the worse for wear, but still alive. Which Arcturus realized was a bloody miracle, remembering the gut-wrenching terror he'd felt as the explosion had torn a monstrous hole in the side of the dropship.

He could recall almost nothing of what followed, save hurricane-force winds roaring through the troop compartment, billowing flames, and the awful sound of battle-hardened marines screaming in agony.

Next thing he remembered, he was lying in a tangle of twisted metal, surrounded by flames and looking up at a pillar of oily black smoke etched on the sky. Hands had grabbed him under his arms and dragged him from the wreckage, and as he'd been propped up against a rock, he saw it had been Chuck Horner who'd rescued him.

"What happened?" he managed.

"Missile," said Horner. "They got a turret set up at the mouth of the valley. Pilot didn't see it and we got a heat-seeker right up our tailpipe. Now at least half the marines are dead, and the damn siege tank ain't here yet neither."

"Emillian?" asked Arcturus. "Where's the captain?"

"Captain's out of the fight, sir," said Yancy Gray, across the gully from Arcturus. "I think her back's broken."

Private Gray's words had focused Arcturus's thoughts, and he pulled himself to his feet using a nearby rock for support. He had to get everyone together and figure out what to do next. Looking over at Emillian's supine form, Arcturus saw that Yancy was dead right: Emillian wasn't going to be joining this fight.

Her armor would keep her alive for a while, but her legs and spine were bent into shapes they weren't designed to make, and Arcturus knew she wouldn't last long if they didn't get her to a medical station.

Twenty meters back down the valley, the gutted hulk of the dropship lay scattered in a mangled pile of fire-blackened steel. The pilot had tried his best to soften their landing, but there was only so much you could do with your engines taken out by an explosion and the nearest piece of flat ground a hundred kilometers away. Thick, billowing clouds of smoke belched from the wrecked craft and the fire crackled and popped as it devoured ammo packs and stim dispensers.

Arcturus had done a quick head count, and found that eleven of the marines who'd accompanied them on the dropship were dead and another eight were too badly injured to fight. Three of the firebats were also dead, immolated by their own weapons when they'd cooked off in the fire of the crash.

That left eleven of Emillian's resoced marines and two firebats to fight alongside Dominion section. No sooner had Arcturus got everyone together than a burst of gunfire ripped down from the rocks above.

"Cover!" he shouted, though the order was unnecessary. High-pitched *pings* of metal on rock echoed deafeningly, like an endless box of nails being emptied onto hard stone from a great height.

Breathing heavily, Arcturus risked a glance out of cover when the fire slackened fractionally, and saw a whole lot of shooters on the rocks above. He guessed about twenty men in body armor, helmets, and tough-wearing outdoor gear.

Certainly not soldiers, but more likely mercenaries or a pirate band hired by the miners.

Arcturus stuck his rifle around the rock and pulled the trigger, not really aiming, but just wanting to return fire. The armor easily absorbed the recoil, and though his shots went well wide, he felt better for shooting back.

Dominion section hugged the rocks, looking up with expressions ranging from the beginnings of panic to relish. More spikes sprayed down at them and Arcturus watched as a concentrated volley tore up one of the injured marines.

The man appeared to jerk as though being electrocuted. His armor was proof against most small-arms fire, but a whole lot of Impaler rifles firing in sync had torn through the weakened portions of his plate.

Whomever these miners had hired to defend them knew their trade.

More shots ricocheted down from above, pinning them in the rocks below their objective, and Arcturus saw they had only two options. They could either retreat, skulking back to the valley mouth, or continue with their mission into the teeth of the gunfire.

Retreat was not an option that appealed to Arcturus, not when so many men were dead, but neither did he want to rush to a glorious death in the face of an unknown number of gunmen.

From his earlier glance, he'd seen that the bulk of the men ahead were lurking behind jagged outcrops of rock in a narrow defile amid a tangle of wiry brush. Above them, the rocks were a vivid white, as though bleached by the sun.

As one group fired, another reloaded. Between them, they kept a near-constant stream of Impaler spikes rattling and chiming from the rocks around Dominion section.

In the quick glance he'd had, Arcturus saw that

the valley narrowed as it neared the gunmen. The ground before their attackers was a sharply inclined, open killing ground that would be close to suicide to charge up, but the rocky walls to either side of where the marines were pinned could be climbed with only a little effort. About four meters above, the ground appeared to become flatter, rocky, and strewn with stunted trees and scattered piles of boulders.

Ideal cover from which to flank their attackers.

Arcturus turned and opened a link to the firebats.

The two surviving firebats were hunched in cover, their hulking suits of crimson armor heavily dented and scarred from the crash, but their Perdition flamethrowers appeared to be in full working order.

"This is Lieutenant Mengsk," he said. "Identify yourselves."

"Private Eugene Malik," came the first reply.

"Private Harper Utley," said the second firebat.

"Malik, Utley, I'm going to need you two to go straight up the middle and give me a screen of fire. When I give the word, head toward the rocks the shooters are using as cover and put a wall of fire between them and us. You understand?"

"Sir, yes, sir!" they replied in unison, and hissing blue cones of heat ignited from the weapon systems fixed to their gauntlets.

Satisfied the firebats understood their task, Arcturus then spoke to the resoced marines who had survived the crash and were still fit to fight. He pointed to the nearest marines and said, "You two stay with the wounded. The rest of you, I want you supporting Malik and Utley. I want a stream of Impalers keeping those bastards' heads down. Got that?"

Nodding heads and snapped salutes assured him they understood, and Arcturus returned his attention to his own soldiers as a ricocheting Impaler spike thudded into his shoulder guard.

"What's the plan, LT?" shouted Dia de Santo as Arcturus brushed the spike from his armor as though it were a piece of lint on his best suit.

"We're going to take out those gunmen and push on," said Arcturus.

"Sir, that's crazy!" cried Chuck Horner. "We ain't got a damn clue how many more of them are waiting for us up there!"

Arcturus shook his head, jabbing his fist at the marines of Dominion section. "We're going and that's an order. When the firebats and what's left of Emillian's marines make their move, I want Horner, Mercurio, and Yancy up and over the rocks on the right. The rest of you with me on the left."

He could see the fear and doubt on their faces, and said, "Listen, soldiers! There's probably more of them moving around our flank already to cut us off."

Given the terrain and the fact that they were pinned down quite neatly here, that probably wasn't true, but it didn't hurt to put the fear of it into them.

"Either we go forward and take this fight to them

or we get cut to pieces like rookies!" shouted Arcturus. "We're Dominion section and we kill anyone who gets in our way."

Chun Leung hefted Mayumi and slammed in a fresh clip.

"Now you're talkin' my language!" he said.

CHAPTER 8

BLAZING PLUMES OF LIQUID FIRE ROARED UP THE valley as Privates Malik and Utley broke from cover. The two red-armored warriors crunched forward, flaming sheets spraying the rocks and brush of the valley ahead. Arcturus could feel the backwash of heat from their flamethrowers through his armor. Impaler spikes hammered the two firebats, but their armor was thicker and heavier than that of an ordinary marine and the two privates pushed on in the face of the gunfire.

The brush around the enemy gunmen went up instantly, crackling and burning with furious glee.

"Go!" shouted Arcturus, scrambling up the rocky slope beside him. Chun Leung and Dia de Santo followed him, their rifles tucked in close to their chests.

More rattling gunfire blazed from below as Emillian's marines followed the firebats, shooting from the hip as they advanced. One marine was cut down the instant he left cover, a hail of razor-tipped spikes splintering his visor and blowing out the back of his helmet.

The others didn't falter and advanced into the teeth of the fusillade.

Arcturus clawed at the rocks, pulling himself up with powerful surges. His armor enhanced his strength and he was able to haul himself over the lip of the canyon walls without difficulty.

He rolled onto his side and brought his gauss rifle up, glancing across to see Yancy, Chuck, and Toby pulling themselves over the rocks and into cover. Below him, the firebats continued to pour flaming gouts of superheated liquid at their foes. One of them—Arcturus didn't know which—was limping badly, his leg armor mangled by gunfire above the knee and blood sheeting down his thigh.

Several other marines were down, but the mercenaries' attention was fixated on the advancing warriors and they hadn't noticed the other inbound enemies. Arcturus opened a link to Dominion section and said, "Get moving, everyone. Fast and low."

"You got it, LT," said Chuck Horner, leading Yancy and Mercurio off. Arcturus nodded to himself. Horner had real potential, naturally assuming command of his small section, and Arcturus made a mental note to see about developing his skills if they survived this encounter.

"Chun, Dia," he said, "let's go."

Arcturus led them off, scuttling forward, hunched over as much as his armor would allow, and keeping to the cover of the rocks. His heart was hammering in his chest as he ran, fully expecting a burst of Impaler spikes to rake him and his soldiers at any moment. Arcturus could hear a near-continual roar of gunfire, screams, and explosions from the canyon and knew the men he'd sent forward were still fighting.

An angry orange fireball mushroomed from below, signaling the death of one of the firebats, followed moments later by a second explosion. The reek of flamethrower fuel filled the air and Arcturus heard more screams of dying soldiers.

Just ahead, he could see a splash of white and recognized the rocks above where their ambushers were fighting. He grinned with feral anticipation, terrified yet exhilarated at the same time.

Arcturus dropped to one knee and jabbed a fist at the white rocks.

"Take up position either side of me," he said. "We get to those rocks and unleash everything we've got."

De Santo and Leung nodded, and Arcturus could see the same relish on their faces he figured they could see on his.

"Let's do this," hissed Chun Leung, patting Mayumi's gleaming barrel.

"You got it, Big Dog," replied de Santo, punching knuckles with Leung.

"Let's go," said Arcturus.

He ran over to the rocks, bracing his foot against a low boulder, and looked down into the canyon as de Santo and Leung took up position. Below them was a scene straight from hell, the valley floor aflame and littered with blackened bodies. A few fallen mercenaries screamed and clutched bloody wounds, but Arcturus didn't care about their pain. These men had tried to kill him and his marines, and that made them less than nothing in his eyes.

As he'd suspected, both firebats were dead, as were about half of Emillian's resoced marines, but they had done their job: keeping the mercenaries' attention firmly fixed on them while Dominion section moved around the flank.

Across the canyon, Arcturus saw Horner, Yancy, and Mercurio rise from the rocks and aim their weapons at the enemy below. A few of the mercenaries looked up as Dominion section appeared above them, and Arcturus relished their look of panic.

"Fire!" shouted Arcturus.

Withering sprays of Impaler spikes ripped through the mercenaries, their lighter body armor no match for close-range gauss fire. Arcturus worked his rifle over the men below him, bloody eruptions fountaining where his spikes blew open skulls or tore limbs from bodies.

Caught in the crossfire, the mercenaries had no chance.

They danced in the vicious bursts of gunfire, trapped in the open and unable to fight back. The echoes of rifles were deafening as they filled the narrow defile in the canyon with screaming hot spikes. A few of the mercenaries managed to bring their weapons to bear, but it was too little too late and they were cut down without mercy.

Realizing that to fight on was hopeless, one man threw down his rifle and held up his hands in surrender.

Arcturus cut him in two with a sustained burst of fire.

It was over in a few seconds, and the canyon was suddenly quiet as the marines of Dominion section ceased firing. Acrid smoke drifted from the heated barrels of their guns as they looked at each other in disbelief—shocked at the carnage they'd caused, but elated to have survived and won their first firefight.

"Good job, everyone," said Arcturus, his heart rate only now beginning to return to normal after the thrill of killing these men. The canyon floor resembled an abattoir, shredded flesh and blood mingling in thick, viscous puddles that were already congealing into sticky pools in the heat.

"Man, we killed those SOBs good!" shouted Yancy, his rifle held triumphantly above his head. Chuck Horner sketched Arcturus a salute and even Toby Mercurio looked pleased for once. Beside him, Dia de Santo and Chun Leung butted helmets and he felt them slap the shoulder guards of his armor in triumph.

"You did it, LT!" cried de Santo. "We killed the whole damn lot of them!"

"That we did," agreed Arcturus, only now beginning to appreciate the slaughter he had orchestrated.

He knew that some men experienced a great and terrible guilt over killing other human beings. But as he looked at the ripped-open sacks of meat and bone that had, only minutes before, been living, breathing human beings, he felt nothing for them.

Nothing at all.

Arcturus looked up at the miners' encampment through the optical viewfinders, seeking any sign of weapons technology like the missile turret that had downed their dropship. Sure enough, another pair of turrets with sweeping dishes, not dissimilar to those they'd left behind at Camp Juno, were placed at the forefront of the encampment.

The mining complex was a well-organized collection of modular constructions built on an artificially created plateau at the mouth of a great scar in the mountainside that resembled the lair of some prehistoric monster. The edge of the plateau had been built up into a defended ridge, with sandbagged foxholes and concrete bunkers.

A pair of goliath combat walkers plodded back and forth behind the barricades on their reverse-jointed legs, the rotary cannons on their weapon arms spooling up and the missile systems above the pilot's canopy trained on the sky. Arcturus wasn't too concerned with the goliaths—they were primarily used to engage airborne targets, though the power of their guns wasn't to be sniffed at if you were a grunt on the ground.

In any case, he had just the thing to fight goliaths.

He smiled as he saw the panicked miners and their mercenaries running back and forth, terrified at the sight that had just come into view on the rutted road that led to the main gate of the mine complex.

The siege tank had finally rumbled into the bloody canyon thirty minutes after the conclusion of the fighting. Since the battle's end, Dominion section had been securing the weapons and ammo of the fallen marines and gathering up the dead.

Of the marines who had charged in the wake of the firebats, only five were left alive, the rest arranged in neat rows alongside the eight wounded and those who had perished in the crash. The bodies of the mercenaries were dragged to the side of the canyon and their weapons taken, but were otherwise ignored.

An evac bird was called in to take Captain Emillian and the wounded back to Camp Juno. Once Arcturus received confirmation that it had been dispatched, he and Dominion section, together with the five resoced marines, rode the tank farther up the valley.

After all, they had a job to finish.

"Oh yeah!" shouted Yancy Gray, standing on the tank's frontal glacis and balancing himself by holding on to its enormous cannon. "Not so cocky now, are ya? Not so tough when you see we got ourselves a tank. Yeah!"

The siege tank had the range to engage the miners'

camp from where they sat now, its main gun more than capable of pounding the camp to smoldering ruin without fear of reprisal.

But Arcturus didn't want to destroy the mining facility if he could avoid it, not if there was a chance it could be taken and put to use.

"Shut up, Yancy," said Arcturus, handing the optical viewers to Toby Mercurio and removing his helmet. He deposited the helmet on the tank's track guard and dropped down to the ground. "Chuck, Dia. You're with me. Shoulder those weapons, and make sure they're safed."

Horner and de Santo dropped to the hard-packed ground as Arcturus marched uphill along the road toward the mining complex, his rifle hanging by its sling from his shoulder. After the frenetic carnage of the battle, this was almost peaceful. The road to the mine was relatively shielded from the fierce winds that swept the lowest reaches of the mountains.

Arcturus watched as a group of five men emerged from the complex above. Three were armed—more mercenaries presumably—while the two others had the weathered, permanently dirty texture of dyed-in-the-wool prospectors.

"LT, what you got in mind?" asked Chuck Horner.

"Yeah, I was kinda wondering that too," said de Santo.

"We're going to talk to them," said Arcturus. "And ask them to surrender."

"Surrender?" said Horner. "I gotta say, LT, they don't look like the surrendering kind."

"You leave that to me, Charles."

The two groups met at a bend in the road, some two hundred meters from the camp's gate, and Arcturus felt the hostility of the miners like a blow. One man was short and thickset, his flesh leathery and pitted from a life in hostile environments. The other was similarly squat, but his eyes had a wary quality to them that told Arcturus he wasn't going to be the one doing the talking.

The mercenaries kept back, though they made a point of showing that they were more than ready to use their weapons.

Before Arcturus could even open his mouth, the first man thrust out a sheaf of grubby, oil-stained papers and said, "This ain't your property, Confed. We own this claim fair and square. Go tell your bosses that we got the paperwork and everything. Y'unnerstand me?"

Arcturus nodded politely and said, "My name is Lieutenant Arcturus Mengsk of the Confederate Marine Corps. Am I speaking with the head of this facility?"

The man with the papers looked at him suspiciously and said, "Yeah, I guess you are."

"And you are?"

"Lemuel Baden—not that it makes a damn bit of difference. We ain't got nothin' to say to each other."

"I beg to differ," said Arcturus. "That's not entirely

correct. I have a siege tank that says we have one very important matter to discuss."

"Yeah? What's that then?"

"Your immediate surrender and relocation to another planet."

Baden snorted with what Arcturus assumed was laughter. "Surrender? Hell, you got some nerve, boy. What are you anyway, twenty? Twenty-one?"

"Nineteen, actually."

This time both prospectors laughed.

"Go home, boy," snapped Baden. "I ain't gonna surrender. Leastways not to a kid that don't even need to shave."

"Oh, I think you'll surrender," said Arcturus. "In fact I'm sure of it."

"And why's that?"

"Because I have a siege tank and if you *don't* surrender, I'll blow this place to hell."

"Don't make me laugh," sneered Baden. "You wouldn't dare."

"Try me," said Arcturus, meeting Baden's hostile stare with one of his own.

Arcturus saw beads of sweat gathering at the miner's temples. He could see courage in Baden's eyes, but also the wariness of not being able to read the young soldier standing before him.

"Right now you're trying to work out if I'm bluffing," said Arcturus. "I can assure you that I am not. I never bluff. If I walk away from this parley without your surrender, you and everyone within your compound will be dead inside of ten minutes. I guarantee it."

"Then maybe we oughta just kill you now," snapped Baden.

"You could, but then my men would kill you and everyone would die regardless," replied Arcturus. "So you see, you really have only one option."

Baden's eyes flicked to his companion, who said, "You goddamn Confeds can't keep doing this to us! This here mine's ours and we ain't gonna let you take it from us."

Arcturus ignored the man's outburst, knowing that Baden was the only man worth talking to in this exchange.

"Easy, Bill, leave this to me," said Baden. The miner looked back to Arcturus. "Gimme twenty minutes to talk to my people?"

"Of course," said Arcturus. "But if I do not have your surrender after that, you're going to see exactly how powerful that tank is. And trust me, you don't want that."

Baden nodded, then stomped back to the mine complex with his companions without another word. Arcturus watched them go and turned on his heel, marching back down the road to where his marines and the siege tank awaited.

Arcturus banged on the tank's side when he finally reached it. "Stand down the gun."

"You *were* bluffing?" asked Dia de Santo.

"No," said Arcturus. "As I told Baden, I never bluff. I already know he's going to surrender."

"You sure?" asked Chuck Horner. "He looked like a stubborn mule, that one."

Arcturus nodded. "Indeed. But he isn't stupid."

"Sir?" said de Santo.

"He knows I'll destroy the mine and kill everyone there if he doesn't surrender," explained Arcturus.

Chuck Horner looked askance at Arcturus. "You ain't kidding, are you?"

"No," said Arcturus. "I'm not. And Lemuel Baden knows that."

The infirmary building of Camp Juno was a sterile, antiseptic place in every sense of the word. Its prefabricated walls were gleaming white and faced with ceramic tiles that reflected the unflattering lights strung from the green-painted girders that formed the roof vault. Its structure resembled a fat tube split down its length and dropped onto the ground.

Pods of beds were spread throughout the open space, with ceiling-mounted extractors trying—and failing—to circulate the stagnant air and diminish the tang of disinfectant. Medics made their rounds of the injured, checking machine readings and administering pain meds, while marines stripped out of their armor and wearing fatigues visited those comrades who weren't too sedated.

Arcturus had expected the infirmary to be noisy, but it was instead subdued, filled with the quiet noise of professionals working hard and a background machine hum. The atmosphere was calm by virtue of the fact that the majority of the wounded marines here were kept heavily sedated, since many of them were resoced. Numerous studies had shown that extreme trauma could have a negative impact on the strength of the neural reprogramming implanted over a subject's original memories, and no one was taking any chances that these marines might relapse to their previous, murderous personalities.

Having heard the lurid details of some of the more outrageous crimes committed by these marines prior to having acceptable behavioral patterns stamped on their brains, Arcturus was pleased to see such precautions in place.

He spotted Captain Emillian lying in a bed pod she shared with three other wounded soldiers—two men and another woman—and made his way over to her.

Emillian smiled as she saw Arcturus approaching, then grimaced as she tried to sit up, the framework of silver steel encasing her pelvis and legs making even that simple act awkwardly painful. The swelling around her eyes and jaw had begun to come down and her bruises had turned an attractive shade of puce. Opposite the scar Emillian had received on Chau Sara was another angry red line of sutures.

Each of the patients in the pod was hooked up to drips and monitored by complicated banks of boxy machinery, and Arcturus carefully negotiated his way through a tangle of wires to get to Emillian's bed.

"Good morning, Captain," said Arcturus.

"Morning, Lieutenant," replied Emillian as Arcturus

took a seat next to her bed, placing a portable console at her feet.

"You're looking well."

"Sure," said Emillian. "I look like crap. Nobody will give me a mirror. What does that tell you?"

"That even when you are nearly killed, you're still incredibly vain?"

"Watch it, buster," said Emillian. "I may be off my feet, but I'm still your superior officer."

Arcturus raised his hands in mock surrender. "Point taken," he said.

"I hear the rest of the op went well."

"Yes," agreed Arcturus. "We got to the Turanga facility and took it without a shot being fired. Apart from the ones in the canyon after we were blown out of the sky."

Emillian's face darkened at the mention of the crash.

"I don't remember anything of that," she said. "They tell me I smashed my head on a stanchion and broke my helmet open. Damn near crushed my skull."

"You were lucky," said Arcturus.

"Yeah, so everyone keeps telling me."

"At least now you have a matching scar," pointed out Arcturus.

"Gee, that's a comfort."

"Sorry."

"So tell me about the rest of the mission," said Emillian. "I got the gist of it from one of the few of my marines you deigned to bring back alive, but they aren't great with the storytelling, you know?"

"To be honest, there isn't much else to tell."

"When someone says 'to be honest' that usually means they're lying."

"I'll keep that in mind," said Arcturus. "But you probably already know the rest. Lemuel Baden came out after his twenty minutes were up and said his people would be leaving. They deactivated their reactor and powered down the turrets, and I arranged for a pair of dropships to escort them back here for a debriefing before they're shipped off world. We secured the complex, and there's a Kusinis mining team swarming over it already. Which I'd like permission to supervise, Captain."

"Still dreaming of being a prospector, eh?"

"Absolutely," said Arcturus.

"So how'd you convince Baden to bring his people out?"

"Simple. I told him I'd level the place with the siege tank."

"That's it?"

"Yes," said Arcturus. "I was very convincing."

"Would you have opened fire if they hadn't come out?"

"Of course," said Arcturus without hesitation. "What's the point of making a threat if you're not willing to back it up?"

"That would have been a very expensive decision, Lieutenant," said Emillian. "A lot of people with higher pay grades than us were very clear that they wanted that place intact."

"And they have it. Baden knew I was serious, and he didn't want to die. It's that simple."

Emillian shook her head. "No, Mengsk, it's not that simple."

"It's not?"

"No. Remember, I've read your file and I know all about you," said Emillian. "I know that you mean what you say, but you don't always say what you think. You keep almost everything of what goes on inside you close to your chest, and you don't let anyone see what you're thinking unless you want them to. And right then, you wanted Baden to know what you were thinking."

"I suppose so," agreed Arcturus. "It worked, didn't it?"

"That it did," said Emillian. "And just for that I might forgive you for getting most of my soldiers killed or maimed in that canyon."

"It was a textbook maneuver," said Arcturus. "One element kept the enemy's attention fixed while others flanked them."

"Almost textbook. Because the guys providing the distraction for the flankers aren't supposed to get killed. Suppression fire? You ever hear of it?"

"I have, but there wasn't any other way to be sure the mercenaries' attention would be firmly fixed to their front."

"Well, you sure as hell managed that," said Emillian, flicking her hair back from her face and reaching for a cup of water beside her bed. She grunted painfully, and Arcturus swiftly moved to lift the cup into her hand.

"Thanks," said Emillian. "Now tell me why you're really here."

"Excuse me?"

"Come on, you didn't come here just to inspect my latest scar, did you?"

Arcturus shrugged, then realized there was no point in beating about the bush. Emillian had read the truth off him, either in his body language or simply via the instincts of a senior officer.

"There *was* one thing I wanted to discuss with you, yes . . . ," began Arcturus.

"Come on, spit it out," said Emillian. "You think I've got nothing better to do than sit here listening to you? There's hot Confederate doctors working these wards, and a girl's got to think of when she musters out . . ."

Arcturus smiled. "And now you're using humor to try and put me at my ease."

"Jeez, way to overanalyze," muttered Emillian. "Pain meds must be kicking in; I'm normally more subtle than that. Okay, so what is it?"

Arcturus lifted the portable console from the foot of her bed and activated it with a touch. A green glow spread over the screen, followed by the insignia of the Marine Corps.

"I observed Lemuel Baden's debriefing," said Arcturus.

"Who was doing the debrief?"

"Captain Graves flew in from Camp Larson to conduct it."

"He's a good man," said Emillian. "Gets the job done quickly and he gets results."

"Well, Baden's debrief was certainly over very quickly. However, whether it could be said that the job was done satisfactorily is another matter."

"What do you mean?"

"Lemuel said the mine legally belonged to him and the other miners, that their claim predated any Confederate interest in Sonyan. He had papers, but it seems they've been confiscated and, wouldn't you know it, no one can find them now."

Emillian shrugged. "Marine Corps admin snafu. Happens all the time."

"I'm sure," said Arcturus dryly, turning the console around for Emillian to see. "The point is, I checked with the Kel-Morian registration database and I found claim dockets for Turanga Canyon registered to one Lemuel Baden of Tarsonis from six years ago."

"What's your point?"

"The first Confederacy ship to make planetfall on Sonyan was the *Jonestown* in '77."

Emillian crossed her arms. "I see. And you think it matters that they were here first?"

"Doesn't it? If his claim to the mine is legal then haven't we just stolen it from him?"

"You secure that crap, soldier," snapped Emillian. "And don't let me hear you repeat it. Lemuel Baden is part of the Kel-Morian Combine, a bunch of good-for-nothing crooks and pirates. Hell, most of their prospectors are wanted criminals anyway."

"That's a bit of a generalization, surely?"

"Is it? Listen, Mengsk, the core worlds depend on the minerals and fuels extracted from mines like this, so do you *really* want us to be beholden to Kel-Morian criminals? Sonyan is part of the Confederacy now, and anything on it belongs to the Confederacy. And the Marine Corps will fight to protect our way of life. You got that?"

"Yes, but how—"

"But nothing, Lieutenant," said Emillian, leaning forward and keeping her voice level. "If you want to survive in the military, you're going to have to stop acting like some damn Boy Scout. In the Marines you follow the orders you're given. And that's it. Period. You go sticking your nose in places it don't belong and you're liable to get it bitten off. That's what being in the Marines is all about, Mengsk. Orders. We start deciding the orders we want to obey and the ones we don't and you know what you get? Anarchy. And I'm not going to allow that in the 33rd."

Anger touched Arcturus and he said, "Sounds like you want everyone to be like one of your resoced marines. Wasn't that exactly why you brought Dominion section in, because we *weren't* mindless automatons? Because we could think for ourselves?"

"I brought you in because I need good officers I can trust to follow orders," said Emillian. "I thought you would understand that, Mengsk, but maybe I was wrong. So, you think you're some kind of rebel like your father? Is that it?"

"What does my father have to do with anything?"

"I've watched the UNN," said Emillian. "I've seen your father speaking out against the Confederacy and stirring up trouble on Korhal. Are you like him, looking for trouble when there's no need to?"

"I'm nothing like my father," said Arcturus.

"Yeah? Sure could have fooled me," said Emillian, pointing toward Arcturus's console.

"I'm nothing like my father," repeated Arcturus, more forcefully this time. "He's an embarrassment, stirring up trouble when there's no need for it."

"Just like you're doing here," said Emillian.

Her tone softened, and she sat back. "Look, I'm not trying to rain on your parade, Mengsk, but, trust me, this isn't an avenue you want to go down. The Marine Corps is a machine and we're all just cogs in that machine. You start messing with that and either the machine chews you up and spits you out or it breaks down. You can get yourself spat out if you want, but I'm not going to allow our part of the machine to break down. It'll be my ass in a sling with Commander Fole if you start pissing off the brass with damn fool questions. You get me?"

"I get you," said Arcturus. "And you're right. I'll stop asking questions."

"Good," said Emillian, searching his face for any sign he was soft-soaping her.

Arcturus knew his captain was good at reading people, but she was dead right when she said that he didn't let anyone see what was going on below the surface. He kept his face utterly blank now, and she relaxed, satisfied she'd quashed his nascent doubts.

"Okay," she said. "Now go enjoy your leave, Mengsk. Go home, relax with the family, eat good food, get drunk, or get laid. I don't care, just come back with your head in the game. Are we clear?"

"Yes." Arcturus nodded. "We're clear."

"Good, now get out of here, soldier, I need to get some sleep."

Arcturus nodded and pushed back the chair as he stood. He saluted Emillian and picked his way through the tangle of cables and wires from the bedside monitors.

As he turned away from Emillian, she asked, "You got any kids, Mengsk?"

Arcturus shook his head. "You know I don't."

"Just as well, eh?"

"What's that supposed to mean?"

"With your family, just imagine what they'd turn out like."

CHAPTER 9

ARCTURUS STEPPED FROM THE GROUNDCAR, A gleaming '79 cobalt blue Terra Zephyr, adjusting the collar of his dress uniform as he did so. He wasn't particularly interested in motor vehicles beyond their ability to get him from point A to point B, but even he had to admit that the Zephyr was a fine piece of machinery, with smooth, graceful lines, a plush leather interior, and an engine that purred like a contented feline.

He turned and offered his hand to Juliana Pasteur, who accepted his gracious gesture and emerged from the groundcar with effortless elegance.

The two years since Arcturus had seen Juliana had been good to her and she had blossomed from a pretty young girl into a beautiful woman. Now eighteen, she had filled out in all the right places and carried herself with a confidence and poise that most other women could only dream of.

Dressed in a simple, backless black dress and tasteful jewelry that matched her eyes, Juliana turned heads as she took Arcturus's arm. The night was balmy and warm, with a salt-tinged breeze blowing in off the ocean, and Juliana wrapped a sheer pashmina around her shoulders as they set off along the tree-lined Cepheid Boulevard toward the restaurant.

Behind them, following at a discreet distance, were two slab-shouldered men in gray suits: Umojan security personnel who accompanied Juliana whenever she traveled off world. Arcturus could sense their dislike of him, or at least what his uniform represented, but wasn't surprised by it. The Confederacy had forever been trying to coerce Umoja into its embrace, but the Umojans were a fiercely independent people and had steadfastly refused to join with the government of Tarsonis.

Cepheid Boulevard was a pedestrianized walkway in the heart of the recreational district of Elsecaro, one of Tyrador IX's most exclusive resort cities, and thus they had to make the rest of the journey on foot. Arcturus didn't mind, for it gave him a chance to bask in the cinnamon-scented air and enjoy the fact that he wasn't being shot at.

Tyrador IX was one of the later colony worlds, a planet that co-orbited its sister world of Tyrador VIII. Ever since its colonization it had been a popular tourist destination, thanks to its distance from the bustle of Tarsonis and its unique ecology.

The orbital dance performed by the two outermost planets in the Tyrador system had blessed Tyrador IX with an incredible variety of ecosystems and climates.

A journey of only a few kilometers could result in a huge change in temperature, humidity, or terrain, which allowed the enterprising colonists to create a wonderland where almost any form of paradise could be replicated.

Ski resorts sat cheek by jowl with jungles and rugged coastal towns, where intrepid holidaymakers could dive in the emerald waters to see the playful Tyradorian narwhal. Achingly beautiful deserts sprawled in the lee of soaring, snowcapped peaks where the rich and famous lived in mountaintop villas accessible only by orbital flyers.

Many of the Old Families kept private enclaves on Tyrador IX, estates where they could enjoy whatever holiday they desired. Rumor had it that it was often a hideaway for family shames, and salacious gossip had many an errant scion sent here, far from Tarsonis and investigative reporters.

Arcturus cared nothing for such things, content just to relax and enjoy his leave far from thoughts of killing. He'd arrived on Tyrador IX that morning and would be heading onward to Korhal in the next day or so. A week later and he'd have to return to his unit, so he wasn't going to waste time thinking about combat suits, C-14 gauss rifles, or blood and death until he had to.

"It's beautiful, isn't it?" said Juliana, threading her arm through his and looking up at the fabulous buildings on either side of them.

Arcturus smiled. "Yes. Certainly an improvement on what I'm used to. SCVs might be an efficient way to build things, but they do tend toward a uniformity of architecture."

"I love it," said Juliana. "There's no two alike."

That was certainly true. The boulevard was paved with irregularly patterned bricks and the structures around them had a rustic charm and individuality that was sadly lacking on the core worlds. They passed wooden-fronted shops selling tourist junk alongside ad hoc art galleries of local painters and delicatessens serving food from all across the sector.

Eateries and bars of all descriptions vied for their attention and the wafting aroma of a dozen different cuisines blended together in a mouthwatering smorgasbord of sensation. Having lived on mess hall slop for so long, Arcturus suddenly realized how much he missed proper food.

Silken lamps hung from ironwork posts and fiber-optic lines of multicolored lights were looped through the branches of trees, giving the boulevard a pleasingly festive air. People thronged the streets, men and women of obvious breeding and wealth. Arcturus saw that many of these faces had a strange, and slightly unsettling, uniformity to them, and guessed that most had been sculpted with augmetic surgery or gene therapy.

Street entertainers amused passersby with music, puppet shows, and conjuring tricks, and the sound of laughter drifted on the breeze.

Farther along the street, Arcturus saw a group of soldiers drinking outside a rough-and-ready bar, their cries for drinks and wolf whistles at passing women out of character with the rest of the boulevard. They spotted Arcturus and, almost immediately, the volume of their shouts diminished.

Arcturus nodded respectfully to the soldiers, their uniform insignias marking them as privates and low-ranked NCOs. One of the soldiers, a young boy who looked barely old enough to be in uniform, stood and saluted Arcturus as he passed.

"Evening, Lieutenant. Evening, miss," said the boy, and Arcturus could smell the alcohol on his breath from several feet away.

"Evening, soldier," replied Arcturus, returning the salute and stopping beside the bar. None of these men would be resoced, and thus it would be bad form not to pass a few words with them, though it wouldn't do to be overly familiar with them.

"What's your name, son?" he asked.

"Private Shaw, sir. 57th Marine Combat Engineers, sir."

"Are you men behaving yourselves?" asked Arcturus with a broad smile. "Upholding the fine tradition of the Corps?"

"Sir, yes, sir!" cried the soldiers, raising their drinks.

"Good work, men," said Arcturus. "Carry on. And behave yourselves."

"Absolutely, sir," said Private Shaw. "Don't you worry about us, sir."

"It isn't you I'm worried about," said Arcturus. "It's the local women I'm thinking of."

The soldiers laughed and Arcturus saluted once more before turning away and continuing onward with Juliana. The noise of the soldiers swelled as Juliana squeezed his arm.

"You look very smart in your uniform," said Juliana. "It suits you."

Arcturus smiled. He *did* look good in uniform. Two years of military service had put meat on his bones and muscle on his limbs. His features had hardened, and he carried himself with a confidence he'd certainly possessed as a young man, but which he now wore like a second skin.

"Thank you, Juliana. I've already told you that you look beautiful tonight, but you can never compliment a lady too much, can you?"

"Certainly not," agreed Juliana. "It's been two years since I've seen you, Arcturus, and I wanted to make an impression."

"You certainly succeeded," said Arcturus, looking around him. "Certainly every man with a pulse seems to think so."

She smiled and said, "Well, if I'm turning heads, I'm not the only one. You're getting your fair share of attention too, you know."

Arcturus had noticed that he was attracting smiles from some of the women—and even a few men—promenading the boulevard, but had modestly chosen not to mention it. Some were plainly lustful, but most were simply nods of respect for his service in the military.

"Well, they do say that women love a man in uniform."

"It's true," said Juliana in a playfully meek-sounding voice. "We are a weak species and are easily undone by the subtle wiles of men."

If only you knew, thought Arcturus.

The restaurant itself was a curious mix of fringe world kitsch and core world chic, and Arcturus couldn't make up his mind whether he loathed it or thought it charming. Juliana made the decision for him when she laughed at the sight of it and clapped her hands, declaring it wonderfully "authentic."

The floor was wooden, scuffed and discolored from the tread of thousands of diners, and the air was smoky with rich, homely smells. Perhaps a hundred people filled the restaurant and the animated buzz of conversation provided a pleasing backdrop.

They were seated without fuss in a cozy booth screened from the tables on either side by wooden dividers pierced by stained glass panels. The seats were comfortable, and they ordered their food from a pretty waitress who seemed genuinely pleased to serve them.

They made small talk for a while, Juliana regaling him with tales of her final year at the Umoja Institute and her new life as a budding lawyer. She had begun working as a paralegal with a firm that specialized in stellar shipping laws, and she hoped to gain her full qualifications within a couple of years at most.

Both Juliana and her father were still making regular trips to Korhal to see Arcturus's father, but, sensing that such a topic would not be conducive to an enjoyable evening, she wisely kept her talk of Korhal light.

In turn, Arcturus spoke to her of his life in the Marines, telling her of his tour on Pridewater and the battle of Turanga Canyon, though he spared her the goriest details and omitted his lack of empathy at the deaths he'd caused.

Some things weren't meant for the dinner table.

The food arrived promptly and Arcturus was mildly surprised to find that it was excellent. He had ordered a dish of andouille sausage and shrimp with spicy mustard sauce, while Juliana had decided upon a creamy polenta with a mushroom-and-sausage ragout. They shared mouthfuls of each other's dinner and drank wine poured from a carafe of translucent blue glass.

As they ate, they flirted outrageously, Arcturus blending just the right amount of compliments and self-deprecating humor to keep Juliana smiling, and she frequently reaching over the table to take his hand or brush his arm.

The conversation flowed naturally and effortlessly, and without even realizing it Arcturus found that he was genuinely enjoying himself.

Juliana took a drink of wine and said, "So do you like being a soldier?"

The question surprised Arcturus, for it was apropos of nothing and he had been careful to keep his depiction of day-to-day life in the military as neutral as possible.

"I suppose so," he said. "I think I enjoy more aspects of it than I don't. As long as you do what you're told, it's not so bad."

"I can't picture *you* liking that," remarked Juliana.

"I don't have a problem with authority, per se," explained Arcturus. "I have a problem when I think the person giving me an order is an idiot. I suppose the Marine Corps is like any other organization, with good people and bad people in its hierarchy. The trouble is that in the Marine Corps the bad ones might get me killed."

"Don't say that," warned Juliana. "It's not good to tempt fate."

Arcturus chuckled dismissively. "Fate? I don't believe in fate. A person makes his own decisions and has to live with the consequences. Logic and order are what determine the shape of our lives, not fate. Anyway, now that I've seen some real combat, it won't be long before I get a promotion and move farther away from the front line."

"I told you so, didn't I?" Juliana said, laughing. "I told you that you'd be a general soon."

"Well, you said six months, but I think it might take a little longer than that."

"Pedant," pouted Juliana.

"Sorry."

"And are you learning about mine-workings? Prospecting and stuff like that?"

Arcturus shrugged. "So far only by taking them by

force from other mining outfits, which seems to be the way of things on the rim territories. The Intelligence Division—an oxymoron if ever there was one—sends in a scout recon force on a given planet to find out what's being mined, who's mining it, and who they're affiliated with. Then the data-hounds scour the networks to try and find a legal loophole or a criminal record that they can use to justify sending in a force of gun-toting marines to bully the miners away."

"That's terrible," said Juliana, shaking her head. "And the Tarsonis Council wonders why Umoja won't make an alliance with them."

"It's not so bad, though. I've supervised a number of Confederate-affiliated mining outfits when they go in to take over, and I've learned a lot from that. Or at least, I've learned a lot of how *not* to run a working mine."

"But the Confederacy is stealing those claims," pointed out Juliana. "My father says that the Council is getting greedier every year, that pretty soon they won't even bother coming up with spurious justifications for their thefts. He says eventually they'll just take what they want by force, and soon there won't be anyone to stop them."

"That sounds like *my* father talking."

"Yes, well, he might be right, you know . . . ," said Juliana hesitantly, knowing that she was risking an angry exchange by bringing up Angus Mengsk.

But thoughts of Angus didn't anger Arcturus so much now. Irritatingly, the more years that passed, the more he found himself thinking back to his father with the uncomfortable realization that a great deal of what he'd said now made sense . . .

Growing up, Arcturus had always thought of his father as the stern, authoritarian patriarch of the Mengsk family, a man utterly unsympathetic to the concerns and ambitions of his young son. In Arcturus's adolescent world, Angus Mengsk had never been young, never run wild or known what it was like to be a teenager, a creature possessed of a deluded belief in its own infinite wisdom and a conceited sense of entitlement and immortality.

"Maybe," conceded Arcturus, and he smiled at the look of astonishment on Juliana's face. "I'm not saying he was right about everything, but the more I see, the more I think that perhaps he knew what he was talking about after all."

"So what does that mean for you now?"

"I don't know," said Arcturus, and that admission was more painful than he had imagined it would be. His self-belief had seen him through his tempestuous relationship with his father, but to know that he hadn't steered his destiny as cleverly as he'd thought was a galling realization.

"I have to finish out my term in the Marines," said Arcturus, "but once that's done, I'm heading out into space and away from all this. Somewhere the Confederacy doesn't care about and where I can live my life away from politicking and corruption."

"That might be a hard place to find."

"It might be," admitted Arcturus. "But when I get back to Korhal I'm going to think long and hard as to where it might be."

"Are you going to see your father when you go back home?"

"Yes," said Arcturus. "It's the first time I've gone back to Korhal on leave, so Mother has arranged a grand family dinner. My attendance is apparently mandatory. I'm dreading it."

"Nonsense," said Juliana, reaching over the table to take his hands. "It will be wonderful."

"I hope so," Arcturus said with a smile, the idea of rapprochement between himself and his family giving him an alien, but not unwelcome, sensation in the pit of his stomach.

"Though, to tell you the truth," he said, "I'm more worried about seeing Dorothy. I think she's still mad at me for leaving, and that little girl can hold a mean grudge."

"She's not so little anymore," said Juliana. "She's a precocious six-year-old now, the grand matriarch of her junior school."

Arcturus smiled with real pleasure at the thought of Dorothy ruling the roost at school.

"She's a Mengsk," he said. "It's what we do."

With the meal finished, Arcturus paid the bill and they left the restaurant and emerged into the fragrant, ocean-scented evening of Tyrador IX. The lights garlanding the trees shone like miniature stars, their brightness waxing and waning, and the silk lanterns bobbed in the freshening wind from the coast. The air had cooled and Juliana pulled her pashmina tightly around her shoulders.

Cepheid Boulevard was busier than it had been earlier, the crowds drawn by the glittering lights, festive feel, and many attractions designed to part them from their cash. Arcturus watched the smiling faces walking past him, attractive men and women, and felt a wave of annoyance that he would have to leave so soon.

Tyrador IX was a place of comfort and respite, and it would be nice to return here sometime soon. Juliana slipped her hand into his and they walked, hand in hand, back along the street, with the two Umojan security personnel following at a discreet distance.

"Thank you," said Juliana.

"For what?"

"For tonight. I had a wonderful time, Arcturus. I like being around you."

Arcturus smiled, pleased at the compliment, and said, "Yes, I enjoyed myself as well."

"You sound surprised," said Juliana.

"I don't mean to," said Arcturus, suddenly finding that he was genuinely sad to be leaving her tomorrow. "It's just that it's been a while since I've been in genteel company. You spend enough time with soldiers, it's easy to forget the simple pleasure of spending an evening with a beautiful woman."

"Well, as long as you think I'm beautiful that's all that matters."

"You *are* beautiful," said Arcturus. "I don't think you know it, and that's what makes it so incredible."

Juliana squeezed his hand tightly and stopped, leaning up to kiss him.

"You realize," she said, "that flattery will get you everywhere?"

"Then you had better get used to it," he said, kissing her back.

A raucous cheer sounded from nearby, and Arcturus looked up to see the soldiers they had passed earlier waving at them from the bar, their glasses raised in salute.

"Just like graduation," said Juliana with a smile.

Arcturus smiled and sketched a roguish salute to his fellow marines.

"Almost," he said. "I think these men are a little tougher than the students of Styrling."

Even as Arcturus formed the thought, the hairs on the back of his neck bristled and he turned to see a group of five men lounging by one of the handcrafted iron benches at the side of the boulevard. They looked out of place, their features rugged and pinched—the faces of men who had grown to adulthood without a properly balanced, nutritious diet.

It was a peculiar facet of human development Arcturus had noticed—that you could tell the quality of a person's upbringing from the briefest glance at their facial bone structure. Even down to their skin, there was a definite difference in the development of the face that distinguished rich from poor.

These men fell into the latter category, without a doubt, and he wondered why they had not moved on. Perhaps they were indentured workers on a break, remembering how Diamond de Santo's family had labored behind the scenes to make the resorts of Tyrador IX such paradises.

Then why were they here, mingling with resort guests and their betters?

One of the men looked straight at him, a man with a bulky trench coat that reached to his shins and whose head was shaven clean with a tattoo of a snake coiled around his ear.

"Is something wrong?" asked Juliana, sensing the sudden tension in his posture.

"Hmmm? No, it's nothing . . . ," he said, not wishing to alarm her.

As she followed his gaze, Arcturus looked behind Juliana to where her security loitered, both men watching a pair of silver-skinned fliers pass overhead. He looked at the shaven-headed man with the snake tattoo, and their eyes met through the laughing crowds.

"Juliana, get inside," he said, recognizing the hard stare of a professional killer.

"What?" she said, but Arcturus was already moving, dragging her back toward her guards while keeping his eyes fixed on the occupants of the bench. The man with the tattoo saw Arcturus move and knew that his cover was blown. He said something to the men next to him, and reached inside his long trench coat.

Arcturus instinctively reached for his slugthrower, but his hand grasped empty air, the pistol resting in its locked, foam-lined case in his hotel room safe. Snake Tattoo raised a long-barreled weapon, an old-model AGR-14 assault rifle, and Arcturus's heart hammered against his ribs as he saw it.

He had gone through boot camp with such a rifle, a no-nonsense gun capable of firing supersonic jacketless slugs that could tear through a human body and leave nothing behind but shredded meat and bone. The four men with the tattooed assassin unveiled a varied mix of pistols and rifles.

"Gun!" shouted Arcturus.

Heads turned, too slowly, and Arcturus bore Juliana down with him as he heard the screams of the crowd upon their seeing the guns. Juliana cried out as she hit the ground, but the deafening roar of gunfire swallowed the sound. The AGR-14 was a powerful weapon, one designed as much to intimidate as to wound, and Arcturus scrambled on all fours, Juliana beside him. He looked over at the gunmen, watching as they played their fire over the front of the bar beside them. The wooden frontage of the bar exploded into splinters, the glass shattering like a million diamonds.

Marines danced in the gunfire, blood sprayed, and the sound of bullets striking flesh was like a hammer repeatedly smacking raw steak. Arcturus saw Private

Shaw hurled backward by the terrible impacts, his chest blown out by a sawing blast of rounds. Other men were hit as well, and Arcturus saw a soldier torn almost in two by a torrent of fire.

Shots sounded from behind Arcturus and he saw one of Juliana's security guards crouched on his knee, his pistol held out in front of him in two hands. One of the gunmen dropped, the back of his head missing, and the guard calmly drew a bead on another.

Before he could shoot again, a burst of rifle fire took him in the chest and he lurched backward, a bloody line of bullet holes tearing him up as though a grenade had gone off inside his rib cage.

Juliana's other guard scooted over to them. "Give me her!" he shouted.

Arcturus nodded and hauled Juliana over to the man.

"Arcturus!" she cried, but he forced himself to ignore her plea as he spotted the fallen guard's pistol on the ground. He scrambled over to the gun and swept it up, twisting onto his back and aiming it toward the bench.

Hordes of people ran in panicked confusion along the boulevard, screaming over the terror that had landed in their midst. The bar was a ruin of shattered timber and glass. Tables had been overturned, chairs scattered, and bloody bodies littered the area in front like multiple victims of a firing squad.

Snake Tattoo and his three comrades continued to rake bullets over the bar's frontage, making the corpses jerk with the impacts. Fury touched Arcturus at the slaughter of his fellow marines. The pistol bucked in his hand and another of the gunmen dropped.

Arcturus rolled to his knees and shifted his aim, putting another enemy on his back, a bloody hole blasted in his chest. His accomplices turned toward the source of this new threat.

Another pistol shot boomed, and Arcturus knew that Juliana's other guard was returning fire. The man's bullet missed, and Snake Tattoo's companion swung his rifle to bear, a look of hatred in his eyes.

Arcturus fired first, but his shot went wide. A bar light that had miraculously survived the initial hail of bullets blew out in a rain of glass. Supersonic slugs ripped toward Juliana's protector and he was punched off his feet in a thudding series of bloody eruptions.

Snake Tattoo opened fire at Arcturus, but a fleeing tourist in a floral-print shirt took the volley. The unfortunate holidaymaker fell as stray slugs tore up the ground next to Arcturus—who didn't give his attacker a second chance. He sighted along the barrel of his pistol and squeezed the trigger.

Snake Tattoo was spun around, his shoulder a pulped mass of shattered bone and geysering blood. He dropped his rifle and toppled backward, screaming in agony.

Arcturus rose to his feet, moving sideways as the last surviving gunman swung his rifle around. Before he could fire, Arcturus put two bullets into his chest. The man toppled, dead before he hit the ground.

Arcturus let out a long, shuddering breath, suddenly realizing how exposed he'd been.

Wearing the heavy plates of combat armor granted a marine almost complete immunity to small-arms fire, but when bullets started flying it was easy to take that immunity for granted and forget that without armor—as Arcturus certainly had been just now—even the lightest handgun was deadly.

He tracked the pistol left and right, keeping on the move. Though he doubted there were other shooters on the boulevard, it didn't pay to be reckless. He ghosted over to the shattered remnants of the bar, crunching on broken glass and through pulverized timber.

Dozens or maybe even scores of bodies filled the bar, torn and mangled by the indiscriminate barrage of gunfire. Soldiers and well-heeled civilians lay together, equal in death if not in life. Arcturus moved through the wreckage until he stood over the architect and sole survivor of this massacre.

Snake Tattoo wept in pain, a gaping, raw crater where his shoulder should have been. He pawed the wound with a glistening red hand, his breath coming in sharp hikes and tortured exhalations. He looked up as Arcturus approached, his flesh waxy and streaked with sweat.

"Confed bastard . . . ," he wheezed between groans of pain.

"What the hell was this?" demanded Arcturus. "What did you think you were going to achieve?"

"I ain't . . . afraid . . . to die," spat Snake Tattoo.

"And . . . I ain't gonna talk . . . You might as well . . . kill me now . . ."

"Fine by me," said Arcturus, and then shot him in the face.

Arcturus held Juliana close as she was wracked with sobs, her shoulders heaving with the force of her distress. Her hand gripped his back, and her tears seemed never-ending. Arcturus had been through the aftermath of combat and knew how to deal with the stress and fear of close brushes with death, but this was new to Juliana and he knew he had to let her vent her fear, anger, and grief.

In the wake of the shooting, Arcturus had dropped his weapon and rushed to her side, holding her close until the Tyrador armed forces arrived in screeching, armored vehicles. Howling orbital flyers—brilliant white and emblazoned with the winged caduceus, the universal symbol of healers—landed in billowing clouds of propwash.

Green-clad paramedics spread efficiently through the crowd, treating the wounded and calming the living as enforcement officers secured the dead attackers and gathered up fallen weaponry. Sirens and screams and shouts blended together, rising into the night sky, forever shattering the aura of invincibility the inhabitants of and visitors to Tyrador IX thought they had.

Until now, this had been a planet everyone believed was far from the concerns of politics and warfare, but the fallacy and naïveté of that illusion had been cruelly stripped away by this atrocity. Nowhere was safe now; the long reach of violence could extend even here, the playground of the rich and powerful.

Arcturus and Juliana answered a barrage of questions from a variety of officials, but after what seemed like a lifetime they were allowed to leave the scene, though Arcturus agreed to report to the local Confederate militia station in the morning to give a fuller account of his role in the night's bloodshed.

Words like "hero," "commendation," and "medal" were already being bandied around.

A police flyer had taken them to Arcturus's hotel, and no sooner had they crossed the threshold of his room than Juliana broke down in tears. Arcturus guided her to the bed and sat next to her, allowing her to cry and knowing that anything he might say right now would be trite and meaningless.

They sat like that for almost an hour before Juliana's sobs became less frequent and she prised herself from his shoulder. Her eyes were puffy and her makeup ran in black streaks down her face. Her golden hair hung limp; her skin was ashen.

She looked achingly beautiful in her vulnerability.

"I'm sorry . . . ," she said. "I look a mess. I—"

Arcturus ran a hand through her hair and kissed her forehead. "You look far better than anyone would expect after what you've been through tonight."

"Oh God . . . all those people," she said. "They killed so many people."

Arcturus nodded. "Yes, they did, but they won't hurt anyone else. They're dead now. I killed them."

"Yes," she said, "you did. You were so brave. You saved my life."

"No," said Arcturus, trying to sound modest, but pleased at the thought of being seen as a hero. "I just did what I had to do. Remember, I'm trained for this kind of thing. I just acted without thinking. If I'd thought about it, I'd have stayed on the ground. Going up against five men armed with assault rifles with only a pistol . . . ? Captain Emillian will have my guts for garters when she hears that."

"She won't," said Juliana, pulling him close. "She'll think you're the bravest man she's ever met. Just as I do."

Arcturus saw that Juliana had control of her emotions now, having come through the horror of the shooting with more aplomb and determination than most soldiers ever did. He saw the core of iron in her, and was reminded of the strength he saw in his mother.

As her sapphire eyes met his, he saw a fierce passion there that reflected his own.

The full force of what had happened tonight rushed to the fore in both of them, and reason was cast aside as they seized one another in a desperate embrace.

Arcturus pressed his lips against Juliana's, and she returned his kiss with hot urgency.

They tore at each other, disrobing one another with

no regard for propriety. The nearness of death and the arousal of killing swept through their mingled flesh in an uncontrollable surge and they fell together with only one thing in mind.

Drowning in desire, Arcturus had wanted this since he had first laid eyes on Juliana, and he gave in to the moment without thought for the consequences—consequences that could bind two lives together forever.

Soon they would be forced to part once more, but for tonight Arcturus and Juliana sought to purge thoughts of their own mortality by affirming their life and humanity in the most primal way possible.

CHAPTER 10

KORHAL. THE PLANET OF HIS BIRTH. UNTIL HE SET foot on it once again, Arcturus hadn't realized how much he'd missed the place. Stepping from the orbital flyer that had brought him from the *John Lomas*, Arcturus followed the crowds making their way to the starport's exit. Given the anti-Confederate unrest the UNN was reporting on Korhal, Arcturus had packed his uniform into his suit-bag, but his CMC ident-tags were hung around his neck to ease his passage through the security checkpoints.

Under normal circumstances, his tags should have allowed him to pass through with the bare minimum of effort, but it took a frustrating two hours to travel from the flyer to the arrivals lounge, the culmination of a several-day journey from Tyrador IX and Juliana.

Their parting had been emotional and heartbreaking.

For her, at least.

When dawn's light had shone through the polarized glass of his hotel window, Arcturus woke with the bitter taste of regret in his mouth. Looking at the sleeping form of Juliana, perfectly outlined by the tousled sheets, he had felt nothing but a profound sense of irritation at his giving in to passion and letting emotion cloud his judgment.

Yes, he had wanted to take Juliana to his bed, and had gone to some effort to do so, but now that the deed was done, he felt a curious regret. Perhaps the previous night's atrocity had touched him more deeply than he had thought, but lying in the half-light of morning, he felt a sense of closure, and yet an awareness of new beginnings. It was a curious sensation.

He had slipped silently from the bed and dressed, then gathered his belongings. Before he could leave, Juliana had woken and smiled. He had stayed long enough to share some breakfast before making his escape, promising that they would see each other soon. She had cried at the thought of his leaving, and he had held her for an appropriate length of time before prising himself from her clinging embrace.

And with that, he had left her.

Arcturus wasn't sure exactly what he now thought of Juliana Pasteur. On the one hand, she was a beautiful woman; but on the other—if he was honest—she had been nothing more than an exercise in satisfying his own vanity. Though it had taken him longer than he would have expected, he had gotten everything he wanted from her and she was therefore of little further interest to him.

Of course, her interest in him was undimmed, but that was a problem for another day.

Putting Juliana Pasteur from his mind, Arcturus had boarded the *John Lomas* and made his way to Korhal.

As he strode toward the arrivals lounge, he saw armed patrols of Confederate militia at every step, groups of hard-eyed men and women scanning the crowds for any potential threat.

Have things really gotten that bad?

There had been a few reports on the UNN of the troubles on Korhal—riots, ambushes, and the occasional bombing—but the media had played these down as isolated incidents perpetrated by lone madmen. Now, here on the ground of Korhal, Arcturus wasn't so sure.

"My father's been busy," he whispered to himself.

The doors to the arrivals lounge opened and he emerged into a crowded concourse of eager faces, men and women and children awaiting reunions with loved ones. Arcturus hefted his suit-bag onto his shoulder and scanned the gathered people, looking for a familiar face.

When he finally saw one, it certainly wasn't one he'd expected.

"Welcome back," said Achton Feld, taking Arcturus's bag.

"Feld?" said Arcturus by way of a greeting. "Where are my mother and father? And Dorothy?"

"They're down the coast," said Feld, "at the summer villa."

"And they couldn't come themselves?"

"Not safely."

Arcturus sighed. He shouldn't have been surprised, but he had held to a faint hope that his parents might have bothered to come and greet the prodigal son back to the family heartland.

He saw Feld sizing him up with a critical eye.

"What?"

"You've changed," noted Feld. "Something about you is different."

"What do you mean?"

"I don't know exactly, but you look better for it, that's for sure."

"I'm so glad you think so."

Feld nodded wearily at Arcturus's sarcasm. "Okay then . . . let's get to the groundcar."

From the bedroom he shared with his wife, Angus watched the silver groundcar as it made its way along the road toward the summer villa, a heavy feeling lurking in the pit of his stomach. It had been two years since he had seen his son, and the emotions of the day when Katherine had tearfully told him that Arcturus had joined the Marines were as strong as ever.

Angus struggled to hold his temper as he thought back to Dorothy's tears that same evening, knowing that Katherine had pinned her hopes on a family reconciliation tonight. Katherine's happiness was the most important thing in the world to Angus Mengsk, and he just hoped he could get through this evening without barking at his errant son.

"Are you ready?" said Katherine from the bedroom door. "He's almost here."

Angus turned and gave his wife a smile. "I don't know if I'm ready, but let's go anyway."

"Please, Angus," said Katherine. "You promised."

"I know," he said, reaching out to her. She came into the room and took his hands. "But I can't forget how he hurt you. How he hurt all of us."

"You have to. Arcturus is our son."

"But joining the military," said Angus, shaking his head. "Of all the ways he could have chosen to disappoint me—"

"Stop it," said Katherine, in a tone that warned Angus he was on thin ice. "He is our son and he will be welcome here, no matter what. Do you understand me?"

"Of course, dear, but the boy infuriates me."

Katherine smiled. "No one gets under our skin quite like the people we love."

"Especially family," said Angus.

"Especially family," agreed Katherine. "They wouldn't get to us so much if we didn't love them."

"I suppose," said Angus. "Where's Dorothy?"

"She's in her room."

"Is she coming down?"

"Not yet," said Katherine sadly. "She's just curled up with Pontius and says she doesn't want to see Arcturus."

"I don't see why she gets out of this and I can't," grumbled Angus.

"Are you *seriously* pouting because you're having to do something a six-year-old won't?"

"No . . ."

"Shame on you, Angus Mengsk," said Katherine. "Now, come on. Let's go downstairs."

"Fine," said Angus, taking a deep breath and straightening his jacket. "How do I look?"

"Like a father," said Katherine.

The groundcar drew to a halt within the villa's courtyard and Arcturus got out in time to see his mother and father emerge onto the steps before the front door. His father was dressed in an immaculate, severely cut suit of ash gray with the wolf-head emblem on the breast pocket, while his mother wore an elegant dress of cornflower blue.

The air was fresh with the tang of saltwater and a pleasing chill blew in off the ocean. As five armed guards stood in the shadows of the courtyard, Arcturus stood straight and with his shoulders back, trying to read the expressions on his parents' faces. His mother smiled warmly, and Arcturus thought he detected a faint hint of welcome even in his father's stern features.

Achton Feld moved past him with his suit-bag and Arcturus followed him.

As he reached the bottom of the steps, his mother came down and embraced him, all her thoughts of reserve forgotten as tears spilled down her cheeks.

"Oh, Arcturus . . . ," she wept. "It's so good to have you home. We've missed you so much."

He returned his mother's embrace, feeling a powerful, forgiving sense of return. He surrendered to it and felt years of bitterness begin to wash away at the simple sincerity of his mother's welcoming love.

Eventually his mother released him and he found himself face-to-face with his father.

The moment stretched and the warmth of the previous welcome faded like a distant memory. At last his father extended his hand.

"Good to see you, son," said Angus.

Arcturus smiled, though it was an effort. "And you, Father."

They shook hands stiffly, but Arcturus could discern that, despite himself, his father was actually pleased to see him.

"You've changed," said Angus.

"So Feld tells me," replied Arcturus. "Though he seems unable to say how."

"It's your eyes. You've gotten older. You've done things that have aged you."

"Is that a good thing?"

"I don't know yet," said his father, releasing his hand.

Arcturus saw his mother narrow her eyes and turned to her. "Where's Dorothy?"

"She's upstairs," said his mother. "Asleep. It seemed a shame to wake her."

Arcturus caught the hesitation in her reply and said, "Come on, Mother. Where is she really?"

"She's upstairs," repeated Katherine. "She's just . . . Well, she's still angry with you."

"After two years?"

"People can hold grudges for longer than that," said his father.

Arcturus nodded. "So I gather. She's in her room?"

"Yes," said Katherine, "but maybe you should let her come down in her own time, dear?"

"I don't think so," said Arcturus. "If there's one thing I've learned, it's that it's almost always best to tackle a problem head-on."

"The Marines teach you that?" said Angus.

"No, I learned that from you," said Arcturus, sweeping past his parents and into the villa.

The entrance hall was exactly as he remembered it, with its checkerboard-patterned floor, dark paneling, and gold-framed portraits. His mother's objets d'art still stood on their white marble columns, and no sooner was he across the threshold than a hundred memories from his childhood returned.

He stood in the warm hallway, letting the smells of the house wash over him in a sustained assault on his senses: the wax rubbed into the wooden floors, the aroma of slowly cooking dinner, the polish used on the silverware. Arcturus could hear the bustle of staff in the kitchens, the creak and groan of an aged house warmed by the sun, and the hum of the generator room deep in the basement.

The house spoke to him in a language of the senses, a combination of a thousand different sights, sounds, and smells, but they all blended into one simple feeling.

He was home.

How many soldiers fantasized about home? All of them, even the ones with nothing much to look forward to at the end of their term of service. Home was an idealized notion to most military men, but here, standing in the house in which he'd spent every summer growing up, Arcturus knew that this was no fantasy.

Arcturus climbed the stairs, avoiding the creaking ones—as he had always done as a child—and made his way toward Dorothy's room. He smiled as he saw that her door was still covered with colorful letters.

He knocked lightly on the door, three slow knocks followed by three quick ones, the secret code they'd used when she was little more than a toddler.

"Go away!" came a voice from beyond the door.

"Little Dot, it's me," he said. "Arcturus."

"I *know*."

Realizing he would get nowhere like this, Arcturus pushed open the door and went in. Inside, he saw that Dorothy's room had changed since the last time he'd seen it. It was still strewn with toys, but there was an order to them now, a hierarchy that had Dorothy clearly at the top.

His sister lay on her back in the center of her bed, Pontius the pony held tightly across her chest. The old pony was looking a little threadbare, but Dorothy plainly wasn't about to let that stop her from hanging on to him.

"Hello, Little Dot," he said. "I'm back home."

"No one calls me that anymore," said Dorothy. "I'm not a baby anymore."

Arcturus crossed the room to stand at the side of her bed, observing that Dorothy had indeed grown since he had seen her last. She had blossomed into a pretty little girl with the distinctive high cheekbones of her mother and the thunderous brow of her father.

She wore a smart dress and her hair was pleated in two pigtails. Even lying down, she looked every inch the Mengsk she was.

He smiled. "Okay. So what do they call you now then?"

"Dorothy, silly," she said, as if it was the most obvious thing in the world, which, he had to admit, it probably was. "What else would they call me?"

"Sorry, yes, should have thought about that," he said, sitting on the edge of her bed.

"I don't want to talk to you," said Dorothy, rolling away from him and onto her side.

"Well, that's too bad," said Arcturus. "I suppose I'll have to keep the present I was going to give you. Maybe I'll give it some poor children."

"I don't care," she said. "I don't want it anyway."

"That's a shame. It was a really nice present."

"I told you, I don't care," said Dorothy, and Arcturus saw he wasn't going to win her over with simple appeals to a child's greed. As always, he'd have to go for the emotional blackmail.

"I wrote to you every day, but you didn't write back," he said. "I missed you. I really missed you, little sister."

"Then why did you leave me?" she cried, rolling over to face him and hurling Pontius at him. The stuffed pony bounced to the floor and Arcturus leaned back as Dorothy rose to her knees and hit him over and over on the chest with tiny fists.

"You went away and left me without saying good-bye," she sobbed.

He let her vent her frustrations on him without protest, and when she was done, he put his arms around her and held her tightly.

"I know I did, and I'm sorry. I never meant to leave you like that."

"Then why did you go? I never saw you to say good-bye."

"I . . . I had to go," he said. "I couldn't stay here."

"Why? Because of Daddy?"

"No, it was because of me. I had to go and do something for *me*, something that wasn't some idea or plan of *his*. Joining up was my way of doing that."

"You could have died," cried Dorothy. "Soldiers get shot at and blown up all the time. I see it on the news every day, even though Mummy and Daddy don't like me watching it. I kept looking for you. I kept watching the news and wondering if you'd been killed."

Arcturus held his sister close as she cried, not having thought about what she must have gone through, wondering if he was alive or dead. His mother and father would no doubt have assured her that he was alive and well, but what force could compete with the imagination of a six-year-old?

"I'm sorry, Dorothy, I really am. I never meant for you to worry about me. I'm your big brother—I can look after myself."

"And who's going to look after me? You're my big brother and you promised you wouldn't let anything happen to me. But then you went away and anything could have happened to me. Those bad men could have come back and shot Mummy and Daddy and me. Or a bomb could have blown us all up or those rebels with guns could have shot us because Daddy has so much money."

The words poured from Dorothy in a rush and Arcturus felt his heart go out to her. Dorothy was a confident, articulate little girl—and a Mengsk to boot—but she was still only six. He realized he had forgotten that.

"Nothing like that could happen," he said as forcefully as he could. "Daddy pays Achton Feld too much money for anything to happen to you. And now that I'm a soldier, I have a big gun and a whole platoon of marines who will protect you, I promise."

She squeezed him tightly and he smiled, knowing he had won her around.

"I missed you," she said. "I cried for a week when you left."

"I'm sorry," he said once more. "But I'm back for a while and I promise I won't go away this time without telling you first."

"Mummy really missed you. I heard her crying too. Daddy missed you as well. He never said it, but I could tell that he did."

Arcturus lifted her face from his shoulder. "I love you, Dorothy. And I always will."

"I love you too," she sniffed. "And it's okay—you can call me Little Dot if you want."

"Thanks."

"You're welcome," said Dorothy. "Now where's my present?"

Dinner was often a lavish affair in the Mengsk household, held in the oak-paneled dining room and comprising several courses, a wide selection of wines, and a grand fire burning in the iron grate. Angus Mengsk sat at one end of the long rosewood dining room table, with Katherine at the other end and Arcturus in the middle to his father's right.

Dorothy sat opposite Arcturus and sipped from a cup of fresh apple juice. As was customary, Pontius sat at the table next to her, with his own place setting. Arcturus and his father had shared a glass of port before dinner, a breach of etiquette under normal circumstances, but Angus had never liked doing things by the book—a trait he seemed not to know that he had passed on to his son.

Angus had drunk a white port, but Arcturus found he preferred a darker, ruby port, and they had sat on either side of the chessboard as his mother cleaned Dorothy up for dinner. The carved pieces were arrayed for battle, but neither man was in the mood for a game.

Arcturus had defeated his father when he was eleven, and they had never played since.

They spoke guardedly, with Arcturus unsurprised to discover that his father was just as vocal as ever in his condemnation of the Confederacy. The special target of Angus's ire these days was the fact that the construction of the new Korhal Assembly Forum had been abandoned and the site bulldozed for some overpriced housing development. Of course, the demolition contract had been awarded to a company owned by one of the Old Families, the Tygores, and the new building contract awarded to a firm owned by a distant nephew of Andrea Tygore.

Times changed, but corruption, it seemed, stayed the same.

Arcturus drained the last of his port as his mother and Dorothy entered the dining room. His father smiled at the sight of his daughter, and Arcturus was reminded that, above all the politicking, the railing against the Confederacy, and his complicity in terrorist activities, Angus Mengsk was still a loving father.

The family seated themselves at the table and dinner began, with the slightly strained atmosphere broken by the excited chatter of Dorothy as she spun tales of her preschool class and the many children she played with.

As he watched the faces of his mother and father come to life, Arcturus realized that it must have been some time since Dorothy had opened up like this. Conversation flowed around the table, though Arcturus saw how his mother skillfully steered them all away from any contentious topics.

The first course arrived, a truffle custard garnished with small slivers of pâté, and Arcturus made appreciative noises as he tasted the food. Like many wives of wealthy men, Katherine Mengsk took a keen interest in the running of the household, and the majority of the dishes served were ones of her own creation, using local ingredients and incorporating her family's favorite flavors. Small glasses of a light, sparkling wine were served with the first course, which was swiftly followed by a mushroom risotto with baby arugula, Manchego cheese, and a lemon-parsley sauce.

Used to living on a diet of ration packs and mess hall dishes, Arcturus found himself struggling with the sheer volume of food, but a lavender sorbet cleared his palate in time for a roasted rosemary pork loin brochette with tomato-port sauce and Gruyère cheese grits.

Finally, a shallow bowl of sweet potato pound cake with a blood-orange-and-bourbon glaze and nutmeg whipped cream was served, and after one portion Arcturus knew he could not eat another mouthful.

Coffees were served and a small bowl of mints placed in the center of the table.

"Mother, that was a triumph," said Arcturus as the last of the plates were cleared.

"Absolutely," agreed Angus, and Katherine smiled to see her son and husband in agreement for once.

"I'm glad you approve," said Katherine. "I planned the menu especially for tonight. I wanted us to have a proper family dinner together. It's been too long since we all sat around a table and just enjoyed each other's company. Don't you agree?"

Arcturus hid a smile at his mother's seemingly innocent question, recognizing an iron fist in a velvet glove when he saw one.

"Of course," said Angus, hearing the same thing, and Arcturus looked over at his father to share a knowing look. The ease of the glance and the natural way he had looked over surprised him as much as it appeared to surprise his father.

"I've missed this," said Arcturus. "It's good to be back home."

"I'm glad you're back," said Dorothy, and the matter was settled.

With the dinner cleared away, Katherine hustled Dorothy off to bed, though not before she had secured hugs and kisses for both herself and Pontius from her father and brother. With the women of the household away, the friction that had fled upon their arrival snuck back into the room like a malignant shadow.

"A glass of port?" asked Angus, and Arcturus nodded.

"Ruby for me," he said.

Angus poured two glasses of port and handed one to Arcturus. They stood in silence for a moment, and Arcturus saw his father struggling to find the right words. With Katherine present, conversation had been light and inconsequential, but without her calming influence, the tension between these two alpha males was resurgent.

"I'm glad you came, son," said Angus at last. "Your mother went to a lot of trouble tonight. And Dorothy, well, you can see how pleased she is to see you."

"And you?" asked Arcturus. "Are you pleased to see me?"

"Of course. You know I am. You are my son."

"I know, but the last time we spoke wasn't exactly friendly."

"You had just gone and joined the Marines," said Angus. "My son the Confederate marine . . . what did you expect?"

"I expected you to respect my damn decision," snapped Arcturus.

Angus sighed and took a sip of his port. "Are you trying to pick a fight, Arcturus?"

"No," said Arcturus. "I'm really not. It's just . . . well, we've never seen eye to eye on lots of things, have we?"

"Not that I can recall, no."

"Exactly, and back when I was living on Korhal,

every time you looked at me, it was like you were *trying* to find faults with whatever I did. Nothing I did was ever good enough for you."

"That's ridiculous," said Angus. "I just wanted the best for you. You see that, surely?"

"The best for me? Are you sure? Or did you want the best for *you*? What I wanted didn't seem important. All you cared about was whether I was a fit successor to you."

Angus poured himself another glass of port, using the time to curb an angry outburst.

Arcturus knew that goading his father could only end one way, but couldn't stop the words from flowing. Two years of pent-up feelings were now coming out and he couldn't stop them.

"Arcturus, you are my son and I have only ever wanted the best for you. You are intelligent and can be the best at whatever you want to be, but to waste your life fighting for a tyrannical, corrupt regime that seeks to take control of everything in the galaxy is just stupid."

"So now I'm stupid?"

"That's not what I said. You're not even listening to me, you're hearing what you want to hear so you can prolong this argument."

Arcturus knew his father was speaking the truth, but the memory of Private Shaw leapt to the forefront of his mind, the image of the boy's torn-up body lying in a pool of blood on the floor of a bar on Tyrador IX fogging his usual clearheadedness.

"No, that's not it at all," said Arcturus.

"Then what is it?" demanded Angus. "Because I'd really like to know."

"It's what you're doing on Korhal," said Arcturus. "The bombings and the riots. You and Feld and your band of revolutionaries are still fanning the flames of hatred here, aren't you?"

"Keep your damn voice down," hissed Angus.

"Why? Afraid this Confederate marine might report you to the authorities?"

"You wouldn't?" said Angus, genuinely horrified at the notion of his son turning on him.

"No, of course not, but I've seen the reality of what people like you are doing," said Arcturus. "I saw the bodies and the blood on Tyrador IX, and I heard the screaming. You can justify what you're doing with talk of corruption and with clever wordplay, but I've seen what's left behind. I saw men shot down without mercy, and God knows how many innocent bystanders were caught in the crossfire. If that's what you're doing, then I want no part of it."

"The attack on Tyrador IX was nothing to do with me, Arcturus," said Angus, taking a step toward him. "I swear it. We only attack military targets. Combatants. Because we're in a war, make no mistake about that."

"Military targets?" said Angus, pulling his marine ident-tags from beneath his shirt. "What do you think these make me? Tell me, would you bomb me or authorize some other attack that might get me killed if it was part of your grand plan?"

"Of course not! Arcturus, why are you doing this? Your mother wanted for us to become a family again tonight. Don't ruin it for her."

"It was a mistake coming here," said Arcturus, putting down his glass and turning toward the door. "I should go."

"No, Arcturus, please stay," said Angus, following him and taking his arm. "For your mother and Dorothy if not for me."

Arcturus turned to face his father. "I'll be gone in the morning."

Far from the glowing jewel that was Styrling, the darkness of the sky was absolute. Arcturus sat on the walnut bench his father had built at the end of the path from the villa, watching the sea explode against the cliffs below in silver cascades. A bronze plaque in the middle of the bench was carved with a memorial inscription to Arcturus's grandfather, Augustus, but the words had been obscured by a green skim of corrosion and could no longer be read.

He sat and looked up at the stars, wondering which ones he would travel to next. The possibilities were endless, and certainly he was likely to see a great many different worlds with the Marines.

And once he was tired of military life, a point he knew was fast approaching, he would muster out and head to the rim, just far enough out to be free.

Arcturus felt a vibration in his pocket and took out

his fone. He waited until the tone had stopped and then flipped it open. Another message from Juliana. That made fifteen since he had arrived on Korhal.

He sighed and replaced the fone in his pocket as he heard footsteps behind him.

"Mind if I join you?" said Achton Feld.

"If you're here to convince me to stay then you're wasting your breath."

"I'm not. I know it's a lost cause trying to convince you of anything."

Arcturus nodded and gestured toward the bench. "Then sit down."

The two men sat in silence for a while, content to simply enjoy the majesty of the view. Farther out to sea, the ocean was like a black mirror, vast and reflecting the stars above in wavering pinpoints. Occasional silver streaks flashed across the sky. Arcturus liked to believe they were shooting stars, though he knew they were simply starships hitting the atmosphere.

"You'll regret this, you know," said Feld eventually.

"What?"

"Leaving like this. You don't know what's going to happen in the future, so do you *really* want this to be the last memory you have of your folks?"

"You're being melodramatic, Feld," said Arcturus. "It doesn't suit you."

"I'm not, Arcturus. Trust me, what's happening on Korhal is more dangerous than you know. The Confederacy is running scared here, and anyone who's seen combat knows that's when the enemy is at its most dangerous. They'll try anything and, as good as I am, I can't guarantee anyone's safety in the face of that kind of desperation."

"Are things really that bad?"

Feld simply nodded and said, "You can never go home. Isn't that what they say?"

"Who?"

"They. Them. Whoever. It doesn't matter."

"What does it mean?"

"When you live here on Korhal, you think it's the center of the world and you believe nothing will ever change. Then you leave and don't come back for a few years. And when you come back, everything's changed. The connection's broken. What you came to find isn't there and what was yours is gone. You'll have to go away for a long time before you can come back and find your people, the world where you were born. But now, for you, it's not possible. You're not ready to come back to Korhal. Or maybe she's not ready for you, I don't know."

"Since when did you become a philosopher, Feld?"

"I've been around," said Feld, "and I picked up a few things along the way. Just don't do anything rash, okay? If you're going to leave, fine, leave, but say good-bye first. Don't leave like last time."

"Don't burn any bridges? Is that what you're saying?"

"Yeah, I guess it is," agreed Feld. "Say your good-byes, and *then* go. And don't come back until you're ready to come back. Make a clean break until then."

Arcturus's fone trilled again and he knew who it was without even looking.

Juliana.

"A clean break, you say?"

"Yeah."

"I think you might be right, Feld."

CHAPTER 11

ARCTURUS LEANED HIS HEAD BACK AGAINST THE plyboard wall of the office and closed his eyes, letting the hum of the air-heaters and the clicking sound of Lieutenant Cestoda's typing lull him into a semi-doze. It would be at least another half hour before he was admitted into Commander Fole's office anyway. Appointments with Brantigan Fole were always late. The bullish commanding officer of the 33rd Ground Assault Division of the Confederate Marine Corps kept very much to his own schedule and no one else's.

Lieutenant Lars Cestoda, the adjutant tasked with keeping track of the commander's appointments, was a waspish and punctilious man who, at first glance, seemed an unlikely soldier, but who positively thrived on the minutiae of army regulations.

Despite the convection heaters warming the office, Arcturus still felt the chill in the air and pulled his uniform jacket tighter. He'd need to request a new one soon; this one barely fit his broad shoulders and wide chest.

The summons to Commander Fole's office in Camp Hastings had come out of the blue, as most orders did in the Marine Corps, but this one had the reek of importance to it and thus Arcturus had arrived early, even though he knew it would be a while before the commander deigned to see him.

The outer office was plain and stark, the only items of furniture an uncomfortable couch on which Arcturus sat, a pair of iron filing cabinets (that looked old and battered enough to have come from the *Sarengo*), and the desk and chair used by Lieutenant Cestoda. A few marine recruitment posters were stuck to the wall with thumbtacks, which seemed a little redundant to Arcturus, since anyone likely to see these posters would already be in the Marine Corps.

Arcturus stood and stretched. He'd been waiting for an hour and had already thumbed through a copy of *Battle Flag*, the magazine of the CMC. The paper version of the magazine had long since been replaced by digi-tome editions—and this copy had seen better days. Cestoda looked up in irritation as Arcturus rose to his feet.

"Something I can do for you, Captain?" asked Cestoda, as though Arcturus had violated some unwritten rule of the office.

"No," said Arcturus. "Just stretching my legs. Do

you have any idea when the commander will be available?"

"Presently."

"That's what you said thirty minutes ago."

"Then you shouldn't have needed to ask again."

Arcturus approached Cestoda's desk and perched on the edge, knowing it would annoy the man. Sure enough, Cestoda glared at him, but Arcturus met his stare with one of his own.

"You are aware of the etymology of your name, I presume?" asked Arcturus, picking up a stylus from the desk. Cestoda snatched it back.

"The what?"

"Etymology," repeated Arcturus slowly. "It means the origins of words and how they arrived at their current meaning. I was asking if you knew what your name means."

"It doesn't *mean* anything," said Cestoda. "It's just a name."

"On the contrary, my dear fellow, in times past, a man's name was what defined him. Many names came from a man's profession, such as Smith or Cooper, while others made reference to his disposition or appearance."

"What does that have to do with me?"

"Ah, well you see, Cestoda is a class of parasitic flatworms that live in the digestive tracts of vertebrates and absorb food predigested by their host. They're ugly creatures, little more than a body with only a rudimentary head for attachment to their host. And one of the most common complaints regarding them is the nausea they cause. Just thought you ought to know."

Arcturus got up from Cestoda's desk before he could reply and moved toward the insulated window that looked out over the barren, blue-lit hinterlands of Onuru Sigma. The outlying buildings of Camp Hastings huddled beneath the cobalt sky, and beyond the defensive turrets, icy tundra spread out for hundreds of miles toward escarpments of glaciers that towered kilometers into the sky.

The sealant around the glass was degrading and the sulfurous chill of the planet's arctic temperatures stole what little heat the convectors were generating.

Arcturus studied his reflection, his features rugged and handsome in the tinted glass. His cheeks were well defined and he now sported a neatly trimmed goatee around his full mouth. His eyes were as piercing as ever they were, though far older than any twenty-four-year-old man's eyes should be, and his dark hair was thick and black. He smiled as he saw he was the image of his father.

A younger, handsomer version of his father, of course.

Though virtually every UNN broadcast was filled with images of Angus Mengsk—the Madman of Korhal, they called him—it had been a long time since Arcturus had consciously thought of his father. Almost five years had passed since he had seen his family and though he had not passed a single word with his father, he kept in regular touch with his mother and Dorothy.

His sister had just turned eleven, an age that made Arcturus feel very old indeed. It seemed like only yesterday Little Dot had been born, but now her conversations over the vidfone were filled with talk of boys and parties and how she hated not being able to leave the house without an escort of soldiers. The trouble on Korhal was on the verge of getting completely out of hand, and the pundits agreed it was only a matter of time until martial law was declared.

Arcturus wasn't worried for his father, who had chosen to live such a dangerous life, but he fretted constantly for his mother and sister. He had once promised Dorothy he wouldn't let anything happen to her, and Feld's warning that their safety couldn't be guaranteed still echoed in his imagination.

He turned as he heard a chime from Cestoda's desk and smiled at the irritated glance that ghosted across the man's features as he listened to Fole's voice through his earpiece.

Cestoda looked up and said, "Commander Fole will see you now."

The commanding officer of the 33rd Ground Assault Division was a short fireplug of a man with a short temper and a quick manner that left many of his fellow soldiers floundering in his wake. His salt-and-pepper hair was kept cropped close to his skull and his skin was tanned the color and texture of worn leather from the rays of a hundred different suns.

An unlit cigar was clamped between his teeth and he chewed a wad of tobacco, a habit he'd picked up while stationed along the outer rim and never saw fit to discard when he'd returned to more civilized space. His uniform was immaculately pressed and decorated with enough stars to fill a decent-sized planetarium.

Arcturus snapped to attention and saluted the commander, who returned the salute without looking up from the papers arranged haphazardly on his desk. Another officer, one with the rank badge of a captain pinned to his white uniform, stood at attention beside the commander.

This captain was broad-shouldered and wore the power of his rank like a threat. His features were arrogant, rugged, and pugnacious. Arcturus disliked him instantly.

He guessed the man was around forty, which made him old for a captain, and his physique was impressive for a man his age.

"Sit down, Captain," said Fole. "I have a job for you."

"Yes, sir," said Arcturus, taking the seat in front of Fole's desk.

"This here's Edmund Duke," said Fole, jerking a thumb in the direction of the man standing beside him. "A captain in Alpha Squadron. His outfit is heading out to the Noranda Glacier vespene mine and I want Dominion section to go with them."

Arcturus nodded. He'd heard of Alpha Squadron, who were supposedly the most efficient fighters in the Confederacy—which meant the most brutal—and whose motto was "First group in, first group out." They were nicknamed the Blood Hawks, which spoke volumes for Arcturus's assessment.

"Yes, sir. What's the mission?"

"Convince the miners it'll be in their best interests to move on and leave the place to us. The Kel-Morians have been busy around this system and the brass thinks something big's in the wind, which they ain't too happy about. We're to keep a lid on things and make sure those damn pirates don't get too uppity. You know, the usual."

"The usual," said Arcturus wearily. If Fole heard his tone, he didn't comment on it, but Arcturus could see Duke bristling.

"If you have Alpha Squadron, why do you need Dominion section?"

"Orders from on high are to combine some of our active squads. I'm thinking of attaching your men to Alpha, so I want Duke to carry out an evaluation in the field, make sure everyone's up to scratch."

Arcturus was horrified at the idea of Dominion section's coming under the command of Edmund Duke. Though he had never met the man before, he instinctively knew he was an arrogant blowhard. As he looked at Duke's smirking face, he realized he recognized him.

He'd seen the same arrogant face on the UNN when

its reporters covered the activities of the Old Families.

"Edmund Duke?" he said. "As in the Tarsonis Dukes?"

"The one and only," drawled Duke. "I hear most of your boys are rim world yokels. That the case? Only two things come from the rim worlds, boy—"

"Yes, yes, I know," interrupted Arcturus, returning his attention to his commander. "Sir, you can't be seriously considering this. You can't put Dominion section under this man's command."

"You telling me what to do with my own division, Mengsk?" asked Fole.

"No, sir," said Arcturus hurriedly, "but—"

"Just as well," carried on Fole, as though Arcturus hadn't spoken. "You're a good officer, Mengsk, and the men respect you, but I'll have you scrubbing latrines in a heartbeat if you try and tell me my business again. Are we clear?"

"Crystal, sir," said Mengsk.

"Anyway, what do you care? You're due to muster out soon, so it doesn't matter who commands them."

"I just want to make sure my men are in good hands," said Arcturus, glaring at Duke.

"Well that ain't your concern no more, Mengsk," replied Fole. "Now get out of here and make sure your men are ready for action. Mission briefing is at 19:00 and dropships are skids up at 20:00."

A spiteful wind scoured the glacial slopes below the Noranda Glacier vespene mine. Arcturus kept his helmeted head down against the force of it, his gaze firmly fixed on the blue ridge of snow ahead of him, beyond which lay the mine itself. The streaked sky above the ridge was squalid with scads of vapor and the emphysemic discoloration of poor emission control.

He marched alongside Edmund Duke, the man's white armor decorated with dozens of rank badges and combat citations. It seemed that for all his bluster, Duke had seen his fair share of battle. It didn't make Arcturus like him any better, but at least he wasn't going into action alongside a rookie.

A hundred marines spread out in combat formation trudged up the rugged slopes toward the ridge. Seven goliath walkers marched in support of them, but even these hardy machines found the terrain challenging, their gyros fighting to keep them stable on the treacherous ice and snow.

Vulture hover-cycles zipped around the flanks and Arcturus could just about hear the engine roar of the two supporting Wraith fighters over the howling winds as they circled above. The dropships that had ferried them from Camp Hastings had been forced to debus them a kilometer back, the crafts' poor aerodynamics unable to cope with the high winds and low visibility.

"Hell of a force, eh, Mengsk?" said Duke over the comms between their helmets. "You ever seen such righteous display of Confederate might?"

"It's impressive," agreed Arcturus. "It's been some

time since I've seen this amount of firepower gathered in one place."

"Yeah, just wish I had me one of them siege tanks."

"The ice here is too unstable," said Arcturus. "In all likelihood we would have lost it down a crevasse before we traveled half a kilometer."

"I know that, but with one of those babies we coulda just scared these damn miners out like the yellow-bellies you ran into at Turanga Canyon."

"You heard about that?"

"Sure did. You handled it pretty well, but you were damned lucky those miners didn't have a pair of balls between the whole lot of them."

Arcturus shook his head at Duke's simplistic reading of the engagement, but didn't reply as his fellow captain continued. "If I had my way we'd just be chasing these dirt-grubbers away at the end of a volley of Impaler fire and that'd be the end of it."

"If a trifle heavy-handed," said Arcturus.

"Heavy-handed? Who do you think you work for, the Boy Scouts? This here's the Confederate Marine Corps, and if you're ever gonna make something of yourself, Mengsk, you're gonna need to get some ruthlessness in you."

"Is that a fact?"

"Damn straight," said Duke, slapping a heavy gauntlet on the side of his gauss rifle. "Ain't no messing with one of these babies."

"Tell me something, Edmund—You don't mind if I call you Edmund, do you? How is it that a scion of one of the Old Families ends up out here pushing miners around as a captain? With your family's influence and the amount of combat it looks like you've seen, I'd have thought they'd have made you a general by now."

Duke stopped and turned to face him, and Arcturus could see the cold anger in his eyes.

"Yeah, I *do* mind you calling me Edmund. And why I'm here is none of your goddamn business. We got our orders and I'm a man who obeys orders, so why don't you shut the hell up and follow yours."

Arcturus smiled as Duke stomped off toward the ridge, letting the man get a goodly distance ahead before embarking himself.

"Gee, Captain, I reckon you done annoyed the big fella," said Chuck Horner, coming alongside him. "What you say to him?"

"Nothing much," said Arcturus. "How's the section, Lieutenant?"

"They're okay," answered Horner. "de Santo's grumbling about the mission, Yancy won't shut up, Chun Leung's bitching about what this weather's doing to Mayumi, and Toby ain't said squat since we touched down, so business as usual, I guess."

Chuck Horner had served as Arcturus's unofficial second in command since the fighting on Sonyan, a position he had fulfilled admirably, eventually earning himself a commission to lieutenant.

Arcturus turned and looked behind him, the blue armored shapes of Dominion section marching a discreet distance away from the marines of Alpha Squadron. Their walks and posture were as familiar to him as his own, and he nodded to each of them as they caught up.

"What's the story, Captain?" said Yancy. "We there yet?"

"Nearly," said Arcturus, pointing to the ridge a hundred meters or so above them. "Just beyond there."

"This is some weather, huh?" said Chun Leung, holding his rifle protectively across his chest to protect it from the worst of the wind. The man's visor was fogged and the plates of his armor were stained with pollutants, yet somehow his weapon was still pristine.

"We saw worse than this on Parragos, remember?" said Yancy.

"I'm trying to forget that one," grumbled Chun Leung. "Took months to get all that grit out of Mayumi's breech."

"This gonna be more of the same?" asked Dia de Santo.

Arcturus didn't have to ask what she meant. Most of their ops in the last few years had involved securing mines or frontier exploration sites from Kel-Morian prospectors. Either that or providing heavily armed backup to local enforcers.

Riots and thousands-strong protests were flaring up throughout the Confederacy with ever more regularity, and you couldn't watch the UNN without some report coming on about a disaffected populace attacking police or marching beneath waving banners.

Of course, these were downplayed as a few malcontents, but Dominion section's experiences and Arcturus's last visit to Korhal told him that things were far worse than anyone suspected. The Confederacy was rotting from the inside out and the powers that be were holding on by their fingertips.

"More of the same?" said Arcturus, as a sudden shiver ran along the length of his spine. "You know, I rather think it won't be."

"What do you mean, Captain?" asked Yancy.

"I have a feeling that Duke isn't playing with a full deck," said Arcturus, disregarding the military protocol of not criticizing fellow officers to lower-ranked soldiers.

"You think he's dangerous?" asked Chuck Horner.

"Very much so, Charles," said Arcturus. "I'm just not sure whom he's dangerous *to*."

Noranda Glacier itself towered over them, a solid escarpment of blue ice on the opposite edge of a shallow-bowled meteor crater gouged into the ice thousands of years ago. The crater's ridge curved away to either side, and its far edge was over three kilometers away. The cliff of the glacier reached thousands of meters into the air, like the dwelling place of gods from ancient legend.

In the center of the shallow bowl a dark fault line

split the ice, and the tendrils of a yellowish green vapor issued from all along its length. A giant, metallic refinery structure of huge pipes, towering collection vats, and flaring exhausts squatted at the center of the crater like a giant, oil-stained spider, surrounded by a host of prefabricated storage sheds and rough-looking living compounds.

Men in hostile-environment suits went about their business below, oblivious to the marines poised to march in and take their livelihood, and huge trucks with spiked wheels crunched over the ice as they loaded up with containers of the precious gas.

It looked as though the place had been built in the midst of what had once been a ruined city, with jagged spires of dark, crystal-veined stone clustered around the more recently built constructions. The architecture of these ruins was a mystery, but there was something about them that looked oddly out of scale with the humans toiling in their shadow.

Brantigan Fole's marines lay in the lee of the crater's edge, looking down into the enormous crater. The goliaths were hunkered down behind them and the vultures did looping circuits of the snow farther back. High overhead, the Wraiths flew figure-eight patterns, lost in the clouds, their engines inaudible.

A thrumming vibration was carried through the ice toward the waiting marines, and Arcturus couldn't help but admire the skill with which the builders of this complex had managed to anchor the refinery over the vespene geyser.

How had they overcome the problem of the shifting ice and the need to keep the collection heads stable? Arcturus couldn't wait to get in and examine the complex.

"Hell, they must have to drill down a ways to get any vespene outta there," said Chuck Horner.

"Indeed they do," said Arcturus. "According to the briefing, the vespene is nearly thirty kilometers beneath the ice."

"Man, that's deep," said de Santo. "Surely there must be easier places to mine?"

"Undoubtedly, but this is an uncommonly large underground geyser," said Arcturus. "And even though it's contaminated with some very noxious chemicals from beneath the ice, it's so vast that it's still worth all the extra effort and danger to get it out."

"Danger?" asked Yancy. "What danger? Aside from drilling over a dirty great crevasse, I mean."

"Look at the color of the gas coming from the extractors," said Arcturus. "You see how it has a yellowish tinge?"

"Yeah."

"That's hydrogen sulfide, a very toxic and flammable gas. Mix it with vespene and you have a highly unstable compound indeed."

"So this place is like one big damn bomb?" asked Dia de Santo.

"Potentially," agreed Arcturus.

"Great," said de Santo. "This just gets better and better."

Leaving his marines to gripe about the danger of

this current mission, Arcturus returned his attention to the target below. The ground was open and inviting, easy to walk over, but with precious little cover. And to reach the central refinery itself, the marines would have to negotiate the tangle of abandoned maintenance sheds and sagging storage hangars.

From the flaring exhaust gases, it was clear the facility was in use, but there seemed precious little activity for so large a refinery. It was almost as though the few workers in view were going through the motions. Something about this whole setup rang false to Arcturus, but before he could give the matter any further thought, Edmund Duke ran over at a crouch and dropped to his knees beside Arcturus.

"Your men ready, Mengsk?" demanded Duke.

"We are," confirmed Arcturus. "How do you want to do this?"

It galled him to defer to Duke's authority, but Commander Fole had been quite clear as to who held the reins of command in this operation.

Duke looked at him as though he'd just asked something stupid. "How the hell do you *think* I want to do it? We go straight toward them and shoot anyone who gets in our way. I'll take most the men out front with the vultures and five of the goliaths. You and your men follow with what's left."

"Captain Duke," said Arcturus, giving Duke his full title as a salve to the man's ego. "That seems a little heavy-handed. We don't know what's down there, and I have just finished telling my soldiers that the gases collecting there are extremely dangerous. We have to be careful here."

"Careful, my ass," said Duke, waving a dismissive gauntlet. "Ain't nothing down there but a bunch of ditch-digging yokels, Mengsk. Nothing we can't handle. Or are you telling me your boys ain't up to the job?"

Arcturus could feel his hackles rise at the insult to his section, but kept his temper in check, knowing that to let Duke see his anger would give him the advantage in this exchange.

"Not at all. Dominion section is ready for action, but we need to think this through. We can't just go in guns blazing."

"Why the hell not?"

Arcturus bellied up to the ridge and gestured to the refinery complex. "Look at the number of maintenance sheds and derelict structures down there. For all we know there could be a hundred or more men waiting for us. It's a ready-made killing ground. I don't like the look of this, Duke. It smells of a trap."

"Mengsk, the only thing I'm smelling here is cowardice," snarled Duke. "Now get your goddamn men ready to move out or I'll haul your ass in front of Commander Fole on a court-martial."

Alpha Squadron formed up and moved out on Duke's order, climbing to their feet and marching over the ridge toward the refinery. Almost immediately, the workers in the mine ceased their labors and withdrew to the central complex. The marines set a punishing stride across the ice, their powered suits allowing them to close the distance to their target at a run.

Five of the goliaths loped across the ice with Duke's men, their heavy autocannons spooled up and ready to fire. Dartlike vultures skimmed over the ice at speed, easily outpacing the marines and moving in to circle the refinery with their grenade launchers locked and loaded.

Arcturus let Duke draw close to the refinery before passing the order to move on to his own men and the twenty his fellow captain had deigned to leave with him. The two remaining goliaths lumbered alongside them, one on either side of their dispersed formation, though Arcturus didn't think they'd be much use back here, where their guns couldn't engage anything for fear they'd hit their own men.

"Man, this stinks worse than that dead guy we found on Pho-Rekh," said Chuck Horner.

"Stay watchful," ordered Arcturus. "And Chuck, keep in contact with the dropships?"

"Sure, but if the winds don't ease back they ain't gonna do us a whole lotta good."

"I'm aware of that. Just do it."

"Sir, yes, sir!" said Chuck, recognizing the authoritative tone of his superior officer.

Arcturus watched as Duke's men reached the outermost building in the refinery complex, passing it at a run and spreading out to secure the target.

Nothing happened, and Arcturus let out the breath he'd been holding.

Vultures scooted in behind the men and the goliaths picked a path over the frozen gravel that served as a level surface. A Wraith screamed overhead, its spiraling white contrails painting the sky and throwing up billowing ice chips as it roared over the refinery at low altitude.

As the Wraith pulled out of its run, Arcturus heard the metallic cough of a missile launch from within the compound. How he could have heard it so clearly over the boom of the Wraith's engines and the thunder of blood in his ears he didn't know, but he would swear on his sister's life that he'd heard it as clearly as if the missile had launched right next to him.

Climbing on a glowing, fire-topped column of white smoke, the missile corkscrewed into the air from one of the dilapidated supply sheds, shreds of camo-netting trailing behind it.

"Oh no . . . ," whispered Arcturus.

At first it seemed as though the missile could not hope to catch the Wraith, but its rocket motor flared and it surged upward at a tremendous velocity. The pilot of the aircraft saw the threat and pushed out the throttle, twisting his vehicle and heading for the open skies.

The missile exploded less than two meters from the pilot's canopy and blew the front of the aircraft off in a bright orange fireball. Spinning wreckage tumbled down on trails of black smoke and slammed into the ice.

As though the downing of the Wraith was a signal, the rattle and pop of distant small-arms fire erupted from the compound ahead. Arcturus saw flashes of gunfire and heard shouted cries of alarm over the comm net in his helmet.

These miners weren't going without a fight.

A column of flame whooshed skyward, followed by a rattling, staccato burst of secondary explosions. Armed men in green powered combat suits poured from the supply sheds previously thought abandoned and opened fire on Duke's men. Goliaths in the same livery stomped into view and streams of fire erupted from the weapon mounts on their arms.

"Everyone forward!" shouted Arcturus, breaking into a run. "Move it!"

While the enemy troops were still tangled up with Duke's marines, they weren't pouring any fire toward Arcturus and his section, but that would soon change if they didn't close the gap. They were headed toward an olive-drab hangarlike structure with a curved roof. If they could get around it, then perhaps they could fall on the soldiers attacking Duke's men from behind.

A vulture screamed around the building, chased by a rippling stream of Impaler spikes fired from loopholes cut in the building Arcturus's men were heading for. The pilot jinked his machine like a snake, weaving in and out of the streams of fire, but he wouldn't last long without help.

"Goliaths!" cried Arcturus. "Engage those shooters. Now!"

The two armored walkers braced themselves and their arms spun up and around. The already rotating barrels suddenly roared and meter-long tongues of flame blasted from the ends of their weapons. Flickering sparks and torn metal exploded from the building's flanks, thousands of rounds carving the sheet metal like a whipping plasma torch. Entire strips of metal fell from the hangar, closely followed by torn-up bodies.

For good measure, a salvo of missiles rippled from the shoulder mounts of the two goliaths, streaking inside the holes their guns had torn. One after another, they exploded inside the building, and the roof boomed upward with each detonation. Flames billowed and smoke boiled from the shattered walls and roof.

The vulture pilot sketched them a quick salute before pulling his hover-cycle in a screaming turn and heading back to the battle.

"Mengsk!" shouted Duke over the comm net. "Where the hell are you? We need help. Now, goddammit, now!"

"On our way, Duke," said Arcturus. "Hold on."

The fighting at the edge of the complex was fierce, groups of armored soldiers dashing from splintered wreckage to piles of stacked steel as they fired quick bursts at one another. Arcturus chopped his hand right—the direction the vulture pilot had flown—and led his men into the complex.

Impaler spikes chimed on steel and armor plates. Explosions flared and shrapnel spanged from the walls of buildings. Thankfully, no one had been foolish enough to shoot anywhere near the refinery, but that was surely a miracle that couldn't last forever. Closer to the complex, the air was greasy and yellow, and a thick fog coiled around their ankles.

Arcturus heard shouts over the comm and skidded into cover at the corner of the building. Closer in, he could see the trap that had been laid for them. The supposedly dilapidated buildings were in fact cunningly constructed strongpoints disguised to look unfinished or abandoned.

An enemy goliath strode around the corner and swiveled its gun mounts toward him.

"Down!" he yelled, and dropped into the fog.

A roaring, sawing line of shells sliced the air like a fiery blade, tearing up the icy ground and sending pulverized chips of gravel flying in all directions. Even through the dampening systems in his helmet, the noise was deafening. Arcturus heard screams and the ringing hammer blows of shells tearing through armor and flesh.

A body fell on top of him, most of its side chewed away. Blood squirted from the torn-up flesh, spraying Arcturus's breastplate in arcing lines. Arcturus gagged back a surge of vomit as he saw Toby Mercurio's lifeless features staring up at him through the smashed ruin of his helmet.

The goliath smashed through a pile of fallen sheet metal, another roaring torrent of shells ripping through the fog toward them. Scattered marines were firing at the armored walker, but their shots were having little effect.

Arcturus pushed Mercurio's body away and rolled to his knees as another hail of explosive 30mm shells reduced what little cover there was to mangled splinters of plascrete and metal shavings.

A series of explosions burst against the goliath's legs and it stumbled, its cannons swiveling to face this new threat. Arcturus saw the vulture they'd saved earlier streak toward the walker. Streams of grenades launched from the hover-cycle's frontal section and a series of explosions burst around the goliath.

It wasn't enough, and Arcturus saw that the pilot had doomed himself in his noble attempt to save them. Then a missile streaked past him and slammed into the pilot's compartment of the enemy walker. As the missile exploded, fire blossomed from the machine and it toppled to the ground in a blazing mass of buckled metal.

Arcturus twisted and saw one of his own goliaths, the blue and red of the Confederate flag a welcome sight on its front glacis. Smoke trailed from its Hellfire missile launchers, and Arcturus let out a shuddering breath at how close they'd come to death.

The vulture pilot looped his vehicle around and sped off into the thick of the fighting without waiting for any thanks.

"Sir!" shouted a voice through the smoke and confusion. "Sir! Are you all right?"

He looked up and saw Dia de Santo, the faceplate of her helmet cracked and scorched. Blood streamed down her arm where her armor had been penetrated, and he saw that her eyes had the glassy look of stim use.

"Yes . . . yes, Dia. I'm fine," he said, pushing himself to his feet.

Chuck Horner ran up to him, his armor similarly dented and battered. "Holy crap," he said when he saw Mercurio's dead body.

Chun Leung and Yancy Gray covered their blind spots as Arcturus shook his head and regained his equilibrium.

"What's the plan, Captain?" shouted Horner. "This here's a real mess now. That idiot Duke really screwed the pooch on this one!"

Arcturus nodded and glanced around the ruined corner of the building once again.

The interior of the mining complex was a hellish war zone. Marines lay dead and dying as Impaler spikes streamed back and forth like horizontal rain. Explosions mushroomed skyward and fires licked at the edges of the habitation compound.

The operation, which had started so simply, had turned into a disaster of epic proportions.

Duke and his men had fought their way into and captured one of the strongpoints, a brutal and heroic action that had probably saved their lives. Gunfire blasted from loopholes, cutting down the armored soldiers who were attempting to rush them.

Smoke and flames obscured much of the battlefield, but Arcturus could already see that it was only a matter of time before Duke and his men were overrun.

He dropped to one knee and turned back to his own men.

"Sound off," he ordered. "How many have we got?"

Altogether he had sixteen marines left alive and one goliath, the other lying in a smoldering heap of flames and popping ammunition. Arcturus hadn't noticed its destruction.

"Charles! Do you still have a line open to the dropships?"

"Yeah, but fat lot of good it's gonna do us under fire like this!" shouted Horner. "Ain't no way those pilots are dumb enough to bring them flying coffins into this shitstorm!"

"Tell them if they don't want to be shot by court-martial they'll come!"

"I'll pass that on, but I'm telling you those flyboys ain't that dumb."

"Just do it!"

Arcturus opened a link to the surviving Wraith pilot and issued her fresh orders. Thus far she had kept her altitude high to avoid any more missiles, but that was going to have to change if they were going to get out of this mess. Next he cycled through the comm channels until he hit upon Duke's.

"Edmund!" he said. "This is Mengsk."

"Where the hell are you?" demanded Duke. "We're getting slaughtered here!"

Quickly Arcturus outlined his plan to the besieged captain, who didn't like it, but was at least savvy enough to realize that it was the only way he was going to see another dawn.

"Okay, Mengsk, we'll do it your way. Duke out."

With his orders issued, Arcturus turned back to his marines and said, "When I give the word, we're going to move forward and form a corridor between us and Captain Duke. We'll babysit him back out of the complex so the dropships can pick us up. Got it?"

They got it, and he could see a fire ignite in their eyes at the thought of hitting back at these Kel-Morians. His earpiece chimed with a shrill buzz and he turned away from the battle.

"Everyone! Incoming!"

A sudden sonic boom announced the arrival of the Wraith as it roared overhead on a strafing run. A streaming cascade of laser fire tore through the middle of the camp in a storm of high-energy bolts, ripping through dozens of the green-armored soldiers and exploding amongst the trucks carrying the barrels of vespene gas.

One of the trucks detonated in a storm of razor-sharp fragments and spraying gas. Fires ripped through the enemy ranks and the shooting ceased as men burned and died. A thunderous salvo of air-bursting missiles hammered the enemy ranks, and bodies flew through the air as billowing pillars of smoke and flame erupted skyward.

"Now!" shouted Arcturus, and his marines broke from cover to rush toward Duke's stronghold. With

Arcturus leading the way, they formed a cordon of soldiers with gauss rifles blazing to keep the survivors' heads down. Arcturus saw an enemy soldier pick himself up from the ground, and shot him through the head with a burst of Impaler spikes.

More soldiers were climbing to their feet. Wraiths lacked a real punch when engaging ground targets, but the shock and noise of the attack had given them some breathing room. Duke and his men were pouring from the wrecked stronghold to join them, and under the covering fire of the few surviving goliaths, the Confederate force began to retreat from the ambush.

Something exploded next to Arcturus and he was slammed into the ground. His rifle spun away and warning lights flashed on the HUD of his visor. A long crack appeared in the plasteel, and the acrid, rotten-egg smell of sulfur clogged his nostrils.

He pushed himself to his knees, and felt a series of ringing hammer blows on his side. He fell back, seeing a pair of green-armored soldiers advancing toward him. They were good, disciplined soldiers and walked their spikes into him, keeping him pinned with the weight of fire. More red icons flashed up on his visor, warning of imminent armor penetration.

Then one of the enemy soldiers fell, his faceplate a mask of red where a stream of Impaler rounds had punched through in one sustained burst. Arcturus looked up to see Chun Leung standing over him, Mayumi pressed tight into his shoulder as he calmly aimed at the second soldier and put him down with another fiendishly aimed stream of spikes.

With the immediate threat neutralized, Leung slung his beloved rifle over his shoulder and offered Arcturus his hand.

"With respect, sir, this probably isn't a good time to be having a lie-down."

Arcturus wanted to laugh at the absurdity of this remark, but accepted Leung's hand and hauled himself to his feet. An explosion burst nearby, and no sooner had Arcturus gained his feet than he saw a strange look enter Chun Leung's eyes.

A froth of blood sprayed the inside of the man's visor.

"Leung!" cried Arcturus, now seeing the plate-sized piece of shrapnel embedded in the back of Leung's helmet. As Chun Leung dropped to his knees, he held his rifle out to Arcturus.

"Look after her," said Leung, and pitched over dead.

Arcturus watched Leung's helmet fill with blood, obscuring the man's features, horrified at the sudden, random nature of his death. He clutched Mayumi tightly to his chest, and with a final glance at Chun Leung's body, turned and ran after his retreating men.

"Captain Mengsk!" shouted a voice in his ear. "This is Lieutenant Wang in Wraith One Fox Three. Over."

"What is it, Lieutenant?" replied Arcturus, running backward and firing Leung's gauss rifle into the regrouping enemy.

"Your dropships are inbound, but you better get your asses moving. I'm picking up a hell of a lot of incoming contacts on your location. Ground and aerial units. Big stuff, too, battlecruiser-sized. Looks like these guys are playing for keeps."

"Understood," said Arcturus. "Can you give us any more cover?"

"I've got fuel and ammo for one more pass," said Lieutenant Wang.

"Then that will have to do. Mengsk out."

Arcturus found himself next to Edmund Duke, the man looking more angry than exhausted by the day's events. Duke looked over at him, glaring in unreasoning bitterness.

"You took your damn time!" was all he said.

Arcturus bit back an angry retort as the last of the goliaths finally toppled, its missiles cooking off in the heat of the explosion and skittering across the ice as they were released from exploding launchers. A vulture smashed into the ice after raking fire from a volley of Impalers blew out its engine. The hovercycle exploded into a thousand pieces as it hit the ice and its pilot bounced across the rocks, every limb in his body broken.

Arcturus hoped it wasn't the same pilot who'd helped them earlier.

The mining complex was ablaze from end to end and Arcturus was amazed the whole place hadn't gone up in one enormous explosion. Looking at the towering glacier above the complex, he saw dark shapes against the midnight blue of the sky.

Starships. Impossibly huge behemoths of neosteel descending from the skies on fiery jets like avenging angels. A fleet of ships was coming in over the glacier and Arcturus knew that the conflict between the Confederacy and the Kel-Morians had moved on from skirmishes and raids. This was something much, much bigger.

He caught up to the survivors of the attack as the howling, lurching forms of their dropships swooped down into the crater, their pilots braving the storm of enemy fire and the elements to rescue their men.

"Angels on our shoulders," said Arcturus, running toward the ramps of the dropships.

Arcturus stepped from the reeking, red-lit dropship almost as soon as it touched down on the gridded landing platform of Camp Hastings. Marines staggered from the bloody, smoky interiors to be met by medics and triage attendants. One dropship had crashed during the extraction, but as Arcturus looked along the line of survivors, he was disappointed to see that Duke hadn't been aboard it.

The camp was in an uproar, as though someone had run an electric current through the entire staff. Arcturus ripped off his helmet and took a deep breath. Even the foul smell of the air here wasn't as bad as that of the blood and sweat inside his helmet.

Chuck Horner, Yancy Gray, and Dia de Santo

marched down the ramp to stand next to him. Horner looked at the rifle Arcturus carried.

"Chun Leung?"

Arcturus shook his head.

"Damn," was all Chuck had to say about that.

Arcturus ran a hand through his hair, watching as SCVs went about the task of dismantling the base. Ground crews were already dragging refueling lines out to the dropships and armored marines were hauling silver steel trunks from the buildings to the large-scale flyers.

"What the hell's going on here?" asked Yancy.

"Looks like we're bugging out," said de Santo. "And in a hurry, too."

Arcturus had to agree with that assessment. Everywhere he looked, he saw military personnel breaking down the base, packing up what could be recovered and destroying what couldn't.

At the center of this controlled chaos, Arcturus saw Commander Fole, clad in a suit of powered combat armor and directing operations with his customary brusqueness. Arcturus slung Mayumi over his shoulder and marched up to him.

Fole saw him coming and nodded curtly. "Glad you made it out, Mengsk."

"Thank you, sir," replied Arcturus. "What's going on?"

"What does it look like? We're pulling out of Onuru Sigma."

"What? Why?"

"Because this conflict just got hotter'n hell," said

Fole. "General Mah Sakai's Kel-Morians are bringing in battlecruisers and brigade-strength forces to push us off this rock."

"Battlecruisers? Where did they get ships that large from?"

"Don't matter how they got them, they got them," snapped Fole as Edmund Duke trudged over to join them.

Fole planted his hands on his hips and said, "Now you're both here I can tell you the bad news. Word from on high is that everyone's term of service just got extended, so I sure hope neither of you was planning on seeing home soon."

"Extended?" said Arcturus. "Why?"

"Because, gentlemen, we are now officially at war with the Kel-Morian Combine," said Fole.

CHAPTER 12

ARCTURUS ADJUSTED THE DIALS AT THE SIDE OF the resonator, wiping a film of moisture from its screen as the green lines of the display shifted and danced. The gravimetric readings were fluctuating, and though he was sure there was a sizable deposit beneath his feet, the machines just weren't confirming what his instincts were telling him.

Looking up from the magnetic resonator, Arcturus cast his eyes over the dig site. Situated in one of the deep, mist-shrouded valleys of Pike's Peak, the cleared terrain was dominated by six tall drilling rigs that cored the dense rock at the base of the river canyon.

Battered hab-units and storage bins were scattered across the drier parts of the valley floor while men in SCVs worked the coring drills and chugging sifters worked night and day to separate what came up.

Which, so far, was absolutely nothing of worth.

Arcturus knew he was risking a lot with this venture,

having sunk most of the money he'd made in the last two mines into this hunk of rock out in the far reaches of the rim. But so far his intuition—which had served him so well in the past—hadn't uncovered the vast seam of valuable minerals he felt sure was buried far below the regolith. The shallower valleys were paying out for other prospectors, but so far this deep one had failed to yield any treasures.

He swore and slammed his palm against the side of the machine as a voice behind him said, "I keep telling you, Arcturus, there's nothing in this valley worth a damn."

"It's here, Dia," said Arcturus, looking up to see Diamond de Santo watching him, her hands planted squarely on her hips. "I can feel it."

Like Arcturus, de Santo wore the heavy-duty work clothes common to most outer rim prospectors: heavy-weave trousers, a quilted jacket with numerous pockets, and a battered hardhat. She wore her dark hair in dreadlocks now and had them pulled in a tight ponytail at the base of her skull.

De Santo bent down to examine the resonator as a jerking sine wave wobbled across its display. At last, Arcturus gave up on the magnetic resonator and stood up straight, wincing as sharp pain flared in his lower back.

"Too much bending over," said de Santo.

"You're probably right," agreed Arcturus, rubbing his hand over his grimy face and then through his hair. There were strands of gray in it now and he knew there was only going to be more of them in the future. He'd seen Angus on the UNN yesterday and his father's hair had gone almost completely silver, so he at least knew he'd likely not be bald when he got older.

"You ain't a young man no more," said de Santo, with a smile. "Nearly thirty."

"I'm only twenty-eight," said Arcturus. "I'm not over the hill quite yet."

"Yeah, but you can see it from here. Soon it'll be all downhill for you."

"You're in a cheery mood today, Dia. What's the matter?"

De Santo shrugged, waving a hand at the work going on around them. "You need to ask?"

"Of course. What's the matter?"

"Look around you, Arcturus," said de Santo. "We've been here two months and we ain't found a damn thing worth sticking around for. I know you think there's a big score in this valley, but there's nothing here."

"There is, Dia. I'm sure of it," said Arcturus. "I can feel it."

"Oh, you can feel it, can you? Then how come the geological mapping, the gravimetric analysis, and the rock assay reports all say the same thing? There ain't nothing here, and you're going to lose everything if we don't cut our losses and move on soon."

Arcturus rounded on de Santo. "*Our* losses? I seem to remember it being mostly my money that started this venture—bought all these machines on credit and hired the workers to use them. We made a little on that first venture, enough to pay back our creditors, and a lot on the following one. You've done well for an ex-marine, Dia, but don't think for a minute that you are taking the same risks as me."

"Damn, but you are one selfish son of a bitch, Arcturus Mengsk," snapped de Santo. "I put all my share of those two mines into this one, and I stand to lose as much as you. Man, I figured once we got out of the Marine Corps you'd become less of an arrogant asshole, but you're getting worse, you know that?"

"Thank you for your candor," said Arcturus. "Now was there anything specific you wanted or did you just come out here to berate me?"

"A little of both," said de Santo wearily.

"Fine, so you have expressed your opinion," said Arcturus. "What else was there?"

"There's a message arrived for you on the vidsys console. Figured you'd want to know."

Arcturus took a deep breath, fighting down his annoyance at de Santo's interruption, but knowing, deep down, that she might be right.

"Fine," he said at last. "Keep working the resonator, I'll go see what it is."

De Santo sat behind the surveying equipment's display as he set off toward the central hab-unit, where the crew gathered for meals and relaxation after the day's labors.

He turned back as he walked. "Any idea whom the message is from?" he asked, expecting it to be from either his mother or Dorothy.

"Signal origin code is Umoja," said de Santo.

"Umoja?"

"Yeah, some guy called Pasteur."

Arcturus shucked off his boots and jacket as he stepped into the entry hall of the hab-unit, letting the flow of dry air cool him down after the humidity of the dig site. As he hung up his hardhat, he saw that his palms were sweating and realized he was apprehensive.

What could Ailin Pasteur want with him after all these years?

It had been nearly a decade since he had seen the man, and their last words were not ones of abiding friendship. Was it perhaps Juliana using her father's console?

He hoped not. He'd taken Achton Feld's advice literally and made a clean break with his previous life when he'd left Korhal all those years ago. Through the hellish years of the Guild Wars, he'd not thought of Juliana or returned home on any of his infrequent periods of leave.

Instead, he had entered the Marine Corps study program, earning himself innumerable qualifications in prospecting and mineral exploration in preparation for the day he could stand before Brantigan Fole and resign his commission.

"Damn, but I hate to lose you, Mengsk," Fole had said when Arcturus slid his discharge papers across the commander's desk. "The Kel-Morians are on the run, and it's only a matter of time until they got no choice but to surrender. You sure you don't want to wait a while, son? You're a colonel now, but they're gonna be handing out promotions like party favors when this is all over. You could be a general if you wanted."

"No, sir," said Arcturus. "As appealing as that is, I've done my time and just want out."

"What you gonna do with yourself, Mengsk? You're a soldier. You were born to be a soldier. I don't think you've got it in you to be a civilian. Come on, son, the things we've done, the things we've seen . . . How can you go back to being an ordinary joe after that?"

"With respect, sir," said Arcturus. "It's *because* of the things we've done that I'm leaving."

"What's that supposed to mean?" said Fole, all civility gone.

Arcturus sighed. "I suppose I just don't believe in what we're fighting for anymore."

Fole had glared up at him and, without another word, signed his discharge papers.

Arcturus shook off the memory and pushed open the door to the rec room. Inside, conditions were spartan, the meager furniture battered from the many times it had been shipped around the rim from potential claim to potential claim. In one corner sat an old cine-viewer where everyone caught up on the latest broadcasts from the UNN or their favorite holo-drama. A number of mismatching chairs were gathered around a chipped Formica table, and a pool table—its felt faded and duct-taped—sat in the corner.

Beyond a bead curtain was a small kitchen unit, and a communal ablutions block lay at the far end of the quarters where Arcturus and a number of others slept and kept their few personal belongings.

Against the far wall was the vidsys console, a battered unit they'd bought secondhand and that had never quite functioned as the seller had promised. But it was serviceable enough, and Arcturus had enough technical savvy to keep it running and allow his prospecting crews some fleeting contact with their homes.

A blinking red light flashed on the grimy, oil-stained panel of the console and Arcturus set himself on the stool before it. Taking a moment to compose himself, he ran his hands through his hair once more and wiped the worst of the grime from his face as he always did before opening any communication. An unnecessary ritual, since the message would have been prerecorded, but Arcturus never liked to begin anything without looking presentable.

Satisfied, he punched the red button, and the screen fuzzed with static before a grainy image of a pair of three-pointed stars, locked together within a circle, flashed on the screen. For all his skill with electronics, Arcturus had never been able to get the color to work properly, but he knew that one of the stars was jet black, the other pure white.

This was the planetary icon of Umoja, and Arcturus took a deep breath as the image faded and was replaced with the face of Ailin Pasteur.

The man had aged, his face deeply lined and his hairline having receded alarmingly. Arcturus saw the years had been a burden to Ailin Pasteur, and that he carried their weight in his eyes.

"Hello, Arcturus," said Pasteur.

"Ailin," replied Arcturus, falling into the habit of most people when viewing such messages and thinking that the other person was actually on the other end of the link.

"It's been some time since we spoke, so I'll keep this brief."

The man might be looking aged, but his voice had lost none of its strength and Arcturus was quietly impressed as Pasteur continued.

"Your mother told me you'd left the Marine Corps and that you're working your way along the outer rim territories as a prospector. Well, you always said that's what you wanted to do, so I suppose that counts for something. But a lot of things have changed since you left your old life behind, Arcturus, things you need to face up to. I haven't contacted you before now, because Juliana asked me not to, but, like I said, things have changed."

Arcturus's brow furrowed at Pasteur's words. What had changed?

"I need you to come to Umoja," said Pasteur. "I know you probably won't want to, but I'm appealing to any shred of humanity you might have left in you. Come to Umoja, Arcturus. As soon as you can."

The image of Pasteur faded from the screen and Arcturus chewed his bottom lip as he considered what he'd just heard. He replayed the message twice more, searching for the meaning lurking behind Pasteur's words, but he could detect nothing beyond their face value.

He shook his head and went into the kitchen to fix a hot drink, and armed with a tin mug of steaming, military-grade coffee, he made his way to his quarters.

Something had changed, and it was something he was going to have to face up to . . .

What in the world could it be?

The room Arcturus had taken within the hab-unit gave a narrow window into his personality. He kept it as clean as was possible in a prospecting camp, which wasn't very clean at the best of times. A narrow cot bed sat against one wall, with a gunmetal gray footlocker at its end. Bundles of clothes in need of washing were piled at the foot of the bed and a number of disassembled pieces of electronic kit lay strewn on a collapsible table in the corner. The walls were largely bare steel, though one wall had a gleaming gauss rifle hung on cloth-wrapped bolts, and another boasted a collection of curling holographic images tacked to it.

In one of these images, Dorothy waved to him and blew him a kiss. The image had been captured on her thirteenth birthday and a cake bedecked with candles flickered in the foreground. Dorothy was fast becoming the apple of every Styrling lad's eye, with boys from all the moneyed families queuing up to court her, only to be sent packing by her father and told to come back when she turned twenty-one.

He reached out and touched the image, as he always did, and scanned the other images: one of him at the graduation ball with Juliana, another of being presented his colonel's stripes by Brantigan Fole, and one of him standing heroically atop the glittering seam of minerals at his first strike.

A final image displayed the entire Mengsk family, standing on the balcony of the Mengsk Skyspire. In this picture, Arcturus had just turned thirteen and his parents stood proudly behind him, his mother holding baby Dorothy in her arms. Styrling's silver towers spread out in back of them. It was the last time Arcturus could remember being truly happy.

He cleared a space on the bed and sat on the lumpy mattress with his back resting on the wall upon which hung the rifle.

Arcturus sipped his coffee and winced as it burned his tongue. He put the cup down to let it cool and reached up to lift the gauss rifle from the wall.

Mayumi. Chun Leung's weapon.

He'd been reluctant to part with it after he'd left the Marines, feeling that it would be somehow wrong to simply get rid of it or pass it on to someone else. He'd kept the weapon clean, and maintained it as best he could, but he knew it was a far cry from the immaculate condition it had formerly known.

Arcturus worked the action and began to disassemble the weapon for cleaning as he thought back to the soldiers who had served under him in the CMC. Despite the constant reminder of de Santo's presence, he hadn't consciously thought of Dominion section for some time, their faces growing hazy in the labyrinth of his memory.

Chun Leung and Toby Mercurio had fallen on Onuru Sigma, killed as much by Duke's headstrong foolishness as the Kel-Morian trap, and Yancy Gray died on Artesia Prime when their convoy had been attacked by a chittering wave of spider mines erupting from the ground. The lad's legs had been vaporized in the blast, and not even the skill of the combat medics could save him. He'd died screaming in the back of a truck sloshing with blood.

Only Chuck Horner and Dia de Santo had survived to reach the end of their extended service along with Arcturus. As Arcturus had expected, Dia mustered out and chose to accompany him to the outer rim territories and help him pursue his dreams of becoming a prospector. She had invested what little money she'd saved while still in the service and had become a pretty damn good prospector, with a nose for when a find was going to pay out and when it wasn't.

"What else am I gonna do? Go back to Tyrador IX and work for rich folks? Not this lifetime," she'd said when he'd once asked her why she'd followed him out of the Marine Corps. He suspected that wasn't the full story, but hadn't pressed her for details.

Chuck Horner had chosen a civilian life, and Arcturus was glad his second in command—who'd reached a captain's salary by the time he left—had come through the wars unscathed. Horner had married a woman he'd met on leave and they planned to start a new life together.

Arcturus had shaken Chuck's hand and wished him luck.

"Thanks, sir," said Chuck as they parted on the docks above the gas giant Dylar IV. "I reckon we could all do with a little extra luck now. My own self, I done believe I used a whole lot more'n I could expect to see during this war, so any extra you got's gratefully received. Me'n Carla are gonna head out to Mar Sara, see if we can't make a life for ourselves. She's a bit young and idealistic, but I guess we all were once."

Arcturus never saw Chuck Horner again.

Captain Emillian had, of course, remained with the Marine Corps, but Arcturus had no idea what had become of her since his departure. Despite her talk of hunting handsome doctors, Arcturus knew Emillian was a career soldier and would no doubt see out her days in the military, either dying on some nameless battlefield or mustering out on retirement.

The odds were vastly in favor of the former, but if anyone could buck those odds, it was Angelina Emillian.

Arcturus and Dia de Santo had taken a ship out to the outer rim territories and set up their prospecting and mining enterprise, taking jobs the bigger outfits didn't like the look of for one reason or another, and had quickly made a name for themselves as skillful and dedicated players. Their first strike had enabled them to clear their debts and acquire bigger, more powerful drilling machines, as well as more advanced survey equipment.

Their second strike had been considerably larger and netted them a hell of a payday, but interference from both the Kel-Morian Combine and the Confederate Exploration Corps had become too onerous, and Arcturus had sold the claim for a small fortune and headed farther out into space.

The worlds at the very edge of the outer rim were less frequented and offered the potential for even bigger unclaimed strikes, but by the same token, they were more isolated and vulnerable to piratical bands or heavily armed competition.

With the money they'd made in their second strike, Arcturus and de Santo had bought an old starship named the *Kitty Jay* and filled her with fresh equipment, skilled workers, SCVs, and even a handful of ex-marines for protection. They had come to Pike's Peak on the strength of prospectors' tales and an old assayer's report Arcturus had found buried within the data architecture of a forgotten Confederate database.

De Santo had balked at risking everything on such scant information, but Arcturus had been insistent, and his instincts had never been proved wrong—yet. For as had been pointed out so bluntly to him not twenty minutes ago, they had found nothing of worth here, and unless they hit paydirt soon, their dwindling capital would soon be exhausted.

It was a depressing thought and Arcturus pushed it aside as he worked an oiled rag along the length of the gauss rifle. The weapon was as clean as it was going to get and he began reassembling it, wondering if he'd be called to use it to defend this claim.

The Guild Wars—as the UNN snappily called it— was entering its fourth year and from what Arcturus had seen of the fighting, he knew that Brantigan Fole was right.

The Kel-Morians were going to lose.

It remained to be seen what that meant for smaller outfits like his, but Arcturus suspected that it wouldn't take long for the Confederacy to turn its attention to the unclaimed resources of the outer rim.

Arcturus snapped the last piece of the weapon into place and clicked the magazine home.

He laid the rifle across his knees and leaned his head back against the wall, looking over at the holographs opposite him. He looked at the image of Juliana and himself smiling for the holocam and smiled at the memory, wondering what Ailin Pasteur could want with him.

It likely wouldn't be anything to do with his family or he'd have heard from his mother or Dorothy.

Perhaps something had happened to Juliana, but then why would Pasteur turn to Arcturus?

He didn't yet know whether he'd even heed the request to travel to Umoja. He owed Ailin and his daughter nothing and had no obligation to make such a journey, but a nagging curiosity gnawed at the back of his mind.

His train of thought was interrupted as he heard running footsteps along the corridor outside and the sound of Diamond de Santo calling his name. He lifted the rifle and placed it beside him on the bed as de Santo burst into his room, her eyes alight with excitement and the breath heaving in her lungs.

"Holy hell, Arcturus, you need to get your ass outside. Now!"

"What is it? What's going on?"

"You were right," gasped de Santo. "Goddammit it, but you were right. It's unbelievable."

"Slow down, Dia," said Arcturus, swinging his legs off the bed and standing up.

De Santo threw herself at him, embracing him in a crushing bear hug.

Arcturus prized her grip from around his neck and held her at arm's length. "Listen to me, Dia. Slow down. What are you talking about? What's unbelievable?"

She took several calming breaths before speaking, but Arcturus saw the thrill in her eyes and felt an electric sense of excitement pass between them.

"The claim," said de Santo. "You were right—there's minerals right below us, but we couldn't see them.

Turns out the resonators were getting some backscatter from a higher stratum of banded ironstone."

"Are you sure?" demanded Arcturus. "Have you checked?"

"Yeah, one of the drills brought up a core sample that showed a layer of magnetite and shale. Once I adjusted the resonator to filter that out . . . Oh, man, you gotta see it. It's the biggest deposit I've ever seen. We're rich, Arcturus!"

"Okay, you need to calm down, Dia."

"No way, man. This is big, Arcturus. I never even heard of a seam this huge; it's still gonna be paying out when our grandkids are drawing their pensions!"

Four days later and the party still hadn't stopped.

If anything, de Santo had underplayed the scale of the find, and with the resonator properly calibrated to reach beyond the banded ironstone layer, there seemed no end to the length, breadth, and depth of the mineral seam. With Arcturus's confirmation of the veracity of the find, and the first samples brought to the surface, the assembled workers and marines had broken out the alcohol and the party had begun in earnest.

Heavier drilling rigs were even now being built to more quickly exploit the enormous find, and Arcturus knew that this strike was going to make him a very rich man indeed. Richer than any prospector in the history of the Confederacy had ever managed after a lifetime of exploration and digging.

The rec room was filled with people: miners,

assayers, and soldiers. The heavier drilling rigs were due to go online tomorrow and the SCVs had made a good start on the construction of an extraction refinery, but tonight everyone was relaxing. This was likely to be the only time off anyone was going to get in the next few months as they established a more permanent facility on the claim, and everyone was making the most of it.

Arcturus sat on one of the chairs around the table, listening to the excited banter of his staff and letting them congratulate him on the intuitive instinct that had led them to this windfall. Everyone expected to get rich from this find, and for once it looked as though that might actually be the case.

Bottles of alcohol were passed around and toasts raised to future fortunes. Arcturus listened to his men's grand plans about how they were going to spend their money and took a proffered mug of lethally strong hooch.

Dia de Santo sat next to him, smiling broadly and flicking through the few channels they received on the cine-viewer. Various images flickered in the corner of the room, adverts mainly, but Arcturus sat up as a familiar face ghosted into focus onto the projection.

He read the caption that scrolled along the bottom of the image and said, "Wait," as he saw de Santo reaching to change the channel. "Turn it up."

The speakers crackled and spat, but eventually Arcturus heard his father's voice, though the sound of revelry in the rec room all but drowned him out.

"Quiet!" barked Arcturus, and the room was instantly silenced.

He stood and walked over to stand right in front of the viewer as the caption repeated across the bottom of the screen.

Martial Law on Korhal as Senator Angus Mengsk Declares War on the Confederacy! Tarsonis Promises Stern Measures of Retaliation!

On the viewer, Angus stood addressing a thousands-strong crowd from a podium erected on what Arcturus recognized as the Martial Field. A sea of adoring faces stared up at his father as he held forth on his favorite subject, the rampant corruption of the Confederacy. Though the UNN had muted his words, Angus's fist hammered the air as he spoke, his call to arms answered by deafening cheers from the crowd.

Arcturus saw his mother and Dorothy standing proudly behind his father as the announcer spoke disgustedly of planetwide riots, the capture of the UNN tower, and attacks on Confederate outposts that had seen thousands dead.

The view rotated between Confederate barracks on fire, vast crowds of people on the streets with brightly painted banners, and Angus shouting to the gathered followers like the fiery demagogue of some ancient fire-and-brimstone faith.

Was this the reason Ailin Pasteur had wanted him to travel to Umoja?

What did Pasteur know that the UNN wasn't reporting?

"Stern measures of retaliation," he said. What did *that* mean?

Arcturus turned from the cine-viewer and marched down the corridor to his room. He pushed open the door and began packing a bag, stuffing in the few clean clothes he had left.

Dia de Santo pushed into his room seconds later, her face betraying her worry. "What are you doing, Arcturus?"

"I'm leaving," said Arcturus. "Isn't it obvious?"

"Tell me you're joking. You can't leave now!"

"Just watch me."

"We're on the verge of digging out the biggest mineral strike this side of the Long Sleep and you wanna leave? Damn it, Arcturus, we need you here. *I* need you here."

"Don't worry, Dia," said Arcturus, reaching out and putting a hand on her shoulder. "I'll be back soon. I'm going to take the *Kitty Jay* to Umoja, but I *will* be back, I promise."

"Umoja? Why the hell do you need to go there?"

"I need to see Ailin Pasteur," said Arcturus. "Then I need to make sure my family is safe."

Arcturus stepped through a haze of steam and oilsmoke onto the surface of Umoja. Or at least onto the heat-resistant ceramic landing platform that had just descended a few hundred meters into the surface of Umoja. A drizzle of moisture clung to his skin like humidity and the heat bleeding from the *Kitty Jay*'s engines warmed the air.

Traveling between worlds always made Arcturus uneasy. The unknown dimensions of deep space and all that might lurk in its vast emptiness fired his imagination with images of as-yet unknown aliens and piratical corsairs.

As master of his own destiny, the placing of his fate in the hands of another, even one as qualified as Morley Sanjaya—the pilot he'd hired when he'd bought the *Kitty Jay*—unsettled him greatly. Though he could not fly a starship, Arcturus felt sure that if he were to try, he would master it quickly enough.

And make better time than the two weeks it had taken them to get here . . .

Ailin Pasteur's private landing platform was empty and its underground walls were a mixture of rock and metal, scorched black by the comings and goings of orbital craft. A flashing amber light rotated above a shuttered blast door, and a low buzz of static poured from a speaker recessed in the wall.

The light flicked off and the blast door began to rumble upward.

A squad of men clad in combat suits of pale blue plate and carrying gauss rifles marched out onto the platform, followed by a man wearing a dark suit and a foul-weather cloak.

Ailin Pasteur.

The last time Arcturus had seen Pasteur had

been at the Close of Session of the Korhal Senate, where the man had berated him for how he had just treated his mother. With the benefit of hindsight, Arcturus now accepted that his actions might have been a little rash that day, which bought Pasteur some goodwill.

Pasteur stopped at the base of the steps that led up to the landing platform.

"Hello, Ailin," said Arcturus, slinging his suit-bag over his shoulder. "I'd say good morning or good evening, but I don't know which it is."

"It's evening, Arcturus," said Pasteur. "Welcome to Umoja."

Though the words were said with formal politeness, Arcturus sensed the rancor behind them. Was this some charade for the soldiers standing at Pasteur's back?

"Thank you," said Arcturus, stepping down from the platform and waving a hand in the direction of the opened blast door. "Shall we?"

Pasteur nodded and turned on his heel, clicking his fingers at the soldiers, who quickly followed, marching in lockstep behind them.

Pasteur led him into a series of rock corridors that looked as though they had been bored through with fusion cutters. Arcturus noted the quality and type of the rock, smiling as he found himself calculating the density of the rock and rate per hour that it could be excavated.

Walking alongside him, Pasteur saw the smile and said, "Something funny?"

"Not really," said Arcturus. "I still have my prospecting head on. Look, tell me what this is all about, Ailin. My outfit's just struck a huge mineral deposit and we need to get our operation up and running before the Confederate Exploration Corps gets wind of it. So come on, what's going on?"

"It's better if you see for yourself," said Pasteur.

Arcturus sighed. "If this has something to do with my family, then I want to know now."

"Oh, it has something to do with your family all right," snapped Pasteur, "but I promised I wouldn't say anything. And I am a man of my word."

This last comment appeared to be particularly barbed, and Arcturus wondered what he had done to deserve such animosity. But Pasteur would not be drawn on the subject and Arcturus left him to his silence as they made their way deeper into the complex. They arrived at an elevator and traveled to the surface within its gleaming, silver-steel interior.

The elevator emerged into the wide hallway of a sizable dwelling, not unlike that of the Mengsk summer villa. The walls were white marble and the floor was a mixture of gleaming hardwood and expensive-looking rugs. An iron screw stair led back down into the rock and a wide set of carpeted stairs led up toward a second story.

A shining dome pierced with panels of stained glass

surmounted the hallway, and a chandelier of flickering candles floated beneath its curve.

"Very nice," said Arcturus as Ailin Pasteur led him toward a thick wooden door.

Pasteur opened the door and indicated that Arcturus should step through.

Arcturus swept past and entered a long room set with expensive furniture and a crackling fire that burned beneath a wide mantel. The smell of hot coffee and sweet fruits hung in the air, and Arcturus saw Juliana sitting in a large chair beside the fireplace.

She looked up as he entered and her face transformed, surprisingly, with genuine pleasure at the sight of him. In the intervening years, Juliana had grown up. Features that were girlish and coquettish when he'd last seen her were now womanly and strong. Juliana had lost nothing of her figure, and when she stood and straightened her dress, Arcturus was again reminded of the poise and grace of his mother.

Arcturus stepped farther into the room, then pulled up short as he saw a young boy sitting on the floor in front of the fire. Dressed in dark trousers and a matching shirt, his shoulder-length golden hair was pulled back in a small ponytail. Arcturus was no expert in such matters, but he guessed the boy's age at around six or seven.

The boy sat in the midst of a pile of colored plastic bricks, built as though he had decided to construct a ruined city. Tiny toy soldiers were scattered through these ruins and Arcturus watched the child move them while making shooting noises with his mouth.

"We have company," said Juliana, and the child looked up.

Arcturus received a dazzling smile from the boy— and felt like he'd been kicked in the stomach.

Startlingly handsome, the child was blessed with high cheekbones, wide gray eyes, creamy skin, and just the hint of a hawkish curve to his nose.

"What's going on here?" hissed Arcturus as Ailin Pasteur shut the door behind him.

"Valerian," said Juliana. "Say hello to your father."

Book 3.

Valerian

CHAPTER 13

VALERIAN'S EYES FLICKERED AND AILIN PASTEUR smiled as he watched the lad fight the tiredness that threatened to overcome him. It had been a long day and emotions had been running high as they awaited the arrival of Arcturus's ship. His grandson had been excited enough for all of them, which wasn't surprising given the inflated stories Juliana had filled his head with over the last seven years.

Ailin sat on the side of Valerian's bed, smiling as his grandson blinked furiously at the onset of sleep.

"But I'm not tired, Grandpa," said Valerian. "Why can't I speak to my dad? I've waited all day for him."

"Then one more night's sleep won't hurt, will it? He'll still be here in the morning."

Ailin dearly hoped that was true, for if he'd learned anything about Arcturus from speaking with Angus and Katherine, it was that their son was inclined to be capricious when it came to remaining in one place for any length of time.

"He's just like I imagined him," said Valerian, and Ailin Pasteur fought to keep the worry from his face. Juliana had built up the boy's expectations of his father since his birth, despite Ailin's warnings to her not to do so. It was a source of constant bafflement to Ailin how Juliana could still hold a torch for Arcturus, given how terribly he had treated her—albeit part of that mistreatment was through ignorance of Valerian's existence.

He still remembered the day Juliana had told him she was pregnant. Pride and joy were mixed with anger and fear as he realized that Juliana wasn't going to tell Arcturus that he was to be a father. To this day he couldn't understand or dent her reasoning, founded as it was on years of adoration from afar. They had argued furiously about her refusal to tell Arcturus of her pregnancy, those arguments only ending when Juliana had threatened to leave and never allow him to see her child should he so much as breathe a word to any of the Mengsks.

Faced with such an ultimatum, what could any father do but accede?

In Juliana's worldview, Arcturus had things he had to do on his quest for greatness, and she couldn't distract him until the time was right. Now that Arcturus had left the military, that time had apparently arrived.

Though it had been galling to see his daughter give up on her nascent legal career in favor of impending motherhood, Juliana was happy and he couldn't deny the pleasure he took from seeing that happiness.

When Valerian had been born, it seemed her joy was complete. Ailin adored the boy—but then, Valerian was easy to love, blessed as he was with his mother's grace and his father's strong features. As Valerian had grown, he began to display a quick wit and a devilish streak that Ailin knew only too well from his trips to Korhal and previous encounters with the Mengsk family.

Only once or twice had Ailin sensed his daughter's regret at her abandonment of her career, but all she had to do was look into Valerian's beautiful face and it was swept away in a rush of adoration.

After the sudden and shocking introduction to his son, Arcturus had gone quite pale and, for once, been lost for a scathing retort. A master of reading people's emotions, Ailin had seen the anger building in Arcturus and whisked Valerian away from the ugly drama that was no doubt unfolding below.

Valerian had protested, but Ailin had learned to be the firm hand in Valerian's life that his mother most certainly was not.

"Is Dad going to live with us now?" asked Valerian, breaking into Ailin's thoughts.

"I don't know, Val," said Ailin, unwilling to sugar his response; Valerian's mother did enough of that. "He's just arrived and I don't know what he's going to do."

"Mum wants him to stay."

"I expect you're right, but try not to worry about it. Get some sleep, eh?"

"Where's my dad been?" asked Valerian with the relentless curiosity of a child.

"He's been in the army, Valerian."

"Fighting bad men? Or aliens?"

Aliens. It always came back to aliens with Valerian. Ever since Ailin had—under protest—read him a bedtime story about invading creatures from another world, the boy had been fascinated by the idea that other life-forms might once have existed (or might still exist) somewhere in the galaxy.

Ailin and Juliana had taken Valerian as a young child—under armed escort, of course—to the far canyons and riverbeds of Umoja in search of relics of those lost civilizations. Undaunted by his singular lack of success, Valerian had nevertheless excavated a host of "ancient" artifacts—oddly contoured rocks, petrified bark, and the shells of dead creatures he proudly claimed to be the remains of aliens.

"No, Valerian, I don't think your father was fighting aliens."

"So who was he fighting?"

"That's kind of hard to answer," said Ailin, trying to think of a way to explain where Valerian's father had been and what he had been doing without upsetting the youngster. As much as Ailin hated the institution of the Confederate Marine Corps, he did not want to rob Valerian of his idealized image of his father before he'd even met the man properly and formed his own opinion.

Arcturus would disabuse the boy of any heroic notions soon enough anyway, he thought.

"I bet my dad's a war hero," said Valerian. "I bet he killed hundreds of men."

"I'm sure he did," said Ailin.

"But he's not a soldier anymore, is he?"

"No, not anymore."

"So what does he do now?" asked Valerian. "Mum just tells me he's doing great work, but I don't really know what that means."

"I'm told he's been a prospector out on the fringe worlds since he left the army," said Ailin. "Quite a good one, too, by all accounts."

"Is he rich?"

"I'm not sure, but from the sound of it, I think he might be soon."

"Good," declared Valerian. "I want to be rich too."

Ailin smiled. "You know, we're not exactly poor here, Valerian."

"I know, but I want to find aliens when I grow up and I'm going to need a lot of money to do that, aren't I?"

"I suspect you might," Ailin said, laughing. "You'll need a fleet of spaceships, the best archaeologists money can buy, and all sorts of tools."

"Oh, I won't need archaeologists. I want to do the digging myself."

"Really?"

"Of course," said Valerian. "If anyone's going to find

aliens I don't want it to be anyone except me. Where would the fun be in that?"

"I suppose you're right; I hadn't thought of that," said Ailin, pride and love filling his heart at the excitement in Valerian's face. "Now, go to sleep, Val. You've got a big day tomorrow."

"Yes . . . ," said Valerian, pulling the covers tightly around him with a contented smile as his eyes drifted shut. "I'm going to meet my dad tomorrow."

Ailin Pasteur rose from the bed and turned off the light beside Valerian's bed. He made his way to the door and slipped from his grandson's room.

"Yes," he said. "You're going to meet your father. I just hope he's all you hope for."

Arcturus still couldn't quite believe it. He was a father . . . ?

He was a father?

How was the first question that leapt to mind, swiftly followed by a mental kick to the backside. *How do you think it happened, idiot?*

He wanted to say something, but the words wouldn't come. He wanted to deny it, but the cast of the boy's countenance was unmistakable. Every curve of feature was that of a Mengsk and the analytical part of Arcturus's brain had seen that the boy was a handsome lad indeed, obscenely gifted with the best genes his parents had to offer.

No sooner had Ailin led the boy away than Juliana said something.

Arcturus didn't hear it.

His head was filled with the white noise of a million questions and the rush of blood around his body. The crackling of the fire was like the roar of a great inferno, and he felt the air in his lungs rasping along his throat and from his mouth.

Juliana rose from her chair with a pained expression and crossed the room toward him with her arms outstretched. Without thinking, he took her in his arms and held her as she rested her head on his shoulder and whispered things he couldn't understand.

He stood like that for several moments before the reality of the situation washed over him in a tsunami of anger and betrayal. Arcturus took hold of Juliana's arms and pushed her away, as though she were contaminated with some vile plague.

"I have a *son*?" he said, striding away from her.

"Yes," said Juliana, smiling broadly. "You have a wonderful son. His name is Valerian."

"A good name," said Arcturus. "Strong."

Juliana nodded. "I knew you'd be pleased with that. It suits him too."

Arcturus *was* pleased with the name, but more pressing concerns needed to be addressed.

"Why the hell didn't you tell me?" he said. "You kept this from me for all these years? Why would you do that, Juliana? Why?"

She recoiled from his anger, and he saw the fear in her eyes. Normally such behavior would have repulsed him, but now he relished it, wanting to hurt her for the insult of keeping a secret from him. And what a secret . . .

"Answer me, damn you!" snapped Arcturus when she turned away from him and stepped close to the fireplace. She held on to the mantelpiece and coughed into a handkerchief before turning to face him.

"I thought you'd be pleased," she said.

"Pleased? That you've lied to me and kept the fact that I . . . that we have a child together? What the hell did you expect? That I'd be pleased with this? That I'd be happy to know I was a father just when my life is taking off the way I've always dreamed?"

"That's why I couldn't tell you before now!" cried Juliana. "All those great plans and dreams you told me—I knew I couldn't get in the way until you were ready to realize them. I know you just joined the Marine Corps to punish your father, and I couldn't tell you about Valerian while you were fighting in the Guild Wars."

"Why not?" said Arcturus, spying a drinks tray on the sideboard and pouring himself a hefty measure of something amber and pungent.

"Knowing you had a son would have made your life so much harder."

Arcturus took a belt of strong liquor. "What are you talking about?"

"I didn't want you thinking of anything except staying alive, Arcturus. I didn't want to do anything that might distract you and get you killed. But now you're out of the military and I asked my father to keep tabs on how you were doing."

Arcturus poured himself another glass of liquor, deciding that it was some kind of brandy. He hoped it was expensive and old.

"If you've been keeping tabs on me then you'll know we just hit the biggest mineral find I've ever heard of. My mining crew are working it as we speak, and I should be with them. I'm on the brink of achieving everything I wanted and you drop this in my lap. Well, thank you *very* much for that, Juliana. Your timing is exquisite!"

A fire flashed to life in her eyes. "You don't think I had dreams too, Arcturus? Remember I had just started with that law firm as a paralegal? I was doing well there, and I had a promising career there until I fell pregnant."

"Not a very progressive firm if they fired you for something like that," said Arcturus. "You should have sued."

"They didn't fire me, thank you very much," snapped Juliana. "They wanted me to come back after Valerian was born, but I wanted to devote myself to our child."

"Very commendable," said Arcturus, pouring a third drink. He could already feel the spikes of his anger being worn smooth by its potency.

"Valerian is very like you, Arcturus. He's brilliant, charming, and utterly determined in everything he does. You'll like him, I know you will."

Arcturus brushed that thought aside, still reeling

from the idea of having a young son and the fact that he didn't know him at all. Seven years of the boy's life had passed and until now, neither he nor Valerian had ever laid eyes on the other.

"Does my father know? My mother? Dorothy?"

Juliana shook her head. "No, I wanted to tell you first. It wasn't my place to tell your family about Valerian."

"True," said Arcturus, lapsing into silence for a moment as a thought occurred to him.

"What is it?" asked Juliana, seeing a dawning realization in his face.

"It was on Tyrador IX, wasn't it?" he said.

"Can you remember any other time you slept with me?"

"Of course not. Don't be so melodramatic; I was thinking aloud," said Arcturus. "Give me a damn moment to get my thoughts straight. You can't spring something like this on me and expect me to be rational just yet."

He reached for another drink, then thought the better of it. He replaced the glass and began to pace the length of the room, running a hand through his hair as he did so.

"Rational?" said Juliana. "What is there to be rational about? You have a son and you have a chance to get to know him. To get to know me again. We can be a family now."

"A family?" said Arcturus, halting before her. "I . . . is that what you want of me? To leave everything behind and come and live on Umoja with you and the boy?"

"His name is Valerian."

"I know what his name is, Juliana."

"Then why are you afraid to say it?" she countered. "Are you afraid that if you say his name you'll have to acknowledge him? That he'll become real to you?"

"No, of course not, don't be absurd."

"Then why won't you say his name?"

"Valerian," said Arcturus. "Valerian, Valerian, Valerian. There, are you happy now?"

Juliana slapped him across the cheek and he had to restrain the urge to slap her back. He remembered a similarly stinging blow delivered by his mother. In hindsight, he'd realized he'd deserved that one, and, he was forced to admit, he probably deserved this one too.

"I'm sorry, Juliana," he said at last. "But I can't leave everything I'm building to come and play happy family with you. I just can't."

"Then what? You're just going to leave like you always do? Run away instead of face up to things?"

"I don't run from things," warned Arcturus.

"Of course you do," said Juliana. "You joined the Marine Corps to run away from your father and you ran away from me just when we were getting close. And now you're going to run away from your son. Your heir."

Juliana's words hit home like hammer blows as he saw the truth of them. Rather than facing up to the events that stood at the crossroads of his life, he had turned from them and chosen the path of least resistance. Would this be another such moment?

Arcturus stood on the brink of everything he had ever wanted, but what good was any of it if it was built on foundations of shifting sand? Perhaps now *was* the time to take stock of his life and look to his legacy. After all, his father had been only a couple of years older than Arcturus was now when he had been handed his son.

"Very well, Juliana," he said at last. "I'll stay. I will talk to the . . . to Valerian. I'll get to know him and he will be my heir, as you say."

She threw herself at him and wrapped her arms around him once more. "I'm so happy. I knew that once you saw Valerian you'd want to be part of his life."

Again, Arcturus prized Juliana from him, though with less force than the last time.

"Don't let's get ahead of ourselves now," he said. "I said I'll get to know him, but I still don't know if I'm ready to just give up on everything I've built."

"I'm not asking you to," said Juliana, cupping his chin in her hands and pressing her face close to his. "Can't you see that? You don't have to give anything up. We can all be together. All of us. We can have everything we ever dreamed of. All those grand plans you told me over the years? They're coming to fruition now. Right now. You just have to want to see it."

Arcturus smiled.

Perhaps Juliana's words had merit or perhaps it was the alcohol flowing around his system, but whatever it was, Arcturus was surprised to find the idea didn't horrify him.

Perhaps they *could* be a normal family after all.

Arcturus awoke with a thick head and a brief dislocation as he wondered where he was. He was refreshed and his limbs felt gloriously rested. The prefabricated crew quarters of a mining claim or the cramped confines of a starship weren't exactly conducive to uninterrupted sleep, and he'd forgotten just how nice it was to spend a night in a soft bed. He stretched and rolled his neck on the pillow, enjoying the warmth and letting the aches of the last six months ease from his bones.

He smiled, and then the blissful forgetfulness of waking was replaced with the cold, hard remembrances of the previous night's events as everything came rushing back.

Juliana.

Valerian.

His son . . .

The gentle ease of morning fled from his body and he pushed himself upright, looking around the wood-paneled room, with its tasteful furniture, heavy curtains, and discreetly situated technology. The functionality of the room was pure Umoja, and the sliver of dusty orange sky he could see through the window only confirmed it.

Arcturus swung his legs from the bed, his earlier desire to wallow in the thickness and warmth of the covers having evaporated once he remembered the purpose of Ailin Pasteur's summons. At least now he understood the source of the man's less-than-friendly welcome.

Quickly and without fuss, Arcturus cleaned himself in the sonic shower, a fine, elegantly designed machine. The brand wasn't one owned by the Old Families; such independence was typical of most homes on Umoja, suspected Arcturus. It was, little to his surprise, efficient and thorough, vibrating the particles of sweat and dead skin from him without peeling off another few layers of skin for good measure.

He shaved with a similarly efficient sonic razor and combed his hair, then dressed in a dark gray suit with knee-height boots. The suit had been cleaned and pressed, the boots polished to a mirror sheen. Ailin Pasteur's servants were thorough, that was for sure.

"Time to face the music," he said, and left the room, making his way along a marble-faced corridor that opened out into the entrance hall he'd arrived in last night. The door to the sitting room was open and Arcturus could hear voices coming from within. He recognized one as belonging to Ailin Pasteur, and entered the room.

Sure enough, the Umojan ambassador was sitting in the same chair his daughter had occupied the night before. He was talking to one of his functionaries, who took notes on a personal console with a wand stylus.

Pasteur, his face an unreadable mask, looked up as Arcturus entered.

"Good morning, Ailin," said Arcturus.

"Indeed," replied Pasteur. "You slept well?"

"You have no idea," said Arcturus. "After nearly a year of sleeping on top of rocks or camp beds, I could have slept anywhere, but, yes, I was most comfortable, thank you."

"Hungry?"

"Ravenous," said Arcturus.

Pasteur nodded to his servant and the man bowed before withdrawing from the room and shutting the door behind him.

"Where's Juliana?" asked Arcturus.

"Outside with Valerian. Digging up the bottom of the garden, no doubt."

"You don't have groundskeepers?"

Ailin smiled, though there was no warmth to it. "I do, but that's not what I meant. Valerian's quite the budding archaeologist. He loves digging in the earth almost as much as another young man I remember."

"Maybe he takes after me," said Arcturus.

"I rather think he does."

"You sound disappointed."

"No, just sad for you that you've missed so much of Valerian's life. The years when Juliana was growing up were some of the happiest I've ever had, but you'll never know that simple joy."

"Hardly my fault, Ailin," pointed out Arcturus. "I didn't know he even existed."

"Would it have made any difference if you had?"

"Honestly? I don't know. I am not blind to my own faults, such as they are, but I said I would stay for a time and get to know the boy. And I'll make sure he has the best of everything."

"We can provide for him," said Pasteur. "I am a wealthy man, Arcturus."

"I know that, but Valerian is *my* son, and I will provide for him. I'll not be beholden to any man, Ailin, and I'll not be accepting charity. Even if this claim I've found is worth only a fraction of what I think it's worth, I'll never need to worry about money again. Therefore, neither will Valerian."

"Very well," said Ailin. "That's good to hear."

Arcturus heard the simmering resentment in Pasteur's voice and said, "You can't hold me responsible for not being here. Juliana never told me of Valerian."

"I know that, but whether she never told you or not, the simple fact remains that you weren't. You didn't see her raise Valerian on her own, you didn't hear her cry in the night, and you missed everything a father is supposed to be part of. It's hard for me to look at you and not pity you for all you've missed."

"Don't pity me, Ailin," said Arcturus. "I'll not have your pity."

"Very well, not pity, but regret. Juliana should have had you next to her through all this, but she didn't. And it wasn't because she never told you about Valerian, it was because you shut her out to pursue your own dreams. We'll never know, but I suspect if Juliana had told you before now, you would have turned your back on her and the baby. Am I wrong?"

"Probably not," admitted Arcturus. "But I'm here now, aren't I?"

"Yes, and that's the only reason I'm maintaining a degree of civility to you. I know you, Arcturus Mengsk. You are a selfish man who I believe cares nothing for anyone else. I think you could be a very dangerous man, but you are the father of my grandson and I'm willing to give you another chance not to disappoint me."

"You're too kind."

"I'm serious," snapped Pasteur, and Arcturus was struck by the vehemence in the man's voice. "You have responsibilities now and if you fail to live up to them, I'll make sure you never see Valerian again."

"That sounds like a threat."

"It is."

"Well, at least we understand each other."

Further discussion was halted as Pasteur's servant reentered the room bearing a silver platter laden with a steaming pot of sweet tea and a plate of pastries, cheese, and cold meat. The man held the platter next to Arcturus's chair and slender metallic legs descended from the platter's base.

Pasteur thanked the man as he left the room.

"These are dangerous times, Arcturus," said Pasteur once the servant was gone. "Battle lines are changing—old wars are drawing to a close and new ones are beckoning."

"Are you talking about the Guild Wars?"

"The Guild Wars are over," said Pasteur. "The Confederacy knows it and the Kel-Morians know it, they just haven't accepted it yet. The Confederacy's too powerful, and if the last shots haven't been fired yet, rest assured they will be soon. And then the Confederacy will be looking for its next target."

"And what do you think that will be? Umoja?"

"Perhaps," said Pasteur, "but there are steps being taken to protect Umoja."

"What steps?"

"Steps I'd prefer not to talk about just yet," said Pasteur.

Arcturus wondered what Pasteur meant, but didn't press the point. If the man wanted to tell his secrets, he'd tell them in his own time.

"Have you spoken to your family recently?" asked Pasteur.

Wondering at the abrupt change of topic, Arcturus said, "Not for a while, no, but that's one of the reasons I came. I saw the broadcast on the UNN about the declaration of martial law."

"Yes, things have become very dangerous on Korhal."

Arcturus poured some tea and helped himself to a cinnamon-topped pastry.

"So tell me what's been happening," he said. "I've watched the UNN reports of bombings, terrorist atrocities, and attacks on Confederate militia, but I imagine they're either wildly exaggerated or half-truths. And every communication I've had from mother is so cryptic as to be unintelligible."

"She's being careful," said Pasteur, pouring himself a cup of tea. "Confederate intelligence agents are monitoring everything that comes off Korhal, especially transmissions from someone in your family. The Skyspire and the summer villa are almost certainly under all-round surveillance."

"I know you and my father were behind most of the attacks against the Confederacy on Korhal, but are you really that dangerous to them?"

"More than you realize," said Pasteur. "Korhal is one of the most important worlds in the Confederacy, a model of what the earliest colonists hoped to build in this sector. For decades, the Old Families trumpeted Korhal as the jewel in their crown, an exemplar world that proudly displayed all they could achieve. They thought Korhal's example would be what would persuade Moria and Umoja to join the Confederacy, but they were wrong. All it did was show us the yoke of tyranny ever more strongly, and now that Korhal's in rebellion, they're terrified that if their most treasured colony could turn against them, others might be tempted to do the same."

"Do you think my family is in danger?"

"I *know* they are in danger," said Pasteur. "They've been in danger ever since your father's Close of Session speech at the Palatine Forum. But then you'd have known that if you had stayed long enough to hear it."

"Please, let's not go down this road again," said Arcturus. "It's old news and frankly I'm bored with your throwing it in my face. Tell me about my family."

Pasteur sat back in his chair, visibly composing himself mentally. "You're right. I'm sorry, Arcturus, but I can still remember your mother's tears that day. It's not an easy thing to forgive."

"She's forgiven me."

"She's your mother," said Pasteur. "That's what mothers do."

Arcturus studied Pasteur's face as he spoke, seeing the deep lines around his eyes and the gleam on his pate, where his hair was little more substantial than thin wisps of gray smoke. The years of clandestine support for his father's rebel faction on Korhal had not been without its price.

"Achton Feld's a good man, but he doesn't have the resources of the Confederacy. He's worked wonders in protecting your family and he's been lucky as well as skilled, but your father's enemies only need to be lucky once and it's all over."

Arcturus was shocked. He had no idea things were so volatile on Korhal. The reports concerning his father had largely belittled his importance or depicted him as some kind of raving madman, which, he now realized, should have told him immediately how seriously the Confederacy viewed Angus.

"Do you think the Confederacy will try and kill him?"

"It's possible," said Pasteur. "Angus is such a valuable figurehead that they might attempt something that direct, but I think maybe his very visibility is what will protect him. If there's anyone with a grain of sense in the Tarsonis Council they'll know that it may do more harm than good to target Angus."

Arcturus snorted in derision. "Yes, and having sense is a quality the Council's known for, after all."

"Hence why I believe things to be so dangerous. Your father and Achton Feld have amassed a popular army that numbers in the millions—tough, disciplined, and loyal men. And the momentum and support your father's built up among the civilian populace and neighboring worlds means it's only a matter of time until the Confederacy's forced off Korhal for good."

"It sounds like they don't need any help then."

"Don't be so naïve," said Pasteur. "This is just when the Tarsonis Council is at its most dangerous, when it thinks it might lose Korhal and have no other option but force."

"Are you talking about an invasion?" said Arcturus, incredulous at the prospect of Confederate marines storming the planet of his birth.

Pasteur shrugged. "Perhaps, but I don't think so. Feld's army is well trained and has the very best weapons we could supply: rifles, explosives, tanks, anti-air missiles, the works. Any invasion would cost the Confederacy dearly and I don't think that's a risk they're willing to take."

"And if you're wrong?"

"Then there will be bloodshed like nothing we've ever seen," said Pasteur.

CHAPTER 14

ARCTURUS FOUND THEM AT THE BOTTOM OF THE garden by the side of a river. Valerian was industriously working within a small cove he had clearly dug by hand with a very small shovel, while Juliana sat nearby on the grass. Walking out to meet them, Arcturus took a deep breath of the faintly spicy Umojan air, enjoying the aroma of an atmosphere unpolluted by the venting of the *Kitty Jay*'s engines or the reek of oil, scorched metal, or turned earth and rock.

Ailin Pasteur's home on Umoja was large and well proportioned, fashioned from white steel and wide panes of bronzed glass, with a pleasing symmetry and elegant design that complemented the natural landscape, with the grass and trees constantly reflected in the glazing. Arcturus knew that such a dwelling would be both rare and expensive on a planet such as Umoja, where the climate was often harsh and land at a premium.

The gardens before the house were kept green and

lush by integrated water atomizers, and an army of robot groundskeepers tended to the numerous hedges and covered arbors that dotted the gently curved slope. The path Arcturus followed led down to a slow, meandering river at the far end of the garden, and tucked discreetly out of sight behind a sweep of hedges was the landing platform on which Arcturus's ship had set down the previous evening.

They hadn't seen him yet, Valerian too intent on his labors in the dirt and Juliana too involved in watching her—*their*, he corrected himself—son at work. Valerian stooped to retrieve something from the mud and proudly held it up for his mother's inspection. She nodded and took it from him, placing it on a tray beside a pile of books as Valerian finally spotted Arcturus.

"Dad!" he cried, dropping his spade and clambering from the cove.

Juliana turned at the sound of her son's shout and smiled as she saw Arcturus. Valerian charged over the grass toward him, and Arcturus realized he was more terrified of this moment than he had been when the goliath had had him dead to rights on Onuru Sigma.

Valerian launched himself like a missile and Arcturus caught him in his arms as the boy wrapped himself around his neck, laughing like a lunatic. Arcturus was surprised at how light he was; the boy weighed next to nothing.

"Dad! You're here! I wanted to talk to you last night, but Grandfather said I was too tired, but I wasn't, I really wasn't, I promise."

Arcturus didn't know what to say. He'd never had any problem speaking to Dorothy when she was younger, but she was his little sister and he had known her and loved her since her birth. Valerian was seven years old, and this was their first meeting.

What do you say to your son when he's seven years old and you've never met him?

"That's quite all right, Valerian," said Arcturus eventually. "I think your grandfather was right. Anyway, I think I was too tired as well."

Arcturus put Valerian down and was summarily led by the hand toward the excavated cove where the boy had been working.

"I want to show you my dig," said Valerian. "Do you want to see it? I'm looking for aliens."

"At the bottom of the garden?"

"Well, not aliens exactly, but fossils of them. You know what fossils are?"

"I do indeed," said Arcturus. "I do some digging myself, you know."

"I know, my mum told me," said Valerian. "She said you're the best miner in the galaxy."

"Did she now?" said Arcturus as they passed Juliana.

"Yeah, she said you were a big soldier and then you became a prospector and that you're going to be rich and that you're the best miner ever and—"

"Valerian," interrupted Juliana, "slow down. Show your father what you've found so far."

"Sure, yeah," said Valerian, dropping to his knees

beside the tray of his finds. Arcturus knelt on the grass beside the tray as Juliana brushed a strand of honey blonde hair from her face. ´Beneath the sunlight, Arcturus noticed how pale her skin was, pallid and without the light golden sheen of Valerian's.

She caught his glance and turned away as though embarrassed.

"I think I'll leave you two boys alone for a while," said Juliana, pushing herself to her feet and ruffling Valerian's hair. "Will you be all right?"

"Yeah," said Valerian, without looking up from his finds.

Arcturus nodded to Juliana, and saw the desperate hope in her eyes. "We'll be fine," he said. "I'm sure we can stay out of trouble for a little while, can't we, Valerian?"

"You bet," agreed the boy.

Juliana made her way back toward the house and Arcturus watched her go. Now that he was over the initial shock of discovering that he had a son, he was reminded of his former desire for Juliana. Ailin Pasteur's daughter had always carried herself with an élan that was wholly natural and effortless, but as Arcturus watched, he saw that elegance had all but vanished.

No, not vanished, but changed . . .

Had motherhood changed her, or was he simply seeing her through different lenses that time and distance had crafted without his noticing? More the latter, he suspected, for, by any objective reasoning, Juliana was still beautiful. In some ways more so.

Last night he had wondered if they might yet be a family, but if he was honest, the burning desire he had once had for her was now cold and dead. The tactless light of day cast its unflattering illumination over the idea, and Arcturus knew that any such notion was wishful thinking at best, dangerous delusion at worst.

Arcturus desired an heir, that was certainly true, but a family life . . . ?

He turned back to Valerian as the boy said something.

"I'm sorry?"

"I think this is alien," said Valerian, holding up a piece of shell that even Arcturus could see was a cracked shard from the shell of one of the domesticated Umojan insect creatures.

"Yes, I think it is. Probably a giant, winged monster from another galaxy."

"You really think so?"

"Oh, undoubtedly," said Arcturus, lifting a piece of fossilized bark. "And this looks like it's a scale from some kind of alien lizard, don't you think?"

Valerian nodded sagely. "Yeah, that's what I thought. A big, man-eating lizard that could swallow a whole squad of soldiers in a single bite. Did you see anything like that when you were a soldier?"

Arcturus shook his head. "No, I didn't, but I'm quite glad about that. I don't think I'd have wanted to be swallowed whole."

"Well, no, I suppose not," said Valerian. "That would be stupid."

Arcturus took a closer look at his son as the boy rummaged through his finds and held each one up for his inspection. Though he bore the genetic hallmarks of a Mengsk, Valerian did not have the physicality of Arcturus or Angus. The lad was thin, much thinner than even Dorothy had been at his age, and his arms were skinny and without definition. By Valerian's age, Arcturus was a fine athlete and had become proficient with the dueling sword.

Not that in this modern age of gauss rifles and missiles Arcturus had much use for an archaic weapon like a sword, but the harsh lessons had taught him balance, honed his muscles, and provided him with a proper appreciation for the martial arts. Given Juliana's disposition, it was unlikely she had encouraged such pursuits, and the sheen of sweat on Valerian's brow was testament to his lack of stamina.

"Are these your books?" asked Arcturus as Valerian finished showing him the junk he'd pulled from the riverbank.

"Yeah, they were Mum's, but she gave them to me to keep."

"May I?" asked Arcturus, reaching for the books.

"Sure."

Arcturus lifted the top volume, a thin picture book on archaeology, complete with diagrams of animal skeletons and geological strata. He remembered reading this book as a child and seemed to remember giving it to Dorothy.

As he examined the next book, Valerian said, "That's my favorite. Mum gave me that for my last birthday."

The book was leather-bound, its cover edged with gold thread and its title printed in elaborate, cursive script.

"*Poems of the Twilight Stars*," read Arcturus, opening the book and turning its pages. The interior was filled with color plates depicting fantastical beasts and verses of escapist nonsense that talked of ancient beings that walked between the stars in ages past. He read one of the poems, a ridiculously trite piece composed of numerous rhyming couplets that used childishly overblown similes.

A quick flick through the book revealed that every single poem was similarly hokey and worthy of nothing but utter contempt. *This* was what Valerian was reading? A quick examination of the spines of the other books revealed one to be a guide to understanding your inner soul, while the other was a history book of Umoja.

At least *that* was something worth reading.

"This is yours?" asked Arcturus, holding up the book of poems.

"Yeah, I've read them all, but that one's my favorite. Mum reads it to me before I go to sleep at night."

"And this is the sort of thing you like? No military books or adventure stories?"

"I'm not allowed books like that. Mum says that the galaxy's a horrible enough place as it is," said Valerian.

"She says I don't need to read that kind of thing. She says it'll just upset me."

"Does she now . . . ?"

"Yeah, she likes that one too."

"But you're a young boy; you should be reading action and adventure stories. Space battles and heroes. My father gave me *Logan Mitchell—Frontier Marshal* when I was about your age. It's a classic. Have you read it?"

Valerian shook his head. "No, what's it about?"

"It's about a man called Logan Mitchell who keeps law and order on one of the fringe worlds. Lots of guns, lots of girls, and plenty of shoot-outs with corrupt officials. Logan's a hard-talking, hard-fighting man who always gets the bad guy. Pretty simple stuff really, but it's good fun and full of blood and guts."

"Why would I want to read about blood and guts and shoot-outs? That sounds horrible."

"I thought most boys liked reading things like that."

"Well, I don't," said Valerian. "I don't like guns."

"Have you ever fired one?"

"No."

"Would you like to?"

Arcturus saw the gleam in the boy's eyes and smiled.

Like most people who professed to dislike guns, Arcturus figured, Valerian had never actually fired one and had probably not even ever held a firearm. There was something about firing a weapon that appealed to the primal urge in everyone, male or female, and even avowed pacifists couldn't deny the thrill of unloading a powerful weapon—even if only into a paper target.

"Come on then," said Arcturus. "I've a gauss rifle and a slugthrower on the *Kitty Jay*. It's time you learned something about being a man."

Valerian lay back on his bed, struggling to hold back tears of frustration and disappointment as he rubbed analgesic ointment into his shoulder where the butt of his dad's gauss rifle had bruised him black and blue. If Valerian hadn't already hated guns, he would have learned to despise them thoroughly during the time his father had spent with him.

The last seven days had to rank as the greatest and worst week of Valerian's life.

The greatest because his dad was here and he was just as he had pictured him: tall, strong, and handsome. Everything his dad said sounded clever and important, even if a lot of it was beyond Valerian's understanding.

The worst because nothing Valerian did seemed good enough for him.

Valerian had greeted every day as a chance to win his dad's approval, and every day he hoped he was going to grow up just like him. He found himself trying to adopt his dad's mannerisms, his walk, his posture, and even his speech.

It was just a pity that his father paid little or no

attention to Valerian's many acts of devotion, seeming only to notice the things he *couldn't* do.

The lessons with the gauss rifle and slugthrower had been a disaster, the savage recoil of the rifle knocking Valerian onto his back and the bucking pistol spraining his wrist. The guns were loud and even when he managed to hold them straight, he couldn't hit any of the targets his dad set up at the edge of the river.

Every failure seemed to irritate his dad, but no matter how he concentrated, squinting down the barrel and pressing his tongue against his upper lip, he could not get the hang or love of firing a weapon.

Not only that, but his favorite books had been consigned to the trash and replaced with freshly uploaded digi-tomes of economics, history, technology, and politics—things he wasn't interested in and which didn't have any aliens in them.

They were confusing and used big words he didn't understand. None of them had any stories in them, apart from the history ones, but even they were really boring and didn't have any pictures of the bits that sounded like they might have been exciting.

The one thing Valerian *did* enjoy was the sparring with wooden swords, which he and his dad engaged in on the lawn before the house. The weight of the sword was unfamiliar, but his dexterous hands could move it quickly and nimbly around his body. Though he was bruised and sore at the end of each of these sessions, his dad would look at him without the more usual expression of disappointment and nod.

"You're fast," said his dad, taking his arm and squeezing it hard, "but you lack power. You need to build up your strength and stamina if you're going to be a swordsman."

"But why do I need to be a swordsman?" Valerian had protested. "Surely no one fights with swords anymore now that we have guns."

"And if you find yourself without a gun, or you run out of ammunition? What will you do then? Anyway, learning how to use a sword isn't just about fighting with one, it also teaches you balance, speed, coordination, discipline. All things you sadly lack, I'm afraid."

That had stung, for it was harsh and unnecessary. His grandpa had argued with his dad after Valerian told him what had been said. Valerian had heard them shouting at each other from behind the closed door of his bedroom.

Grandpa had left the house yesterday, and though Valerian didn't know what was going on, he had seen that his grandpa looked really worried. His mum told him that the Ruling Council of Umoja had been called to an emergency sitting (whatever that was) and that something very important was going on.

She didn't say what that might be, but Valerian could read his mum's moods as easily as if she had spelled them out, and he could tell she was worried.

As well as what was worrying her about Grandpa,

he knew she wasn't too pleased with his dad, either. But she had kept her opinions to herself, as far as Valerian knew.

At least, he hadn't *seen* them argue.

With Ailin Pasteur gone from the house, Arcturus helped himself to another measure of the man's brandy and sank into one of the leather seats before the fireplace. He sipped his drink, its taste pleasant enough, and remembered his first sip of brandy: the night the Confederate assassins had come to kill them at the summer villa. Thinking back to that night, Arcturus remembered sitting in the dining room and talking to his father, and felt a sudden, and wholly unexpected, pang of nostalgia for those long-ago days.

Back then everything was simpler, he mused, then realized this kind of thinking was just the rosy mist of memory softening problems that, at the time, had been huge and calamitous. Time, he knew, had a way of distorting the truth of experience, embellishing past pleasures and diminishing hardships.

Though he was still a young man, Arcturus felt old now. Part of that was no doubt the fact that he had a son, a factor surely designed to make any man feel as though he had advanced in age—if not maturity—by an order of magnitude.

Arcturus wondered if his own father had felt like this when presented with his newborn son. He didn't think so, since Angus would have had nine months and more to get used to the idea. Fatherhood had been sprung on Arcturus like a bolt of lightning from an open sky.

The idea had taken root, though, and instead of railing against the idea of a son, Arcturus had begun to feel that perhaps it was for the best he now had an heir (and had skipped the messy years of nappy changing and midnight feeds).

He had sent a message to Korhal—tagged specifically for his mother and Dorothy—telling his parents of this latest development, though it had taken him several days to work out exactly how to tell them of Valerian's existence without casting himself in an unfavorable light.

That hadn't been easy.

Arcturus had fought Kel-Morian pirates, been shot at by angry miners, and faced furious superior officers, but composing himself to record a message to send home and inform his family he was now a father had been the most nerve-wracking experience of his life.

Arcturus remembered when he'd been about eight or nine and had broken one of his mother's ornamental dancers with a poorly thrown padball. He'd sweated for days to pluck up the courage to tell her he'd broken it.

The sensation engulfing him as his finger hovered over the Record icon on the vidsys was uncomfortably familiar to the cold dread he'd felt as he stood before his mother's drawing room bathed in a guilty sweat.

He smiled, realizing it didn't matter how old you were—your parents would always be figures of authority, and it never got any easier telling them something difficult. Just as you would always be their child, no matter that you grew up, fought battles, made a life for yourself, and perhaps even started a family of your own.

The evolutionary dynamic between parents and their children was inescapable.

In any case, he'd sent word of Valerian to Korhal and three days had passed without a response, which surprised him. He had expected his mother to respond more or less instantly to the news that she was a grandmother.

And Dorothy . . . she was now an auntie. If anyone should have reacted with glee, he would have expected it to be her. Arcturus knew Dorothy would love Valerian. But what kind of relationship could *he* expect to have with the boy? Would they bond or would they remain distant, as Arcturus and his own father had?

The last week had given him an inkling as to how their relationship would go, and it was not a pleasant realization to discover it would likely be one of disappointment. The boy was weak and displayed no aptitude for the skills and enthusiasms a man needed to prosper.

Arcturus would journey to Korhal soon to formally present Valerian to his family, and the boy would need toughening up if he was to become a worthy successor.

In the meantime, he'd received word from Diamond de Santo regarding the claim, and the news was all good. The initial core samples brought up by the rigs was about as pure as it ever got and the yield from the rocks was like nothing any of the workers had ever seen. Arcturus smiled as he recalled the excitement in de Santo's voice as she spoke of the value of the claim. She'd also mentioned a rumor going around the inter-guild networks that the Guild Wars were in fact over: that the Kel-Morians had lost.

Arcturus hadn't heard anything of that news, since Ailin Pasteur had no cine-viewers in his home, claiming they showed nothing but Confederate propaganda and mindless, brain-rotting melodramas anyway. Arcturus could sympathize with that view, so he'd connected remotely to a UNN satellite feed via the *Kitty Jay*'s console and, sure enough, the channel carried the triumphant news of the defeat of the Kel-Morians.

Images of marching marines and hundreds of gleaming siege tanks rolled across the screen and the gushing announcer spoke of the craven capitulation of all enemy forces, as though the Confederate military machine had just defeated the most bloody regime imaginable instead of a loose alliance of pirates and miners.

Was this why Ailin Pasteur had been called away?

Bored—and slightly disgusted—by the relish the UNN was taking in its paymasters' victory, Arcturus had disconnected with the feed and returned to Pasteur's home to pour himself the brandy that warmed him as surely as the crackling fire in the hearth.

Arcturus was enjoying this rare moment of solitude when he heard Juliana enter the room behind him.

He recognized the hesitancy of her step and knew it signaled another argument about the boy.

"What is it, Juliana?" he said without turning.

"Your son is in tears again," she said.

"Why doesn't that surprise me?"

"Why are you being like this?" said Juliana, coming around the chair to stand before him.

"Like what?"

"Why are you being so hard on Valerian?" she asked, ignoring his question. Her face was hard and pinched with anger. "Can't you see he adores you? Even though you belittle him every time you see him. He's just met his dad and all you can do is tell him how bad he is at everything."

Arcturus put down his brandy, angry with her now. "That is because he *is* bad at everything. He can't even hold a gun, let alone fire one. The books you've been foisting on him are turning him into a flower-wearing believer in universal harmony, and he's as skinny as a rake. There's no meat on his bones and he gets tired after even light calisthenics. If I'm hard on him it's because I'm trying to undo the damage your mollycoddling has done."

"We love him here, Arcturus," said Juliana. "We don't force him to do what *we* think he should do. I thought you, of all people, would respect that. Our son is free to choose what he wants to learn and what he wants to be passionate about."

Arcturus shook his head. "That's just the kind of woolly-headed nonsense that'll leave him unprepared for life beyond this cozy little bubble you've built around him. You're raising a bookish, effeminate weakling, Juliana. The galaxy is a hard, ugly place and if you carry on raising him like this, he'll not survive when he has to face it alone, do you understand me?"

"I understand all right," snapped Juliana. "You want to make a carbon copy of yourself!"

"And would that be so bad?" retorted Arcturus, surging to his feet. "At least I've made something of myself. I've gone out into the galaxy, gained real experience, and forged my destiny with my own two hands. What's the boy ever going to manage on his own? He's a Mengsk and he's made for great things, but he'll never amount to anything like this."

"Whatever he wants to do with his life is up to him," said Juliana. "We can't choose the path of his life for him."

"Utter rubbish," said Arcturus. "Children need discipline, and you have conspicuously failed to give him that. He's too young to know the right path when he sees it, so it behooves us to make sure we put him on it."

Juliana balled her fists, and Arcturus saw the strength he thought she'd lost resurface in her. "I wish you could hear yourself, Arcturus. I really wish your younger self could hear what you're saying now."

"What are you talking about?"

"Everything you rebelled against when you were younger, that's what you've become. You've become your father."

"Don't be foolish, Juliana; I am nothing like my father."

She laughed bitterly. "For someone so clever, Arcturus, you can be so blind. I listened to all the things you'd tell me over the years, the grand plans for the future and your ambitions for greatness, and I believed them. I think on some level I still believe you will do great things, but you won't be doing it alone anymore. You have a son, and he needs his father."

"And I'm doing what a father needs to, Juliana. I'm giving him the benefit of my experience to turn him into a man."

"He's only seven—let him be a child," pleaded Juliana. "Does he need to grow up just yet?"

Arcturus was about to deliver a withering reply when the door opened and one of Ailin Pasteur's servants entered. Immediately, Arcturus could sense the man's urgency.

"What is it?" asked Juliana, turning and snapping at the man.

"A communication for Mr. Mengsk," said the servant.

"A message?" said Arcturus. "And you had to interrupt us for *that*? I'll open it later."

"No, sir," said the man. "It's not a message, it's a real-time communication from Korhal."

Arcturus frowned. To communicate in real time between worlds was incredibly expensive and could only be done by those with access to the most powerful and advanced equipment.

"From Korhal? Is it my mother?" he asked.

"No, sir, it's a Mr. Feld," said the man. "And I'm afraid he says he has some bad news."

Arcturus cradled the brandy bottle in his lap, knowing that draining the last of its contents was the wrong thing to do, but not caring for right and wrong anymore. His tears had long since dried, but the grief still tore his heart with cold steel claws. The words Feld had spoken echoed within his skull.

They're dead . . . all of them . . .

They were etched into his memory with a permanency that could never be erased.

It was impossible, surely.

No one could have penetrated the security around them.

No one could have defeated the manifold security systems that protected them from harm.

It was impossible.

They killed them. Oh, God, Arcturus . . . I'm so sorry . . .

He'd known something was wrong the minute he'd seen Achton Feld's face. His image on the vidsys had been grainy and static-washed, the signal degraded after so immense a distance piggybacking along myriad relays, boosters, and carrier waves.

A communication like this was the equivalent of your fone ringing in the middle of the night and jerking you from sleep with a deep, gnawing fear in your belly. No one foned with good news in the dark; no one went to the expense and trouble of a real-time communication with good news.

"What is it, Feld?" Arcturus had said, sitting in front of the vidsys unit he'd used to send the news of Valerian's birth to Korhal.

"I'm sorry, Arcturus, I'm so sorry . . . ," said Feld, tears running down his cheeks.

"Sorry . . . ? For what? Listen, Feld, spit it out. What's wrong?" said Arcturus, a lead weight of cold fear settling in his stomach.

"They're dead . . . all of them . . . ," wept Achton Feld.

"Who?" said Arcturus when Feld didn't continue.

"All of them . . ." sobbed Feld, struggling to form the words. "Angus . . . your mother. Even . . . even Dorothy."

Arcturus felt as though a great black void had opened up inside him. His hands began to shake and he felt cold. His mouth was dry and his mind stopped functioning, unable to process the reality of what Feld had just said.

"No," he said at last. "No, you're wrong. This can't be right. You've made a mistake. You *must* have made a mistake, Feld! They can't be dead! No, I won't allow it!"

"I'm so sorry, Arcturus. I don't know how it happened. Everything was normal . . . All the security systems were functional. They're *still* functional . . . I just don't know."

Arcturus felt his limbs go numb, as though they were no longer his to control. A rushing sound, like the sea crashing against the cliffs below the summer villa, roared in his head. Feld's mouth moved on the screen, but Arcturus no longer heard the words. His hands pressed against his temples and tears of grief, anger, and sucking, awesome loss flowed with them.

As if he'd taken an emotional emetic, his humanity flowed from him in his tears, and every petty feeling he'd ever harbored toward his family, every feeling of compassion, and every shred of restraint was washed away in a tide of hot tears.

The sheer, unimaginable scale of what had happened settled upon him. It was too much. No one could suffer such a crippling loss and remain whole. The power of his grief tore through him like a hurricane, breaking chains of restraint, honor, and mercy, scouring away all thoughts except one shining beacon that offered a ray of hope, a slender branch of survival to which he could cling.

Revenge.

The people that had caused him this hurt were going to die. All of them.

Arcturus knew that killings like this could only be the work of the Confederacy.

Only they had agents with the skill and gall to perpetrate something so heinous.

Only they had the temerity to think they could get away with it.

Well, Arcturus Mengsk was going to disabuse the Confederacy of *that* notion.

What was it his father had said?

When all you have is a hammer, everything starts to look like a nail . . .

The diamond clarity of the thought swept away the drag of his grief and he took a great draft of air, feeling himself fill with righteous purpose as he did so. His tears ceased and his back straightened.

"Tell me what happened," said Arcturus, his voice icy and controlled.

"I . . . They're dead, isn't that enough?" said Feld. "You need to come back to Korhal."

"Oh, I'll be coming back soon enough," promised Arcturus. "But tell me what happened."

Feld saw the urgent need in his eyes and nodded, wiping a hand across his face. Arcturus was impressed. Say what you liked about Achton Feld, he was a professional.

"I came up in the morning with the daily security brief, just like I always do," said Feld, shoring up his own walls against the grief with commendable discipline. "I passed through the biometric identifiers, swiped my card, and went through into the penthouse. Angus is usually waiting for me, but he wasn't there this morning, which immediately made me suspicious. Katherine . . . I mean, your mother normally has a pot of java on, but I didn't smell it. That's normally the first thing I notice, you know? The smell of fresh java. But not this morning. I knew something was wrong, so I made a sweep of the apartment."

"What did you find?"

Feld took a deep breath. "I couldn't see anyone. There was no sign of forced entry—I mean *nothing*. But the door to the balcony was open."

"And?" said Arcturus, when Feld didn't go on. He

could see it was taking all of Feld's self-control to keep speaking, and Arcturus prepared himself for the worst. His jaw tightened. He'd already *had* the worst . . . what else could there be?

Feld nodded. "I went out on the balcony. And that's where I found them. The damn force field had shorted out and they were just lying there . . . like they were asleep. Your mother, Dorothy, and your father. Dead."

"How did they die?"

"Does it matter?" snapped Feld. "Why the hell do you need to know something like that?"

"I need to know," said Arcturus. "I don't know why, I just do . . ."

"They were shot," said Feld. "Katherine and Dorothy were shot. One in the heart and one in the head."

"And my father? Was he shot too?"

Again Feld paused, his face averted as though unwilling to meet Arcturus's gaze. "No, he wasn't shot. He was decapitated."

"What?" cried Arcturus. "Decapitated? What are you talking about?"

"You heard me," shouted Feld. "They cut his damn head off, Arcturus! And we can't find it. The sick bastards took it with them!"

He'd terminated the communication soon after, telling Feld to wait to hear from him, that he'd be in touch to sort out what their next move would be. He'd marched from the room and returned to the drawing room where he'd lately been arguing with Juliana and swept up the bottle of brandy.

An hour passed, maybe more, but Arcturus didn't feel the passage of time, his brain whirling in a million different directions as he tried to process the gaping emptiness in his soul.

He took mouthfuls of the brandy, the liquor as potent as ever, but seeming to leave him unaffected. His entire body was numb to its powers, and he drained half the bottle before hurling it into the fire with a splintering crash of glass.

"Waste of good brandy . . . ," he hissed as the alcohol burned off in bright flames.

He heard the door open behind him.

"Arcturus," said a man's voice. "I'm so sorry. I came as soon as I heard."

He turned to see Ailin Pasteur and Juliana standing at the entrance to the room, as though afraid to intrude on his grief, but happy to watch from the sidelines. His heart twisted with contempt.

Juliana's face was streaked with tears and she held Valerian close to her. The boy's eyes were wide and fearful, not quite comprehending what was going on. Valerian untangled himself from his mother and came over to stand next to Arcturus.

"Is your mum and dad dead?" he asked.

Arcturus nodded. "Yes, Valerian, they are. And my sister, too."

"How did they die?" asked Valerian.

"Hush, Valerian!" said Juliana. "Don't ask such things."

"The Confederacy killed them," said Arcturus, his voice low and threatening. "They killed them because my dad spoke out against them. They killed them because they are animals."

Valerian reached out and hesitantly put his hand on Arcturus's shoulder.

"I'm sorry they're dead," whispered Valerian.

Arcturus looked into his son's eyes and saw the honest sincerity of a child, his expression uncluttered by adult notions of propriety or reserve.

"Thank you, Valerian," he said.

Ailin Pasteur approached and guided Valerian back to his mother. He took the seat opposite Arcturus and said, "Whatever you plan to do next, I can promise you that you'll have the support of Umoja."

"Like my father did?" said Arcturus bitterly.

"More than that," said Pasteur. "Arcturus, I've just come from an emergency sitting of the Ruling Council, and in the wake of the Kel-Morians' defeat, Councilor Jorgensen has announced the formation of the Umojan Protectorate. It will be an organization to keep our colony free from Confederate tyranny, to resist their expansionist policies and offer a safe haven to those who stand for freedom."

"Very noble of you," said Arcturus. "If a little belated."

"You might be right," admitted Pasteur, "but it's a start."

"A start . . . ," said Arcturus, staring into the crackling fire. "Yes, a start."

A sudden, terrible thought lanced into Arcturus's brain with the force of an Impaler spike, and he looked over at Valerian and Juliana. Fear clenched in his guts and took the breath from him.

"What is it?" said Pasteur, seeing the urgency in his eyes.

"Juliana . . . you and Valerian have to leave," said Arcturus, rising to his feet. "Right now."

"What? I don't understand, what are you talking about?"

"They know," said Arcturus, pacing the room, his thoughts crashing together like a convoy of groundcars rear-ending one another. "Or if they don't yet, they will soon."

"Slow down, Arcturus," said Pasteur. "Who knows what?"

"The Confederacy," snapped Arcturus. "The message I sent to my family about Valerian. If they're good enough to defeat Feld's security systems without breaking a sweat, then it's a mathematical certainty they know where I am and that I have a son. We're loose ends, and the Confederacy doesn't like loose ends when it comes to murder."

"You think they'd come here? To Umoja?" said Juliana, holding Valerian even tighter.

Arcturus laughed, the sound hollow and coming from the bleakest, emptiest part of his soul. "Don't think for a moment they won't. They will do whatever it takes to destroy their enemies. You have to get out of here and stay on the move or they'll find you. And that can't be allowed to happen."

"Don't be ridiculous," said Pasteur. "We are well protected here."

"Ridiculous?" said Arcturus. "If my family's killers can penetrate the Skyspire's security, they will simply walk in here and kill you all in a heartbeat. No, the only way to evade people like that is to not be here when they come for you."

"He's right, Daddy; we need to go," said Juliana, her voice brittle with fear, though Arcturus knew that fear was for Valerian and not herself. "I won't let anything happen to Val."

Pasteur hesitated and then nodded reluctantly. "I'll have a ship here within the hour."

"Stay on the move," warned Arcturus. "Don't stay in any one place too long."

"You're not coming with us?" said Juliana.

"No," said Arcturus. "They don't know it yet, but the Confederacy has just created the greatest enemy they will ever know."

"What are you going to do?" asked Pasteur.

"I'm going to burn the Confederacy to the ground," hissed Arcturus.

CHAPTER 15

THE SWORD CAME AT HIM IN AN ARCING LINE of silver and Valerian twisted his wrists to bring his own weapon up to block. The blades connected with a shriek of steel and he spun from the reverse stroke as Master Miyamoto's sword darted forward. Valerian's sword came down, deflecting the stroke as he backed away from the relentless attack.

Sweat ran down his face in runnels and his breathing came in short, sharp gasps. In contrast, Master Miyamoto looked as serene and unflappable as he always did, no matter whether he was pouring tea or executing flawless sword movements.

Dressed in a simple cream-colored keikogi and hakama, Master Miyamoto was as unreadable as ever, no trace of expression betraying his intended movements in this dangerous ballet called a sword bout.

Valerian wore identical training clothes, though tailored for his smaller, nine-year-old frame, which had finally begun to fill out as he grew older and took more exercise. He was still slender and ascetic-looking, but the last two years had seen his shoulders and arms begin to strengthen and offer promising hints of the man he might become.

They were alone in the garden; Master Miyamoto allowed no one to observe their training, not even Valerian's mother. Roughly built walls of high stone enclosed the garden, a rectangular courtyard of gently swaying plants, freshly tended herb patches—and a slate-paved sparring area next to the eastern wall.

A fountain gurgled peacefully in the center of the garden and the cold air was thin, scented with the earthy smell of ripe crops. This region of Icarus IV always smelled, due to the loamy richness of the soil that made it such a fertile world for agriculture, and the faint yet unmistakable hint of chemical fertilizer.

Birds perched on the high walls, the only spectators able to observe Valerian's grueling training rituals, and their twittering conversations were like a chorus of amused theatergoers enjoying a boy's humiliation at the hands of a fencing master.

"What is the meaning of victory?" said Miyamoto, slowly lifting his sword up and back.

"To defeat your enemy," said Valerian, circling as Master Miyamoto slid sideways.

"No," said Miyamoto, launching a lightning-fast thrust toward Valerian. "That is not enough."

Valerian averted the attack, his speed impressive, and slashed his sword at his trainer's side. His blade struck empty air and he realized he'd been lured into the attack as the flat of Master Miyamoto's blade struck him painfully on the bicep.

"Then what is it?" he yelped. Every time he failed to answer a question correctly, Valerian received a stinging rebuke from Master Miyamoto's weapon.

"It is to destroy him," said Master Miyamoto. "To eradicate him from living memory. You must leave no remnant of his endeavors. Utterly crush his every achievement and remove from all record his every trace of existence. From such defeat no enemy can ever recover."

Master Miyamoto's sword looped around his body in a series of perfectly executed maneuvers that, had Valerian attempted them, would have seen him limbless, earless, and dead.

"That," said Master Miyamoto, "is the meaning of victory. You would know this if you had paid attention to the books on your father's reading list. Or the one I gave you."

"I read that one," said Valerian, returning to the guard position and bowing to Master Miyamoto.

"Not closely enough. Again."

Valerian nodded and once more dropped into the *en garde* position, his long blade extended before him. After three hours of training with Master Miyamoto, Valerian's arms burned with fatigue and his chest felt as though a fire had been set in his lungs.

Master Miyamoto returned Valerian's bow and the

two of them circled one another, their swords shining in the afternoon sun.

"The enemy comes at you in a great horde," said Master Miyamoto. "How do you fight?"

Valerian cast his mind back to the text his tutor was referencing. It was a treatise recovered from the data vaults of the *Reagan*, the supercarrier that had brought the colonists to Umoja. Supposedly written by an ancient warrior king of Earth, its words were instructions in the arts of war, diplomacy, and personal discipline.

The book had no official title, but Master Miyamoto called it *The Book of Virtues*, and seemed to know its text verbatim. Valerian had read the book, as it was high on the list of approved texts his father had set him, but he found it difficult to recall its teachings while trying to avoid a stinging slap from the flat of Master Miyamoto's blade.

"Quickly," said Master Miyamoto, his sword raised to strike. "Do not think. *Know*!"

Valerian lifted his blade, letting his mind float back over the many evenings he'd sat at his desk with the pages swimming before his tired, gritty eyes. He had read the book a dozen times or more, and as he let his thoughts concentrate on the tip of his tutor's sword, the words came to him without conscious thought.

"It's best to try and direct them into a narrow defile or enclosed space," Valerian said.

"Why?" A slash to the body.

"So that their numbers work against them." A rolling block.

"How will they do that?" A thrust to the chest.

"Crowded together, those at the front will impede those behind." A parry and riposte.

Valerian shifted left and launched his own attack. "The push from the rear will prevent those at the front from retreating or finding a better path."

"Very good," said Master Miyamoto, easily deflecting Valerian's attacks. "And what of balance?"

"It is the key to success," said Valerian, smiling as yet again the words came easily to him.

"Why?" repeated Master Miyamoto, parrying a clumsy attack and rolling his blade around Valerian's sword.

"A leader who puts his faith in his guns will be outmaneuvered," said Valerian, deflecting the blow and circling around to his right.

"Then he must train all his warriors in close-quarters combat," offered Miyamoto.

"No, for then he will lose his force to enemy fire," countered Valerian.

"Very good. So what does it mean to have balance?"

"It means that every element of an army must work in harmony, so that its effectiveness is greater than the sum of its parts."

Master Miyamoto nodded and lowered his blade. He spun the weapon quickly and sheathed it in the scabbard at his belt.

"We are done for the day," he said.

Valerian was relieved, for his body was aching, but he was also disappointed, for he had finally begun to appreciate the lessons of *The Book of Virtues* and how to access them while he trained. It was just a beginning, but it was an important beginning, he felt.

He returned Master Miyamoto's bow and sheathed his sword, running his hands through his blond hair. He wore it long, pulled tightly into a ponytail during sword practice, and its golden hue was no less bright than it had been when he was a youngster.

Master Miyamoto turned on his heel and made his way along a stone-flagged path toward the fountain at the garden's center. He took a seat on the ledge around the fountain and dipped his hand into the cold water.

Valerian followed the swordmaster and sat next to him, taking a handful of water and splashing his face.

"You are improving," said Master Miyamoto. "It is good to see."

"Thank you," said Valerian. "It's hard work, but I think I'm beginning to get it."

"It will take time," agreed Miyamoto. "Nothing good ever comes without effort. I remember telling your father the same thing."

Valerian's interest was suddenly piqued, for Master Miyamoto had never spoken of his dad before now, save when he had first arrived. Miyamoto had arrived a few weeks after Valerian and his mother had fled Umoja, informing Juliana that Arcturus Mengsk had retained him to become the boy's tutor in all matters martial and academic.

His mother had been furious at his dad's presumption, but the matter was not up for discussion. Master Miyamoto had only been persuaded to leave his position at Styrling Academy to teach the boy for an exorbitant fee, and only Valerian's desire to win his father's approval had persuaded Juliana to let Miyamoto stay.

"You taught my dad to use a sword?" asked Valerian.

"I did." Miyamoto nodded. "He casts a long shadow, Valerian, but it is my hope that you will be able to escape it and fulfill your potential."

"I bet he was good with a sword," said Valerian. "He looks like he could fight."

"He was a fair swordsman," conceded Miyamoto. "He was strong and won most of his bouts before even a single blow was struck."

"How?"

"There is more to fighting than simply wielding a sword," said Miyamoto. "More often than not, a man is defeated by his own doubts."

"I don't understand."

"In any contest of arms where life and death rest on the outcome, most men's fear will see their opponent as stronger, faster, and more capable," explained Miyamoto. "Such doubts only serve to make it so. To win, you must have utter belief in your abilities. No doubt must enter your mind."

"Is that what my dad did?"

Miyamoto stood, as though deciding that he had said too much. "Yes, your father had complete faith in his abilities. But victory is not the only measure of a man."

"It isn't?"

"No, there is honor. A man may lose everything he has, yet still retain his honor. Nothing is more important. Always remember that, Valerian, no matter what anyone else tries to teach you. Even your father."

"Honor is more important than dying?"

"Absolutely," said Miyamoto. "Some things are worth dying for."

"Like what?"

"Defending noble ideals or fighting for the oppressed. The honorable man must always stand firm before tyrants who would dominate the weak. The abuse of power must always be fought, and men of honor do not stand idly by while such evils are allowed to exist."

"Just like my dad," said Valerian proudly.

Master Miyamoto bowed to him. "No," he said sadly. "Not like your father."

Valerian stripped off his training garments and dumped them on the floor of his bedroom. He grabbed a towel and made his way into the bathroom, turning on the tap and stepping back from the tub as chilly water gurgled and spurted from the showerhead. Eventually the water warmed and Valerian stepped under the hot spray.

Over the last year he and his mother had spent on Icarus IV, Valerian had gotten used to a liquid shower as opposed to the sonic ones he'd grown up with on Umoja. The hot water soothed his muscles and refreshed him in a way the vibrational removal of dirt molecules and dead skin from his body just couldn't. Even though it was wasteful to use water this frivolously, Valerian decided it was entirely worth it.

He stepped from the shower and began toweling himself dry, stopping for a moment to look at himself in the full-length mirror on the back of the door. Though he was young, his body was developing quickly and his upper body strength was growing every day. Accompanied by a squad of soldiers, he ran every other morning, jogging around the patrolled perimeter of the Umojan agrarian complex—a distance of some six kilometers—and was pleased with his increased endurance.

He flexed and posed in the mirror, enjoying the fantasy that he was some dashing interplanetary hero like his dad. Despite Master Miyamoto's words, Valerian was proud of what his dad was doing.

Valerian returned to his bedroom, a cluttered space filled with books, digi-tomes, an unmade bed, and silver-skinned trunks full of clothes. His collections of fossils, rocks, and alien artifacts were proudly on show in a number of display cabinets and a number of antique weapons were hung on the wall.

They had belonged to the previous owner of the mansion in which they now dwelled—surely the most salubrious accommodation they'd stayed in since leaving Umoja—and Valerian had liked them so much, he had left them there. He'd asked Master Miyamoto if he could train with some of the more exotic-looking weapons—a falchion, a glaive, or a falx—but his tutor had forbidden him to touch any more weapons until he was competent with a sword at least.

Still, it did no harm to have them around, as many were plainly hundreds of years old and gave him a connection to times long gone. In a small way, they made it easier to hold on to the concept of alien civilizations existing in forgotten ages of the past. The concept of millions of years ago was almost impossible to grasp, but a few hundred years was easy, and by such small steps he could imagine larger spans of time.

Valerian cleared a space on his bed and dressed himself in loose-fitting trousers and a blue shirt of expensive silk. He settled back on the bed and lifted the copy of *The Book of Virtues* Master Miyamoto had given him and began to read. Unlike the majority of Valerian's other books, this was an old-fashioned one of paper pages bound together within a leather cover, which bore an inscription on the inside in letters he couldn't read.

Master Miyamoto had said his own father had written the words on the morning of his death. Only after much cajoling had Master Miyamoto told Valerian what the words meant.

Valerian's tutor had lifted the book, and though he clearly knew the inscription by heart, his eyes had nevertheless followed the path of the words on the page; his voice choked with emotion as he read his father's valediction.

"What is life?" read Master Miyamoto. "It is the flash of a firefly in the night. It is the little shadow which runs across the grass and loses itself in the sunset."

Valerian had found the words wonderfully uplifting and looked down at the wolf head picked out in gold thread over the breast pocket of his shirt. The symbol was that of the Mengsk family, and Valerian bore it proudly whenever he was in a place of safety. On those rare occasions they ventured into public, he had been warned not to display anything that might link him to his dad.

Given how his dad was portrayed in the media, that was a sensible precaution.

It had been two years since he had seen his father, standing on the underground platform where his ship, the *Kitty Jay,* was berthed.

It was a moment of confused emotions for Valerian. He had been sad to see his dad leave, but, even as a youngster, he had sensed the tension between his mum and dad and grandpa. He sensed a familiarity to the drama before him: his dad leaving and his mother left behind, with his grandpa there to deal with the emotional fallout. Even though he hadn't thought of that moment in such terms, he'd sensed the reality of them as though they'd been spelled out.

His father had knelt beside him and fixed him with his gaze.

"I would have liked to spend more time with you, Valerian," said his dad.

"Yeah," agreed Valerian. "I'd have liked that."

"There is much to be done if you are to be a worthy heir, but I have work to do and you cannot be part of it yet. You are not strong enough or wise enough, but you will be. You are going to hear a lot of bad things said about me in the coming years, but I want you to know that none of it will be true. What I'm doing is for the good of humanity. Always remember that."

And Valerian *had* remembered it.

Despite his mother's reservations, Valerian eagerly watched every report on the UNN concerning his dad. He saw bombings, assassinations, and the spread of revolution throughout the sector. Some of those reports were plainly so ridiculous that even a nine-year-old could see through them, but others appeared to be unvarnished truth that needed no embellishment.

Images of burned bodies and mangled corpses being carried from wrecked Confederate buildings that had been torn apart by explosives. Burning Confederate vehicles targeted by one of the many insurgent groups that were slowly, but surely, accreting under his father's banner and leadership.

Factories belonging to the Old Families were bombed, each target carefully chosen to cause maximum disruption to the economic infrastructure of the Confederacy. Of course, none of the news broadcasts spoke of this, but Master Miyamoto made Valerian always look to answer the most important question of all when looking at his dad's handiwork: *Why?*

Why was that particular factory destroyed?

Why was that particular official killed?

Each question forced Valerian to think beyond the simple, bloody facts of the act itself and to search for deeper purpose than simply the causing of harm. Though it was hard watching so many images of death and suffering, Valerian felt sure it was for a higher cause. These people were part of the Confederacy and they had murdered his dad's parents and sister in cold blood.

Master Miyamoto had urged Valerian not to see things in these black-and-white terms, but such deeper considerations stood little chance of recognition in the face of a youngster's loss. High-minded ideals were all very well until you were put to the test of having to hold on to them in the face of personal tragedy.

The Confederacy had robbed his dad of his parents and his sister, and Valerian had lost two grandparents and an aunt he had never met, never got the chance to know, and now never would. If that wasn't worth some bloodshed, then what was?

Valerian knew that his dad was wanted throughout Confederate space, a wanted terrorist and murderer, but these were labels hung on him by his enemies, so Valerian didn't pay them much attention. He knew who his dad was and knew that when he saw him again—whenever that might be—he would not be the disappointment he now realized he had been when they'd first met.

He recalled his mother tearfully telling him that his dad had called him bookish, effeminate, and weak, an admission she later regretted, but which could not be taken back. In that moment, Valerian had made a personal vow to himself that he would never be thought of that way again, and had thrown himself into physical exercise as though his life depended on it.

There had been some communication with his father, but it had all been done through his grandfather, and was sporadic at best. Icarus IV was the fifth place they had lived in two years and looked like it wouldn't be the last. Valerian tried not to get comfortable in any once place, knowing an imperious command could be delivered at any time, instructing them to move on.

Valerian's grandfather would sequester yet another outlying Umojan outpost or colony to hide them and the process would begin again.

The necessity of this was brutally demonstrated when Valerian had once complained about the need to move incessantly and begged his mother to not uproot them again. She had agreed not to move on for a little longer, but one night Valerian had woken to the sound of shouting soldiers, gunfire, and the flash of explosions.

"Not a word, not a whimper, Val my darling," said his mother, dragging him from his bed and handing him over to an Umojan soldier in battered combat armor.

Valerian's memories of that night were confused and fragmented, but he remembered being carried through the night, its darkness split with stuttering flashes of fire. He'd taken a tumble as the man carrying him collapsed, but was picked up again, realizing at the same time that the first soldier had been killed.

They'd been hustled onto the dropship that was always prepped nearby, and as it lifted off in a screaming, rocking ascent, Valerian clung to his mother and said, "Mommy? Will Daddy ever come for us?"

"Yes, honey," she'd replied. "He will. One day."

As the pilot flew them to safety, Valerian had lain with his head in his mum's lap for hours, letting her stroke his golden hair and soothe away his worries. He heard her crying and pretended to be asleep, letting her think she had succeeded.

Valerian never again complained about their need to keep on the move.

It was hard to be always on the move, but as hard as it was for him, with no real friends and no sense of stability to his life, he knew it was harder still for his mum.

She tried to hide it, and denied it whenever he brought it up, but Valerian knew she was quite ill. Exactly what was wrong with her he didn't know, but he could see the gray pallor of her skin and the way the weight seemed to melt from her bones, no matter how much she ate—which wasn't very much at the best of times.

At night, he heard her racking coughs and cried as

he thought of her pain and his inability to do anything about it. Through all of this, Valerian's most pressing question was *Why*. Why did his dad not come to see her?

He knew his grandfather must have sent word to him that Juliana was ill, but the weeks and months passed with no sign of his dad. Didn't he care?

It was hard for Valerian to reconcile the mounting evidence of his dad's indifference to their plight against the image he'd cultivated since a youngster.

The subject of his mum's illness was always quietly dismissed whenever he brought it up, but Valerian knew that if whatever was wrong with his mum was serious enough to warrant its being kept from him, it must be extremely serious indeed. A succession of physicians had come and gone, but none of them appeared to offer anything that stopped his mum's terrible, hacking cough or enabled her to put on weight.

He'd heard words like *"long term," "inoperable," "terminal," "nonviable," "immedicable,"* and yet others he didn't understand, but the meaning was all too clear. As each doctor arrived, Valerian felt a flutter of hope, but as each one left, that hope was crushed. Evidently, his grandfather was not about to give up, even if it seemed his dad already had.

Valerian felt his anger grow and tried to suppress it.

One of the few teachings of his dad that had stuck was that anger was a wasted emotion.

"Angry people do stupid things, Valerian," his dad had said. "Speak when you're angry and you'll make the best speech you'll ever regret. So when your anger rises, think of the consequences before you act."

He put down his book and closed his eyes, trying to calm his seesawing emotions, but finding it difficult with all the noise coming from downstairs. It took a second to dawn on him that the noises from downstairs were not normal for this time of day, and he sat up as he caught a measure of the urgency in them.

Valerian heard the sound of someone crying and made his way quickly to his bedroom door. Something was definitely going on, so he made his way downstairs, heading toward the large room at the rear of the house that served as a warm gathering place in the evening.

He heard shouted oaths and more crying, and a cold hand seized his heart as he suddenly wondered if something had happened to his mum. Valerian broke into a run and skidded into the room from which the sounds of crying were issuing. The room was full of people, all staring in rapt attention at something displayed on the flickering holographic image of the cine-viewer in the corner of the room.

Valerian's first feeling was relief as he saw his mum standing in the center of the room; but then he noticed that there were a lot of people here who looked as though they'd just been given the worst news imaginable.

A few heads turned to face him, their faces streaked with tears, then quickly turned back to the unfolding drama on the cine-viewer. The image was fuzzy and dark, but from here it appeared to be showing a large black ball.

"What's going on?" he asked. "Why is everyone so sad?"

"Oh my darling, Val," said his mum, rushing to him and sweeping him up in a hug. "Oh honey, it's Korhal."

"Korhal? The planet dad comes from? What about it?"

His mum pulled back, as though not sure she should tell him what was going on.

"It's okay, Mum," he said. "Just tell me."

"Korhal's gone, honey."

"Gone? How can a planet be gone?" said Valerian. "It's too big to be gone."

His mother struggled with her words, her eyes streaming with tears. "I mean . . . not gone, exactly, but . . ."

"The Confederacy has launched a thermonuclear strike against Korhal," said Master Miyamoto, appearing at his mum's side. "A thousand Apocalypse-class nuclear missiles, according to a military press release."

Valerian felt his stomach lurch and terrible fear freeze his limbs. "Korhal's destroyed? Dad? Is Dad dead?"

"No! No, he's alive," said his mum. "We had word from your grandfather not long after the first news reports came through. Your dad's fine."

Relief flooded him and he disengaged himself from his mum's arms as everyone in the room continued to watch the image on the cine-viewer. He stood before the flickering image of Korhal, watching the black disc of the world as nuclear firestorms raged across its surface with elemental fury. The once bountiful and green world was now a superheated sphere of blackened glass and phantoms.

Even with his limited understanding of the physics of nuclear detonations, Valerian knew that a thousand missiles was an inordinate amount of overkill. Such an overwhelming attack would have killed every living thing on the planet's surface.

"How many people lived on Korhal?" he asked.

"More than thirty-five million," said Master Miyamoto. "All dead."

The thought of such devastation was humbling. That so many people could be wiped from existence in such a short period of time was unbelievable.

What manner of madman could ever think to unleash such wanton destruction?

"The Confederacy did this?" asked Valerian.

"Men without honor did this," replied Master Miyamoto.

CHAPTER 16

FLAMES BURNED WITH A GREENISH GLOW FROM
the bombed-out munitions plant, but Valerian couldn't
tell if the color was the result of ignited chemical
spillage or a fault of the cine-viewer. Fire crews fought
a futile battle with the blaze and medics dragged
screaming men and women from the wrecked interior
of the building.

Valerian felt no sympathy for these people—they
were employees of the Old Families and therefore part
of the system that maintained the bloated, corrupt
form of the Confederacy, the same men who had
destroyed Korhal six years ago.

The image panned from the blazing plant to a
sandy-haired young man standing at the edge of a
perimeter enforced by Confederate marines clad in
full combat armor and looking eager to use the heavy
gauss weapons they carried.

"Another atrocity unleashed by Arcturus Mengsk
and his Sons of Korhal that forces us to number the

dead in the thousands," said the reporter, his voice appropriately outraged, and mixed with not a little relish, thought Valerian. "An unknown number of bombs placed with uncanny skill throughout the Ares munitions factory has resulted in its complete destruction. There's no word yet from official sources of the number of people murdered in this latest act of terrorism, but one thing is certain: It will be high. Back to you, Michael."

Valerian muted the sound and shook his head as the image of the burning factory was replaced with the neon-lit, chrome interior of the UNN studios on Tarsonis. The broadcast was a few days old and he was under no illusions that much of what the reporter had said was true, which was a rarity these days.

The Sons of Korhal . . .

An appropriate name, thought Valerian, one apparently coined by his father in the wake of the nuclear attack on Korhal as he began rallying fragmented and scattered bands of revolutionaries to him in his bid to topple the Confederacy. Those ragtag soldiers had been molded into an army that was—if what he was hearing from his grandfather was true— proving to be a grave threat to the continued existence of the current regime.

Though to hear the reports of the UNN, Arcturus Mengsk was a madman, a lunatic who made raving pronouncements over the airwaves of his supposed divinity and the alien creatures that used mind-controlling drugs on the Tarsonis Council.

On those rare occasions where the UNN played snippets of his father's broadcasts, they were so chopped up, edited, or manipulated that even a child could tell they bore no resemblance to their original content.

It had been eight years since Valerian had last seen his father, eight years of forced relocations and moving from planet to planet as they kept one step ahead of Confederate assassins and kill teams. Whether or not such killers were still after them was a moot point—it did not do to take chances when their lives hung in the balance.

This hideaway was a particularly bleak refuge, thought Valerian, though it at least had the benefit of relative proximity to Umoja for covertly delivered supplies and a steady stream of news that wasn't weeks, if not months, out of date.

Valerian got up from his bed and stretched, thinking that perhaps he would go for a run, doing a few circuits of the orbital along its outer ring before returning to his medical digi-tomes of oncological research. Tethered in orbit above an inhospitable rock named Van Osten's Moon (despite the fact that it was not a moon, having nothing to orbit), Orbital 235 didn't even warrant a name, such were its remoteness and insignificance to anyone else.

He supposed he had only himself to blame for the tedium of the orbital; it was a destination he had picked from a list of suitable candidates after recognizing the name from an archaeological report penned by a Dr.

Jacob Ramsey that Valerian had read two years ago. Ancient ruins had been discovered on Van Osten's Moon, and Orbital 235 had been shipped across space and converted from its original function as a base for mining operations to one of archaeological discovery.

The expedition had been abandoned due to lack of funding, and the ruins never fully explored, much to Dr. Ramsey's chagrin, from the frustrated tone of the report.

But Ramsey's loss had been Valerian's gain, and he had leapt at the chance to discover ruins that might be genuinely alien, having long ago discarded his collection of "fossils" unearthed in various gardens and riverbanks.

So far he'd made a single trip to the barren rock, a desolate craggy wasteland with the merest scrap of an atmosphere to its name, with an escort of soldiers to view the ruins.

The surface of Van Osten's Moon felt as though one were walking on something that ought to be a piece of something far larger, but where this intuition had come from, Valerian had no idea. The atmosphere was gritty and cold, like breathing in on a frozen winter's day. Though breathing apparatus was not required, the thin air made it all too easy to become light-headed and disorientated.

To avoid arousing the attention of the Confederate Exploration Corps, shipments of exploratory equipment were coming in piece by piece, and it would be some time before Valerian had assembled enough kit to begin a full examination of the ruins.

But what he had seen so far had been awesome in its breathtaking scale—"awesome" in the original sense of the word, as in "capable of producing awe, wonder, or admiration," not the watered-down colloquialism it had become, where a pair of new shoes could be called "awesome."

Perched on the edge of the world overlooking what might once have been an ancient seabed, the ruins towered over the mesas around them, spiraled nubs of broken-down towers and collapsed caverns that were too enormous and geometrically perfect to have been created by anything but an intelligent hand.

In everything Valerian saw, there was a curious fusion of the organic and the artificial: Weathered walls were laced with strange-looking alloys within the natural rock, and canyons, mountains, and caverns had been artfully engineered to their designers' needs. He found vast and airy caverns roofed by rounded, riblike vaults and curved tunnels that stretched deep into the surface of Van Osten's Moon.

Though he was glad the site had been left largely unexplored, Valerian had to wonder at the stupidity of the bureaucrats who had withheld funding for such a wondrous find.

The sense of scale and the seeming age of the site were astounding, the deterioration of the rock suggesting spans of time more akin to geological ages rather than that of any time period comprehensible to humans.

Who had built the structures was a mystery, one that Valerian felt he could solve, had he but the resources and time. Though his father ensured that he and his mother were never short of money—the mineral find he had discovered just before their first meeting had turned out to be a seemingly never-ending source of funds, one that was now jealously guarded by a veritable army of soldiers, tanks, and goliaths—Valerian knew that time was against him.

With his father the most wanted man in the galaxy, it was only a matter of time until the hounds were snapping at their heels again and they were forced to move on. His mother's sickness had already forced him to halt his exploration of the alien ruins, but the actions of his father force him to leave them behind.

Either way, the end result was the same.

Valerian continued with his stretches, knowing that a hard run would work out some of his stress and anger toward his father. It was difficult to be angry with someone you hadn't seen for so long, but Valerian only had to think of his mother's condition and the familiar smoldering coal of his bitterness would flare into life once more.

A nervous knock came at the door to his room and he said, "Come in, Charles."

The door opened and a young man, only a few years older than Valerian, entered the room. He was dressed in an immaculately cut suit and his head was crowned with a shock of wild red hair that seemed at odds with the blandness of his features.

Charles Whittier had become part of their roving band of fugitives a year ago, an aide, servant, equerry, and general manservant who had arrived at the instruction of his father. Valerian was sure Whittier was reporting to his father, but what was not so clear was why.

Valerian played dumb, but for all that he did not trust Whittier; the man was a capable valet who attended to Valerian's needs with alacrity and competence.

"Good morning, sir," said Whittier. "I hope I'm not disturbing you."

"Not at all," said Valerian. "I was just about to go for a run."

"Ah, then I fear I may have come with a summons that might inconvenience you."

"What is it?"

"Your mother asks to speak with you," said Whittier.

Valerian made his way along the steel-walled corridors of the orbital, the fluorescent strips set into the ceiling and walls bleaching everything of life and color. It had once been a mining installation, and on such a facility visibility was more important than aesthetics, a concept Valerian could understand, even if he didn't subscribe to it.

Everything on board Orbital 235 was simple and functional, as was to be expected where space was at a premium and burly, largely unskilled men were expected to spend a great deal of their time.

The air had a dry, recycled quality to it, and Valerian found himself wishing for the hundredth time to be back on Umoja, with its scented air and copper skies. He walked at a brisk pace, his body now in the throes of its teenage development and changing daily.

He was still handsome to the point of beauty, his skin flawless and his hair golden. His features were in transition from boy to man, but he could already visualize the form they were going to take and knew they would be perfect.

Whittier walked alongside him, his legs seeming to move at twice the speed of Valerian's just to keep up with him. He was slender and apparently fit, but there was little vigor to the man, a trait Valerian was blessed with in abundance.

"How was she when you spoke to her?" asked Valerian.

"Much the same, sir. Though there was a certain animation to her today."

"Really? That's good. Any idea why?"

"No, sir," replied Whittier. "Though she did receive a communiqué from her father."

"How do you know who it came from, Charles?" asked Valerian. "Did you look at it first?"

"I most certainly did not," replied Whittier. "The very idea! Your grandfather always sends a communication at the beginning of the month. It is the beginning of the month; ergo, it is from your grandfather."

"Beginning of what month? We're in space, Charles."

"I keep a record of the diurnal rotations on Umoja and Tarsonis to keep track of our time relative to them. In such dislocated circumstances, I find it helps fix oneself if there is a predetermined point of reference to cling to."

"You've traveled a lot in space?"

"More than I have cared to," was Whittier's noncommittal answer.

Valerian wanted to ask more, but felt he would get little in the way of an answer that meant anything, so let the matter of Whittier's previous travels go and concentrated on the summons issued by his mother.

Juliana Pasteur was not a well woman, and her health had only deteriorated over the last six years. After his fifteenth birthday, Valerian had demanded to know what was wrong with her, and at last she had told him the truth of what the doctors had discovered, though sometimes he wished she hadn't.

His mother had been diagnosed with a carcinoid tumor, a rare cancer of the neuroendocrine system. The cancer had arisen in her intestine and grown slowly over the years, which was why it had taken so long for her to suspect there was more wrong than she realized.

By the time she'd consulted a physician, the cancer had already spread to her liver and begun to attack other parts of her body with unthinking biological relentlessness. Its progress had been slow, but steady, robbing her of her vitality and stripping the meat from her bones. Not even the most advanced surgical techniques could defeat the cancer without killing her in the process.

Valerian had cried with her as she told him and gently guided him through the same reactions she had experienced: denial, shock, anger, sadness, guilt, and fear.

She was going to die, and had made her peace with that.

It was more than Valerian could do.

He had immediately ceased his visits to the surface of the planetoid they circled and thrown himself into researching his mother's condition, despite the apparent hopelessness of the endeavor. Perhaps because she had been told she could live for several more years before death finally claimed her, his mother had tried to dissuade him from wasting his time looking for a miracle cure.

"Sometimes fighting to hold on to something you love can destroy it in the process," she had said to him one evening, holding him as he cried. "Let's enjoy the time we have left, Val. Let me watch you grow and live your life. Don't waste it chasing windmills."

But nothing she said to him could penetrate his need to *do* something, no matter that this was an enemy he had no means to fight. He discovered that not even the most advanced intrascopic lasers—devices capable of targeting specific areas of the body with precise amounts of heat—nor the latest drugs or even nano-brachytherapy could defeat this foe without first killing its victim.

Valerian, however, was a Mengsk, and he did not give up easily, requesting fresh digi-tomes and the latest researches from the top medical institutes on Umoja and Tarsonis (via safe routes to avoid compromising their security, of course).

"Sir?" said Whittier, and Valerian started. He hadn't realized they'd reached his mother's room, and wondered how long he'd been standing here.

"Are you going in?" asked Whittier.

He took a deep breath. "Yes. Of course I'm going in."

Valerian sat beside his mother's bed and held her hand, wishing he could pass some of his own vitality on to her. He had plenty to spare, so where was the cosmic harm in evening the balance? But the universe didn't work that way, he knew. It didn't care that bad things happened to good people, and was entirely indifferent to the fate of the mortal beings that crawled around on the debris of stars, no matter what those who believed in divine beings might claim.

His mother sat upright on her bed, her skin pale and translucent, as though pulled too tightly across her skull. Her hair fell around her shoulders, its golden luster now the sickly, jaundiced yellow of a chronic smoker. She was still beautiful, but it was a serene beauty bought with the acceptance of death.

Valerian found it hard to see her, fearful that if he looked too long he might lose grip on his emotions. At times like this he cursed his father for the lessons of emotional control.

"Have you been to your ruins today, Val?" she asked.

"No, Mum," he said. "I haven't. I don't go to them anymore, remember?"

"Oh yes, I forgot," she said, waving a bony arm before her. "I have trouble remembering things now, you know."

Valerian looked around the room, its austere functionality putting him in mind of a mortician's workspace. He hated the reek of defeat that filled the room.

"Are you thirsty?" he asked, in lieu of something meaningful to say.

She smiled. "Yes, honey. Pour me some water, would you?"

Valerian filled two plastic cups with tepid water and handed one to her, making sure she had it held in both hands before releasing his grip. She lifted the cup to her gaunt face and sipped the water, smiling as she handed it back to him.

"Charles told me you received a message today."

"I did," she said with a smile that served only to make her face look even more cadaverous than it did already. "It's from your grandfather."

"What does he have to say for himself this month?"

"He says your father is coming to see us."

The cup of water fell from Valerian's hands.

The spire of rock soared above Valerian like the horn of some massive, buried narwhal, its surface pitted and worn smooth by uncounted centuries. He ran his hand across the surface, feeling tingling warmth through the fluted surface of the rock that was quite at odds with the chill of the air around him.

Sheer cliffs of curving rock arched up overhead, a natural canyon that Valerian suspected had once been roofed by ribbed beams of stone, but which now lay scattered and broken at his feet.

Frozen, gritty winds howled as they funneled through the canyon, lamenting the fall of so mighty a structure, and Valerian wondered what great catastrophe had occurred here to cast it down. The sky rippled through the thin atmosphere, stars pulsing in the far distance, their light already millennia old.

He pulled his thick jacket tighter about himself and adjusted his goggles as he descended the loose-rubble-and-scree slope that led to the colossal cave mouth ahead. He had ventured within this cave before and felt a deep sense of connection to the past within its shimmering, hybrid walls.

To know that long-forgotten hands had crafted this palace with ancient artifice was an electrifying sensation—proof that life had existed in the galaxy long before the arrival of human beings. The secrets that might yet be buried here were beyond measure and Valerian longed for the opportunity to plumb the depths of those mysteries, both for the sake of knowledge and for the rewards it would bring.

Valerian paused as he took a moment to savor the solitude, smiling to himself as he realized that this was probably the most alone he had been in his entire life. He was the only human being on this rock, and the freedom of that sensation was intoxicating.

The news that his father was coming to Orbital 235 had made Valerian surly and irritable. He found himself unable to concentrate on his researches, and his mother had even berated him—something she almost never did.

The only peace he found was on the surface of Van Osten's Moon, alone with his thoughts and the ruins of a forgotten race of alien builders. What had brought them here and what had become of them? These were mysteries Valerian felt sure he could unlock were he but given the time.

Time. It all came back to time.

Time he, and more especially, his mother, didn't have.

He'd managed to persuade Charles Whittier that he could travel to the surface of Van Osten's Moon without escort and had landed one of the orbital's two flyers at the mouth of the largest canyon complex on the surface.

He wore a pair of loose-fitting cargo pants and a heavy, insulated jacket. Over his back was slung a rucksack filled with a comm unit, surveying equipment, and food and water. He wore a slugthrower in a shoulder holster and his favorite sword was belted at his hip. He wanted solitude, but he wasn't about to venture into alien ruins without taking some precautions.

The journey down the rocky canyon had been easy going so far, but his breath was still tight in his chest, and he slipped the mouthpiece of a small aqualung canister over his nose and mouth.

A squall of dust blew off the ground and Valerian looked up to see the Orbital's second lander flash overhead, circling and coming in to alight at the mouth of the canyon. He cursed at the interruption and had half a mind to just carry onward, to hell with the new arrival, but he forced the thought down.

The lander touched down without fuss and within moments, the side hatch opened and a tall figure emerged into the twilight world of Van Osten's Moon.

Valerian recognized him immediately, and his heart hammered on the cage of his ribs.

There was no mistaking the powerful cut of the man, even from this distance.

His father.

Arcturus Mengsk descended the ladder and began the trek to meet his son. Valerian saw that the man was dressed similarly to himself, with heavy-duty work wear and rugged boots. Like Valerian, his father carried a pack over his shoulders and moved with the natural assurance of a man used to being in control.

As his father approached, Valerian took the time to

study him. Arcturus's hair was still dark, but the first signs of gray were appearing at his temples and in his beard. Only in his mid-thirties, his father's ongoing war against the Confederacy was evidently aging him prematurely—though he was still an imposing, proud figure.

Despite the thin atmosphere, his father seemed untroubled by his exertions, and maintained a steady pace toward him over the rough terrain.

He waved at his son and, despite himself, Valerian waved back.

His mother had once told him that people often found themselves going out of their way to please his father for no reason they could adequately explain. Valerian wondered if he too had been affected by that reality-warping effect.

Arcturus dropped over a fallen slab of rock and took a deep breath of the thin air.

"Bracing, isn't it?" said his father.

Valerian removed the aqualung canister and said, "That's it? That's your greeting after eight years?"

"Ah, you're angry," said Arcturus, pausing and taking a seat on a smooth boulder. "A natural reaction, I suppose. Do you need to berate me for a while before we talk as men? It won't do any good, but if you feel you must, then go ahead."

Valerian felt the angry outburst he had planned to deliver wither in his breast and the angry retort on the tip of his tongue become stillborn.

"Right," he said. "I might as well get mad at these rocks for all the good it would do."

"Words spoken in anger are just hot air, Valerian. They rarely hurt, so what's the point of them? There are no words as ultimately destructive as those which are ultimately considered."

"You'd know about that," said Valerian. "The UNN is making you look like some kind of crazed madman."

Arcturus waved his hand. "No one believes what's on the UNN anyway, and the more they vilify me, the more people are waking up to see that I have the Confederacy worried."

"And do you? Have them worried?"

His father stood and came over to him, looking him up and down as though inspecting a prime specimen of livestock. "Oh, I'd say I do. The Confederacy is about to fall; I can see the cracks widening with every day that passes. My father and your grandfather knew what they were doing, but they weren't thinking big enough."

"And you are?"

"Very much so," said Arcturus, nodding in the direction of the cave mouth Valerian had been heading for. "Now what say you show me what's been occupying your time on this barren rock?"

Valerian nodded and set off without another word, picking his way down the slope toward the yawning cave. Its scale was immense and it took them a further hour to reach the bottom of the canyon, the towering cliffs wreathing them in shadow and cold.

The surfaces of the rocks were smooth and glassily transparent, as though vitrified by intense heat and striated with what looked like gleaming metal. Perfectly round gemstones were buried within the heart of the rock.

"Fascinating," said his father. "The surface has an igneous look to it, but appears to be metamorphic. Do you know the substance of the protolith?"

"No," said Valerian, suddenly wishing he knew more about the formation of rock and had more specialist equipment here. "I don't even know what that means."

"Ah, no, I suppose you wouldn't," said Arcturus. "Metamorphic rocks come about when a preexisting rock type, the protolith, is transformed into something altogether new."

"What sort of thing could cause that change?"

Arcturus pressed his hand against the rocks, resting his forehead on the smooth face of the stone. "Usually it's caused by high temperatures and the pressure of rock layers above, but tectonic processes like continental collisions would do it as well. Any sufficiently large geological force that causes enormous horizontal pressure, friction, and distortion could cause this, but I don't think we're looking at any natural phenomenon here."

"Why not?"

"Because whatever caused this transformation—if it even *was* a transformation, didn't take place over geological spans of time; I think it happened virtually overnight. But then, I've just arrived. I'm sure you've looked more deeply into the geological formations already."

Valerian hadn't had the chance to go any deeper than observational study, but suspected his father already knew that, and was bandying about his knowledge in an unconscious display of superiority.

"Of course," said Valerian, attempting to reassert his power. "My studies have shown that this formation is a blend of natural forces and artificial engineering. See here, where the natural camber of the rock has been molded and interfaced with what looks like some kind of metal reinforcement."

Arcturus looked closely at the rock Valerian indicated. "Yes, like a neosteel rebar in plascrete."

Valerian waved his father onward. "Come on, let's go inside; it's quite something. You'll not have seen anything like it."

"Don't be so sure—I've seen a lot these last few years."

"Nothing like this," promised Valerian.

His father stood in the center of the cave, though to call it such was to vastly diminish its unbelievable, incomprehensible scale. It was a gargantuan cathedral of light and stone and metal, fashioned deep in the heart of a mountain by an ancient race of gods. For surely no beings but gods could have hollowed out so massive a peak and not have it collapse in the millions, probably billions of years since they had first devised the means of its construction.

Gracefully curving ribs of rock soared overhead, each one thicker than the hull of a battlecruiser. Corbels the size of siege tanks jutted out of the walls and airy flying buttresses supported hanging finials and graceful descending archways of stone. Distance rendered them slim and delicate, but Valerian guessed most were at least twenty meters thick.

The very walls seemed to shimmer with internal bioluminescence, scads of light darting along the lengths of metal set in the stone like flickering embers of electrical current. Gems pulsed with a faint glow, as though in time with an infinitely slow and inaudible heartbeat.

Fluted stalactites descended in tapering spears, penetrating the roof like an inverted crown of ice pushed through the mountain's summit. A light mist hung in the upper reaches of the enormous cavern, a cloud system that kept the air moist and reduced the internal humidity.

The interior of the cave seemed to point even more conclusively to a deliberate hand in its creation, its scale making a mockery of any such human constructions. Entire fleets could fit within this enormous cavern and, for all Valerian knew, perhaps they had.

"It's incredible," said Arcturus, and Valerian was surprised to hear genuine emotion in his voice. "I've never seen the like."

"Told you," said Valerian, pleased he had been able to surprise his father.

"And you think this is alien?"

"Don't you?" replied Valerian, surprised at the question.

"I suppose it's possible," conceded his father, "but even if it's true, what does it matter? Whoever built this is long dead and gone."

"Aren't you curious about who built it? What great secrets we might learn from them?"

"Not especially. They are nothing but dust now and no one remembers them. How great could they have been?"

Valerian's frustration at his father's obstinate refusal to grasp the enormity of such revelations grew with every word Arcturus uttered, and his temper began to fray. He realized he'd been sucked into his father's reality by the man's apparent interest in the ancient cave. Valerian shook himself free of it as all the things he had wanted to say to his father suddenly rushed to the forefront of his mind.

"Where have you been all these years?" he blurted. "Why did you never come for us? Didn't you care for us?"

His father turned from his contemplation of the vast cavern, its majesty forgotten in an instant as he saw that the pleasant fiction of a father and son bonding was at an end.

"It was too dangerous," he said simply. "The

Confederacy wants me dead and if they knew where you were, they would use you to get to me. There's no great mystery to it, Valerian."

"My mother is ill," said Valerian. "Did you know?"

"Yes, I know."

"Do you care?"

"Of course I care," snapped Arcturus. "What kind of childish question is that?"

"Childish? Is it childish to wonder where you were when the mother of your son is dying?"

"Ailin told me your mother's cancer was inoperable," said Arcturus. "Is he right?"

"He is," confirmed Valerian, fighting to control his anger and hurt. "And all this running from planet to planet and moon to moon isn't doing her any good. It's just making her worse."

"And what would it have achieved if I had come rushing to your side, save put you both in danger?" said Arcturus. "Did you want me to come and help you hold your mother's hand as she lay on her deathbed? Is that it? Well, Valerian, I'm sorry, but that would have achieved nothing. I have greater concerns than comforting you. Or your mother."

Valerian wanted to launch himself at his father and wipe the uncaring expression from his face with his fists, but he kept his anger locked tightly within himself. Though he hated to admit it, Valerian found himself admiring the man's ability to think logically and focus in the face of what would have broken the composure of a lesser man.

But still, he had things to say to his father that needed saying, regardless of whether or not they would penetrate his armor of conceit.

"Greater concerns? Like overthrowing the Confederacy?"

"Exactly," said Arcturus. "And such a goal requires sacrifice. We have all lost people in the course of this war, son, including me: my parents, Dorothy, Achton."

"Who?"

"He was my father's head of security, and a good man."

"What happened to him?"

"He was on Korhal when the missiles hit."

"Ah."

"But their deaths will gain meaning when the Confederacy lies in ruins and you and I step in to fill the void. We can do it, Valerian. I have an army behind me that is the equal of anything the Confederacy can field. It's only a matter of time until they break and we can rule what they leave behind. But we can do it *right,* and found an empire for the good of humanity."

"The good of humanity?" spat Valerian. "You mean the benefit of the Mengsk dynasty."

Arcturus shrugged. "I see no difference between the two," he said.

"And you'd want me beside you?" said Valerian, trying to keep the hope from his voice.

"Of course," replied Arcturus, coming over and gripping his shoulders. "You are my son and you are a Mengsk. Who else would be worthy to stand at my side as my successor?"

"You didn't think so before," pointed out Valerian. "I heard what you said about me. You called me bookish, effeminate, and weak."

"Words spoken in anger long ago," said Arcturus, dismissing the hurt his words had done with a wave of the hand. "But look at you now! You have done me proud, boy. And I'm impressed; I can't pretend I'm not. You have achieved a lot since I saw you last."

"I didn't do it for you, Father," he said. "I did it for me."

"I know that, and that's good. A man should never do anything to impress others; he must always do things on his own and for his own sense of validation."

"And what if I don't want to your successor?" said Valerian. "You've been controlling my life from afar for so long now, I think you've gotten used to the idea that I'll always jump at your command. Well, I'm not like that, Father. I am my own man and I make my own decisions."

His father smiled and nodded, letting go of his shoulders and sitting on a nearby hunk of fallen rock. "I remember saying something similar to my father long ago."

Valerian felt the anger drain from him and took a long drink of water from a plastic canteen he removed from his pack.

"Did it do you any good?"

"Not really," said Arcturus, accepting the canteen

from Valerian. "I called him a terrorist and a murderer, but now I've done far worse than he ever did. I guess if someone does something truly terrible to you, it's easier to justify your retaliation, no matter how vile it is. The Confederacy killed my family and obliterated my homeworld; what could I possibly do that would approach an atrocity of such magnitude?"

"I don't know," said Valerian. "I don't think I *want* to know."

"Then what *do* you want, Valerian?"

"I want to be part of your life, but I want to make my own destiny."

"I said *that* to my father too," replied Arcturus. "However, I have since found that time and history have a way of sweeping us up and making use of our talents, irrespective of what we might want."

"What do you mean?"

"I mean that destiny will sometimes force us down the road it intends for us and there's nothing we can do about it."

"Is that what you think happened to you?"

"Maybe, but I don't think so."

"Why not?"

"Because destiny dances to *my* tune," said Arcturus.

Valerian laughed at that, but the laugher died when he realized his father wasn't joking.

CHAPTER 17

DESTINY DANCES TO MY TUNE . . .

The words came back to Valerian as he watched the gigantic AAI holo-screen in the main commercial square of Gramercy City, capital of Tyrador VIII. Fully thirty meters wide and nine high, the artificial advertising intelligence projected an image atop a shimmering podium before a giant skyscraper.

Normally, the AAI advertised clothes, soft drinks, or the latest model of groundcar, but today promised to be quite different.

A flickering, three-dimensional image of his father's face hovered over the podium, for once speaking to those who watched without interference from Confederate censors or UNN editors. Upward of ten thousand people filled the square—traders, shoppers, businessmen, refugees, criminals, and enforcers of the law—all silent and filled with nervous excitement as they listened to the words blaring from the speakers set within the podium.

The voice of Arcturus Mengsk spoke over a magnificent tableau of stirring imagery, sweeping landscapes, and Wraith fighters flying in formation.

"Fellow terrans," began his father, his voice booming its pronouncement like that of a stern but magnanimous god. "I come to you in the wake of recent events to issue a call to reason. Let no human deny the perils of our time. While we battle one another, divided by the petty strife of our common history, the tide of a greater conflict is turning against us, threatening to destroy all that we have accomplished."

Valerian watched the faces of the people of Gramercy City around him, feeling slightly in awe of being in so vast a crowd. Until recently, the largest number of people he'd seen gathered in one place had been a dozen or so servants in his grandfather's home on Umoja, which seemed so long ago it was like another life.

Taking refuge on Tyrador VIII had been Valerian's idea—hiding in plain sight in the midst of a populous planet, though given the fate of the Confederacy in recent months and this current announcement, it looked like their enforced flight was now at an end.

"It is time for us as nations and as individuals to set aside our long-standing feuds and unite," continued the stentorian voice of his father as the image on the screen changed to mighty battlecruisers sweeping majestically over Korhal. "The tides of an unwinnable war are upon us, and we must seek refuge on higher ground, lest we be swept away by the flood."

An image of a Confederate battlecruiser on fire from stem to stern filled the viewer and the crowd cheered, a collective outpouring of decades of repressed anger and frustration.

Valerian's father continued. "The Confederacy is no more; whatever semblance of unity and protection it once provided is a phantom . . . a memory. With our enemies left unchecked, who will you turn to for protection?"

The montage of images moved on as the cheering continued, the shattered Confederate vessel replaced with juddering shots of what Valerian now knew were a protoss ship and a snapshot of a zerg higher organism drifting in space.

"The devastation wrought by the alien invaders is self-evident. We have seen our homes and communities destroyed by the calculated blows of the protoss. We have seen firsthand our friends and loved ones consumed by the nightmarish zerg. Unprecedented and unimaginable though they may be, these are the signs of our time."

Flashing, violent images of battling Wraiths sped across the screen, though what they were shooting at wasn't clear.

"The time has come, my fellow terrans, to rally to a new banner," demanded his father. "In unity lies strength; already many of the dissident factions have joined us. Out of the many, we shall forge an indivisible whole, capitulating only to a single throne. And from that throne I shall watch over you."

A tingle ran up Valerian's spine, but he couldn't tell whether it was one of relief or dread. His father's words had sounded more like a warning than a promise of protection. The image returned to the soaring spires that were even now being rebuilt on Korhal amid the ashen devastation of the Confederates's spiteful attack. The camera closed on the buildings, finally settling on a huge black flag bearing a symbol that had become familiar to everyone over the last few years: a red arm holding a whip in its fist, the whip forming a circle around the arm.

The Sons of Korhal.

The camera lingered on the flag as his father delivered his closing words. "From this day forward let no human make war upon any other human; let no terran agency conspire against this new beginning; and let no man consort with alien powers. And to all the enemies of humanity, seek not to bar our way, for we shall win through, no matter the cost."

Static formed a glittering column of white noise as the voice of Arcturus Mengsk faded and was replaced by the unwavering symbol of the Sons of Korhal.

Valerian turned away from the enormous AAI as he heard the familiar snap and sizzle of the holo-projectors firing up to repeat the message once more. Valerian had no need to hear it again; he had memorized the words as soon as he'd heard them.

He turned and made his way along the crowded thoroughfares, pushing against the tide of jubilant people making their way toward the central square.

Valerian found a side street he knew, and on it a small coffee house he frequented. The shop was empty when he reached it, and Valerian helped himself to a hot drink, making sure to leave a few credit notes on the scuffed wooden bar.

He took a seat by the window and watched the cheering crowds pass by, their faces alight with joy. Valerian knew that the people here would, for a while, remember this day with golden memories: the day the hated Confederacy was overthrown and replaced with . . .

Well, no one had been sure until today who would step into the void of authority left by the Confederacy's sudden, shocking demise.

No one except Valerian Mengsk. He had known *exactly* who it would be.

Today's sectorwide broadcast had only confirmed it. His father had declared himself Emperor Arcturus Mengsk I of the Terran Dominion, but no one was yet sure of the legitimacy of his claim. Valerian had heard some people talk of elections, while others cried out in support of a man who had, until recently, been condemned throughout human space as a terrorist.

Never more was the aphorism about history being written by the victors about to be proven correct.

Destiny dances to my tune . . .

In the three years since he had heard his father speak those words, Valerian had come to understand his ultimate aim. He'd seen his suspicions turn to certainty as, over and over again, his father had defeated every force the Confederacy sent against him with a combination of guile, brute force, and displays of utter ruthlessness that still had the power to stagger Valerian when he thought of them.

Indeed, the last year had seen a multitude of changes, all of which had come with such unprecedented speed that it was hard to process them with any degree of comprehension.

Humanity's first system shock had come with the news that the worlds of Chau Sara and Mar Sara had been destroyed by a fleet of ships belonging to an alien race known as the protoss.

The second had followed soon after when it became apparent that both worlds had been destroyed to ensure the destruction of a *second* alien species, a species whose name soon became synonymous with wholesale destruction and parasitic infestation of world after world: the zerg.

Valerian's initial excitement concerning the now indisputable evidence of alien life had been dampened somewhat with the realization that neither the protoss nor the zerg were likely candidates as the builders of the ancient structures—he'd decided they were temples of some sort—that he'd explored on Van Osten's Moon.

The zerg were a vile agglomeration of genetically mutable creatures driven by bloody instinct and an insatiable hunger to devour, while the protoss were a strange, aloof race of psionic warriors. Though this latter race possessed technology far in advance of and just plain *different* from that of the terrans, it did not seem likely they were a resurgent branch species of the temple's builders.

The news that humanity was no longer alone was greeted with horror in some quarters, religious ecstasy in others. Some people wanted to greet these new arrivals with open arms and hearty welcomes, while others—savvy to the current zeitgeist—armed themselves for war. This latter group were to be proved the more perceptive.

With the arrival of these alien races, open warfare ignited throughout Confederate space, with local brushfire skirmishes flaring into full-scale revolts. And, of course, Arcturus Mengsk was there to fan the flames.

Refugees fled before the tides of this increasingly ferocious war, and conflicts revved up from terrorist attacks to full-fledged planetary battles throughout the sector. Thousands were dying every day and calamity followed calamity for the Confederates as they lost their grip on their colony worlds one by one.

Then came the destruction of Antiga Prime.

The truth had been suppressed, of course, but Valerian had it on good authority from his grandfather that the great Arcturus Mengsk had used stolen psi-emitter technology to lure the zerg to the Confederate colony to defeat his enemies, which had in turn drawn the protoss there to scour the planet bare of all life.

The terror that had followed this catastrophe spread through what remained of the Confederate colonies like a virus through a fringe world shantytown. The stream of refugees became a raging torrent, and freighters crammed with terrified people fled in thousands from the epicenters of the fighting to the outer rim territories.

Valerian remembered his mother's reaction to the news of his father's complicity in the death of Antiga Prime, seeing her visibly sag at what the man she had once loved was becoming. Valerian had realized some time ago that his father's once noble ideals of throwing off the yoke of Confederate tyranny and ending the corruption of the Old Families had withered and been replaced with a desire for an empire of his own.

His mother despised what his father had become, but Valerian secretly admired the single-mindedness with which Arcturus pursued that one ambition, knowing that one day it was destined to be his.

The thought still struck an ambivalent chord within him.

Not long after the destruction of Antiga Prime, his father had ordered Valerian and his mother to find a new refuge, one far from the core worlds of what remained of the Confederacy. It was typical of his father to send such a blunt message, but Valerian had sensed something deeper behind it, as though some terrible event was about to be set in motion that required Valerian and Juliana to be as far from it as possible.

He hadn't known what that was until news reached them of the fall of Tarsonis, capital world of the Confederacy. Like Antiga Prime before it, Tarsonis was overrun by the zerg, drawn there by his father to destroy his enemies—the Old Families who had murdered his parents and sister and consigned millions people to death on Korhal.

As acts of vengeance went, Valerian had to admit it was a masterstroke.

Bold, without mercy, and unstoppable.

The Confederacy died with Tarsonis. It had been the linchpin of human space for so long that without it, the colony worlds folded and collapsed, leaving Arcturus Mengsk's Dominion triumphant in the ruins of his enemies' defeat.

No sooner had the Confederacy fallen than his father had made contact, telling him that the time was approaching when he would bid Valerian step into the light as his son.

Valerian couldn't deny the attraction of that idea, for he was now eighteen and ready to take his place on the galactic stage as a force in his own right. He was his own man now: intelligent, erudite, charming, and capable, able to fight with sword, rifle, or rhetoric as the occasion and honor demanded.

But whether he would be the successor his father imagined . . .

Well, that was another matter altogether.

Valerian finished his drink and left the deserted coffee shop.

"Time to go home," he said.

In the end, it was another six months before Valerian was to see his father again, the demands of building the Dominion from the ashes of the Confederacy taking longer and placing more demands on the newly installed emperor than had been foreseen. Valerian hadn't minded at first, content to spend time back on Umoja at his grandfather's house with his mother now that they were free of the need to move from place to place to avoid Confederate kill teams.

But as the weeks turned to months, his impatience grew and the enforced idleness of life on Umoja began to grate on him. He was the son of an emperor, yet had nothing of importance to do.

His mother's condition had progressed, with every remission followed by a resurgence of the invisible sickness that was consuming her. New technologies had slowed her descent but hadn't been able to stop it, and the doctors had solemnly informed him that she could last only another six months at most. They had been saying that for years, though, and his mother had surprised them all with her dogged tenacity and courage.

Between periods of caring for his mother, Valerian's days were spent honing his already fearsome skills with a blade and gun under the stern gaze of Master Miyamoto. His old tutor had accompanied him back to Umoja and had declared Valerian the best student he had ever taught.

He devoured every digi-tome he could get hold of, learning everything he could of the protoss and zerg. He scoured the information networks for any sign of fresh alien ruins, but in the aftermath of war, archaeology was no one's priority save his.

On this evening, Valerian walked behind his mother in the gardens of his grandfather's house, following the path toward the river, which glittered like molten copper in the sunset.

She had bid him accompany her to the riverbank and they had set off as the servants prepared the evening meal. Juliana ate little these days, but Valerian's appetite was as hearty as ever.

He wore a form-fitting suit of charcoal gray, knee-high boots of gleaming black leather, a double-breasted jacket with more than a hint of the soldier to it, and a scarlet cloak draped around his shoulders. His hair was unbound and fell about his shoulders in a cascade of gold, the image of his mother's in her prime.

Now that there was no reason to hide his ancestry, and every reason to display it, Valerian proudly wore a bronze wolf-head medal of the Mengsk family upon his breast.

His mother sat in an automated wheelchair, controlling its movements with an alpha wave reader fitted just behind her right ear. Returning to Umoja had done more to restore his mother's constitution than all the years of drugs and painful chemotherapy. Intramuscular nano-stimulators had prevented her muscles from atrophying completely, and it was wonderful to see some of her vitality restored to her. Even though Valerian knew she could not last much longer, he loved that she smiled again now that she was home.

The air was clear and crisp, the umber sky warm and like honey over the distant horizon as the day drew to a close. The scent of the air was heavy, and Valerian took a deep breath, instantly transported back to his boyhood and a time where he was innocent of the wider scope of the galaxy around him.

"It's good to be home, isn't it?" said his mother, her voice thin, but stronger than it had been in many years. "Back on Umoja, I mean."

Valerian nodded. "Yes, though I still find it hard to think of anywhere as home now."

"I know, honey," said his mother. "And I'm sorry— it was no way to grow up, being shunted from pillar to post like that."

"It was hardly your fault. After all, what choice did we have?"

"I know, but I want you to understand that I wish I could have given you a normal childhood."

"'A normal childhood'?" said Valerian. "What is that, anyway? Does it even exist?"

"Of course it does. I had a perfectly normal childhood growing up here."

"I guess," said Valerian as they rounded a bend in the path next to a stand of poplars and the river came into view. "And I remember this place fondly—though too much has happened for me to think of it as home anymore."

"That's sad," said Juliana, pointing to an irregular chunk taken out of the otherwise smooth course of the riverbank. "You remember that little cove there?"

Water had since filled the cove, where it gamboled in miniature whirlpools, but Valerian remembered kneeling in the mud with a small shovel and a tray of unearthed treasures.

"Yes," he said with a smile. "I remember. I used to dig there for alien fossils."

"I was so proud of you," said Juliana. "I *am* proud of you, Valerian. You've grown up into such a wonderful, handsome boy. My heart almost breaks every time I look at you."

"Mother, don't go on!" said Valerian, embarrassed by her praise, but enjoying it nonetheless.

"I mean it," she said, more urgently this time. "I might not have much time left and there are things I need to say to you, my darling boy. And I wanted you to remember something good from your childhood before I say them."

"What is it?" he asked, instantly alert as he sensed finality at the implication of his mother's words.

"You've had to grow up so quickly, and I know that's been hard on you, but you're going to have to grow up some more soon. I'm not going to be around much longer—"

"Quiet, Mother," said Valerian, keeling beside her and taking her hand. "Those doctors don't know what they're talking about. Not one of them has been right about your condition. You've confounded them all and I know you'll outlive every one of us."

"You're so sweet," she said, running a hand along the side of his face, "but we both know that this will get me in the end, no matter how fast I run."

"Please," said Valerian, his voice trembling. "Don't talk like this."

"I have to; I'm sorry," said Juliana, tears welling in the corners of her eyes.

"Why?" cried Valerian.

"Because soon your father will be here and I'm not strong enough to stand up to him anymore, if I ever was." This last comment was said bitterly and seemed to give her the strength to continue.

"Your father is a dangerous man," said his mother. "And I don't just mean to his enemies. He uses people, Valerian. He uses them and he chews them up and when he's done with them he spits them out. I wasted my life believing in him, and my heart would break if I thought you were about to become the same kind of man he is. I gave up my dreams for your father, thinking he needed me and that he'd come for me when the time was right, but he never did."

"Why are you saying these things, Mother? I don't need to hear them."

"Yes," she said, squeezing his hand with all her strength. "Yes, you do. You have to be strong enough to resist your father's influence. By all means admire him—he has many admirable qualities—but don't try to be like him, no matter what happens. Be your own man in all things and don't let him maneuver you like one of his chess pieces."

Valerian felt the strength of her purpose pouring from her with every word, as though she were channeling every last bit of her energy into making sure he understood her. He could understand the cause of her bitterness toward his father, but did she truly appreciate the grand designs his father had set in motion, and the sacrifices necessary to realize them?

Valerian looked into his mother's sunken eyes, seeing the pain and sorrow that filled them, and suddenly thought that maybe she understood the price of his father's ambition all too well . . .

"Do you understand me?" she said urgently. "Please tell me you understand."

"I understand," said Valerian, though in truth he did not. "I do. Father may be many things, but he wouldn't sacrifice his own son to further his ambitions."

"I hope you're right, Val," she said, opening her arms and taking him into her embrace. "I really hope you're right."

They sat in silence for many minutes, holding on to one another and letting cathartic tears fall without inhibition. Valerian took a breath, then released his mother's skeletal frame.

"I love you, Valerian," she said. "My wonderful, handsome boy. You are the best thing I have done with my life."

Valerian tried to answer her, but his throat was too choked to speak, his mind too overwhelmed at the thought of losing his mother.

He wiped his eyes with a handkerchief and dabbed away the last tears with the heel of his palm. This was not the way of a Mengsk, he thought. A Mengsk was stronger than this, his heart a fortress . . .

Valerian turned as he heard the crunch of gravel on the path behind him, recognizing the diffident tread of Charles Whittier, who remained his constant companion still. Accompanying Whittier was Valerian's grandfather, Ailin Pasteur.

"What is it, Charles?" asked Valerian.

"I'm sorry to intrude, sir, but we've just received confirmation from General Duke."

"And?" said Valerian when Whittier did not continue.

"He wasn't too happy about keeping his ships beyond the outer shipping markers. He demanded to bring his ships into Umoja's orbit before allowing the emperor to descend to the planet's surface."

"And I told him to shove his demands up his ass," said Ailin Pasteur.

Valerian was shocked at his grandfather's outburst, knowing he detested expletives as a sign of poor upbringing and a lack of vocabulary.

"I'll bet that went down well with Duke," said Valerian.

He'd never met Edmund Duke, but his grandfather had told him of his reputation and how he'd defected to the Sons of Korhal when his ship crashed amid a ravenous zerg swarm.

Valerian had taken an instant dislike to him, recalling the teachings of Master Miyamoto and his notions of honor. As antiquated as such beliefs might be now, they still had a hold on Valerian's soul.

"I don't care how it went down," continued his grandfather. "The Ruling Council is concerned at the direction Arcturus is taking his Terran Dominion. To say we're unhappy at the idea of a fleet of Dominion warships parked in orbit around Umoja is an understatement."

"And what did Duke say?"

"Duke didn't say anything, sir" said Whittier. "It was the emperor himself who sent word."

Valerian's head whipped up at the mention of his father.

"The emperor agreed to the Umojan conditions," said Whittier, and Valerian could hear the sycophancy in his aide's voice.

"So when will he get here?"

"He will travel to us aboard an in-system gun cutter. He has arranged to be here first thing in the morning."

Valerian nodded and watched the sun set over the horizon, the descending orb bathing the landscape in a russet glow the color of blood.

"Did it work?" asked the armored figure standing in the doorway of the ship's bridge. The voice was muffled by the helmet, but the aching *need* was clear.

"It worked," confirmed the tech in oil-stained overalls hunched over a battered, jury-rigged comm unit. "The stuff we got on Braxis was the real deal. I've been able to decode all the Dominion datalinks. We got it all: his flight plan, IFF codes, full manifest, and arrival point. Pilot's already plotting us a course."

The figure nodded, hands curling into fists. "Good. Stay on it; listen for any more chatter."

"Will do."

The figure turned and made its way along a metal-framed corridor that led deeper into the starship, the CMC-300 Powered Combat Suit emblazoned with the red and blue flag of the Confederacy painted on several of the armored plates. A gauss rifle was slung over one shoulder and a long-bladed combat knife was sheathed in a leg holster.

The corridor's walls were dented from small-arms fire, scorched by the impacts of ship-to-ship lasers, and corroded from bio-organic weapons of the zerg. The interior of the ship had clearly seen better days.

It was a miracle the ship was spaceworthy at all, considering the damage it had taken during the battle around Tarsonis when Mengsk had unleashed those hellspawn monsters on them all.

The figure made its way into the depths of the ship, passing barrack rooms where Confederate marines cleaned their armor and stripped their weapons down for the hundredth time. There was no garrulous banter between these warriors anymore; the fall of the Confederacy and death of everything they held dear had seen to that.

At last, the figure came to a metal doorway and rapped a heavy gauntlet on the shutter.

"Come in," said a voice with a laconic, almost liquid accent.

The figure entered the room and removed the armor's helmet.

Captain Angelina Emillian shook her head and ran a hand through her tousled hair.

"We got what we need," she said, addressing the man who sat on the edge of the room's only bed. His white uniform jacket was unbuckled, revealing a hairless, slab-muscled chest, and he polished a large rifle that lay across his lap.

"Everything?" he said, putting down the rifle.

"Yeah," said Emillian. "The codes we got on Braxis are still active. They don't know we hit the base at Boralis yet, so they haven't bothered to change them."

"Excellent work, Angelina," he said, standing and buckling his jacket. "Assemble the marines and warn them this one's going to be hard. When we launch your dropship, you'll be going in hot. We won't be able to extract you unless you kill him."

"That don't matter," said Emillian. "As long as that bastard Mengsk is dead I don't care."

"I know," he said. "Believe me, I understand hatred very well."

"I trained him, did you know that?"

"Yes," he said. "And that's why I know you'll kill him. You're better than him."

Emillian nodded toward his rifle. "You sure you don't want to go in with us? I know how you like to use that bad boy."

"Not this time," he said. "Our new allies are readying another mission as well as the assassination of Mengsk, and I need to help them coordinate."

"Oh? And where might that be?"

"The shipyards at Dylar IV," said Samir Duran.

CHAPTER 18

THE LAST TIME VALERIAN HAD WAITED FOR HIS father on Umoja, he had been seven years old. He remembered his wide-eyed optimism at the thought of meeting the heroic man who stood head and shoulders above lesser mortals. This occasion shared similarities with that day, in that Arcturus Mengsk was now literally head and shoulders above lesser men.

Emperor Arcturus Mengsk the First. It had a strange sound to it, as though it had not yet settled and was yet to earn its rank as a title.

Valerian stifled a yawn and wished he'd been able to sleep last night. He'd told himself it was simply that he'd drunk too much caffeine, but he knew it was the thought of his acknowledgment as the emperor's son that had caused his sleepless night. With the resources of the Dominion at his disposal, nothing would lie beyond his grasp. He could lead archaeological teams back to Van Osten's Moon or any number of sites that had recently come to light.

The day had dawned bright and warm, as though Umoja itself were preparing to welcome the new emperor, and the sun was a bloated red orb in the coppery sky. Valerian stood on the lawn before his grandfather's house, dressed in his finest suit and boots, with his ubiquitous scarlet cloak that accentuated his broad shoulders like armor. His sword was slung low by his left leg and a handcrafted blaster pistol was holstered on the opposite hip. He presented a perfect image of an emperor's son, and despite his mother's reservations about today, he could see she was pleased with how fine he looked.

She sat in her wheelchair, wearing the most flattering clothes that could be tailored for her painfully thin form. Her hair was washed and cleaned and, even after all she had said about his father at the riverbank last night, Valerian could see she had put on a little makeup.

Even those cast aside by his father still made an effort to look presentable for him.

Standing with them was his grandfather, Charles Whittier, and Master Miyamoto—resplendent in his finest fighting robes—and behind them a line of Ailin Pasteur's servants. It had been Whittier's idea to have the serving staff stand ready to greet the new emperor, and though Valerian's grandfather had balked at the idea of putting on such a dog-and-pony show, Valerian had persuaded him that it couldn't do any harm.

"The great emperor likes to make us wait," grumbled Pasteur.

"Well, the Ruling Council did make him halt his ships beyond the outer marker," pointed out Whittier. "And gun cutters aren't exactly the fastest ships. A battlecruiser would have arrived here much sooner."

His grandfather mumbled something under his breath; Valerian didn't catch it, but could guess its substance. Ailin Pasteur and Charles Whittier had gotten off on the wrong foot and had never bothered to try and find the right one. He suspected his grandfather was unsure as to which of the Mengsks Whittier owed his loyalty, proving to Valerian that Ailin Pasteur was a shrewd judge of character.

"There," said Master Miyamoto, pointing to a spot of light in the orange-flecked clouds.

Valerian looked up, feeling his heartbeat shift up a notch as he saw the glowing cruciform shape of an aircraft dropping through the atmosphere. Two lighter ships swooped protectively around it, flying figure-eight patterns above and below the larger ship. Valerian felt a hand take his and looked down to see his mother staring in apprehension at the approaching flyers.

"It'll be all right," said Valerian.

She looked up at him with a weak smile. "Remember what I told you," she said.

"I will," he promised.

The shapes resolved themselves from the clouds and Valerian saw that the central craft was a heavy gun cutter, a wide-bodied, pugnacious-looking aircraft long ago rendered obsolete by the development of the Wraith fighter. But it had range and was capable of interplanetary travel within a system, so had never quite vanished from the inventory.

With the losses taken in the war against the Confederacy, he guessed his father could not afford to be too choosy when it came to weapons of war. The other two ships were Wraiths, sleek air-superiority fighters that could engage ground and air targets with equal lethality.

The gun cutter slowed its descent and rotated in to land, its ventral thrusters kicking in as it approached the ground. Its bulbous engine nacelles were too wide to allow the craft to fit into the underground hangar, but the pilot contented himself with landing next to the platform's open hatchway. The Wraiths continued to fly overhead patrols as the gun cutter settled its heavy bulk onto the ground.

"That's never going to grow back," grumbled Pasteur as the cutter's jets seared the grass.

"You use robots to tend the garden, so where's the harm?" said Valerian with a smile.

"Not the point," replied his grandfather. "Lack of respect for others is what it is."

Further discussion was halted as the side hatch of the gun cutter rumbled open in a haze of steam. Smoke swirled as a dozen soldiers in combat armor jogged down the assault ramp and took up the position of honor guard on either side of it.

A shape appeared in the smoke and Valerian smiled at the theatricality of his father's emergence into the Umojan sunlight.

Emperor Arcturus Mengsk wore a long brown duster edged in gold thread and a brocaded internal lining. His suit was styled like a marine's dress uniform and finished with a glittering, wolf-head belt buckle. His boots were polished and a long sword was buckled at a rakish angle on his hip.

As Arcturus marched down the ramp, Valerian saw his father had aged, the silver in his beard and hair more pronounced than when he had last seen him. Yet for all the signs of maturity, his father was still a year shy of forty and carried himself with the confidence and power of a man half his age.

Everything about him radiated his absolute belief in himself, and Valerian knew that though in any other man this would be arrogance, with his father it was simply a statement of fact.

The soldiers fell in behind Arcturus as he crossed the lawn toward them with a purposeful stride. Valerian noticed the shock in his eyes at the sight of Juliana. In that one, quickly masked window, Valerian caught a glimpse of his father's fear of infirmity and things he could not call on his fearsome intellect and power to fight.

Valerian's grandfather stepped forward to meet Arcturus, his ambassadorial mask slipping into place as he shook hands with a man with whom he had run the gamut of emotions: admiration, mistrust, anger, forgiveness, and finally mistrust again.

"Arcturus, welcome to Umoja."

"I remember the last time you said that to me, Ailin," said Arcturus. "You didn't mean it then and I suspect you don't entirely mean it now."

"So long as you are here in peace, then you are welcome," replied Pasteur.

"Ever the diplomat, eh?" said Arcturus, turning to greet Valerian.

His father came forward with his arms open and his face alight with genuine pleasure. "My boy, it does my heart good to see you. You look well, very well."

"I am, Father," said Valerian, embracing him and enduring a series of hearty slaps on the back for his trouble. His father was at his ease with such comradely gestures, but Valerian had always found them awkward and forced.

Valerian broke the embrace and his father turned to Juliana.

"If you dare say I look well, I'll take that sword and stick you with it," she said.

"I was going to say that it was good to see you," replied his father. "But you look better than I was led to believe, so that's good."

"I'm flattered," said Juliana, but his father had already moved on to greet Charles Whittier and Master Miyamoto, playing the role of the approachable man of the people. Valerian saw the falseness of it and wondered how others could not. Perhaps he was more like his father than he knew, able to see through the charade as if it were his own.

At last his father stepped back and said, "You are al very dear to me, my friends, and it means a great deal, after all we have been through together, that we should meet like this in the wake of my great triumph."

Arcturus came forward and put his arm around Valerian, pulling him forward to stand at his side before the assembled onlookers.

"We live in momentous times," said Arcturus. "But going forward together, we can achieve anything we desire. Father and son, we will build a better world for everyone."

Polite applause rippled from the serving staff and Valerian dearly wanted to believe his father's words, feeling somewhat swept up in the grandeur of his vision for the future.

Only Master Miyamoto looked unimpressed, staring in consternation at the sky.

"Are those yours?" he said, shading his eyes from the sun.

Valerian followed Miyamoto's gaze, and a hot rush of adrenaline flooded his system.

Four Wraith fighters. Emblazoned with the flag of the Confederacy.

Diving in on an attack run.

"Everyone inside!" shouted Arcturus.

The assembled crowd needed no encouragement and bolted for the house.

The two Wraiths tasked with patrolling the skies above the emperor reacted as soon as their pilots realized the codes they were receiving on their IFF threat panels were a lie, but by then it was already too late. The first fighter exploded as a stream of bright laser bolts stitched a path over its fuselage and ripped off its right wing.

The second Wraith avoided the initial volley of gunfire and was able to return fire. Amazingly, the pilot's shots impacted on one of the attackers, blowing out the cockpit in a shower of superheated blood and glass.

The enemy fighter spiraled toward the ground, plowing into the grass in a spectacular fireball, cartwheeling across the lawn, and smashing into the house, drowning out the screams of panic that filled the air. Shattered glazing and buckled steel caved inward and black smoke billowed upward from the wreckage buried in the structure of the house.

The Dominion pilot's defiance was short-lived, however, as the remaining three Confederate fighters boxed him in and blew his craft apart in a hail of laser fire.

Burning wreckage fell into the river, sending up huge spouts of water as it crashed.

Valerian grabbed his mother from her chair and carried her close to his chest as he ran for the house, knowing there wasn't time to get her to safety with more dignity. Sizzling bolts of energy sawed across the lawn as the first Wraith flew in low on a strafing run. Half a dozen of his grandfather's serving staff were scythed down, bodies blown apart from inside by the passage of violently hot lasers through their flesh.

Valerian dropped to the ground as the ruby bolts ripped up the ground on either side of him. He tasted earth and blood and smelled the stink of seared meat. His mother cried out in pain and he rolled onto his side, seeing her lying helpless next to him. The Confederate Wraiths screamed overhead, their wing-mounted weaponry firing upon the helpless targets below them.

His father's marines returned fire on the Wraiths as they fell back toward the house, but the pilots weren't worried about small-arms fire from the ground. Impaler spikes sparked from the fighters' fuselages or missed altogether, but they at least gave the semblance of a fight back.

The gun cutter that had brought his father to Umoja was powering up its engines, but before it could lift off it was struck by a withering salvo of gunfire from the predatory Wraiths. One of the engine nacelles exploded, spraying white-hot fragments in all directions.

Whickering, razor-edged shrapnel cut down fleeing men and women in a bloody storm as the gun cutter lurched sideways. It plowed a huge furrow in the ground, throwing up sprays of earth and clods of mud as its one remaining engine roared into life and spun it around on its axis.

The gun cutter lurched one last time and vanished from sight, tumbling down into the open shaft of the landing platform it had previously been too big to fit within.

With one of its engines blown off, that was no longer a problem.

Valerian heard someone shout his name and looked over the corpse-strewn lawn toward the house, seeing his father and grandfather crouched in the shelter of a recessed doorway. Both men were furiously beckoning to him as the Wraiths circled around for another strafing run.

Valerian didn't waste time looking up and simply scooped his mother off the ground and ran as fast as he could to safety.

"Oh God, Val, I'm so scared!" she cried.

"Don't worry," he gasped. "I won't let anything happen to you."

The house suddenly seemed impossibly far off, as though his every step carried it farther and farther away from him. His father's soldiers were painting the sky with Impaler fire, and Valerian risked a glance over his shoulder as he heard the distinctive, chopping-air sound of a dropship on a fast insertion run.

A heavy lander in the colors of the Confederacy was dropping rapidly through the clouds, a midsized assault boat capable of carrying around twenty to thirty soldiers, depending on their loadout. Valerian forced himself to run faster, and suddenly he was at the doorway.

His father grabbed him and hauled him into the house. The breath heaved in his lungs and his heart rate was racing like never before. From eight years of age, he had trained to fight with gun and sword, but this was the first time he'd been exposed to real combat. Valerian handed his mother off to Charles Whittier, who set her down on a carved wooden bench as Ailin Pasteur slammed the door shut and engaged the mag-lock.

They were in the east wing hallway, a terrazzo-floored vestibule that linked the main receiving rooms and the guest quarters. Along with his mother and father, Master Miyamoto, Whittier, and Ailin Pasteur, there were five soldiers and a handful of weeping domestics.

"What the hell is going on, Mengsk?" demanded Ailin Pasteur. "Who is trying to kill us?"

His father took a breath and placed his hands on Valerian's shoulders, his relief at his son's survival plain for all to see.

"There has been some . . . opposition to the institution of my reign," he said, turning and drawing his sword as his soldiers formed up around him. "I can only assume that this is a manifestation of that opposition."

"Opposition?" exploded Ailin. "This is more than bloody opposition—those men are going to kill us!"

Arcturus laughed in Pasteur's face. "Kill us? Don't be foolish, Ailin."

"This isn't a fortress, Arcturus. That door isn't going to keep them out for long."

"They're not going to kill us, Ailin," repeated Arcturus.

"You sound very sure," snapped Pasteur.

"I am," replied Arcturus. "I may die one day, but it won't be today. Not at the hands of fools who can't accept they're beaten. Charles, what's the comm situation? I need reinforcements."

Charles Whittier, still holding Juliana Pasteur upright, had one hand pressed to his ear, in which was nestled the blinking light of a comm bead.

"All the local networks are jammed, sir," he said. "Our assailants appear to have cast an electromagnetic pulse net around us, and I do not believe any of the house comm units are strong enough to burn through it, at least not before we are dead. Also, I'm picking up hundreds of channels of white noise across a wide spectrum. Even if someone could pick up our broadcast, there's too much interference for anyone to understand the signal."

Arcturus nodded. "They're using a Cassandra scrambler. So we can't expect any local help, then. Well, we're going to have to look elsewhere for aid."

"There *is* nowhere else," said Ailin Pasteur.

"There's always somewhere else you can turn," said Arcturus.

As his father spoke, Valerian pressed himself to the outer wall and looked through the glass panel at the side of the door. Flying shrapnel had punched a neat hole in the glass and he saw the Confederate dropship hammer into the lawn, its skids gouging great chunks from the soft earth. Its assault ramp dropped and a host of armored marines emerged. They spread out and began moving cautiously toward the house in pairs.

"Incoming," he said, turning back to face his father. "Marines. At least thirty."

His father nodded and addressed Ailin Pasteur. "Do you have a refuge here? A safe room?"

"Yes, in the central service core."

"Get to it. Take Valerian, Juliana, and Charles and two of my soldiers," ordered Arcturus. "Lock yourselves in and wait for the cavalry. Understood? You three soldiers and Miyamoto, you're with me."

"Arcturus," cried Juliana. "What are you going to do?"

"I'm going to get us some help," he said. "The only comm unit strong enough to penetrate a Cassandra screen is on the gun cutter. If we can get to it, I can call in Duke and his boys."

"I'm going with you," said Valerian. "I'm not running."

"No," said his father. "You're getting to safety."

"I'm going with you," repeated Valerian. "That's the end of it, no argument."

Arcturus looked set to dispute him, then saw his determination. Valerian felt his heart soar at the pride he saw in his father's eyes.

"The cutter went down the landing shaft, yes?" said Arcturus.

"Yeah," said Valerian. "Its engine blew out and it fell in."

"Which means we can reach it from the house."

"Arcturus, that's insane!" said Juliana. "Edmund Duke's ships are too far away to reach us in time and for all you know the cutter's comm unit is destroyed."

"If I know Duke, he'll be halfway here already," said Arcturus. "Sorry, Ailin. You didn't really think I'd leave my ships that far out, did you?"

"Damn you, Arcturus," said Pasteur. "You go too far."

Arcturus gave a hollow laugh. "If Duke gets here in time, you'll be glad I do."

Valerian straightened as his father turned and handed him a gauss rifle. "You ready?"

He racked the slide of the weapon. "I'm ready."

His father led the way and Valerian, Master Miyamoto, and the three marines dashed after him. The flaming wreckage of the crashed Wraith blocked their initial route through the house, but Valerian guided them around it to reach the concealed elevator in the main hall.

The power was out, so they took the stairs, clattering down flight after flight in their desperate hurry. Valerian heard gunfire from above and paused in his descent, torn between his desire to follow his father and his need to protect his mother.

He realized he hadn't even said good-bye, and took a step back up the stairs.

"Don't be foolish!" shouted Arcturus. "We can only help them by reaching the cutter."

Valerian hesitated, but he knew his father was right and headed down once more, taking the stairs two at a time. Eventually they reached the bottom and emerged into the system of corridors, maintenance caves, and stores of the landing facility.

Wretched smoke billowed and heaved throughout the underground complex, and sprays of water drizzled from the sprinklers set into the roof. Valerian coughed at the acrid stench of burning fuel, rubber, and plastic, pressing his hand over his mouth to avoid the worst of it.

He flinched at the sound of breaking glass and turned to see Master Miyamoto at an emergency fire point, hauling a trio of breathing apparatus facemasks from within. He handed one to Valerian and one to his father before fitting his own mask.

"Which way to the platform?" asked Arcturus, his voice echoing and artificial-sounding through the mask. "I don't remember the layout."

"That way," pointed Valerian, heading off down a side corridor, running bent over to keep out of the smoke. His eyes still stung from the fumes and his mouth tasted of tar, but he couldn't deny the exhilaration he felt going into battle alongside his father.

Valerian negotiated them through the network of tunnels until they arrived at the blast door that led out onto the platform. The neosteel door had been torn from its mounting by the enormous impact of the gun cutter's fall and lay buckled on the concrete floor.

They clambered over the shattered door and entered the cavern of the landing platform. The gun cutter lay canted at an angle, its fuselage torn open where it had been peeled back by the rock walls of the shaft. Smoke billowed upward from its remaining engine toward the bright oblong of daylight, and burning pools of fuel collected beneath the wrecked craft.

"We're going to have to be quick," said Arcturus.

"Damn right," agreed Valerian. "I don't want to get blown to bits by an exploding gun cutter, thank you very much."

"Yes, it wouldn't be a very epic way to meet your end, would it?" said his father. "Let's make sure we don't then, eh?"

With that, his father began clambering up the slope of twisted metal and debris toward the tear in the fuselage. As he reached the gaping wound in the side of the cutter, he turned and called down to Valerian.

"Keep watch above us and back along the corridor. If our enemies pick up the signal from the cutter you can be sure we're going to have company . . ."

CHAPTER 19

VALERIAN FOUND COVER BEHIND A TWISTED SHEET of the gun cutter's fuselage, training his rifle down the length of the passageway they had come from. Master Miyamoto took up position across from Valerian, and his father's three marines found cover that would allow them to enfilade the enemy.

Eventually their attackers would realize that their target was not in the house. Once the enemy marines figured out where their quarry had gone and what they were doing, they'd throw everything they had at them.

Valerian and his soldiers had dragged piles of debris back toward the cutter to form rudimentary barricades and shared out what ammunition they had for the gauss rifles. The clock was ticking, but for what it was worth, they were ready.

Or at least as ready as five men could be to hold off thirty trained soldiers.

The heat in the cavern was stifling and sweat ran down Valerian's face inside his facemask. His breathing sounded incredibly loud and his peripheral vision was practically nonexistent. In frustration, he tore the mask off and dropped it next to him.

The air was tight and oxygen-depleted, but much of the smoke from the wrecked cutter was being vented up through the wide landing shaft. Not the best conditions in which to fight a battle, but who ever got to fight a battle in ideal conditions?

And Valerian was willing to risk some respiratory difficulty to actually see the men he was going to have to kill.

He wiped a hand over his face, trying to keep his breaths shallow, and blinked regularly to keep his eyes moist. He could just about make out the echoing sound of gunshots and wondered where they were coming from. Had his grandfather and Charles managed to get his mother to safety while his father's marines fought back? Or was he hearing echoes of shots being fired execution style, like those that had ended the life of his father's parents and sister?

The thought that his mother was in real danger almost sent him running back along the corridor, but he forced himself to remain where he was. Allowing emotion to rule his actions would only get him killed and that would do no one any good, least of all himself.

He glanced up toward the cutter. What was taking so long?

Was the comm unit broken? Was his father even now trying to repair it?

How long had passed anyway?

Valerian found he couldn't even begin to guess how long it had been since the attack began. It felt as though several hours had elapsed, but he suspected that it was one at best. The elasticity of time in a combat situation was something he'd read about, but had never expected to experience firsthand.

He felt the hairs on the back of his neck rise and looked over to where Master Miyamoto crouched. His former tutor was staring at him, jabbing a finger down the corridor, and Valerian felt his mouth go dry as he heard the clatter of boots and the bark of shouted orders.

This was it. The enemy he'd run from all his life was finally here.

But this time Valerian Mengsk wasn't running.

This time he was fighting.

He shouldered his gauss rifle and licked his lips as he saw shadows moving through the ruptured aperture of the blast door. Risking a quick glance back at the cutter, he silently willed his father to get a damn move on.

A pair of Confederate marines ducked around the edge of the torn doorway. Master Miyamoto rose from cover and opened fire, a meter-long tongue of fire blasting from the muzzle of his weapon. The first marine dropped, Master Miyamoto's expertly aimed fire punching unerringly through his visor and filling the inside of his helmet with iron spikes.

Valerian pulled the trigger, working his fire over the second marine. The recoil of the gauss rifle was fearsome, designed to be absorbed by a powered combat suit, which Valerian conspicuously wasn't wearing. The roar of the weapon was deafening, but Valerian kept the rifle on target, knowing that his target's armor would defeat all but the most concentrated clusters of impacts.

The man fell as the three soldiers opened up as well, the additional weight of their firepower tearing through the marine's armor and spraying the wall behind him with blood. Valerian ducked back into cover as return fire sawed through the doorway. Impaler shots rattled from the metal around him and he flinched as a ricochet sliced across his arm.

He heard shouts and rose once more, sending a blast of fire toward the doorway.

Shots filled the air, smacking from the debris and rock walls as the enemy marines laid down a curtain of suppressive fire. Valerian heard something skitter across the ground and his heart leapt into his mouth as he saw a gently wobbling oval disc come to rest no more than a few feet from him.

Without thinking, he dropped to one knee and scooped up the grenade, lobbing it back the way it had come. It exploded an instant later, the noise agonizingly loud and the wave of overpressure swatting him onto his back. He scrambled to his knees, coughing and trying to force the air to return to his lungs.

Valerian heard screams and cries for medics, sounding tinny and impossibly distant. He felt warm wetness in his ears and reached up, his fingers coming away bloody. A greasy fog bank of acrid smoke swirled upward from the grenade's detonation. Valerian felt around for his rifle, only now realizing it had been snatched from his grip by the blast.

More blasts of gunfire sounded, but he couldn't tell who was shooting.

He found his rifle and swept it up. The top portion of the barricade he'd been sheltering behind had been torn away by the explosive force of the detonation. Valerian realized if he'd stood to throw the grenade back, his upper body would have been vaporized.

Perhaps seven marines were lying screaming on the ground, ripped open and their guts spilled out over the floor. Fragments of armor and ruptured body parts littered the ground, but it was impossible to tell exactly how many men had died. Shouting marines tried to drag their wounded comrades to safety, but Valerian and Miyamoto gave them no respite, cutting them down in a deadly crossfire.

Valerian experienced a surge of exhilaration and felt the urge to laugh well up within him with almost uncontrollable force. Amid all this killing and death, the sensation was ludicrous, and he suddenly realized how ridiculous this notion of battle was. Men who had never met were trying to kill one another.

Valerian knew why *he* was fighting: to protect his loved ones and save his own life.

But these marines? What were *they* fighting for?

A fallen regime that had lied to them and probably erased the truth of their own lives with invasive brain surgery.

That was no reason to die, yet here they were, fighting a battle to the death.

As he was contemplating such weighty thoughts, a trio of grenades arced into the chamber. Valerian saw them coming and dropped, cursing at his stupidity. The middle of battle was no place to meditate on the absurdity of war, yet it had seemed the most natural thing in the world at the time.

Strange what the mind will do in times of stress, he thought.

Clearly the marines had learned their lesson and the grenades exploded almost as soon as they landed. Grenades explode up and out, so Valerian pressed his face to the floor as the enormous force of the blast roared over him.

Two of his father's soldiers vanished in a seething orange fireball and the gun cutter lurched dangerously as the blast's shock wave dislodged the rubble holding it in place. More choking clouds of smoke billowed upward, and Valerian knew their defiance was at an end.

He heard the sound of charging marines and the ripping-cloth sound of sustained gauss fire. Impaler spikes zinged from sheet metal and neosteel armor plates and the last of his father's soldiers cried out in pain as he was brought down.

Valerian coughed and rolled to his feet. He'd hung on to his rifle this time and, though he knew it was futile, aimed it toward the marines assaulting their position.

A continuous roaring howl, like the thunder of the mightiest storm front, filled the enclosed landing platform chamber. Valerian dropped to his knees with his hands pressed against his ears at the overwhelming, unbelievable volume.

The marines in front of Valerian disintegrated in a storm of blazing light, chewed up by hypervelocity slugs and exploding like wet, red sacks of meat. He looked up to see the dorsal-mounted cannon turret of the gun cutter spewing shells from its quad-barreled weapon mount. Armor and bone and flesh vaporized under the holocaust of cannon fire. The sheer killing power of the guns at such close range was utterly terrifying.

Valerian could just make out his father sitting behind the weapon, working its fire over their attackers in merciless arcs. Even as he watched, sparks and ricochets hammered the upper fuselage of the cutter, and Valerian looked up to see half a dozen marines firing down into the landing platform's shaft from above.

The armored Plexiglas of the turret held long enough for his father to drop out of the gunner's compartment, but within seconds the interior was a shattered ruin of broken plastic and metal. More shots rained down from above and Valerian ducked back as Impaler spikes hammered into the ground beside him.

He felt a hand seize his arm and, with his rifle raised, swung to face his assailant.

Master Miyamoto slapped the barrel away and Valerian let out a shuddering breath at how close he'd come to cutting the man down in a point-blank burst of fire.

"Need to get into the cutter," gasped Miyamoto. Blood streamed from a cut on his head and his robes were soaked with red at his shoulder and hip.

"You're hurt."

"I know," replied Miyamoto, with typical brevity. "Nothing I can do about it, though."

Valerian nodded and pressed himself against the buckled hull of the cutter. They couldn't break from cover—the marines on the surface would pick them off. Valerian could hear more shouts coming from beyond the doorway.

"These ones don't know the cutter's turret is out of action," hissed Miyamoto, guessing why none of their enemies were showing themselves. "That will not last. We need to move."

"Yeah," agreed Valerian. "Damn it, I hope my father got a message through to Duke."

"Either he did or he did not," said Miyamoto.

"He should be here by now."

"But he is not, so we still need to fight."

"Always the teacher, eh?" said Valerian, scrambling

around the edge of the cutter, keeping low and making sure he didn't expose himself to the marines up top.

"Always there is more to learn," countered Miyamoto. "The man who thinks he knows everything in fact knows nothing."

Valerian let out a laugh, though there was a slightly desperate quality to it. Despite the precariousness of their situation and the undoubted pain of his wounds, Master Miyamoto *still* found the time to dispense a bon mot.

"There," he said, bending over and pointing to a hole ripped in the cutter's underside. "We can climb in through there."

Master Miyamoto nodded, glancing back toward the doorway for any signs that their attackers were moving in.

"You go in first," said Miyamoto. "I will cover you."

Valerian didn't argue and slung his rifle over his shoulder, dropping to his belly and crawling toward the hole. He jumped as he heard a blast of gunfire, spinning around in time to see Master Miyamoto drop his rifle and sink to his knees with a gaping, raw wound in his stomach.

His former tutor's eyes were shut and his face was serene as he crumpled to the ground beside him. Valerian looked up and saw a marine in scarred and dented armor behind Miyamoto, and raised his hands.

Entire plates had been torn from the marine's combat suit and Impaler impacts and shrapnel scoring covered almost every inch of the armor. The marine's helmet had been ripped off and blood clotted the cropped hair. The hair was blonde, and Valerian realized that Miyamoto's killer was a woman in her early forties, and even through the mask of blood, grime, and sweat, he saw she was exceptionally attractive.

Was it better to be killed by a good-looking marine or an ugly one?

The thought made him smile, and he giggled in her face.

"Man, you are one crazy son of a bitch," said the marine, limping toward him with her rifle aimed unwaveringly at his chest. "I'm gonna enjoy killing you."

Valerian wanted to reach for his rifle, but knew he would be dead in a heartbeat if he so much as twitched a muscle in its direction.

He was dead anyway, and they both knew it.

As she approached, her eyes narrowed and she let out her own bark of laughter.

"I don't believe it," she said. "You're Mengsk's kid, aren't you? With that face, you gotta be related to him somehow. Hell, we got ourselves a twofer!"

"I am Valerian Mengsk," he said proudly. "Son of Emperor Arcturus Mengsk the First."

"That figures—you got that same damned arrogance."

Valerian tensed. "Who are you?" he demanded. "Why are you doing this?"

"What do you care who I am? I'm going to kill you is all you need to know."

"I want to know the name of my murderer," he said.

"Angelina Emillian," she said. "I recruited your old man into the Marine Corps and taught him all he knows. So you might say I'm making up for that mistake now."

Emillian brought her weapon up and said, "So long, Valerian."

Before she could pull the trigger, a blur of silver steel flashed and the rifle exploded as Master Miyamoto sliced his sword through the magnetic accelerator pack with the last of his strength. Valerian blinked away the brilliant afterimages as Emillian staggered and dropped her useless weapon, drawing the combat knife sheathed on her leg.

She leapt at him with a feral snarl of rage.

Valerian swept up his rifle and unloaded the last of his clip into her.

Most of his spikes flattened themselves on her breastplate, but a squirting spray of blood arced from her neck and she landed next to him with a gurgling scream. Valerian kept his finger pressed to the trigger, his breath heaving as the firing mechanism whined and the magazine clicked dry.

"Nice shot," said a voice behind him, and he turned his head to see his father emerge from the hole in the cutter's belly.

"Thanks," gasped Valerian, dropping the rifle and looking over to Master Miyamoto.

Valerian could see the man was dead and silently thanked his tutor for saving his life.

His father squatted next to Angelina Emillian, and Valerian could almost read the expression on his face: part anger, part regret.

"I never expected to see you again," he said, and Valerian was amazed to realize the marine wasn't dead. His Impaler spikes had punctured her neck and ripped open her carotid artery. She was still alive, but had moments left at best.

"I kinda wish you hadn't . . . ," she gasped, her words wet and gurgling.

"You died for nothing," said Arcturus. "You know that, don't you?"

"Screw you, Mengsk," replied Emillian with a cough of blood. "It don't matter now anyway—the UED are going to clean your clock but good."

"Who?" said his father. "Who are the UED?"

Emillian turned her head toward Valerian. "Damn, I was right about you, Mengsk. I knew if you had kids they'd be trouble . . ."

"Angelina, who are the UED?" demanded his father.

But Angelina Emillian was dead.

The inside of the cutter smelled of fuel, burned meat, and iron. Valerian coughed a few times, then slammed a fresh clip of Impaler spikes into his rifle. The craft's keel was buckled, and sections of deck plating had popped from the framework. Sparks crackled worryingly from broken panels and spurting cables frothed with leaking hydraulic fluid.

Lights flickered and fizzed, the electrics buzzing and spitting as the cutter's batteries shorted in and out. The contents of stowage lockers were spilled over the deck: playing cards, canteens, fresh magazines, and the personal effects of the marines who had accompanied his father to Umoja.

Valerian braced himself against a groaning stanchion. "Did you get a message to Duke?"

"I think so," said his father, looking through a tear in the cutter's side.

"You *think* so? Don't you know?"

His father shook his head, quickly checking the load on his rifle. "With a Cassandra scrambler it's hard to tell what goes in or out, but I think Duke heard me. I certainly heard him swearing enough to make me think he knows what's going on."

"Do you think he'll come?"

"I do, yes. Edmund Duke may be many things, but while he believes he'll benefit from his association with me, he'll be loyal. And right now, he knows I'm his best shot at making something of himself."

"I hope you're right," said Valerian, joining his father at the torn bulkhead.

"I'm sure I am," said his father. "If Edmund has a grain of sense, he'll have been keeping his sensor suite trained on Umoja since I left the command ship. With any luck, he'll have come running as soon as he picked up the weapons' discharges."

Valerian cocked his rifle as they heard the sound of voices from outside.

He peered through a shrapnel hole and saw marines, ten of them—fully armored and loaded for bear—negotiating their way through the blasted debris that filled the chamber.

Valerian and Arcturus were on their own now, and with only two gauss rifles between them, Valerian knew they didn't stand much—or indeed any—chance of defeating their foes. He decided there were worse ways to end his allotted span than to die fighting next to his father.

"We won't stop them all," said Valerian.

Arcturus grinned. "Speak for yourself."

Valerian nodded, emboldened by his father's attitude, and shouldered his rifle.

The marines saw them and charged.

Valerian and Arcturus opened fire at the same time, their Impaler spikes hammering the nearest of their attackers. The marine stumbled and fell, but his armor protected him from injury. Valerian ducked back as a spray of spikes hammered the cutter, tiny pyramids punched into the internal skin of the fuselage by their impacts.

His father squeezed off a burst of fire and whipped back into cover. The roar of gauss fire filled the cutter's interior, a shrieking howl of metal slamming on metal. Once again, Valerian aimed his rifle through the ruptured hull of the cutter, opening up on a red-armored marine as he clambered over the remains of one of their jury-rigged barricades. Impaler spikes hammered the man, but he shrugged off the impacts and kept coming.

More fire sparked off the cutter's hull and Valerian knew they could not hope to stop these marines. Where their previous attackers had come at them with fatally misplaced confidence, these were taking no chances, operating in pairs and covering each other's advance with suppressive fire.

Valerian slammed in a fresh magazine, his last, and took a deep breath.

This was it, this was the end, and what better way to go out than in a blaze of glory.

He looked over at his father and saw the same determination to make their ending one worthy of remembrance.

"You ready?" he asked.

"I'm ready," replied Arcturus.

They whipped around together, rifles raised, and opened fire.

And the landing shaft was suddenly filled with a cascade of incandescent bolts of blistering light that slammed down from above. Percussive explosions bloomed skyward and the cutter rocked backward as a wave of heat and pressure washed over it.

The tremendous impacts shook the damaged vessel so violently its keel split in two. Arcturus and Valerian were thrown to the deck as the streaming torrent of light hammered the world beyond the interior of their refuge to oblivion.

At last the waterfall of molten light ceased and

Valerian blinked away the starbursts behind his eyes. His ears rang with the concussion of the explosions, but he was alive, and that was something he hadn't expected.

His father lay across from him, looking dazed but otherwise unhurt.

"What the hell?" gasped Valerian, seeing nothing but blackened walls and complete annihilation outside.

Arcturus laughed. "Told you . . . ," he said.

Valerian looked up.

Blocking the light from the open shaft was an enormous steel behemoth that floated above the landing hatch in defiance of the laws of gravity.

As a monstrous, rippling heat haze surrounded its engines, Valerian covered his ears against the teeth-loosening rumble. The insignia of a red arm holding a whip on a black background was emblazoned on either side of a cavernous docking bay, and it took Valerian a moment to realize he was looking at the underside of a Dominion battlecruiser.

A voice, heavily accented and with a thick drawl, blared from an external loudspeaker.

"Someone order a heroic rescue?" said General Edmund Duke.

In the immediate aftermath of the fighting, no clue could be found as to how these Confederate die-hards had managed to learn the particulars of the emperor's visit to Umoja. Nor could any light be shed on the identity or allegiance of the UED that Angelina

Emillian had spoken of before her death—though this mystery would have a bloody answer soon enough.

Arcturus promised Ailin Pasteur that a full and thorough investigation would be undertaken, and while no direct accusations were made, it was clear the emperor suspected the Umojans of a degree of complicity in the attack.

More Dominion ships were on their way to the emperor, and in response, capital ships of the Protectorate were en route to persuade him that it would be in his best interests to withdraw them as soon as possible.

The survivors of the attack gathered in Ailin Pasteur's cavernous dining room, shaken and bloodied, but glad to be alive. When Valerian saw his mother he raced toward her, dropping his rifle and embracing her as she wept tears of joy to see him alive.

"I thought you were dead," she sobbed.

"I'm a Mengsk," he said. "We don't die easy."

ENDINGS

BUT FIRST WE HAVE TO BURY HER . . .

Valerian sat in the leather armchair before the dying coal fire, swirling another tawny port in his glass as his father poured himself another rich amber brandy. That wasn't his usual drink of choice, but he'd always drunk brandy when in Ailin Pasteur's home and didn't see any need to change now.

The funeral service of Juliana Pasteur had been brief, but dignified, attended by the majority of the Umojan Ruling Council and a few of the emperor's closest advisers. Ailin Pasteur had read his daughter's eulogy and no one had been surprised when he did not ask Arcturus to say anything.

Valerian had planned to speak, but when the moment came he had been unable to move, such was the weight of grief pinning him to his seat.

His mother's death was the most painful thing Valerian had ever endured.

It had taken a further eighteen months after the

attack on her father's house for her to die, her last breath taken a month before Valerian's twenty-first birthday. It had not been an easy death; her last year had been spent confined to bed with only infrequent bouts of lucidity.

Valerian had spent those months at her side, holding her hand, mopping her brow, and reading passages from *Poems of the Twilight Stars*. Often she forgot who he was or believed him to be her long-lost love, Arcturus: her great and glorious prince.

That had been hard to bear, for she recalled a man who no longer existed, if he ever had.

Her last morning had been glorious, the sun a brilliant bronze disc in the sky and the wind fresh off the river, carrying scents of far-off provinces and the promise of undiscovered countries.

Valerian had opened the curtains and said, "It's wonderful out there today."

"You should go for a run," replied his mother. "It's been so long since you went outside."

"Maybe I will," he answered. "Later."

She nodded and propped herself up in bed.

Though her illness had robbed his mother of much of her former beauty, the copper light from the newly risen sun bathed her in a pearlescent glow that most healthy people, never mind cancer sufferers, could only dream of.

"You look beautiful today," said Valerian.

She smiled and said, "Sit with me."

Valerian sat in the chair next to her bed, but she shook her head. "No, on the bed."

He did as he was bid and she slipped her arms around him, pulling him to her as she had done so many times when he was a little boy. She stroked his golden hair and kissed his forehead.

"My dear boy," she said. "You are everything I wished for. Do you remember that day beside the river before the attack on your grandfather's house?"

"Yeah, I remember. What about it?"

"Do you remember what I said to you there?"

"I do," he said, wary as to where this conversation was going.

"You've been so good to me since then, honey, but it's time for you to live your own life now. You can't be tied to me anymore."

"What do you mean?"

"I mean that it's time for you to be your own man now, Val," said his mother urgently, and he could hear her heartbeat flutter like a caged bird in her chest. "You tried so hard to make me better and fought against something that can't be fought, but it's time to let go."

"No," he said, tears gathering in his eyes as he held her tightly.

"You have to," said Juliana. "Acceptance is the only way you can defeat death, my beautiful boy. I've made peace with it and now you have to as well. Tell me you understand . . ."

Valerian closed his eyes, unwilling to say the words,

but knowing that she was right. He had fought against the inevitable for so long that he had forgotten there was nothing he could do to prevent it. His mother was dying and part of him would die with her, but so long as he lived, part of her would live on.

That was her legacy to him. Her goodness and her compassion had always been part of his character, her life and beauty and vitality part of his soul. But so too was his father's ruthlessness and determination to succeed at any cost. Those qualities passed on by his parents had blended within him to make him who he was, and only now did he understand what that meant.

He was neither his mother nor his father; he was Valerian Mengsk, with all the qualities and faults such a state of being entailed. The things he had inherited and learned from both of them would forever guide his steps, but the final choice of where his life would lead was down to him.

"I understand," he said, and he knew she felt the truth of his words.

"I know you do, my dear. You make me so proud."

"I love you," he said as tears streamed freely down his face.

"I love you too, Valerian," said his mother.

Those had been the final words she said to him, her heart finally giving out as she held him on that last glorious morning on Umoja.

Valerian had stood and folded her arms in her lap, smiling at the serenity he saw in her, the lines of care, worry, and pain erased from her face in death. She was at peace, and she was beautiful.

His father had come to Umoja a week later and they had circled one another like the largest wolves in a pack, each gauging the other's strength as mourners arrived for the funeral. Now, with the burial concluded and the guests sipping expensive wine and eating canapés, father and son retired to Valerian's study.

"Your grandfather spoke well," said his father, pouring a glass of brandy and taking the seat opposite Valerian. "It was a moving eulogy."

"Yes, but you'd expect that," said Valerian, his voice hollow and empty, "what with him being a politician."

"I suppose so," agreed Arcturus.

"So?" said Valerian, when his father lapsed into silence. "You were going to tell me of Korhal. Of your father. And my mother."

"Yes," mused Arcturus, swilling brandy around his glass. "Are you sitting comfortably?"

His father then went on to speak for several hours, telling him of his youth on Korhal, his time with the Confederate Marine Corps, and what had transpired between him and Juliana. Valerian had been surprised by his father's candor, but soon realized that Arcturus Mengsk had no need to lie to anyone anymore.

His father had done most of the talking, but as the tale had caught up to the present, Valerian had spoken, injecting his father's story with his own memories. At the conclusion of the narrative both men lapsed into silence.

It was a silence that wasn't uncomfortable, simply a space between two men who had not yet decided what to say to one another.

Valerian broke the silence first. "I won't be like you," he said.

"I'm not asking you to be like me," said his father, taking a mouthful of brandy. "I never wanted that, I just wanted you to be someone I could be proud of."

"And are you? Proud of me."

His father considered the question for a moment before answering. "Yes. I am proud of you. You are intelligent and have courage, two qualities that will get you far in this galaxy, but you have more than that, Valerian. You have greatness within you, just as I do, and everything we have talked about today only reaffirms my belief that we Mengsks are made for greater things than the common herd can expect of their lives."

"I am my own man, Father, and I'll not live my life in your shadow."

His father chuckled. "Nor do I expect you to. Ah, Valerian, so many of the things you say remind me of the arguments I had with my father all those years ago."

Arcturus stood and drained the last of his brandy. "Sometimes I think we're doomed to repeat the mistakes of our fathers throughout eternity."

"I won't make the same mistakes you made," promised Valerian.

"No, I'm sure you won't," agreed Arcturus. "You'll make new ones."

"That's not very reassuring."

"It wasn't meant to be, son," said Arcturus. "Now come on, pull yourself together: We have an empire to build."

ABOUT THE AUTHOR

Hailing from Scotland, **GRAHAM McNEILL** narrowly escaped a career in surveying to join Games Workshop in 2000, where he worked for six and a half years as a games developer. In 2006, he took the plunge to become a full-time author, which seems to be going pretty nicely. As well as fourteen novels, Graham has written a host of science fiction and fantasy short stories and comics. He lives in Nottingham, United Kingdom.

You can check out Graham's work, what he's up to, and where he'll be by going to his website at:

www.graham-mcneill.com